REGENCY
Betrayal

Julia
Justiss

First Published in Great Britain 2016
By Mills & Boon, an imprint of HarperCollins*Publishers*
1 London Bridge Street, London, SE1 9GF

REGENCY BETRAYAL © 2016 Harlequin Books S.A.

The Rake to Ruin Her © 2013 Janet Justiss
The Rake to Redeem Her © 2013 Janet Justiss

ISBN: 978-0-263-92373-5

52-1016

Our policy is to use papers that are natural, renewable and recyclable products and made from wood grown in sustainable forests. The logging and manufacturing processes conform to the legal environmental regulations of the country of origin.

Printed and bound by
CPI Group (UK) Ltd, Croydon, CR0 4YY

1 2 0595497 1

A REGENCY

Collection

Carole Mortimer — REGENCY Scandals

Bronwyn Scott — REGENCY Gamble

Julia Justiss — REGENCY Betrayal

Annie Burrows — REGENCY Rumour

Margaret McPhee — REGENCY Desire

Sarah Mallory — REGENCY Beauty

Michelle Styles — REGENCY Bride

Lucy Ashford — REGENCY Seduction

Ann Lethbridge — REGENCY Proposal

Diane Gaston — REGENCY Reputation

Christine Merrill — REGENCY Temptation

Gail Whitiker — REGENCY Disguise

The Rake to Ruin Her

Julia Justiss wrote her first ideas for Nancy Drew stories in her third-grade notebook and has been writing ever since. After publishing poetry in college she turned to novels. Her Regency historical romances have won or been placed in contests by the Romance Writers of America, *Romantic Times* magazine, National Readers' Choice and the Daphne du Maurier Award. She lives with her husband in Texas. For news and contests visit www.juliajustiss.com.

Prologue

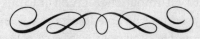

Vienna—January 1815

The distant sound of waltz music and a murmur of voices met his ear as Max Ransleigh exited the anteroom. Quickly he paced toward the dark-haired woman standing in the shadowy alcove at the far end of the hallway.

Hoping he wouldn't find on her more marks of her cousin's abuse, he said, 'What is it? He hasn't struck you again, has he? I fear I cannot stay; Lord Wellington should arrive in the Green Salon at any moment and he despises tardiness. I would not have come at all, had your note not sounded most urgent.'

'Yes, you'd told me you were to rendezvous there; that's how I knew where to find you,' she replied. The soft, slightly French lilt of her words was charming, as always. Lovely dark eyes, whose hint of sadness had aroused his protective instincts from the first, searched his face.

'You've been so kind. I appreciate it more than I can say. It's just that Thierry told me to obtain new clasps for his uniform coat for the reception tomorrow and I haven't any idea where to find them. And if I fail to satisfy my cousin's demands…' Her voice trailed off and she shivered. 'Forgive me for disturbing you with my little problem.'

Disgust and a cold anger coiled within him at the idea of a man—nay, a *diplomat*—who would vent his pique on the slight, gentle woman beside him. He must find some excuse to challenge Thierry St Arnaud to a boxing match and show him what it was like to be pummelled.

Glancing over his shoulder toward the door of the Green Salon, the urgent need to leave an itch in his shoulder blades, he tried not to let impatience creep into his voice. 'You mustn't worry. I won't be able to escort you until morning, but there's a suitable shop not far. Now, I regret to be so un-chivalrous, but I must get back.'

As he bowed and turned away, she caught at his sleeve. 'Please, just a moment longer! Simply being near you makes me feel braver.'

Max felt a swell of satisfaction at her confidence, along with the pity that always rose in him at her predicament. All his life, as the privileged younger son of an earl, others had begged favours of him; this poor widow asked for so little.

He bent to kiss her hand. 'I'm only glad to help. But Wellington will have my hide if I keep him waiting, especially with the meeting of plenipotentiary officials about to convene.'

'No, it wouldn't do for an aspiring diplomat to fall afoul of the great Wellington.' She opened her lips as if to add something else, then closed them. Tears welled in her eyes. 'I'm so sorry.'

Puzzled, he was about to ask her why when a pistol blast shattered the quiet.

Thrusting her behind him, Max pivoted toward the sound. His soldier's ear told him it had come from within the Green Salon.

Where Wellington should now be.

Assassins?

'Stay here in the shadows until I return!' he ordered over his shoulder as he set off at a run, dread chilling his heart.

Within the Green Salon, he found chairs overturned, a case of papers scattered about and the room overhung by the smell of black powder and a haze of smoke.

'Wellington! Where is he?' he barked at a corporal, who with two other soldiers was attempting to right the disorder.

'Whisked out of the back door by an aide,' the soldier answered.

'Is he unharmed?'

'Yes, I think so. Old Hookey was by the fireplace, snapping at the staff about where you'd got to. If he had not looked up when the door was flung open, expecting you, and dodged left, the ball would have caught him in the chest.'

I knew where to find you...

Those French-accented words, the tears, her apologetic sadness slammed into Max's gut. Surely the two events couldn't be related?

But when he ran back into hallway, the dark-haired lady had disappeared.

Chapter One

Devon—Autumn 1815

'Why don't we just leave?' Max Ransleigh suggested to his cousin Alastair as the two stood on the balcony overlooking the grand marble entry of Barton Abbey.

'Dammit, we only just arrived,' Alastair replied, exasperation in his tones. 'Poor bastards.' He waved towards the servants below them, who were struggling to heft in the baggage of several arriving guests. 'Trunks are probably stuffed to the lids with gowns, shoes, bonnets and other fripperies, the better for the wearers to parade themselves before the prospective bidders. Makes me thirsty for a deep glass of brandy.'

'If you'd bothered to write that you were coming home, we might have altered the date of the house party,' a feminine voice behind them said reproachfully.

Max turned to find Mrs Grace Ransleigh, mistress of Barton Abbey and Alastair's mother, standing behind them. 'Sorry, Mama,' Alastair said, leaning down to give the petite, dark-haired lady a hug. When he straightened, a flush coloured his handsome face; probably chagrin, Max thought, that Mrs Ransleigh had overhead his uncharitable remark. 'You know I'm a terrible correspondent.'

'A fact I find astonishing,' his mother replied, retaining Alastair's hands in a light grip, 'when I recall that as a boy, you were seldom without a pen, jotting down some observation or other.'

A flash of something that looked like pain passed across his cousin's face, so quickly Max wasn't sure he'd actually seen it. 'That was a long time ago, Mama.'

Sorrow softened her features. 'Perhaps. But a mother never forgets. In any event, after all those years in the army, always throwing yourself into the most dangerous part of the action, I'm too delighted to have you safely home to quibble about the lack of notice—though I fear you will have to suffer through the house party. With the guests already arriving, I can hardly call it off now.'

Releasing her son's hands with obvious reluctance, she turned to Max. 'It's good to see you, too, my dear Max.'

'If I'd known you were entertaining innocents, Aunt Grace, I wouldn't have agreed to meet Alastair here,' Max assured her as he leaned down to kiss her cheek.

'Nonsense,' she said stoutly. 'All you Ransleigh lads have run wild at Barton Abbey since you were scrubby schoolboys. You'll always be welcome in my home, Max, no matter how…circumstances change.'

'Then you are kinder than Papa,' Max replied, trying for a light tone while his chest tightened with the familiar wash of anger, resentment and regret. Still, the cousins' unexpected appearance must have been an unpleasant shock to a hostess about to convene a gathering of eligible young maidens and their prospective suitors—an event of which they'd been unaware until the butler warned them about it upon their arrival half an hour ago.

As he'd just assured his aunt, had Max known Barton Abbey would be sheltering unmarried young ladies on the prowl for husbands, he would have taken care to stay far away.

He'd best talk with his cousin and decide what to do. 'Alastair, shall we get that glass of wine?'

'There's a full decanter in the library,' Mrs Ransleigh said. 'I'll send Wendell up with some cold ham, cheese and biscuits. One thing that never changes—I'm sure you boys are famished.'

'Bless you, Mama,' Alastair told her with a grin, while Max added his thanks. As they bowed and turned to go, Mrs Ransleigh said hesitantly, 'I don't suppose you care to dine with the party?'

'Amongst that virginal lot? Most assuredly not!' Alastair retorted. 'Even if we'd suddenly developed a taste for petticoat affairs, my respectable married sister would probably poison our wine were we to intrude our scandalous presence in the midst of her aspiring innocents. Come along, Max, before the smell of perfumed garments from those damned chests overcomes us.'

Thumping Max on the shoulder to set him in motion, Alastair paused to kiss his mother's hand. 'Tell the girls to visit us later, once their virginal guests are safely abed behind locked doors.'

Max followed his cousin down the hallway and into a large library comfortably furnished with well-worn leather chairs and a massive desk. 'Are you sure you don't want to leave?' he asked again as he drew out a decanter and filled two glasses.

'Devil's teeth,' Alastair growled, 'this is *my* house. I'll come and go when I wish, and my friends, too. Besides, you'll enjoy seeing Mama and Jane and Felicity—for whom the ever-managing Jane arranged this gathering, Wendell told me. Jane thinks Lissa should have some experience with eligible men before she's cast into the Marriage Mart next spring. Though she's not angling to get Lissa riveted now, some of the attendees did bring offspring they're trying to marry off, bless Wendell for warning us!'

Sighing, Alastair accepted a brimming glass. 'You'd think my highly-publicized liaisons with actresses and dancers, combined with an utter lack of interest in respectable virgins, would be enough to put off matchmaking mamas. But as you well know, wealth and ancient lineage appear to trump notoriety and lack of inclination. However, with my equally notorious cousin to entertain,' he inclined his head toward Max, 'I have a perfect excuse to avoid the ladies. So, let's drink to you,' Alastair hoisted his glass, 'for rescuing me not only from boredom, but from having to play the host at Jane's hen party.'

'To evading your duty as host,' Max replied, raising his own glass. 'Nice to know my ruined career is good for *something*,' he added, bitterness in his tone.

'A temporary setback only,' Alastair said. 'Sooner or later, the Foreign Office will sort out that business in Vienna.'

'Maybe,' Max said dubiously. He, too, had thought the matter might be resolved quickly…until he spoke with Papa. 'There's still the threat of a court-martial.'

'After Hougoumont?' Alastair snorted derisively. 'Maybe if you'd defied orders and *abandoned* your unit before Waterloo, but no military jury is going to convict you for throwing yourself *into* the battle, instead of sitting back in England as instructed. Some of the Foot Guards who survived the fighting owe their lives to you and headquarters knows it. No,' he concluded, 'even Horse Guards, who are often ridiculously stiff-rumped about disciplinary affairs, know better than to bring such a case to trial.'

'I hope you're right. As my father noted on the one occasion he deigned to speak with me, I've already sufficiently tarnished the family name.'

It wasn't the worst of what the earl had said, Max thought, the memory of that recent interview still raw and stinging. He saw himself again, standing silent, offering no defence as the earl railed at him for embarrassing the family and complicating his job in the Lords, where he was struggling to sustain a coalition. Pronouncing Max a sore disappointment and a political liability, he'd banished him for the indefinite future from Ransleigh House in London and the family seat in Hampshire.

Max had left without even seeing his mother.

'The earl still hasn't come round?' Alastair's soft-voiced question brought him back to the present. After a glance at Max's face, he sighed. 'Almost as stubborn and rule-bound as Horse Guards, is my dear uncle. Are you positive you won't allow me to speak to him on your behalf?'

'You know arguing with Papa only hardens his views—and might induce him to extend his banishment to you, which would grieve both our mothers. No, it wouldn't serve…though I appreciate your loyalty more than I can say—' Max broke off and swallowed hard.

'No need to say anything,' Alastair replied, briskly refilling their glasses. '"Ransleigh Rogues together, for ever,"' he quoted, holding his glass aloft.

'"Ransleigh Rogues,"' Max returned the salute, his heart lightening as he tried to recall exactly when Alastair had coined that motto. Probably over an illicit glass of smuggled brandy some time in their second Eton term after a disapproving master, having caned all four cousins for some now-forgotten infraction, first denounced them as the 'Ransleigh Rogues.'

The name, quickly whispered around the college, had stuck to them, and they to each other, Max thought, smiling faintly. Through the fagging at Eton, the hazing at Oxford, then into the army to watch over Alastair when, after the girl he loved terminated their engagement in the most public and humiliating fashion imaginable, he'd joined the first cavalry unit that would take him, vowing to die gloriously in battle.

They'd stood by Max, too, after the failed assassination attempt at the Congress of Vienna. When he returned to London in disgrace, he'd found that, of all the government set that since his youth had encouraged and flattered the handsome, charming younger son of an earl, only his fellow Rogues still welcomed his company.

His life had turned literally overnight from the hectic busyness of an embassy post to a purposeless void, with only a succession of idle amusements to occupy his days. With the glorious diplomatic career he'd planned in ruins and his future uncertain, he didn't want to think what rash acts he might have committed, had he not had the support of Alastair, Dom and Will.

'I'm sure Aunt Grace would never say so, but having us turn up now must be rather awkward. Since we're not in the market to buy the wares on display, why not go elsewhere? Your hunting box, perhaps?'

After taking another deep sip, Alastair shook his head. 'Too early for that; ground's not frozen yet. And I'd bet Mama's more worried about the morals of her darlings than embarrassed by our presence. Turned out of your government post or not, you're still an earl's son—'

'—currently exiled by his family—'

'—who possesses enough charm to lure any one of Jane's innocents out of her virtue, should you choose to.'

'Why would I? I'd thought Lady Mary would make me a fine diplomat's wife, but without a career, *she* no longer has any interest in me and *I* no longer have any interest in marriage.' Max tried for a light tone, not wanting Alastair to guess how much the august Lady Mary's defection, coming on the heels of his father's dismissal, had wounded him.

'I wish I could think of another place to go, at least until this damned house party concludes.' With a frustrated jab, Alastair stoppered the brandy. 'But I need to take care of some estate business and I don't want to nip back to London just now, with the autumn theatre season in full swing. I wouldn't put it past Desirée to track me down and create another scene, which would be entirely too much of a bore.'

'Not satisfied with the emeralds you brought when you gave her her *congé*?'

Alastair sighed. 'Perhaps it wasn't wise to recommend that she save her histrionics for the stage. In any event, the longer I knew her, the more obvious her true, grasping nature became. She was good enough in the bedchamber and possessed of a mildly amusing wit, but, ultimately, she grew as tiresome as all the others.'

Alastair paused, his eyes losing focus as a hard expression settled over his face. Max knew that look; he'd seen it on Alastair's countenance whenever women were mentioned ever since the end of his ill-fated engagement. Silently damning once again the woman who'd caused his cousin such pain, Max knew better than to try to take him to task for his contemptuous dismissal of women.

He felt a wave of bitterness himself, recalling how easily *he*'d been lured in by a sad story convincingly recited by a pretty face.

If only he'd been content to save his heroics for the battlefield, instead of attempting to play knight errant! Max reflected with a wry grimace. Indeed, given what had transpired in Vienna, he was more than half-inclined to agree with his cousin that no woman, other than one who offered her talents for temporary purchase, was worth the trouble she inevitably caused.

'I've no desire to return to London either,' he said. 'I'd have to avoid Papa and the government set, which means most of my former friends. Having spent a good deal of time and tact disentangling myself from the beauteous Mrs Harris, I'd prefer not to return to town until she's entangled with someone else.'

'Why don't we hop over to Belgium and see how Dom's progressing? Last I heard, Will was still there, looking after him.' Alastair laughed. 'Leave it to Will to find a way to stay on the Continent after the rest of us were shipped home! Though he claimed he only loitered in Brussels for the fat pickings to be made among all the diplomats and army men with more money than gaming sense.'

'I don't know that Dom would appreciate a visit. He was still pretty groggy with laudanum and pain from the amputation when I saw him last. After he came round enough to abuse me for fussing over him like a hen with one chick, he ordered me home to placate my father and the army board.'

'Yes, he tried to send me away too, though I wasn't about to budge until I was sure he wasn't going to stick his spoon in the wall.' Setting his jaw, Alastair looked away. 'I was the one who dragged the rest of you into the army. I don't think I could have borne it if you hadn't all made it through.'

'You hardly "dragged" us,' Max objected. 'Just about all our friends from Oxford ended up in the war, in one capacity or another.'

'Still, I won't feel completely at ease until Dom makes it home and…adjusts to life again.' With one arm missing and half his face ruined by a sabre slash, both knew the cousin who'd always been known as 'Dandy Dominick', the handsomest man in the regiment, would face a daunting recovery. 'We could go and cheer him up.'

'To be frank, I think it would be best to leave him alone for a while. When life as you've always known it shatters before your eyes, it requires some contemplation to figure out how to rearrange the shards.' Max gave a short laugh. 'Though *I*'ve had months and am still at loose ends. You have your land to manage, but for me—' Max waved his hand in a gesture of frustration. 'The delightful Mrs Harris was charming enough, but I wish I might find some new career that didn't depend on my father's good will. Unfortunately, all I ever aspired to was the diplomatic corps, a field now closed to me. I rather doubt, with my sullied reputation, they'd have me in the church, even if I claimed to have received a sudden calling.'

'Father Max, the darling of every actress from Drury Lane to the Theatre Royal?' Alastair grinned and shook his head. 'No, I can't see that!'

'Perhaps I'll join John Company and set out for India to make my fortune. Become a clerk. Get eaten by tigers.'

'I'd feel sorry for any tiger who attempted it,' Alastair retorted. 'If the Far East don't appeal, why not stay with the army—and thumb your nose at your father?'

'A satisfying notion, that,' Max replied drily, 'though the plan has a few flaws. Such as the fact that, despite my service at Waterloo, Lord Wellington hasn't forgotten he was waiting for *me* when he was almost shot in Vienna.' The continuing coldness of the man he'd once served and still revered cut even deeper than his father's disapproval.

'Well, you're a natural leader and the smartest of the Rogues; something will come to you,' Alastair said. 'In the interim, while we remain at Barton Abbey, best watch your step. Mrs Harris was one thing, but you don't want to get *entangled* with any of Jane's eligible virgins.'

'Certainly not! The one benefit of the débâcle in Vienna is that, with my brother to carry on the family name, I'm not compelled to marry. Heaven forbid I should get cornered by some devious matchmaker.' And trapped into a marriage as cold as his parents' arranged union, he thought with an inward shudder.

Picking up the decanter, Alastair poured them each another glass. 'Here's to confounding Uncle and living independently!'

'As long as living independently doesn't involve wedlock, I can drink to that,' Max said and raised his glass.

Chapter Two

'No, no, you foolish creature, shake out the folds before you hang it!'

Caroline Denby looked up from her comfortable seat on the sofa in one of Barton Abbey's elegant guest bedchambers to see her stepmother snatch a spangled evening gown from the hapless maid and give it a practised shake.

'Like this,' Lady Denby said, handing the garment back before turning to her stepdaughter. 'Caroline, dear, won't you put that book away and supervise Dulcie with that trunk while I make sure this girl doesn't get our evening dresses hopelessly wrinkled?'

'Yes, ma'am,' Caroline replied, setting down her book with regret. Already she was counting the hours until the end of this dreary house party so she might return to Denby Lodge and her horses. She hated to lose almost ten days' training with the winter sales approaching. The Denby line her father had bred had earned a peerless reputation among the racing and army set, and she wasn't about to let her stepmama's single-minded efforts to marry her off get in the way of maintaining her father's high standards.

Besides, while working in the fields and stables in a daily regimen as comfortable and familiar as her father's old riding boots, she could still feel the late Sir Martin's kindly presence, watching over her and the horses that had been his life. How she still missed him!

Sighing, she closed her book and dutifully cast her gaze over at Dulcie, who was currently lifting a layer of chemises, stays and stockings out of a silken rustle of tissue paper. She should be thankful she'd been delegated to supervise the undergarments and leave the gowns to her stepmother. At least she wouldn't have to cast her eyes on them again until she was forced to wear one.

Better to appear in some hideously over-trimmed confection of unflattering colour, she reminded herself, than to end up engaged.

'I'll help with the unpacking, but afterwards, I intend to ride Sultan before the light fades.' As her stepmother opened her lips, probably to argue, Caroline added, 'Remember, you agreed that if I consented to come to Mrs Ransleigh's cattle auction, I'd be allowed to ride every day.'

'Caroline, please!' Lady Denby protested, her face flushing. Leaning closer and lowering her voice, she said, 'You mustn't refer to the gathering in such terms! Especially...' She angled her head toward the maids.

Caroline shrugged. 'But that's what it is. A few gentlemen in search of rich wives gathering to look over the candidates, evaluate their appearance and pedigree, and try to strike a bargain. Just as they do at cattle fairs, or when they come to buy Papa's horses, though I suppose the females here will be spared an inspection of their teeth and limbs.'

'Really, Caroline,' her stepmother said reprovingly, 'I must deplore your using such a vulgar analogy. Just as the ladies wish to ascertain the character of prospective suitors, gentlemen want to assure themselves that any lady to whom they offer matrimony possesses suitable background and breeding.'

'And dowry,' Caroline added.

Ignoring that comment, Lady Denby said, 'Couldn't you, for once, allow yourself to enjoy the attentions of some handsome young men? I know you don't want to spend another Season in London!'

'You also know I'm not interested in getting married,' Caroline said with the weariness of long repetition. 'Why don't you forget about trying to lure me into wedlock and concentrate on making a match for Eugenia? My stepsister is beautiful and wealthy enough to snare any suitor she fancies, and she's eager enough for both of us. Only think how much blunt you'd save, if you didn't have to take her to town in the spring!'

'Unlike you, Eugenia is eagerly anticipating *her* London Season. Besides which, though I don't wish to be indelicate, you are…getting on in years. If you don't marry soon, you will be considered quite on the shelf.'

'Which would be quite all right with me,' Caroline retorted. 'Harry won't care a fig for that, when he comes back.'

'But, Caroline, India is such an unhealthy, heathenish place! Marauding maharajas and fevers and all manner of dangers. Difficult as it is to consider, you must acknowledge the possibility that Lieutenant Tremaine might not return.' Lady Denby's eyes widened, as if the notion had only just occurred to her. 'Surely he wasn't so heedless of propriety as to ask you to wait for him!'

'No,' Caroline admitted. 'We have no formal understanding.'

'I should think not! It would have been most improper, with him leaving for Calcutta while everything was still in such an uproar after your papa's…demise. Now, I understand you've known Harry Tremaine for ever and are comfortable with him, but if you would but give the notion a chance, I'm sure you could find some other gentleman equally…accommodating.'

Of her odd preferences for horses and hounds rather than gowns and needlework, Caroline silently filled in the unstated words. With Harry she'd had no need to conceal her unconventional and mannish interests, nor did she have to pretend a maidenly deference to his masculine opinions and decisions.

For her dearest childhood friend she might consider marrying and braving the Curse—though just thinking about the prospect sent an involuntary shudder through her. But she certainly wasn't willing to risk her life for some lisping dandy who had his eyes on her dowry…or the Denby stud.

Unfortunately, she was wealthy enough that, despite her unconventional ways, there'd been no lack of aspirants to her hand during her aborted Season, before news of her father's sudden illness had called them home. Caroline remained sceptical of how 'accommodating' any prospective husband might be, however, once he gained legal control over her person, property—and beloved horses. With the example of her now much-wiser and much-poorer widowed cousin Elizabeth to caution her, she had no intention of letting herself become dazzled by some rogue with designs on her wealth and property.

If she must marry, she'd wait to wed Harry, who knew her down to the ground and for whom she felt the same sort of deep, companionable love she'd felt for her father. Another pang of loss reverberated through her.

Gritting her teeth against it, she said, 'In the five years since Harry joined the army, I've not found anyone I like as well.'

'Well, you certainly can't claim to have seriously looked! Not when you managed to talk your dear father, God rest his soul, out of taking you to London, or even attending the local assemblies, until I managed to convince him of the necessity last year. It's just not…natural for a young lady to have no interest in marriage!' Lady Denby burst out, not for the first time.

Before Caro could argue that point, her stepmother's expression turned cajoling. 'Come now, my dear, why not allow Mrs Ransleigh's guests to become acquainted with you? It's always possible you might meet a gentleman you could like well enough to marry. You know I have only your best interests at heart!'

The devil of it was Caroline knew the tender-hearted Lady Denby did want only the best for her, though what her stepmother considered 'best' bore little resemblance to what Caroline wanted for herself.

Her resolve weakening in the face of that lady's genuine concern, Caroline gave her a hug. 'I know you want me to be happy. But can you truly see me mistress of some *ton* gentleman's town house or nursery? Striding about in breeches and boots rather than gowns and dancing slippers, stable straw in my braids and barn muck on my shoes? Nor do I possess your sweetness of character, which allows you to listen with every appearance of interest even to the most idiotic of gentlemen. I'm more likely to pronounce him a lackwit to his face, right in the middle of the drawing room.'

'Fiddle,' her stepmother replied, returning the hug. 'You're often a trifle…impatient with those who don't possess your quickness of wit, but you've a kind heart for all that and would never be so rag-mannered. Besides, it was your papa's dying wish that I see you married.'

When Caroline raised her eyebrows sceptically, Lady Denby said, 'Truly, it was! Though I suppose it's only natural of you to doubt it, since he made so little effort to push you towards matrimony while he was still with us. But I promise you, as he breathed his last, he urged me to help you find a good man who'd make you happy.'

Caroline smiled at her stepmother. 'You brightened what turned out to be his last two years. Knowing how much you did, I suppose I shouldn't be surprised that, at the end, he urged you to cajole me into wedlock.'

Lady Denby sighed. 'We were very happy. I've always appreciated, by the way, how unselfish you were in not resenting me for marrying him, after it had been just the two of you for so long.'

Caroline laughed. 'Oh, I resented you fiercely! I *wished* to be sullen and distant and spiteful, but your sweet nature and obvious concern for us both quite overwhelmed my ill humour.'

'You're not still concerned about that silly notion you call 'the Curse'?' Lady Denby enquired. 'I grant you, childbirth poses a danger to every woman. But when one holds one's first child in one's arms, one knows the risk was well worth it! I want you to experience that joy, Caroline.'

'I appreciate that,' Caro said, refraining from pointing out again just how many of her female relations, including her own mama, had died trying to taste that bliss. Her stepmother, ever optimistic, chose to see their deaths as unfortunate chance. Caro did not believe it to be mere coincidence, but there was no point continuing to argue the matter with Lady Denby.

Her stepmother's genuine concern for her future usually kept Caroline from resenting—too much—Lady Denby's increasingly determined efforts to push her towards matrimony…as long as the discussion didn't drag on too long. Time to end this now, before her patience, always in rather short supply when discussing this disagreeable topic, ran out altogether.

'Enough, then. I promise I will view the company with an open mind. Now, I must change if I am to get that ride in before dinner.' She gave Lady Denby an impish grin. 'At least I'll don a habit, instead of my usual breeches and boots.'

Caroline was chuckling at her stepmother's shudder when suddenly the chamber door was thrown open. Caro's stepsister, Eugenia, rushed in, her cheeks flushed a rosy pink and her golden curls tumbled.

'Mama, I've heard the most alarming news! Indeed, I fear we may have to repack the trunks and depart immediately!'

'Depart?' Lady Denby echoed. With a warning look at Eugenia, she turned to the maids. 'Thank you, girls; you may go now.'

After the servants filed out, she faced her daughter. 'What calamity has befallen that would require us to leave when we've only just arrived? Has Mrs Ransleigh fallen ill?'

'Oh, nothing of that sort! It seems that her son, Mr Alastair Ransleigh, just arrived here unexpectedly. Oh, Mama, he has the most dreadful reputation! Miss Claringdon says he always has an actress or high-flyer in keeping, or is carrying on a highly publicised affair with some scandalous matron! Sometimes both at once!'

'And what would you know of high-flyers and scandalous matrons, Eugenia?' Caro asked with a grin.

'Well, nothing, of course,' her stepsister replied, flushing. 'Except what I learned from the gossip at school. I'm just relating what Miss Claringdon said. Her family is very well connected and she spent the entire Season in town last spring.'

'Poor Mrs Ransleigh!' Lady Denby said. 'What an embarrassing development! She can hardly forbid her son to enter his own home.'

'Yes, it's quite a dilemma! *She* cannot send him away, but if any of us should encounter him…why, Miss Claringdon said merely being seen conversing with him is enough for a girl to be declared *fast*. How enormously vexing! I was so looking forward to becoming acquainted with some of the ladies and gentlemen that I shall meet again next Season in London. But I don't want to remain and have my reputation tarnished before I've even begun.' She sighed, a frown marring her perfect brow. 'And that's not all!'

'Goodness, more bad news?' Lady Denby asked.

'I'm afraid so. Accompanying Mr Ransleigh is his cousin, the Honourable Mr Maximillian Ransleigh.'

'Why is that a problem?' Caro asked, dredging out of memory some of the details about the *ton* Lady Denby had drummed into her head during her short stay in London. 'Isn't he the Earl of Swynford's younger son? Handsome, wealthy, destined for a great career in government?'

'He *was*, but his circumstances now are sadly changed. Miss Claringdon told me all about it.' Eugenia gave Caroline a sympathetic look. 'It's no wonder you didn't hear about the scandal, Caro, with Sir Martin falling ill and you having to rush back home. Such a dreadful time for you both!'

'What happened to Mr Ransleigh?' Lady Denby asked.

'"Magnificent Max", they used to call him,' Miss Claringdon said. 'Society's favourite, able to persuade any man and charm any lady. He'd served with distinction in the army and was sent to assist General Lord Wellington during the Congress of Vienna—the perfect assignment, everyone believed, for someone poised to begin a brilliant diplomatic career. But then came the affair with the mysterious woman and the attack on Lord Wellington, and Mr Ransleigh was sent home in disgrace.'

Caroline frowned, remembering now that Harry had told her before leaving for Calcutta how the English commander, then in charge of all the Allied occupation troops in Paris after Napoleon's first abdication, had been forced to station a personal guard because of assassination threats. 'How did it happen?'

'Miss Claringdon didn't know the details, only that he returned to London under a cloud. Then, if that wasn't bad enough, when Napoleon escaped from Elba and headed to Paris, gathering an army as he marched, Mr Ransleigh disobeyed a direct order to remain in London until the Vienna matter was investigated and sailed to Belgium to rejoin his regiment.'

'Did he fight at Waterloo?' Caroline asked.

'I suppose so. There's still talk of a court-martial, though. In any event, Miss Claringdon says his father, the Earl of Swynford, was so incensed, he ordered his son out of the house! Lady Mary Langton, whom everyone thought he would marry, refused to see him, which ought to have been a vast good fortune for some other lucky female. Except that it's now said that he has vowed never to marry and has been going about London with his cousin Alastair, always in the company of some actress or…or lady of easy virtue!'

A glimmer of a memory stirred in Caroline's mind…Harry, talking about the 'Ransleigh Rogues', four cousins who'd been at school with him before they all joined the army and served in assorted regiments on the Peninsula. Brave, strapping lads who could always be found in the thick of the fight, Harry had described them approvingly.

'Miss Claringdon was nearly in tears as she told me the story,' Eugenia continued. 'She'd quite thought to set her cap at him before he began making up to Lady Mary…but now, with him dead set against marriage and keeping such scandalous company, no well-bred maiden would dare associate with him.'

'An earl's son, too.' Lady Denby sighed. 'How vexing.'

'Well, Mama, must we leave? Or do you think we can remain and avoid the Ransleigh gentlemen?'

For a moment, Lady Denby stared thoughtfully into the distance. 'Mrs Ransleigh and her elder daughter, Lady Gilford, are both eminently respectable,' she said at length. 'In fact, Lady Gilford is the most influential young hostess in the *ton*. I'm sure they will talk privately with the gentlemen who, once the situation has been explained, will either take themselves off, or remain apart, so as not to compromise any of Mrs Ransleigh's guests.'

'So they don't inadvertently ruin some young innocent before she even begins her Season?' Caro asked, winking at Eugenia.

'Exactly.' Lady Denby nodded. 'Though I'm convinced it will be handled thus, just to make certain, I shall go at once in search of Mrs Ransleigh and make enquiries.'

Caroline laughed. 'Goodness, Stepmama, how are you to phrase such a question? "Excuse me, Mrs Ransleigh, I just wished to make sure your reprobate son and disgraceful nephew aren't going to hang about, endangering the reputation of my innocent girls!"'

Eugenia gasped, while Lady Denby chuckled and batted Caroline on the arm. 'To be sure, it will be more than a little awkward, but I'll word my question a good deal more discreetly than that!'

'Perhaps she will lock the gentlemen in the attic—or the wine cellar, so none of the young ladies are at risk of irretrievable ruin,' Caroline said.

'Caro, you jest, but it is a serious matter,' Eugenia insisted, a worried frown on her face. 'A girl's whole future depends upon her character being thought above reproach! A ruined reputation *is* irretrievable, and I, for one, don't find the discussion of so appalling a calamity amusing in the least... especially after Miss Claringdon told me Lady Melross arrived this afternoon.'

Lady Denby groaned. 'The worst gossip-monger in the *ton*! What wretched luck! Well, you must both be extremely careful. Lady Melross can winkle out a scandal faster than a prize hound scents a fox. She'd like nothing better than to uncover some misdeed she can report back to her acquaintances in town.'

'Very well,' Caroline said, sobering at the sight of her stepmother's agitation. 'I shall behave myself.'

'And I shall go and make discreet enquiries of our hostess,' Lady Denby said. 'Eugenia, let me escort you to your room, where you should remain until dinner, while I…acquaint myself with the arrangements.'

'Please do, Mama. I shan't stir a foot from my chamber until you tell me it is *safe*!'

'You'd best make haste,' Caroline said, anxious to see them out of the door before her stepmother recalled her intention to ride and forbade *her* to leave her room. She didn't intend to let adherence to some silly society convention get in the way of riding the best horse she'd ever trained.

The two ladies safely dispatched, Caroline tugged the bell pull to summon Dulcie to help her into her habit. Extracting the garment from the wardrobe, she sighed as she thought of the much more comfortable breeches and boots she'd sneaked into her portmanteau. Though she was sensible enough not to don them when her hostess or the guests might be about, she did intend to wear them on her daily dawn rides.

Might she encounter one of the scandalous Ransleigh men this afternoon? If Mrs Ransleigh was going to banish them from the house, the stables were a likely place for them to retreat.

Despite Eugenia's alarm, Caroline felt no apprehension about encountering either Alastair or Max Ransleigh. She doubted either would be so overcome by her charms that they'd try to ravish her in the hayloft. As for having her reputation ruined merely by chatting with them, Harry would consider that nonsense, and his was the only opinion besides her own that mattered to her.

A knock at the door heralded Dulcie's arrival. Caroline

hurried into her habit, anxious to be changed and gone before her stepmother finished her errand and returned, possibly to ban her from riding for the duration.

She didn't slow her pace until she'd escaped the house and made it safely down the lane leading to the stables. Curious now, she looked about the grounds as she walked and peered around the paddock, but saw no sign of anyone besides the groom who had saddled Sultan for her.

She had enjoyed the ride tremendously, thrilled as always to order Sultan through his paces and receive his swift and obliging responses. As she turned him back towards the stables, she had to admit she was a bit disappointed she hadn't caught so much as a glimpse of the infamous Ransleigh men.

It would be interesting to come face to face with a real rogue. Her stepmother, however, would be aghast if she were to converse with either of them, given their terrible reputations and the fact that Lady Melross was now in residence. Were that woman to observe her exchanging innocuous comments about the weather with either Mr Ransleigh, she'd probably find herself branded a loose woman by nightfall.

Although, Caroline thought with a grin as she guided Sultan back into the stable yard, being pronounced 'ruined' in the eyes of society might be positively advantageous, if it relieved her of having to suffer through another Season and made her unacceptable as a bride to anyone save Harry.

The idea struck her then, so audacious that her heart skipped a beat and her hands jerked on the reins, causing Sultan to toss his head. Soothing him with a murmur, she took a deep breath, her pulse accelerating. But outrageous as it was, the idea caught and would not be dislodged.

For the rest of the way back to the stables and from there to her chamber, she examined the idea from every angle. Stepmother would probably be appalled at first, but soon enough, she and Eugenia would be off to London, where Caro's small scandal would be swiftly forgotten in the excitement and bustle of Eugenia's first Season.

By the time she'd summoned Dulcie to help her change out of her habit into one of the unattractive dinner gowns, she'd made up her mind.

Now all she needed to do was track down one of the Ransleigh Rogues and convince him to ruin her.

Chapter Three

In the late afternoon three days later, Max Ransleigh lounged, book in hand, on a bench in the greenhouse, shaded from the setting sun by a bank of large potted palms, his nose tickled by the exotic scents of jasmine and citrus. Alastair had gone off to see about purchasing cows or hens or some such for the farms; armed with an agenda prepared by his aunt that detailed the daily activities of her guests, he'd chosen to spend his afternoon here, out of the way.

A now-familiar restlessness filled him. Not that he wished to participate in this petticoat assembly, but Max missed, and missed acutely, being involved in the active business of government. His entire life, he'd been bred to take part in and take charge at a busy round of political dinners, discussions and house parties. To move easily among the guests, soliciting the opinions of the gentlemen about topics of current interest, drawing out the ladies, setting the shy at ease, skilfully managing the garrulous. Leaving men and women, young or old, eloquent or tongue-tied, believing he'd found their conversation engrossing and believing him intelligent, attentive, masterful and charming.

Skills he might never need to exercise again.

Anguish and anger stirred again in his gut. Oblivious to

the amber beauties of the sunset, he stared at the narrow iron framework of the glasshouse. Somehow, somewhere, he had to find a new and worthwhile endeavour to which he could devote his energy.

So abstracted was he, it was several minutes before he noticed the muffled pad of approaching footsteps. Expecting to see Alastair, he pasted on a smile and turned towards the sound.

The vision confronting him made the jocular words of greeting die on his lips.

Instead of his cousin, a young woman halted before him, garbed in a puce evening gown decorated with an eruption of lace ruffles, iridescent spangles and large knots of pink-silk roses wrapped in more lace and garnished with pearls. So over-trimmed and vulgar was the dress, it was some minutes before his affronted senses recovered enough for him to meet the female's eyes, which were regarding him earnestly.

'Mr Ransleigh?' the lady enquired, dipping him a slight curtsy.

Only then did he remember, being young and female, she must be one of Aunt Grace's guests and therefore should not be here with him. Especially unchaperoned, which a quick glance towards the door of the glasshouse revealed her to be.

'Have you lost your way, miss?' he asked, giving her the practised Max smile. 'Take the leftmost path to the terrace; the French doors will lead you into the drawing room. Hurry, now; I'm sure your chaperon must be missing you.'

He made a little waving motion towards the door, wishing her on her way quickly before anyone could see them. But instead of turning around, she stepped closer.

'No, I'm not looking for her, I'm looking for you and very elusive you've proven to be! It's taken me three days to run you to ground.'

Max stirred uneasily. Normally, when attending a gathering such as this, he'd have taken care never to wander off alone to a location that screamed 'illicit assignation' as loudly as this secluded conservatory. He couldn't imagine that he and Alastair had not been the topic of a good deal of gossip among the attendees—hadn't the girl in the atrocious gown been warned to stay away from them?

Or perhaps she was looking for Alastair? Though he couldn't imagine why a respectable maiden would agree to a clandestine rendezvous with as practised a rogue as his cousin—or why his cousin, whose tastes ran to sensual and sophisticated ladies well skilled in the game, would trouble himself to lead astray one of his mother's virginal guests.

'I'm sorry, miss, but I'm not who you are seeking. I'm Max Ransleigh and it would be thought highly inappropriate if anyone should discover you'd spoken alone with me. For your own good, I must insist that you depart imm—'

'I know which Ransleigh you are, sir,' the young woman interrupted. 'That's why I sought you out. I have a proposition for you. So to speak,' she added, her cheeks pinking.

Max blinked at her, sure he could not have heard her properly. 'A *"proposition"*?' he repeated.

'Yes. I'm Caroline Denby, by the way; my father was the late Sir Martin Denby, of Denby Stables.'

Thinking this bizarre meeting was getting even more bizarre, Max bowed. 'Miss Denby. Yes, I've heard of your father's excellent horses; my condolences on your loss. However, whatever it is you wish to say, perhaps Mrs Ransleigh could arrange a meeting later. Truly, it's most imperative that you quit my presence immediately, lest you put your reputation at risk.'

'But that's exactly what I wish to do. Not just risk it, but ruin it. Irretrievably.'

Of all the things the lady might have said, that was perhaps the most unexpected. The glib, never-at-a-loss Max found himself speechless.

While he goggled at her, jaw dropped, she rushed on, 'You see, the situation is rather complicated, but I don't wish to marry. However, I have a large dowry, so any number of gentlemen want to marry *me*, and my stepmother believes, like most of the known world—' her tone turned a bit aggrieved at this '—that marriage is the only natural state for a woman. But if I were to be found in a compromising situation with a man who then refused to marry me, I would be irretrievably ruined. My stepmother could no longer drag me about, trying to introduce me to prospective suitors, because no gentleman of honour would consider marrying me.'

Suddenly, in a blinding flash of comprehension, he understood her intentions in seeking him out. Chagrin and outrage held him momentarily motionless. Then, with a curt nod, he spat out, 'Good day, Miss Denby', turned on his heel and headed for the door.

She scurried after him and snagged his sleeve, halting his advance. 'Please, Mr Ransleigh, won't you hear me out? I know it's outlandish, and perhaps insulting, but—'

'Miss Denby, it is without doubt the most appalling, outlandish, insulting and crack-brained idea I've ever heard! Naturally, I shall say nothing of this, but if your doubtless long-suffering stepmother—who has my deepest sympathies, by the way—should ever learn of it, you'd be locked up on bread and water for a month!'

The incorrigible female merely grinned at him. 'She is long suffering, the poor dear. Not that it would do her any good to lock me up, for I'd simply climb out of a window. You've already been outraged and insulted. Could you not allow me a few more moments to explain?'

He ought to refuse her unconditionally and beat a hasty exit. But the whole encounter was so unexpected and preposterous, he found himself as intrigued as he was affronted. For a moment, curiosity arm-wrestled prudence…and won.

'Very well, Miss Denby, explain. But be brief about it.'

'I realise it's an…unusual request. As I said, I possess a substantial dowry and I'm already past the age when most well-dowered girls are married off. It wasn't a problem while my father lived—' sorrow briefly shadowed her brow '—for he never pressed me to marry. Indeed, we've worked together closely these last ten years, building the reputation of the Denby Stables. My only desire is to continue that work. But since Papa's death, my stepmother has grown more and more insistent about getting me wed. Because of my dowry, she has no trouble coming up with candidates, even though I possess almost none of the attributes most gentleman expect in a wife. If I were ruined, the suitors would disappear, my stepmother would be forced to give up her efforts and I could remain where I wish to be, at Denby Lodge with my horses.'

'Do you never want to marry?' he asked, curious in spite of himself.

'I do have a…particular friend, but he is in India with the army, and won't return for some time.'

'Wouldn't this "particular friend" be incensed if he were to discover you'd been ruined?'

She waved a hand. 'Harry wouldn't mind. He says most society conventions are contrived and ridiculous.'

'He might feel differently about something that sullied the honour of the woman he wished to marry,' Max pointed out.

'Oh, I'd have to explain, of course. But Harry and I have been the closest of friends since we were children. He'd understand that I only meant to…to save myself for him,' she finished.

'Let me see if I understand you correctly. You wish to be found in a compromising situation with *me*, then have me refuse to marry you, so you would be ruined, which would prevent any honourable gentleman but your friend Harry from ever seeking your hand in wedlock?'

She nodded approvingly, as if he'd just worked out a particularly difficult proof in geometry. 'Exactly.'

'First, Miss Denby, let me assure you that though the world may call me a rogue, I am still a gentleman. I do not ruin innocents. Besides, even if I were obliging enough to agree to this scheme, how could I be sure that in the ensuing uproar—and there would be considerable uproar, I promise you—that you would not change your mind and decide you had better wed me after all? Because—no offence meant to present company—I have no wish at all to marry.'

'Nor do I—no offence meant either—wish to marry you. But no one can *force* us to marry.'

Leaving aside that dubious claim, he said, 'If it's ruination you seek, why did you not approach my cousin Alastair? His reputation is even more scandalous than mine.'

'I considered him, but thought he wouldn't suit. For one, it's his mother's house party and he wouldn't wish to embarrass her. Second, I understand that since being disappointed in love, he's held females in aversion, whereas you are said to genuinely like women. And finally, since your plans for your career were recently shattered, I thought perhaps you would understand what it is like to have your future dictated by the decisions of others, with little control over your own destiny.'

His eyes widened, for the observation struck home. Despite the impossible nature of her request, he felt a rush of sympathy for this young woman who'd lost the only advocate who could guarantee her the life she wanted, while everyone else was trying to force her into a role not of her choosing.

She must have seen the realisation in his eyes, for she said, 'You do understand, don't you? Despite the setback in your choice of career, you are a man; you can make new plans. But when a woman marries, everything she owns, even power over her very body, becomes the possession of her husband, who can sell it, game it away, or ruin it, as he pleases. You must admit, few gentlemen would permit their wives to run a horse-breeding farm. I don't want to see Papa's lifetime of work pass into the hands of a man who would forbid me to manage it, who might neglect, ruin—or even sell it! *My* horses! There's no one I trust with Papa's legacy, except for Harry. So…won't you help me?'

The whole idea was outlandish, as she herself had admitted. He ought to refuse categorically and send her on her way…before someone discovered them and she was compromised in truth. But he hadn't been so intrigued and amused for a very long time. 'You're in love with this Harry, I suppose?'

'He's my best friend,' she said simply, her gaze resting on the glass panes behind them. 'We're comfortable together and we understand each other.'

'What, no passionate declarations, or sighs, or sonnets to your eyebrows? I thought all females dreamt of that.'

She shrugged. 'It might be lovely, I suppose. Or at least my stepsister, who always has her nose in a Minerva Press novel, says so. But I'm not a beauty like Eugenia, the sort of delicate, clinging female who inspires gentlemen to poetry. Harry will marry me when he gets back from India, but that's no help now.'

'Why don't you just contact him about entering into an engagement?'

She sighed. 'If I'd been thinking rationally at the time, I would have asked him to announce we were affianced before he left for India. But Papa had just died unexpectedly and I…' her voice trembled for a moment '…I wasn't myself. Not until weeks later, when my stepmother, fearing Harry might never return, began pressing me to marry, did I realise what Papa's demise would mean to my work and my future.

Meanwhile, Stepmama keeps trying to thrust me into society, hoping I will meet another gentleman I might be persuaded to marry. I shall not.'

'I sympathise—' and he truly did '—with your predicament, Miss Denby. But what of your family, your stepmother and stepsister? Do you not realise that if I were to agree to ruin you, the scandal would devastate them as well? Surely you wouldn't wish to subject them to that.'

'If we were discovered embracing in the garden at a London ball during the height of the Season and refused to marry, it might embarrass Stepmother and Eugenia,' she allowed. 'But I can't believe anything that happens here would even be remembered by the time next Season begins. In any event, Eugenia's a Whitman, not a Denby, so there'll be no contagion of blood and her dowry is handsome enough to make gentlemen overlook her unfortunate connection of a stepsister. By next Season, any stain on your honour for not marrying a girl you were thought to have compromised would have faded also.'

Max shook his head. 'I'm afraid you don't know society at all. So, though I am, ah, honoured that you considered me for your…unusual proposal—'

She chuckled, that unexpected reaction throwing him off the polite farewell he'd been about to utter.

'It's rather obvious you were not *"honoured"*,' she retorted. 'But speaking of honour, did you serve with the Foot Guards at Waterloo?'

'Yes, in a Light Guard unit,' he replied, wondering where she meant to go now with the conversation.

'Then you were at Hougoumont,' she said, nodding. 'The courage and valour of the warriors who survived that engagement will have earned you many admirers. Once most of the army returns home, you will have supporters aplenty to champion your cause. If you cannot be a diplomat, why not rejoin the service? But while you are lounging about, being naught but a rogue, why not do something useful and rescue me?'

'Rescue you by ruining you?' he summarised wryly, shaking his head. 'What an extraordinary notion.' But even as the words left his lips, he recalled how he'd told Alastair earlier that he'd be glad if his aborted career were good for *something*.

Despite the dreadful dress, Miss Denby was an appealing chit, perhaps the most unusual female he'd ever encountered. Spirited and resourceful, too, both factors that tempted him to grant her request, no matter how imprudent. Because despite what she seemed to believe, compromising her *would* cause an uproar and he *would* be honour-bound to marry her.

A realisation that should speed him into giving her a firm refusal and sending her away. But as his thoughtful gaze travelled from her hopeful face downwards, he suddenly discovered the hideous dress's one redeeming feature.

Miss Denby might be a most unusual young woman, but the full, finely rounded bosom revealed by the low-cut bodice of her evening gown was lushly female.

His senses sprang to the alert, flooding his body with sensation and filling his mind with images of ruining her... the scent of orange trees and jasmine washing over them as he tasted her lips...caressing the full breasts straining at her bodice, rubbing his thumb over the pebbled nipples while she moaned with pleasure...

He jerked his thoughts to a halt and his gaze back to her face. She might be startlingly plainspoken, but she was unquestionably an innocent. Did she have any idea what she was asking, wanting him to compromise her?

Instead of bidding her goodbye, he found himself saying, 'Miss Denby, do you know what you must do to be ruined?'

Confirming his assessment of her inexperience, she

blushed. 'Being found alone in a compromising position should be enough. You being a gentleman of the world, I thought you would know how to manage that part. As long as you don't go far enough to get me with child.'

For an instant, he was again speechless. 'Have you no maidenly sensibility?' he asked at last.

'None,' she replied cheerfully. 'Mama died giving birth to me. I was my father's only child and he treated me like the son he never had. I'm more at home in breeches and top-boots than in gowns.' Catching a glimpse of herself reflected in the glass wall, she shuddered. 'Especially gowns like this.'

He couldn't help it; his gaze wandered back to that firm, rounded bosom. Despite the better judgement urging him to dismiss her before someone discovered them and the parson's mousetrap snapped around him, a pesky thought started buzzing around in his mind like a persistent horsefly, telling him that compromising the voluptuous Miss Denby might almost be worth the trouble. 'Some parts of the gown are quite attractive,' he murmured.

He hadn't really meant to say the words out loud, but she glanced over, her eyes following the direction of his gaze. Sighing, she clapped a hand over the exposed bosom. 'Fiddle—I shall have to add a fichu to the neckline. As if the garment were not over-trimmed enough!'

The shadowed valley of décolletage just visible beneath her sheltering fingers was even more arousing than the unimpeded view, he thought, his heartrate notching upwards. Adding a fichu to mask that delectable view would be positively criminal.

Shaking his head to try to rid himself of temptation, he said, 'Your speech is so forthright, I would have expected your dress to be…simpler. Did Lady Denby press the style upon you?'

She laughed again, a delightful, infectious sound that made

him want to share her mirth. 'Oh, no, Stepmama has excellent taste; she thinks the gown atrocious. But I put up such a fuss about being forced to waste time shopping, she let me purchase pretty much whatever I selected. Although I couldn't manage to talk her into the yellow-green silk that made my skin look so sallow.'

The realisation struck with sudden clarity. 'You are deliberately dressing to try to make yourself unattractive?' he asked incredulously.

She gave him a look that said she thought his comment rather dim-witted. 'Naturally. I told you I was trying to avoid matrimony, didn't I? The dress is bad enough, but the spectacles are truly the crowning touch.' Slanting him a mischievous glance, from her reticule she extracted a pair of spectacles, perched them on her nose and peered up at him.

Huge dark eyes stared at him, so enormously magnified he took an involuntary step backwards.

At his retreat, she burst out laughing. 'They make me look like an insect under glass, don't you think? Of course, Stepmama knows I don't wear spectacles, so I can't get away with them when she's around, which is a shame, because they are wondrous effective. All but the most determined fortune hunters quail at the sight of a girl in a hideously over-trimmed dress wearing enormous spectacles. I shall have to remember about the fichu, however. The spectacles can't do their job properly if gentlemen are staring at my bosom.'

Especially when the bosom was as tempting as hers, Max thought. Still, the whole idea was so ridiculous he had to laugh, too. 'Do you really need to *frighten* away the gentlemen?'

Probably hearing the scepticism in his tone, she coloured a bit. 'Yes,' she said bluntly, 'although I assure you, I realise it has nothing at all to do with the attractions of my person. Papa's baronetcy is old, the whole family is excessively well-connected and my dowry is handsome. As an earl's son, do you not need stratagems to protect yourself from matchmaking mamas and their scheming daughters?'

She had him there. 'I do,' he acknowledged.

'So you understand.'

'Yes. None the less,' he continued with genuine regret, 'I'm afraid I can't reconcile it with my conscience to ruin you.'

'Are you certain? It would mean everything to me and I'd be in your debt for ever.'

Her appeal touched his chivalrous instincts—the same ones that had got him into trouble in Vienna. Surely that experience had cured him for ever of offering gallantry to barely known females?

Despite his wariness, he found himself liking her. The sheer outrageousness of her proposal, her frank speech, disarming candour and devious mind all appealed to him.

Still, he had no intention of getting himself leg-shackled to some chit with whom he had nothing in common but a shared sympathy for their inability to pursue their preferred paths in life. 'I'm sorry, Miss Denby. But I can't.'

As if she hadn't heard—or couldn't accept—his refusal, she continued to stare at him with that ardent, hopeful expression. Without the ugly spectacles to render them grotesque, he saw that her eyes were the velvety brown of rich chocolate, illumined at the centre with kaleidoscope flecks of iridescent gold. A scattering of freckles dusted the fair skin of her nose and cheeks, testament to an active outdoor life spent riding her father's horses. The dusky curls peeping out from under an elaborate cap of virulent purple velvet glowed auburn in the fading light of the autumn sunset.

Miss Denby's ugly puce 'disguise' was very effective, he realised with a something of a shock. She was in fact quite a lovely young woman, older than he'd initially calculated, and far more attractive than he'd thought upon first seeing her.

Which was even more reason not to destroy her future—or risk his own.

'You are certain?' she asked softly, interrupting his contemplation.

'I regret having to be so disobliging, but…yes.'

For the first time, her energy seemed to flag. Her shoulders slumped; weariness shadowed her eyes and she sighed, so softly that Max felt, rather than heard, the breath of it touch his lips.

Those signs of discouragement sent a surge of regret through him, ridiculous as it was to *regret* not doing them both irreparable harm. But before he could commit the idiocy of reconsidering, she squared her shoulders like a trooper coming to attention and gave him a brisk nod. 'Very well, I shan't importune you any longer. Thank you for your time, Mr Ransleigh.'

'It was my pleasure, Miss Denby,' he said in perfect truth. As she turned to go, though it was none of his business, he found himself asking, 'What will you do now?'

'I shall have to think of someone else, I suppose. Good day, Mr Ransleigh.' After dipping a graceful curtsy to his bow, she walked out of the conservatory.

He listened to her footfalls recede, feeling again that curious sense of regret. Not at refusing her absurd request, of course, but he did wish he could have helped her.

What an unusual young woman she was! He could readily believe her father had treated her like a son. She had the straightforward manner of a man, with her frank, direct gaze and brisk pace. She took disappointment like a man, too. Once he'd made his decision final, she'd not tried to sway him. Nor had she employed anything from the usual womanly arsenal of tears, pouts or tantrums to try to persuade him.

He'd always prided himself on his perception. But so well did she play the overdressed spinster role, it had taken an unaccountably long time for him to realise that she was a potently alluring female.

She didn't seem to realise that truth, though. In fact, it appeared she hadn't the faintest idea that if she wished to tempt a man into ruining her, her most powerful weapons weren't words, but that generous bosom and that kissable mouth.

Now, if she'd slipped into the conservatory and caught him unawares, still seated on the bench...pressed against him to whisper her request in his ear, leaning over to place those mounded treasures but a slight lift of his hand away...lowered her face in invitation...with the potent scent of jasmine washing over him, he'd probably have ended up kissing her senseless before he knew what he was doing.

At the thought, heat suffused him and his fingers tingled, as if they could already feel the softness of her skin. Damn, but it had been far too long since he'd last pleasured, and had been pleasured by, a lady. He reminded himself that he didn't debauch innocents—even innocents who asked to be debauched.

If only she were not gently born and not so innocent. He could easily imagine whiling away the rest of his time at Barton Abbey with her in his bed, awakening to its full potential the passion he sensed in her, tutoring her in every delicious variety of lovemaking.

But she *was* gently born and marriage was too high a price to pay for a fortnight's pleasure.

The ridiculousness of her request struck him again and he laughed out loud. What an outrageous chit! She'd made him smile and forget his own dissatisfaction, something no one had done for a very long time. He hoped she found a solution to her dilemma.

Her last remark echoed in his ears then, dashing the smile from his lips. Had she said she meant to try some*thing* else? Or some*one* else?

The last of his warm humour leached away as quickly as if he'd jumped into the icy depths of Alastair's favourite fishing stream. Her proposal could be considered merely outlandish…if delivered to a gentleman of honour. But Max could think of any number of rogues who'd be delighted to take the luscious Miss Denby up on her offer…and would be deaf to any pleas that they halt the seduction to which she'd invited them short of 'getting her with child'.

Were there any such rogues present at this gathering? Surely Jane and Aunt Grace would not have invited anyone who might take advantage of an innocent. He certainly hoped not, for he had no doubt, with the same single-minded directness she'd employed with him, Miss Denby would not flinch from making her preposterous offer to someone else.

He tried to tell himself that Miss Denby's situation was not his concern and he should put her, enchanting bosom and all, from his mind. But despite the salutary lesson of Vienna, he found he couldn't completely ignore a lady in distress.

Not that he meant to accept her offer, of course. But while he remained at Barton Abbey, shooting, fishing with Alastair, reading and contemplating his future, he could still keep an eye—from a safe distance—on Miss Caroline Denby.

Chapter Four

Still brooding over her failed interview with Mr Ransleigh, Caroline rose at the first faint light of dawn, quickly donned the hidden boots and breeches, and crept silently to the stables before the tweenies were up to light the fires. She encountered only one sleepy groom, rousted from his bed above the tack room when she went in to retrieve Sultan's saddle.

After last night's dinner, the guests had stayed up playing interminable rounds of cards, so she felt fairly assured they would all be abed late this morning. Her peep-of-dawn start should give her at least an extra hour to ride Sultan before prudence required her to slip back to the house and change into more acceptable clothing.

He flicked his ears and nickered at her as she entered the stables, then nosed in her pockets for his usual treat as she led him from his stall. She fed him the bit of apple, quickly saddled him and led him to the lane, then gave him his head. Eagerly the gelding set off at a gallop, the calming effects of which she needed even more than the horse.

For the next few moments, she gave herself over to the unequalled delight of bending low over the neck of the magnificent animal beneath her, heart, mind and soul attuned to his effort as the ground flew by beneath his pounding hooves.

All too soon, it was time to pull up. Crooning her approval, she schooled him to a cool-down walk while her attention, no longer distracted by the pleasure of riding, returned inexorably to her dilemma.

Unwise as it was, it seemed she'd pinned her hopes on the mad scheme of being ruined. She hadn't realised until after he had turned her down just how much she'd been counting on coaxing Max Ransleigh to accept her offer and put an end to her matrimonial woes.

Though she had to admit to being a little relieved he *had* refused. Miss Claringdon had called him 'charming', but he exuded more than charm. Though she'd rather liked his keen wit, some prickly sense of awareness had flooded her as she'd stood under his gaze, some connection almost as real as a touch, that made her feel nervous and jittery as a colt eyeing his first bridle. When he'd asked her if she knew what he must do to compromise her, she'd blushed like a ninny, while visions of him drawing her close, covering her mouth with his, flashed through her mind. Thank heavens her garbled reply had made him laugh, but though the fraught moment had passed, she'd still felt his eyes examining her, heating her skin even as she walked away from him.

He certainly did not inspire her with the same ease and confidence Harry did.

Perhaps that's why she'd remained so tense and sleepless last night, tossing and turning in her bed as she ran through her mind all the gentlemen present at the house party who might be possible alternatives to Max Ransleigh.

Only Mr Alastair's reputation was scandalous enough to guarantee that being found in his presence would be enough to ruin her. She supposed she could try her luck with him, but she doubted he could be persuaded to throw his mother's house party into an uproar by compromising one of her guests.

She could approach him back in London next spring. But though she was fairly confident ruining herself here wouldn't create any long-lasting problems for her family, doing so at the height of the Season probably would, as Max Ransleigh had asserted. She certainly didn't wish to repay the kindness Lady Denby and Eugenia had always shown her by spoiling in any way the Season that her stepsister anticipated so eagerly.

Which brought her back to the guests at this house party.

Unless she could work out some way to turn one of them to account, the future stretched before her like a grimly unpleasant repetition of her curtailed London Season: evening after evening of dinners, musicales, card parties, balls and routs, crowded about by men eager to relieve her of her fortune.

Was there any way she could avoid being dragged through all that? Maybe she should write to Harry after all, proposing a long-distance engagement. But would Lady Denby consider such an informally made offer binding?

By the time they reached the end of the field bordering the paddock, she was no closer to finding an answer to her problem. Thrusting it aside in disgust, she turned her attention back to putting Sultan through his paces.

If only, she thought as she commanded him to a trot, life could be schooled to such perfection as a fine horse.

Blinking sleep from his eyes, Max shouldered creel and rod and followed Alastair to the stables. His cousin, having learned from his factor in the village that the fish were running well in the river, had dragged him from his bed before first light so they might try their luck at snagging some trout.

They were tromping in companionable silence down the path leading to the river when Alastair suddenly halted. 'By Jove, that's the finest piece of horseflesh I've seen in a dog's age, trotting there in the paddock,' he declared, pointing in that direction. 'Whose nag is it, do you know?'

Max peered into the distance, where a stable boy was guiding a showy bay hack in a series of high-stepping motions. His eyes widening in appreciation, he noted the horse's deep chest, broad shoulders, glossy sheen of coat and steady, perfect rhythm. His interest piqued as well, he said, 'I have no idea. The bay is a magnificent beast.'

'That's not one of our grooms, either. Horse must belong to one of Mama's guests, who brought his own man to exercise it.' Alastair laughed. 'I might resent providing the food and drink these man-milliners consume while they loiter here, but an animal as magnificent as that is welcome to my largesse.'

'Aunt Grace's largesse, to be fair.'

'Not that I truly begrudge Jane the expense of their party. I just wish the guests were less tedious and the timing not so inconvenient.'

At least one guest, Max thought, had not been 'tedious' in the least. He smiled as images of Miss Denby ran through his head: staring up at him with a grin, bug-eyed in her spectacles; the atrocious puce gown she'd employed to 'disguise' her loveliness; and ah, yes, the luscious breasts whose rounded tops enticed him above the low neckline of her dinner dress…

Desire rose in him, surprising in its intensity. Reminding himself that seducing Miss Denby was not a possibility, he thrust the memories of her from his mind and turned his attention back to the horse, now being put through several intricate manoeuvres.

Finally, the groom pulled up and leaned low over his mount's head, probably murmuring well-deserved compliments in his ear. Straightening, the lad kicked him to a trot across the paddock towards the lane leading back to the stables.

'I'd like a closer look at that horse,' Alastair said. 'If we cut back at the next crossing, we should reach the stable lane about the same time as the groom.'

Max nodding agreement, the two cousins set off. Confirming Alastair's prediction, after hurrying down the path, they emerged from behind a stand of trees just as the rider trotted past.

Apparently startled by their unexpected appearance, the horse neighed and reared up. With expert ease, the lad controlled him.

'Sorry to have frightened your mount,' Alastair told him. 'We've been admiring him from the other side of the paddock.'

Max was about to add his compliments when his assessing eyes moved from the horse to the rider. With a shock, he realised the 'groom' was in fact no groom at all, but Miss Caroline Denby.

Alastair, no sluggard where the feminine form was concerned, simultaneously reached the same conclusion. 'Devil's teeth! It's a girl!' he muttered to Max, even as he swept his hat off and bowed. 'Good morning, miss. Magnificent horse you have there!'

Miss Denby's alarmed gaze leapt from Alastair to Max. As recognition dawned in her eyes, her face flamed. 'Stepmother is going to be furious,' she murmured with a sigh. Apparently accepting that she'd been well and truly caught, she nodded to him. 'Good morning, Mr Ransleigh.'

Alastair's brows lifted as he looked enquiringly from Miss Denby back to Max, then gestured to him to perform the introductions. Bowing to the inevitable, Max said, 'Miss Denby, may I present my cousin, your host, Mr Alastair Ransleigh.'

She made a rueful grimace. 'I wish you wouldn't. I thought surely I'd be able to return before anyone but the grooms were stirring. Couldn't you just pretend you hadn't seen me?'

'Don't fret, Miss Denby,' Max said. 'We're not supposed to let *you* see *us*, either. Shall this unexpected encounter remain our secret?'

She smiled. 'In that case, I shall be pleased to meet you, Mr Ransleigh.'

'And I am absolutely charmed to meet you, Miss Denby,' Alastair replied, his rogue's eyes avidly roving her form.

Max restrained the strong desire to smack him. Hitherto he'd thought nothing could accentuate a lady's body like a silk gown, preferably thin and cut low in the bosom. But though he'd be delighted to see Miss Denby garbed only in the sheerest of materials, there was no escaping the fact that, in male riding attire, she looked entirely delectable.

Tight-knit breeches hugged her slender thighs and the curve of her trim *derrière* upon the saddle, while riding boots outlined her shapely calves. Beneath her unbuttoned tweed jacket, her shirt, open at the top since she wore no cravat, revealed a swan's curve of neck, kissable hollows at her throat and collarbones, and a lush fullness beneath that made his mouth water. Several lengths of the glossy dark hair she'd thrust up under her cap had tumbled down during the ride and lay in damp, tangled curls upon her face and neck—looking much as they might, he thought, if she were reclining against her pillows after a night of lovemaking.

The heated gleam in Alastair's eyes said he was envisioning exactly the same scene, damn him.

'Bargain or not, I'd best return immediately and get into more proper clothing,' Miss Denby said, pulling Max from his lusty imagining. 'Good day, gentlemen.'

'Wait, Miss Denby,' Alastair called. 'There wasn't a soul stirring when we left the house but a short time ago. Tarry with us a minute, please! I'd like to ask about your mount. You were training him, weren't you?'

She'd been looking towards the stables, obviously anxious to be away, but at Alastair's expression of interest, she turned back, her eyes brightening. 'Yes. Sultan is the most promising of our four-year-olds. Father bred him, Cleveland

Bay with some Arabian for stamina and Irish thoroughbred
for strength in the bone. Easy-going, with wonderful paces.
He'll make a superior hunter or cavalry horse…although I've
about decided I cannot part with him.'

'Your father…you mean Sir Martin Denby, of the Denby
Stud?' Alastair asked. When she nodded, he said, 'No wonder
your mount is so impressive. Max, you remember Mannington brought several of Sir Martin's horses to the Peninsula.
Excellent mounts, all of them.'

'Lord Mannington?' Miss Denby echoed. 'Ah, yes, I remember; he purchased Alladin and Percival. Geldings who
are kin to Sultan here, having the same dam, but a sire with
a bit more Arabian blood. I'm so pleased to know they performed well.'

'Mannington said their stamina and speed saved his neck
on several occasions,' Alastair said. After giving her a second, more thorough appraisal, he said, 'You seem very knowledgeable about your father's operation.'

'I've helped him with it since I mounted my first pony,'
she responded, pride in her voice. 'In addition to training
the foals, I kept the stud books and sales records, as Papa
was more concerned with charting bloodlines than plotting
numbers.'

Sympathy softened Alastair's face. 'You must miss him
very much. My condolences on your loss.' While, her lips
tightening, she nodded a quick acknowledgement, Alastair
said, 'A sad loss for the stud as well. Who is running it now?'

'I am,' she replied, lifting her chin. 'Papa involved me
in every aspect of the business, from breeding the mares to
weaning the foals to breaking the yearlings and beginning
the training of the two-year-olds.' Her chin notched higher.
'Denby Stud is my life. But…' she gestured toward the fishing gear looped across their shoulders '…I mustn't keep you
from the trout eager to sacrifice themselves to your lures.'

She turned her mount's head towards the stable, then paused. 'I *can* count on your discretion, I trust?'

'Absolutely,' Alastair assured her.

Giving them a quick nod, she touched her heels to the gelding and rode off. Alastair, Max noted with disgruntlement, was following the bounce of her shapely posterior against the saddle as closely as he was, devil take him.

After she disappeared around the curve in the lane, Alastair turned to Max, grinning. 'Well, well, well. Don't think I've ever seen you so silent around a female. Here I thought you'd been moping about, mourning your lost career. Instead, you're been perfecting your credentials as a rogue, sneaking off to secret assignations with a tempting little morsel like that.'

Max struggled to keep his temper in check. 'Let me remind you,' he said stiffly, 'that "morsel" is one of your mother's guests and an innocent maid.'

'Is she truly innocent?' Alastair shook his head disbelievingly. 'Lord have mercy, riding astride in breeches like that! I can't believe I didn't immediately realise she was female. Just shows how one doesn't recognise what is right before one's eyes when one's not expecting it. Though she *is* an excellent rider: fine hands, great seat.' With a chuckle, he added, 'Wouldn't mind having her in the saddle, those lovely long legs wrapped around *me*.'

A flash of fury surging through him, Max whacked his cousin with his fishing pole. 'Stubble it! That's a *lady* you're insulting.'

'Fancy her for yourself, do you?' Alastair asked, unrepentant. 'With her going about like that, her limbs and bottom outlined for any red-blooded man to ogle, it's not my fault she evokes such thoughts. Nor are we the only ones watching.' He pointed toward the opposite side of the field. 'Some bloke over there is ogling her, too.'

His gaze following the direction of his cousin's extended arm, Max squinted into the morning sunlight. 'Who is it?'

'How should I know? Probably another one of those damned macaroni merchants hanging about, measuring up the female flesh on display. Not a man's man among them— petticoat-string dandies all,' he concluded in disgust. 'But this girl...she's truly an innocent, you say?'

'Absolutely.'

'How do you know so much about her?'

Knowing he'd have to explain, but not wishing to reveal too much—certainly not her scandalous proposition—Max gave Alastair an abbreviated version of his meeting with Miss Denby in the conservatory.

'Devil's teeth, she's a luscious armful in breeches. What a mistress she'd make!' Alastair exclaimed, then waved Max to silence before he could deliver another rebuke. 'Don't get your cravat in a knot; I know there's no chance of that. She is a "lady", amazing as that seems to a man seeing her for the first time garbed like that. If *marriage* is her stepmoth-er's object, pulling it off is going to be difficult if word gets out of her offending the proprieties by riding about in boy's dress. Though it would almost be worth wedlock, to get one's hands on the Denby Stud.'

'So she fears. She doesn't want to marry, she said, and risk losing control over it.'

Alastair nodded. 'I suppose I can understand. One wouldn't wish to turn such a prime operation over to some hamfisted looby who couldn't housebreak a puppy.'

'How infuriating to see everything you'd worked on, worked for, the last ten years of your life given over to some-one else. Ruined, perhaps, and you unable to do anything about it.'

Alastair gave him a searching look, as if he thought Max were speaking more about himself than Miss Denby. 'Well,

I wish her luck. She's an odd lass, to be sure. But undeniably attractive, even without the inducement of the Denby Stud. Now, if we're going to catch breakfast, we'd better be going.' At that, Alastair kicked his mount into motion.

Lagging behind for a moment, Max studied the man across the field, who was now striding back toward the stables. He'd better find out who that was. And continue to keep an eye on Miss Denby.

Chapter Five

After a most satisfactory session at the stream, Max and Alastair returned the trout to the kitchen for Cook to turn into breakfast. While Alastair went on to change out of his fishing garb, Max hesitated by the door to his aunt's room.

All during their mostly silent camaraderie at the river, rather than concentrate on fish, Max had thought about his aunt's unusual guest. He'd had, he was forced to admit, to exercise some considerable discipline to keep his thoughts from turning from the serious matter of her situation and the man watching her to memories of her inviting gurgle of a laugh, that enticing bosom and the wonderfully suggestive up-and-down motion of her *derrière* on the saddle.

Making enquiries of Aunt Grace might seem odd, but while Alastair was otherwise occupied, he probably ought to risk it. If he discovered that the gentleman guests included none but paragons of honour and virtue, he could stop worrying about Miss Denby and dismiss her situation from his mind.

Decision made, he knocked and was bid to enter. 'Max! This is a pleasant surprise!' Mrs Ransleigh cried, her expression of mild curiosity warming to one of genuine pleasure.

'Will you take chocolate with me, or some coffee? I confess, I do feel terrible, I've been so poor a hostess to you.'

'Nonsense,' he said, waving away her offer. 'I'll not stay long enough for coffee; we're just back from the river, and I'm sure you'd as lief I not leave fish slime on your sofa. You know Alastair and I are quite able to keep ourselves well entertained.'

She flushed. 'I do appreciate your…discretion. Even as I absolutely deplore the necessity for it! Is there truly no hope of your finding another diplomatic position?'

'I have some ideas, but there's no point initiating anything yet while Father is still so angry. You know he has the influence to block whatever I attempt, should he wish to.'

'That's so *James*!' she cried. 'Brilliant orator and skilled politician your father may be, but he can be so bull-headed and unreasonable sometimes, I'd like to shake him!'

Though he appreciated his aunt's sympathy, he'd just as soon not dwell on the painful topic of his ruined prospects. 'I didn't stop by to talk about me,' he parried. 'How goes your party? Has Jane succeeded in leg-shackling any of the guests? Has Lissa found her ideal mate?'

'Felicity is enjoying herself immensely, which is all I wished for her, since I have no desire to give her up to a husband just yet! Among the other guests, there are some promising developments, though it's too early to tell yet whether they will result in engagements.'

Trying for a nonchalant tone, Max said, 'I happened to encounter one of your young ladies. No, nothing scandalous about it,' he assured her hastily before, her eyes widening in alarm, she could speak. 'I met her briefly and by chance one afternoon in the conservatory, where she darted in, she told me, to escape some suitor. A most unusual young woman.'

Aunt Grace laughed. 'Oh, dear! That must have been Miss Denby! Poor Diana—her stepmother, Lady Denby, an old friend of mine—is quite in despair over the girl. Perhaps you didn't notice in your quick meeting, but the lady is rather... old.'

Were he pressed to describe what he'd noticed about Miss Denby during that first meeting, Max thought, 'old' would not be among the adjectives that came to mind. 'I must confess, I didn't notice,' he replied in perfect truth.

'She should have had her first Season years ago,' his aunt continued. 'But she was her widowed father's only child. Now that I face having *my* last chick leave home, I can perfectly understand why he didn't wish to lose her. She's a great heiress, though, so Diana hasn't given up hope yet of her making an acceptable match, even though at five-and-twenty she's practically on the shelf.'

'A doddering old age, to be sure.'

'For a female of good birth and fortune to remain unwed at such an age *is* unusual,' his aunt said reprovingly. 'With her being practically an ape-leader, you'd think she'd be eager to wed, but apparently it's quite the opposite! Though the poor dear seems intelligent enough, she's terribly shy in company and possesses not a particle of conversation unrelated to hunting and horses. To make matters worse, though I hesitate to say something so uncharitable about a guest, her taste in clothing is atrocious. I expect, arbiter of fashion that you are, you did notice the dreadful gown.'

'I did,' he said drily. *Though my attention focused more on the neckline than the trimming.* 'So, there is no one here who wishes to coax her into matrimony?

'I had high hopes of Lord Stantson. A very knowledgeable horseman, he's a mature man with a calm demeanour I thought might appeal to her.' At Max's raised eyebrow, she said, 'Many young ladies prefer to entrust their future to the steady hand of an older gentleman, rather than risk all with such dashing young rakes as *some* I might mention!

Mr Henshaw has also been pursuing her, though I have to admit,' his aunt concluded, 'she has given neither man any encouragement.'

Henshaw! That was the man who'd been watching her in the paddock this morning, Max realised.

Aunt Grace sighed. 'Lady Denby is quite determined to get her settled before her own daughter Eugenia makes her début next spring. The poor girl's chances for making a good match will diminish drastically if she must share her Season with her stepsister, for Eugenia Whitman is nearly as wealthy as Miss Denby and far outshines her in youth, wit and beauty.'

Miss Denby was hardly an antidote, Max thought, indignant on her behalf before he recalled the great pains she'd been taking to ensure she created just the sort of negative impression his aunt was describing.

'If she seems so unwilling and unsuitable, I wonder that her stepmother keeps pushing her to wed. Why not let her remain at Denby Lodge, with her horses?'

'Well, she must marry *some time*,' Mrs Ransleigh said. 'What else is she to do? And she's very, very rich.'

'Which explains the gentlemen's pursuit of someone who gives them no encouragement.' Max had been feeling more hopeful, but some niggle of memory made him frown.

Having spent so much time away with the army, he hadn't visited London very often the last few years, but he vaguely recalled from his clubs the tattle that Henshaw was always pursuing some heiress or other. 'Is Henshaw a fortune hunter?'

Aunt Grace coloured. 'I should never describe him in such uncomplimentary terms. Mr Henshaw comes from a very good family and is perfectly respectable. If he wishes to marry a wealthy girl, such a desire is hardly unusual.'

Definitely a fortune hunter, Max concluded. 'Anyone else angling for the reluctant Miss Denby?'

His aunt fixed him with an assessing look. 'Did the young lady catch your interest?'

'Does she look like a lady who would attract me?' Max asked, feeling somehow guilty for disparaging a woman he admired even as he imbued his voice with the right note of disdain.

Fortunately, his previous flirts had always been acknowledged beauties, so the hopeful light in his aunt's eyes died. 'No,' she admitted.

'I merely found her amusingly unconventional.'

Aunt Grace laughed ruefully. 'She is certainly that! Poor Lady Denby! One can only sympathise with her difficulties in trying to get the girl married.'

Having discovered what he'd come for, he'd best take his leave, before Aunt Grace tried to spin some matrimonial web around *him*. 'I'll leave you to your dresser and return to my breakfast, which Cook is now preparing.'

'Go enjoy your fish, then. I'm so glad you stopped by. I do hope you'll stay long enough that we can have a good visit, after all the guests leave. Felicity and Jane are eager to have more from you than a few hurried words.'

'I would like that.'

'Enjoy your day, then, my dear.'

Max kissed her hand. 'Enjoy your guests.'

After bowing himself out, Max walked towards the study he and Alastair had turned into their private parlour, running over in his mind what he'd learned from Aunt Grace about Miss Denby.

So none but Stantson and Henshaw had set their sights on the heiress. If Aunt Grace believed both to be gentlemen, he had nothing to worry about. He might enquire and see what Alastair knew about the men, just to be sure, but unless his cousin disclosed something to their discredit, he had no reason to involve himself any further in the matter of her future.

Though, as he'd assured his aunt, the lady was nothing at all like the women who usually attracted him, he had to admit to a feeling of regret at the idea that he'd seen the last of Miss Denby, the only unusual member of what was otherwise a stultifyingly conventional gathering of females.

Several days later, while Alastair occupied himself in the estate office, Max repaired to his bench in the conservatory to while away the afternoon with some reading.

No sun gilded the tropical plants today, but the morning's rain had left a soft mist dewing the grass, greying the greens of the trees, shrubs and vines. Within the warm, heated expanse of the glasshouse, the soft swish of swaying palms and ferns and the sweet exotic scent of citrus and jasmine were infinitely soothing.

Alastair had informed him the previous evening that he'd heard the colonel of Max's former regiment had just returned from Paris. He'd recommended that Max speak with him about a position, sound advice Max meant to follow. The calm and beauty surrounding him here further lifted his spirits, filling him with the sense that much was still possible, if he were patient and persistent enough.

He was absorbed in his book when, some time later, a lavender scent tickled his nose. At the same moment, a soft 'Oh!' of surprise brought his head up, just in time to see Miss Denby halt abruptly a few yards away down the pathway.

A warm wave of anticipation suffused him, even as she hastily backed away. 'I'm so sorry, Mr Ransleigh! I didn't mean to disturb you!'

'Then you didn't come here to seek me out?' he asked, his tone teasing.

'Oh, no! I wouldn't have intruded on your privacy, sir. Your cousin Miss Felicity, who has become great friends with my stepsister, Eugenia, told her you and Mr Alastair would be away all day.'

'You truly are not pursuing me, then?' He clapped a hand to his chest theatrically. 'What a blow to my self-esteem.'

For an instant, her brow furrowed in concern, before her ear caught his ironic tone and she grinned. 'I dare say your self-esteem can withstand the injury. But I told you I would not tease you and I meant it. I shall leave you to your book.'

It was only prudent that she leave at once…but he didn't want her to, not just yet.

'Since you've already interrupted my study, do stay for a moment, Miss Denby.'

She raised her eyebrows. 'For a chat that will become another of our little secrets?'

He grinned, pleased that she would joke with him. 'Exactly.' Come, sit.'

He motioned her to the bench…and found himself holding his breath, hoping she would come to him. Already his pulse had kicked up and all his senses sharpened, his body quickening at her nearness—which should have been warning enough that urging her to linger was not wise. He thrust the cautionary thought aside.

And then in a graceful swish of fabric, she sat down beside him. Max inhaled deeply as her faint lavender scent washed over him. It must be soap; he'd be astonished if she wore perfume. She was garbed against the misty chill in a cloak that covered her from head to toe, masking whatever hideous gown she'd selected along with, alas, that fine bosom. Even so, close up, he was able to drink in the fine texture of her face, the soft glow of her skin, the perfect shell of ear outlined by a mass of auburn-highlighted brown curls, tamed under her hat on this occasion. She tilted her face up to him and he lost himself in her extraordinary eyes, watching the golden centres shimmer within their dark-velvet depths.

Her lips, full and shapely, bore no trace of artificial gloss or colour. Would her mouth taste of wine, of apple, of mint?

Make conversation, he reminded himself, pulling back abruptly when he realised he'd been lowering his head toward their tempting surface. Devil's teeth, why did this young woman of no outstanding beauty evoke such a strong response from him?

'How goes your campaign?' he managed.

She made a moue of distaste, curving back the ripe fullness of her mouth. He wanted to trace the twin dimples that flanked it with his tongue.

'Not well, I'm afraid. As one might expect, all the men—the ones your aunt *invited*, in any event,' she added, tossing him a mischievous glance, 'are unmistakably gentlemen. I've considered each of them, but some are actively pursuing other ladies. Of the two pursuing *me*, neither is likely to refuse to marry, should I find some way to get myself compromised. Then there's the inhibiting presence of Lady Melross, whom I suspect Lady Claringdon inveigled to be present just to ensure that if any gentleman coaxed a maiden to stroll with him where she shouldn't, he'd be fairly caught—unless he was too dishonourable to do the proper thing and abandoned the girl to her ruin.' She sighed. 'Would that I might be!'

'Lady Melross is a dreadful woman, who delights in spreading bad news,' Max said feelingly. She'd been the first to trumpet the rumours of his disgrace, even before he reached London after leaving Vienna, then to whisper that his father had banished him. Though he knew she was zealous about reporting the failings of anyone of prominence whose missteps happened to reach her ears, it seemed to him she took a particularly malevolent interest in his affairs.

If he ever managed to secure a prominent position in government, hers would be the first name he would see struck from the invitation list at any function he attended.

Miss Denby drummed her fingers absently on the bench. 'I wish I could marry my horse. He's the most interesting male here, present company excepted, of course. Even if he has, ah, been deprived of the tools of his manhood.'

Surprised into a bark of laughter, Max shook his head. 'You really do say the most outlandish things for a lady.'

She shrugged. 'Because I'm not one, really. I wish I could convince all the pursing gentlemen of the fact that I'd make them a sadly deficient wife.'

With her seated there, tantalising his nose with her subtle lavender scent and his body by her nearness, Max thought that, for certain of a wife's duties, she would do admirably.

Before his thoughts could stampede down that lane, he reined himself back to more proper conversational paths. 'Still training your gelding every morning?'

'Yes.'

'In breeches and boots?' *A lovely image, that!*

'No more breeches and boots, alas; you and your cousin taught me to be more cautious. Though I still ride early, it's getting more difficult to avoid company. Lord Stantson has been pressing me to let him ride with me of a morning, but thus far has honoured my wishes when I firmly decline. He's a fine enough gentleman, but I've heard he came here specifically looking for a second wife. Since I'm not angling for the position, I'm trying to give him no encouragement.'

Wrinkling her nose in distaste, she continued, 'Mr Henshaw, however, not only requires no encouragement, he positively refuses to be *dis*couraged! He's turned up each of the last two mornings, despite my continued insistence that I prefer to ride alone. How am I to train Sultan properly, with him interrupting us?'

For a moment, her eyes focused unseeing on the glasshouse wall and she shivered. 'Though I was garbed in a stiflingly proper habit, he seems to be always *staring* at me. I don't care for his expression when he does so, either—as if I were a favourite pudding he meant to devour.'

Max frowned. She might have worn a proper habit every day since that first one, but she hadn't been the morning he'd seen Henshaw watching her. How close a look at her had the man got? Close enough to get an eyeful of the shapely form he and Alastair had so appreciated?

If so, Max could hardly fault any man for staring at her like a 'pudding one meant to devour'. Which didn't reduce one whit the strong desire rising in him to blacken both Henshaw's eyes for making her feel uncomfortable.

'He insisted on riding with me, despite the fact that I was quite obviously trying to work with Sultan,' Miss Denby continued. 'Honestly, he possesses terrible hands and the worst seat I've ever been forced to observe. I've taken to riding even earlier to avoid him.'

'I've never seen him astride, only observed his…remarkably inventive dress. He must make his tailors very rich.'

She chuckled. 'A man milliner indeed. One would think, with his exacting tastes in garments, sheer disgust over my atrocious gowns would be enough to dissuade him from pursuing me.'

She looked up at him, smiling faintly, those great dark eyes inviting him to share her amusement. Her lavender scent wrapped itself around him like a silken scarf, pulling him closer. He wanted to trace the scent to its origin, lick it from her neck and ears and the hollows of the collarbones he'd seen that day she'd ridden in an open-collared shirt and breeches.

As he gazed raptly, her dark eyes widened and her smile faded. She seemed as mesmerised as he, her lips parting slightly, giving him the tiniest glimpse of pink tongue within the warmth of her mouth.

Desire shot through him, pulsing in his veins, curling his fingers with the itch to cup her chin and taste her.

'Well,' she said, her voice a bit breathless, 'I suppose I should leave you now, lest someone come by and see us. Unless…' she smiled tremulously, brushing a curl back from her forehead as her cheeks pinked '…you'd like to…reconsider my proposition?'

Her cloak fell open at that movement. Beneath the fabric of another overtrimmed, pea-green gown, he saw the rapid rise and fall of her breasts as her breathing accelerated.

His certainly had. All over his body, things were accelerating and rising and pulsing. The need to kiss her, learn the taste of her mouth, the contour of her ears and shoulders and the hollow of her throat, thrummed in his blood. His gaze wandered back to the mesmerizing shimmer of gold in her eyes and halted.

In his head, that persistent fly of temptation buzzed louder, almost drowning out good sense.

Almost.

It took him a full minute to shoo it away and find his voice.

'A tempting offer. But I fear I must still decline.'

Despite the words, he couldn't make himself stand, bow, put an end to this interlude, as prudence demanded.

She, too, remained motionless, her eyes studying his, the current of attraction pulsing between them almost palpable. As he watched intently, the embarrassment she'd displayed upon repeating her offer changed to uncertainty and then, yes, he was certain, to desire. Confirming that assessment, slowly she leaned towards him and tilted her face up, bringing her lips tantalisingly close.

Max forced himself to remain motionless, while every nerve and sense screamed at him to lower his head and take her mouth. In some distant corner of his brain, honour and common sense was nattering that he should move away, end this before it began.

But he couldn't. He would not cross that slight boundary

and touch her first, but, shutting out the little voice insisting this was madness, he waited, aflame with anticipation, confident she would close the distance between them and kiss him.

Her eyelashes feathered shut. His eyes closed, too, as her warm breath washed over him, the first tentative wave from an incoming tide of pleasure.

Just as his eager body whispered 'now, now', she straightened abruptly and scooted backwards on the bench.

'I—I should go,' she said unsteadily.

Max shook his head, trying to drown out the buzzy little voice that urged him to lure her into remaining.

And he could do it; he knew he could.

Over the protest of every outraged sense, he wrestled his desire back under control. 'That would be wisest…if not nearly so pleasant.'

'Wisest…yes,' she repeated and belatedly bobbed to her feet. 'Thank you for the, ah, chat. Good day, Mr Ransleigh.'

He stood as well and bowed. 'Good day, Miss Denby.'

Regretfully, while his body yammered and scolded at him like a disgruntled housewife cheated by a market vendor, he watched her retreat down the pathway. Just before turning the corner to exit the glasshouse, she halted.

Looking back over her shoulder, she said softly, in tones of wonder, 'You tempt me too, you know.'

A surge of delight and pure masculine satisfaction blazed through him. Before he could reply, she turned and hurried out.

He jumped to his feet and paced after her. Fortunately, by the time he reached the door to the glasshouse, sanity had returned.

Good grief, if he couldn't rein in his reaction to her, he'd better avoid her altogether, lest he find himself being quickstepped to the altar. Had he not committed idiocies enough for one lifetime?

So he made himself stand there, watching her trim figure retreat through the mist down the pathway back to the
house. But as she took the turn leading to the drawing-room
terrace, a man stepped out.

Henshaw.

Max gritted his teeth. Frowning, he watched the exchange,
too far away to hear their voices, as Henshaw bowed to Miss
Denby's curtsy. Offered his arm, which she declined with a
shake of her head and a motion of her hand in the direction
of the stables. Henshaw, giving a dismissive wave, offered
his arm again, which, after a few more unintelligible words,
she reluctantly accepted.

They'd just set off on the path to the house when Alastair
came striding up. Putting a hand to his forehead, he peered
into the distance and declared, 'That looks like the chap who
was watching Miss Denby ride the other morning.'

'It is. David Henshaw. Do you know him?'

'Ah, yes, that's why he looked familiar. He's a member
at Brooks's. Too concerned with the cut of his coat and the
style of his cravat for my taste. He the front runner for Miss
Denby's affections?'

'Not if she has anything to say about it.'

'Ah, had another little chat with the lady, did you? Sure
you don't fancy her for yourself?'

He made himself give Alastair a withering look. 'Does she
look like a woman I'd fancy?' he drawled, feeling more uncomfortable about uttering the disparaging remark this time,
after he'd practically devoured her on the greenhouse bench,
than when he'd been trying to throw Aunt Grace off the scent.

'Not in your usual style,' Alastair allowed, 'but there is
something about her. Devilishly arousing in her own way…
like when riding astride in breeches! What a shame she's an
innocent; don't forget, my friend, that the price for tasting
that morsel is marriage.'

'So I keep reminding myself,' Max muttered, grimly aware that the moment she'd sat down beside him, his instincts for self-preservation had gone missing.

'I'm not surprised Henshaw is on the scent,' Alastair continued. 'The latest word at the London clubs was he's run so far into debt, he can't even go back to his town house for fear of meeting the bailiffs. The Denby girl's fat dowry would put all his financial problems to rest.'

Max had never given much thought to the fact that a husband gained control over all his wife's wealth, but after hearing Miss Denby lament the fact, such an arrangement now struck him as little short of robbery. 'Doesn't seem quite sporting that he could float himself down River Tick and then use her money to paddle out of danger.'

Alastair shrugged. 'It's done all the time.'

The fact that it was didn't make it any more palatable, Max thought. 'Does Aunt Grace know about Henshaw's current monetary difficulties?'

'I don't know. But he's been angling to marry a fortune ever since he came up from Cambridge, so there's nothing new about it, except perhaps the degree of urgency. Come now, enough about Henshaw. The man's a pretentious, ill-dressed bore. How about a game of billiards before dinner? If any guests approach the room, I'll have Wendell scare them off.'

Absently Max agreed, but as they walked back to the house, he couldn't get out of his mind the image of Henshaw compelling Miss Denby to take his arm.

Were Henshaw's circumstances difficult enough that he'd be willing to coerce an heiress into matrimony?

Most likely, he was letting his dislike for the dandified Henshaw colour his perceptions. The man *was* a gentleman of good family and Aunt Grace would never have invited him if there were any doubt about his integrity.

However, just to be safe, he'd ride out early tomorrow and warn Miss Denby to be on her guard with him.

Feeling better about the matter, he followed his cousin into the house and focused his mind on the best strategy for beating Alastair for the third evening in a row.

Chapter Six

The next morning, Max rose before dawn and headed to the stables before even a glimmer of dawn lightened the treeline, determined not to risk missing Miss Denby. But though he trotted his mount up and down the stable lane for so long that the grooms must have wondered what in the world he was doing, she did not appear.

Perhaps she was being prudent, abstaining from her morning ride so as not to be pounced upon by Henshaw. Alastair had told him over billiards the previous evening that his mother said the party was wrapping up; Jane had boasted to him of its successes, two matrons having managed to get offers for their daughters. Felicity, she added, had made a great new friend of Miss Denby's stepsister, Eugenia Whitman, and was giddy about the prospect of sharing her upcoming Season with the girl.

The same Miss Whitman who, his Aunt Grace had informed him, 'far outshines her stepsister in youth, wit and beauty'. Max still resented that comment on Miss Denby's behalf.

In any event, it appeared she would soon be relieved of Mr Henshaw's pursuit, Max concluded, turning his probably puzzled mount to the stable and returning to the house.

But what of next spring? Would she, as she feared, have to suffer through another Season, dragged off to participate in a round of social activities for which she had no inclination, forced to neglect her beloved horses?

What a shame her childhood beau Harry was so far away. She deserved to marry a man who appreciated her unique talents and interests, who supported rather than discouraged her desire to carry on her father's legacy.

He toyed with the idea of trying to seek her out and bid her goodbye, but couldn't come up with a way to do so that would not shock the gathering by revealing she was well acquainted with a man she wasn't supposed to know. Perhaps, once he had his life sorted out, he could call on her in London, maybe even seek her out at Denby Lodge and purchase some of her horses.

With Alastair away on another of his lord-of-the-manor errands, Max fetched his book and headed for what might be his last afternoon hidden away at the conservatory. He'd rather miss the place, whose warm scented air and soothing palm murmurs he would probably never have discovered had he not been forced to vacate the house. With the guests soon departing, he and Alastair would have free run of the estate again.

He halted just inside the threshold of the glasshouse, inhaling the tangy-sweet scent of jasmine that seemed always to hang in the air, insubstantial as a whisper. He was about to proceed to his usual bench when a murmur of voices reached his ears, the words as indistinct as the gurgling of a brook over rocks.

He halted, trying to identify the speakers. Aunt Grace, conferring with the gardener? Or one of the affianced couples, stealing one last tryst before the party broke up?

In either case, his presence would be an impediment. He was silently retracing his steps when a feminine voice reached his ears, its increased volume making the words suddenly clear.

'Mr Henshaw, I *do* appreciate the honour of your offer, but I'm absolutely convinced we will not suit!'

Miss Denby's voice, Max realised, halting in mid-step. Had Henshaw tracked her there?

His first impulse was to set off in her direction, but she'd probably not thank him for interfering. Still, though he felt confident she could handle her disappointed suitor without his assistance, some deep-seated protective instinct made him linger.

After a masculine murmur whose words he could not make out, Miss Denby said, 'No, I shall not change my mind. You must admit, sir, that I have tried in every possible way to discourage you, so my refusal can hardly come as a surprise. You will oblige me by leaving now.'

'Waiting here for someone else, were you?' Henshaw replied, his angry tones now comprehensible. 'Max Ransleigh, perhaps? He'd never marry you. Despite his father's banishment, he has money enough, and if he ever does wed, it will be a woman from a prominent society family. In any event, his taste runs to sophisticated beauties, which you, I'm forced to say, are not. Nor are you getting any younger. If you've any hopes at all of marrying, you'd better accept my offer.'

Why, the mercenary little weasel, Max thought, incensed. Only the certainty that Miss Denby would not appreciate having him witness this embarrassing scene kept him from setting off down the pathway to plant a fist squarely on the jaw of that overdressed excuse for a gentleman.

'You're quite correct,' she was saying. 'I possess none of the virtues and talents a gentleman looks for in a wife. As you so kindly noted, I'm hardly a beauty and am hopeless at making the sort of polite chat that makes up society conversation. Worst of all, I fear I have no fashion sense. You can do so much better, Mr Henshaw! Why not wait until the Season and find yourself a more suitable bride?'

Despite his ire, Max had to grin. Had any female ever so thoroughly disparaged herself to a prospective suitor?

'I'm afraid, my dear, the press of creditors don't allow me the luxury of waiting. Though admittedly you possess neither the style nor the talents I would wish for in a wife, you do have...a certain charm of person. And wealth, of which I'm in desperate need.'

No style? No talent? His mirth rapidly dissipating, Max reconsidered the prospect of cornering Henshaw, shaking him like a dog with a ferret and then tossing him out of the glasshouse like the refuse he was.

But alerting them to his presence would not only distress Miss Denby, it might give the thwarted suitor an opportunity to claim he'd caught *Max and Miss Denby* alone together. His self-protective instincts on full alert now that Miss Denby wasn't within touching distance, Max didn't want to risk that.

His decision not to intervene, however, wavered when he heard a sharp, cracking sound that could only be a slap.

'Keep your hands to yourself,' Miss Denby cried. 'You followed me without my leave or encouragement. If you will not quit this place, then I will do so. Since I do not anticipate seeing you again before the party ends, I will say goodbye, Mr Henshaw.'

'Not so hasty, my dear. It might not be an arrangement either of us want, but you *will* marry me.'

'Let go of my arm! It's useless for you to detain me, for I promise you, nothing on earth would ever induce me to marry you!'

'I'd hoped you would consent willingly, but if you will not, you force me to employ...other measures. Before you leave this spot, you'll be fit to be no one's wife but mine.'

At that threat, Max abandoned discretion and set off at

a run. If he hadn't already been prepared to tear Henshaw limb from limb, the scuffling, panting sounds of a struggle that reached him as he rounded the last corner, followed by the unmistakable rip of fabric, had him ready to do murder.

Seconds later, he lunged over a potted fern to find Henshaw trying to pin a wildly struggling Miss Denby down on the bench, his free hand clawing up her skirts. As a clay pot fell over and shattered, Henshaw looked up, his hands stilling.

The smirk on his face and the lust in his eyes turned to surprise, then alarm as he recognised Max. But before Max could seize him, Miss Denby, taking advantage of Henshaw's distraction, kneed him in the groin, then caught him full on the nose with a roundhouse left jab of which Gentleman Jackson would have been proud.

Howling, Henshaw released Miss Denby and staggered backwards, one hand on his breeches front, the other holding his nose. Blood oozing through his fingers, he snarled, 'Bitch! You'll regret that!'

Max grabbed him by the arm and slammed him against the wall, regrettably with less force than he would have liked, but he didn't want to break a glass panel in Aunt Grace's conservatory.

Securing him against it with a stranglehold on his cravat, Max growled, 'Miss Denby will not regret her rejection. But you, varlet, will regret this episode for the rest of your life unless you do exactly what I say. You will apologise to Miss Denby, then pack your bag and leave immediately, before I tell the world and Lady Melross how you tried to attack an innocent and unwilling young lady.' Giving Henshaw's cravat a final twist, he released the man.

Henshaw shook his arms free and retreated several steps, trying to repair his ruined cravat before giving it up as hopeless. 'You dare to threaten me?' he blustered. 'Who will believe you? A flagrant womaniser, sent away from Vienna in disgrace, disowned by your own father!'

'Who will believe me?' Max echoed, his voice silky-soft. 'Your hostess, my aunt, perhaps? Or Lady Melross, seeing your elegant attire as it now appears?'

Fury and desperation might have briefly clouded Henshaw's judgement, but the reference to his dishevelled clothing snapped him back to reality. Obviously realising he could not hope to prevail over the nephew of his hostess, especially in his present incriminating state of disorder, he clamped his lips shut and looked down the pathway, eyeing the exit.

More concerned with assisting the lady, Max resigned himself to letting him go. 'Are you unharmed, Miss Denby?' he asked, stepping past Henshaw to her side.

'Y-yes,' she replied, her voice breaking a little.

The path to the doorway free, Henshaw backed cautiously away, his wary gaze fixed on Max. After retreating a safe distance, he tossed back, 'I won't forget this, Ransleigh. I'll have retribution some day…and on the bitch, too.'

'You don't follow instructions very well,' Max said softly, an icy contempt filling him. 'Now I'm going to have to thrash you like the cur you are.'

But before he could take a step, abandoning any pretence of dignity, Henshaw bolted for the door. Much as he would have liked to give chase and thrash the man, Max concluded his more urgent duty was to see to Miss Denby, who stood trembling by the bench, holding together the ripped edges of her bodice.

Her cloak had fallen off during the struggle and her pelisse, now lacking its buttons, gaped open over her white-knuckled hands. Her beautiful dark eyes, wide with shock and outrage, looked stricken.

Max cursed under his breath, wishing he'd tossed the bounder through the glass wall after all. 'I entered a few minutes ago and heard voices, but didn't realise what was transpiring until…it was almost too late. I'm so sorry I didn't intervene earlier and spare you that indignity. Say the word and I'll track down Henshaw and give him the drubbing he deserves.'

'Beating him further will serve no useful purpose,' she said, attempting a smile, which wobbled badly. 'Though I might wish to hit him again myself. He has ruined one of my best ugly gowns.'

Thankfully, some colour was returning to her pale cheeks and her voice sounded stronger, so Max might not have to pursue the man and rearrange his skeleton after all. 'You did quite a capital job on your first round, though I don't believe you succeeded in breaking his nose, more's the pity. Who taught you to box? That roundhouse jab was worthy of a professional.'

'Harry. He took lessons with Jackson in London while he was at Winchester. Satisfying as it was to land the blow exactly where I wished—on both parts of his anatomy—that won't help my biggest problem now, which is how to get back to my chamber and out of this gown. My stepmother would have palpitations if she saw me like this. Not that I would mind being ruined, but I should be indignant if anyone were to try to force me to marry *Henshaw.*'

'That sorry excuse for a man?' Max said in disgust. 'I should think not.'

'A sorry excuse indeed, but stronger than I anticipated,' she said, looking down at the fingers clutching her torn bodice. 'I thought I could handle him, but…' She took a shuddering breath, as if shaken by the evidence of how close she'd come to being ravaged. 'If only *you* had accepted my first offer! I'm certain you would have c-compromised me much more g-genteelly.'

She was trying to put on a brave face, but tears had begun slipping down her cheeks and she started to tremble again.

Making a vow to seek out Henshaw wherever he went to ground and pummel him senseless, Max abandoned discretion and drew Miss Denby into his arms. 'If *I* were to compromise you, I would at least make sure you *enjoyed* it,' he said, trying for a teasing tone as he cradled her, gently chafing her hands and trying to use his warmth to heat her chilled body. 'And it would have been done with much more expertise and finesse. Like this,' he said and kissed just the freckled tip of her nose.

The last time he'd encountered her in the conservatory, he'd burned to plunder her mouth and let his lips discover every wonder of nose, chin and eyelids. As indignant as his aunt would be that a guest of the Ransleighs had been assaulted, all he wished for now was to erase from her memory the outrage that had just been perpetrated against her.

To his relief, she gave herself into his hands, snuggling with a broken little gasp against his chest. For long moments, he simply held her, one finger gently stroking her cheek, until at last the tremors eased and she pulled back a bit, still resting in the circle of his arms.

'You do compromise a lady most genteelly,' she said. 'Thank you, Mr Ransleigh. I shall never forget your kind assistance.'

'Max,' he corrected with a smile. 'I should be honoured to have you call on me at any time.'

Before she could reply, a loud shriek split the air. *'Miss Denby!'* a shrill female voice exclaimed. 'Whatever are you about?'

A sense of impending disaster stabbing in his gut, Max looked over Miss Denby's head to see Lady Melross hurrying toward them.

Chapter Seven

Clutching the ragged edges of her bodice, Caroline stared in horror as Lady Melross marched up to them, her eyes widening with shock, then malicious glee as she perceived Caro wrapped in Ransleigh's arms, her bodice in ruins.

A sick feeling invaded Caro's stomach. How could things have gone so hideously wrong? In Lady Melross's accusing eyes, Mr Ransleigh, who had protected and comforted her, must now appear to be the one who'd tried to ravish her. And the old harpy would lose no time in trumpeting the news to all and sundry.

'This isn't what you think!' Caro cried, furious, frustrated, knowing the denial was hopeless. Oh, that she might run after Henshaw and rake her fingers down his deceitful face!

Ransleigh had never wanted to compromise her. Now, through the hapless intervention of the detestable Henshaw, the scandal he'd scrupulously avoided would fall full upon him.

It was all her fault…and she couldn't think of a single way to stop it.

'Not what I think?' Lady Melross echoed. 'Gracious, Miss Denby, do you believe me a simpleton, unable to comprehend what I see right before my eyes? No wonder a little bird told me I might find something interesting in the conservatory.'

'A little bird?' Caro echoed. 'What do you mean?'

'Oh, I had a note…from someone who knew about your rendezvous. Or maybe you sent it yourself, Miss Caroline?'

'Henshaw,' Caro whispered, her eyes pleading with Max, who'd already stepped away from her, his face going grim and shuttered the moment he saw Lady Melross charging toward them down the glasshouse path, Lady Caringdon trailing behind.

Henshaw must have sent the note, wanting Lady Melross to find them with her gown in tatters, ensuring a scandal public enough that they'd be forced to marry.

Surely Max Ransleigh understood that?

'You, Ransleigh,' Lady Melross said, turning to Max, 'I wouldn't have expected something this lacking in taste and finesse…although after Vienna, I suppose maybe I should have. What a sly thing you turned out to be, Miss Denby,' she continued as she snatched up Caroline's cloak and tossed it over her shoulders. 'There, you're decent again.'

Lady Caringdon stared at them both accusingly. 'Aren't you a rum one, Ransleigh, sneaking around, keeping your distance from the company while you plotted to seduce an innocent right under the nose of her chaperone! And you, young lady, have got exactly what you deserve!'

'Indeed!' Lady Melross crowed. 'Don't you understand, you stupid girl? Ruining yourself with Ransleigh won't earn you the elevated position in society you expect, for his father isn't even receiving him! While you were immured in the country at that dreary horse farm, he was creating a scandal—'

'Lady Melross,' Max broke in on the lady's tirade, 'that is quite enough. Abuse me as you will, but I cannot allow you to harass Miss Denby. She has suffered a shock and should return to the house at once to recover. Miss Denby,' he continued, turning to Caroline, his voice gentling, 'will you allow these ladies to escort you back to your chamber? We will talk of this later.'

'I should like to settle it now—' Caro said.

'No, in this at least, Ransleigh has the right of it,' Lady Melross broke in. 'You cannot stand there chatting in that disgrace of a garment! Come along, both of you. Though I cannot imagine what you could say that might excuse your behavior, Ransleigh, before you present yourself to Lady Denby, you'd best go and make yourself respectable.'

'Perhaps it would be better if I talk with Stepmother first,' Caroline conceded. Poor Lady Denby would be close to hysterics if the outcry about this disaster reached her before Caro did. She'd need to explain and calm her down before Max called on her.

Lady Caringdon sniffed. 'Poor Diana. What a tawdry, embarrassing predicament—and with dear Eugenia set to make her bow next spring! Dreadful!'

'Dreadful indeed,' Lady Melross said, sounding not at all regretful. 'Come along now, and wrap that cloak tight about you, miss. I shouldn't want to shock any of the *proper* young ladies we might encounter on the way. Doubtless Lady Denby will summon you later, Ransleigh. Perhaps you'd better go and acquaint your aunt with the débâcle you've created in the midst of her party.'

'Don't worry,' Ransleigh said to Caro, ignoring Lady Melross's disparaging remarks. 'Get some rest. I'll see you later and make everything right.' Giving her an encouraging smile, he stepped back to allow Lady Melross to take her arm.

Having a sudden change of heart, Caroline almost reached out to snag his sleeve and beg him to walk in with her. If only they could face Lady Denby now, together, and explain what had happened, surely they could sort it out and keep the dreadful Lady Melross from spreading her malicious account of the events!

But she suspected Ransleigh wouldn't deign to explain himself with Lady Melross present, and there was no chance whatsoever that the lady would let herself be manoeuvred out of escorting her victim into the house.

'I will call on Lady Denby soon,' he told Caro, then moved aside to let them pass.

'Speak with me first!' she tossed back as, Lady Caringdon seizing her other arm, the two women half-led, half-dragged her down the path.

They marched her into the house and up the stairs, relentless as gaolers. Initially they peppered her with questions, but her refusal to provide any details eventually convinced them she intended to remain silent.

With a final warning that it was useless to turn mute now, as her character was already ruined, they ignored her and spent the rest of the transit speculating about how devastated Lady Denby and Mrs Ransleigh would be and how fast the scandalous news would spread.

While they chattered, Caro's mind raced furiously. Should she ask Max Ransleigh to seek out Henshaw, drag him in so they might jointly accuse him? Was Henshaw still at Barton Abbey to be accused?

Trapped between the two dragons, she had no way of determining that. Should she try to explain immediately to Lady Denby, or wait until after she'd consulted with Mr Ransleigh?

She had only a short time to figure out what *she* wanted, while her whole life and future hinged on her making the right decision.

When she reached her rooms and her erstwhile 'rescuers' discovered neither her stepmother nor her sister was present, they finally stopped plaguing her and rushed off. Doubtless anxious to compete over who could convey the interesting news to the most people the fastest, Caro thought sardonically.

She hoped her stepmother would not be one of those so informed, vastly preferring to break the dismal story herself. In any event, Lady Denby's absence gave her the opportunity to summon Dulcie and change before the tattered evidence of the disaster could further upset her stepmother. Reassuring her maid, who gasped in alarm upon seeing her in the ruined gown, that she was quite unharmed and would explain later, Caro sent her off to dispose of the garment.

Watching the girl carry out the shreds, Caro smiled grimly. It certainly wasn't the way she would have chosen to do it, but the escapade in the glasshouse *had* effectively ruined her. At least now she'd be able to purchase gowns that didn't make her wince when she saw her image in a mirror. With that heartening thought, she scrawled a note asking Mr Ransleigh to meet her in Lady Denby's sitting room at his earliest convenience.

As she waited for her stepmother to return, she tried to corral the thoughts galloping about in her mind like colts set loose in a spring meadow. How could she turn Henshaw's despicable conduct to best advantage, managing the scandal so she would be able to return to Denby Lodge and her horses, while leaving Mr Ransleigh's good name unblemished?

Only one thought truly dismayed her: that having heard Lady Melross testify that she'd received a note bidding her come to the conservatory, Max might think, in blatant disregard of his wishes, *she* had arranged for Lady Melross to find them, trapping him with treachery into compromising her after persuasion had failed.

Trapping herself?

How to avoid that fate? Too unsettled to remain seated, she paced the room. In the aftermath of Henshaw's unexpected attack, her still-jangled nerves were hampering her ability to think clearly. The bald truth was she'd underestimated the man, dismissed him as a self-indulgent weakling she could easily handle.

It shook her to the core to admit that, had Max Ransleigh not rushed to her rescue, she probably could not have successfully resisted Henshaw.

How understanding Max had been, lending her his warmth and strength as she had struggled to compose herself. Bringing her back from the horror of what might have been to a reassuring normalcy with his gentle teasing. Renewed gratitude suffused her.

They must find some way out of this conundrum. She refused to repay his generosity by trapping him in a marriage neither of them wanted.

But when she recalled his parting words, a deep sense of unease filled her.

'I'll make everything right,' he'd said. Initially, she'd thought he meant to track down Henshaw and force him to confess his guilt. However, if Henshaw had already scuttled away from Barton Abbey, leaving Max bearing the blame for her disgrace, Ransleigh's sense of honour might very well force him into making her an offer.

And that wouldn't do at all. For one, he'd told her quite plainly he had no wish to marry and she could think of few things worse than being shackled to an uninterested husband. The image of her cousin Elizabeth came forcefully to mind.

Nor did she want to cobble her future to a man with whom she had little in common, whose wit engaged her but who agitated and discomforted her every time she was near him, filling her with powerful desires she had no idea how to manage.

Before she could analyse the matter any further, a rapid patter of footsteps in the hallway and the buzz of raised voices announced the imminent return of her stepmother.

Praying Lady Melross had not accompanied her, Caro braced herself for the onslaught.

A moment later, the door flew open and Lady Denby burst into the room, Eugenia at her elbow. 'Is it true?' her stepsister demanded. 'Did Mr Ransleigh truly…debauch you in the conservatory, as Lady Melross claims?'

'He did not.'

'Oh, thank heavens!' Lady Denby exclaimed. 'That dreadful woman! I knew it had to be naught but a malicious hum!'

'There was an…altercation,' Caro allowed. 'But events did not unfold as Lady Melross supposed.'

'Surely she didn't find you wrapped in Mr Ransleigh's arms, your gown in disarray, your bodice torn?' Eugenia asked.

'My gown had been damaged, but it was not—'

'Oh, no!' Eugenia interrupted with a wail. 'Then you *are* ruined. Indeed, we are *both* ruined! I shall never have my Season in London now!' Clapping a hand to her mouth, she burst into tears and rushed into her adjoining room, slamming the door behind her.

Lady Denby stood pale-faced and trembling, tears tracking down her own cheeks as she looked at Caro reproachfully. 'Oh, Caro,' she said faintly, 'how *could* you? Even if you had no concern about your own future, how could you jeopardise Eugenia's?'

'Please, ma'am, sit and let me explain. Truly, it is not as bad as you think. I'm certain that virtually nothing the detestable Lady Melross told you is accurate.'

Lady Denby allowed herself to be shown to a seat and accepted a glass of sherry, which she sipped while Caro related what had actually transpired. When she got to the part about how Mr Ransleigh's timely arrival had prevented Henshaw from overpowering her, Lady Denby cried out and leapt to her feet, wrapping Caro in her arms.

'Oh, my poor dear, how awful for you! Bless Mr Ransleigh for having the courage to intervene.'

'I owe him a great debt,' Caro agreed, settling her stepmother back in her chair. 'Which is why we need to somehow stop Lady Melross from circulating the falsehood that he compromised me. I can hardly repay Mr Ransleigh's gallantry by forcing him to offer for me, a girl he hardly knows. That would not be fair, would it?'

'It doesn't seem right,' Lady Denby admitted. 'But if you don't marry *someone*…how are we to salvage anything? And my dear, the truth is, this scandal could ruin Eugenia's Season as well!'

'Surely not! She's not even a Denby! Once Lady Gilford and Mrs Ransleigh learn the truth, I'm certain they will enlist their friends to ensure my difficulties do not reflect badly on my stepsister.'

That hope seemed to reassure Lady Denby, for she nodded. 'Yes, perhaps you are right. Grace and Jane would think it monstrous for poor Eugenia to suffer for Henshaw's villainy. But how are we to salvage your position, my dear?'

'I don't know yet,' Caro evaded, guiltily aware that she had no desire to 'salvage' it. 'Will you allow me to discuss this alone with Mr Ransleigh first, before he speaks with you? I expect him at any moment.'

'Very well,' Lady Denby agreed with a sigh. 'It's all so very distressing! I must go and comfort Eugenia.'

After giving her a final hug, Lady Denby walked out. Knowing that she would be meeting Max Ransleigh again any moment set every nerve on edge.

The fact that, despite her agitation, an insidious little voice was whispering that wedding Max might not be so disastrous after all filled her with a panicky agitation that drove her once again to pace the room.

From the very first, he'd affected her differently than any

other man she'd ever met. Being near him filled her with a tingling physical immediacy, a consciousness of her breasts and lips and body she'd never previously experienced.

Yesterday in the conservatory, that strange but powerful attraction had urged her to touch him, kiss him, feel his mouth and hands on her. Thought and reason vaporised into heat and need, into a burning, irresistible desire to know him, to let him know her. She'd *craved* that contact with a force and single-mindedness she would never have believed possible.

Even with the threat of the Curse hanging over her, she wasn't sure she would have been able to bring her rioting senses under control and walk away if he'd made any move at all to entice her to stay.

The power Henshaw had exerted over her while she struggled to escape him had frightened her, but what Max inspired in her was even more terrifying…because she hadn't wanted to escape it. Indeed, recalling him poised motionless on the bench, inviting her kiss, making no move to cajole or entice, letting her own desire propel her to him, was more coercive than any force he could have employed.

She'd been as powerfully in his thrall as…as her cousin Elizabeth had once been to Spencer Russell, the reprobate she'd married. The man who'd charmed and wed and betrayed, and almost bankrupted her cousin before a fortuitous racing accident had brought to an end Elizabeth's humiliating existence as a disdained and abandoned wife.

Caro did not want to be ensnared by an emotion that dazzled her out of her common sense, nor be held captive by a lust so strong it paralysed will and smothered rational thinking.

Just as she reached that conclusion, a rap sounded at the door.

Her heartbeat stopped, then recommenced at a rapid pace

as a stinging shock rippled through her, setting her stomach churning. Wiping her suddenly sweaty palms on her gown, she took a deep breath and walked to open the door.

Chapter Eight

As expected, Max Ransleigh stood on the threshold. Looking solemn, he took her hand and kissed her fingers.

A second wave of sensation blazed through her. Clenching her fists and jaw to try to dampen the effect, she mumbled an incoherent welcome and led him to a chair. Though she was still too agitated to want to sit, knowing he would not unless she did so, she forced herself into the place opposite him.

'I'm so sorry to have involved you in this,' she began before he could speak. 'Though I did invite you to compromise me, I hope you realise I had no part in setting up the situation in the conservatory today! I would never have gone behind your back to create a scandal in which you'd already assured me you wanted no part.'

'I believe you,' he said, calming her fears on that matter, at least. 'I expect it was Henshaw who sent Lady Melross the note, wanting her to find you with him in a state dishevelled enough to ensure you'd be coerced to wed him.'

'Thank you. I would hate to have you think I'd use you so shabbily. Lady Denby has agreed to let me speak with you privately before she comes in, so shall we discuss what is to be done?'

'Let us do so. You did get your wish, you know. You are quite effectively ruined.'

'Yes, I know. I certainly didn't enjoy being mauled by Henshaw, but it might turn out for the best. We need only tell people what really happened, establishing that you had no part in it, and all will be well. I'll still be ruined, but with Henshaw showing his character to be so despicable, no one could fault me for refusing to marry him.'

Frowning, Ransleigh shook his head. 'I'm afraid that is not the case. Society would still believe the only way to salvage your reputation would be for you to marry your seducer. However deplorable his present conduct, Henshaw was *born* a gentleman, so much would be forgiven as long as you end up wed.'

'But that's appalling!' Caro cried. 'The *victim* is expected to marry her attacker?'

'Rightly or wrongly, the blame usually attaches itself to the female. But it won't come to that. Accusing Henshaw isn't possible; he's already left Barton Abbey. Any evidence that might confirm he was your attacker—bloody nose, ruined cravat—will have been put to rights by the time I could run him to ground. Since he can now have no doubt that you'd refuse to marry him, he has no reason to corroborate the truth, especially since Lady Melross is circulating a version of events that relieves him of responsibility. Indeed, he will probably think it a fine revenge to see me blamed for his transgressions.'

Caro nodded, distressed but not surprised that Ransleigh's assessment of Henshaw's character matched her own. 'I imagine he would, though I have no intention of allowing him the satisfaction. Whether he admits his guilt or not, I still intend to accuse him. Why should you, who intervened only to help me, suffer for his loathsome behaviour?'

'I don't think accusing him would be wise.'

Puzzled, Caro frowned at him. 'Why not?'

'You were discovered in *my* embrace. I'm the son of an earl who exerts a powerful influence in government; you are the orphaned daughter of a rural baron. If you accuse Henshaw, who will justly claim he was in his room, preparing to depart when Lady Melross found us, there will be many who will whisper that I coerced you into naming another man to cover up my own bad conduct. Lady Melross in particular will be delighted to embellish the details of my supposed ravishment and assert such behaviour is only to be expected after my…previous scandal.'

'You really think no one would believe me if I tell the truth?' Caro asked incredulously.

'What, allow such a salacious act to be blamed on some insignificant member of the *ton* rather than titillate the masses by accusing the well-known son of a very important man? No, I don't think anyone would believe you. I can see the scurrilous cartoons in the London print-shop windows now,' he finished bitterly.

'But that's so…unfair!' she burst out.

He laughed shortly, no humour in the sound. 'I have learned of late just how unfair life can be. Believe me, I like the solution as little as you do, but with your reputation destroyed and the blame for it laid at my door, the only way to salvage your position is for you to marry me.'

Alarmed as she was by his conclusion, Caro felt a flash of admiration for his willingness to do what he saw as right. 'A noble offer and I do honour you for it. But I think it ridiculous to allow society's expectations—based on a lie!—to force us into something neither of us desire.'

'Miss Denby, let me remind you that you are *ruined*,' he repeated, his tone now edged with an undercurrent of anger and frustration. 'Fail to marry and you risk being exiled altogether from respectable society. Being cast out of the company of those with whom you have always associated is not a pleasant condition, as I have good reason to know.'

'First, I've never really "associated" with the *ton*,' she countered, 'and, as I've assured you several times, polite society's opinion does not matter to me. Certainly not when compared with losing the freedom to live life how—and with whom—I choose.'

'But Lady Denby does live and move in that society and Miss Whitman's future may well depend upon its opinions. We may be far removed from London here, but I assure you, Lady Melross will delight in dredging up every detail of this scandal when your relations arrive in London next spring.'

Caroline shook her head. 'I've already discussed that problem with my stepmother. If they band together, I'm certain Lady Denby, your aunt and Lady Gilford can manage this affair so that no harm comes to Eugenia's prospects. Since you are already accounted a rake, it shouldn't much affect your reputation and ruining mine has been my goal from the outset.'

She'd hoped to persuade Max to accept her argument. Far from looking convinced, though, his expression turned even grimmer and his jaw flexed, as if he were trying not to grit his teeth.

'Miss Denby,' he began again after a moment, 'I don't mean to seem overbearing or argumentative, but the very fact that you have not much associated with society means you are in no position to accurately predict its reaction. I have lived all my life under its scrutiny and I promise you, once Lady Denby has thought through the matter, she will agree with me that our marriage is the only solution that will safeguard the reputations of everyone involved.'

He paused and took a deep breath, as if armouring himself. 'So you may assure her that I have done the proper thing and made a formal offer for your hand.'

If the situation had not been so serious, Caro might have laughed, for he spat out the declaration as if each word were a hot coal that burned his tongue as he uttered it. His obvious reluctance might even have been considered insulting, if her own desire to avoid marriage hadn't exceeded his.

But then, as if realising that his grudging offer was hardly lover-like, he shook his head and sighed. 'Let me try this again,' he said, then reached over to tangle his fingers with hers.

Immediately, heat rushed up her arm, while her heart accelerated so rapidly, she felt dizzy.

'Won't you honour me by giving me your hand?' he said. 'I know neither of us came to Barton Abbey with marriage in mind. But during our brief acquaintance, I've come to admire and respect you. I flatter myself that you've come to like me, too, at least a little.'

'I do like and…and admire you,' she replied disjointedly, wishing he'd release her fingers. They seemed somehow connected to her chest and her brain, for she was finding it hard to breathe and even harder to think as he retained them.

His thumb was rubbing lazy circles of wonderment around her palm, setting off little shocks of sensation that seemed to radiate straight to the core of her.

She should pull free, but she didn't seem able to move. So he continued, his touch mesmerising, until all the clear reasons against marriage dissolved into a porridge-like muddle in her brain. She couldn't seem to concentrate on anything but the press of his thumb and the delights it created.

'I think we could rub together tolerably well,' he went on, obviously not at all affected by the touch that was wreaking such havoc in her. 'I admire you, too, and from what I've seen of your Sultan, you are excellent with horses. You could run Denby Stud with my blessing.'

That assurance was as seductively appealing as the thumb

caressing her palm, which was now making her body hot and her nipples ache. An insidious longing welled up within her, a yearning for him to kiss her, for her to kiss him back.

Without question, he knew society better than she did, and, for a moment, her certainty that she ought to refuse him wavered. She struggled to recapture her purpose and remember why marrying him was such a bad idea.

Unable to order her thoughts in Max's disturbing presence, she pulled her fingers free, sprang up and paced to the window.

How could she become his wife and not let him touch her? Was she really ready to test the power of the Curse for a man who merely 'admired' her? Besides, the experience of their last two meetings suggested that her ability to resist him, if he did make overtures toward her, would be feeble at best, regardless of how tepid his feelings for her might be.

She could tell him why she was so opposed to marriage. But after his courage in rescuing her and resolutely facing the consequences, she really didn't wish to appear a coward by admitting that it was the strong probability that she would die in childbed, as so many of her maternal relations had, that made her leery of wedlock.

No, the very fact that he affected her so strongly was reason enough not to marry Max Ransleigh.

Reminding herself of her conviction that Lady Denby could protect Eugenia, she said, 'I know you make your offer hastily and under duress. If you will but think longer about it, you will agree that it isn't wise to take a step that will permanently compromise our futures in order to avoid a scandal that will soon enough be overshadowed by some other.'

'It will have to be some scandal,' he said drily.

'Only think if I were to accept you!' she continued, avoiding his gaze in the hope that not meeting his eyes might lessen the disturbing physical hold he exerted over her. 'I'm not being modest when I assert that a huge divide exists between Miss Denby, countrified, unfashionable daughter of minor gentry, and Max Ransleigh, an earl's son accustomed to moving in the first circles of society. I have neither the skills nor the background to be the sort of wife you deserve.'

Before he could insert some patently false reassurance, she rushed on, 'Nor, frankly, do I wish to acquire them. My world isn't Drury Lane, but the lane that leads from the barns to the paddocks. Not the odour of expensive perfume, but the scent of leather polish, sawdust and new hay. Not the murmur of political conversation, but the jingle of harness, the neighing of horses, the clang of the blacksmith's hammer. I have no desire to give that up for your world, London's parlours and theatre boxes and its endless round of dinner parties, routs and balls.'

His expression softened to a smile. 'You are quite eloquent in defence of "your world", Miss Denby.'

'I don't mean to disparage yours!' she said quickly. 'Only to point out how different we are. All I want is to remain at Denby Lodge, where I belong, sharing my life with someone who loves and appreciates that world as I do.' *Someone to whom*, she added silently, *I have long been bound by a comfortable affection, not a man as disturbing and far-too-insidiously appealing as you.*

Turning from the window, she said, 'Though I am fully conscious of the honour of your offer, as I told you from the beginning, I wish to marry Harry. By the time he returns from India, this furore will have calmed. And even if it has not, Harry will not care.'

'I don't know that you can be certain about that,' he objected. 'If it doesn't, and he marries you, he will share in your notoriety. Being banished from society is no little thing. Would you choose exile for him? Would he suffer it for you?'

'Harry would suffer anything for me.'

'How can you commit Harry to such a course without giving him a choice?'

'How can you ask me to give him up without giving him a chance? No, Mr Ransleigh, I will not do it. I will leave it to ladies better placed than I to protect my stepsister and to Harry to settle my future when he returns. And lest you think to argue your position with her, Lady Denby would not compel me to marry against my will.'

Hoping to finally convince him, she chanced gazing into his eyes. 'It really is more sensible this way, surely you can see that! Some day you, too, will encounter a lady you *wish* to marry, one who can be the perfect helpmate and government hostess. You'll be happy then that I did not allow you to sway me. So, though I am sorry to be disobliging, I must refuse your very flattering offer.'

He studied her a long moment; she couldn't tell from his face whether he felt relief or exasperation. 'You needn't give me a final answer now. Why not think on the matter for a few days?'

'That won't be necessary; I am resolved on this. As soon as my stepmother recovers from the shock, we will pack and leave for Denby Lodge.'

For another long moment he said nothing. 'I am no Henshaw to try to force your hand, even though I believe your leaving here without the protection of an engagement is absolutely the wrong course of action. However, if you insist on refusing it, know that if at any time you decide to reconsider, my offer will remain open.'

Truly, he was the kindest of men. The shock and outrage and dismay of the day taking its toll, she felt an annoyingly missish desire to burst into tears.

'I will do so. Thank you.'

He bowed. 'I will send a note to Lady Denby, offering to

call and tender my apologies if she permits. Will you let me know before you leave, so I might bid you goodbye?'

'It would probably be wiser if we go our separate ways as quickly as possible.'

'As you wish.' He approached her then, halting one step away. Her body quivered in response to his nearness.

'It has been a most…interesting association, Miss Denby.' He held out his hand and reluctantly she laid hers in his as he brought her fingers to his lips. Little sparks danced and tingled and shivered from her fingernails outwards.

'I will remain always your most devoted servant.'

Snatching back the hand that didn't want to follow her instructions to remove itself from his grasp, she curtsied and watched him stride out of the room, telling herself this was for the best.

And the sooner she got back to Denby Lodge, the better.

Chapter Nine

Max stalked from Lady Denby's sitting room towards the library, anger, outrage and frustration churning in his gut. Encountering one of the guests in the hallway, avid curiosity in his eyes, Max gave him such a thunderous glare, the man pivoted without speaking and fled in the opposite direction.

Stomping into his haven, he went straight to the brandy decanter, poured and downed a glass, then poured another, welcoming the burn of the liquor down his throat.

What a calamity of a day.

Throwing himself into one of the wing chairs by the fire, he wondered despairingly how everything could have gone so wrong. It seemed impossible that, just a few bare hours ago, he'd halted on the threshold of the conservatory and breathed deeply of the fragrant air, his spirits rising on its scented promise that life was going to get better.

Instead, events had taken a turn that could end up anywhere from worse to disastrous.

Reviewing the scene in the glasshouse, he swore again. Hadn't Vienna taught him not to embroil himself in the problems of females wholly unrelated to him? Apparently not, for though, unlike Madame Lefevre, he acquitted the Denby girl of deliberately drawing him into this fiasco, by watching over her he'd been dragged in anyway.

And might very well be forced into wedding a lady with whom, by her own admission, he had virtually nothing in common.

True, Miss Denby had turned down his offer. But he placed no reliance on her continuing to do so, once her stepmother brought home to her just how difficult her situation would be if they didn't marry.

His wouldn't be as dire, but the resulting scandal certainly wouldn't be helpful. With a sardonic curl of his lip, he recalled Miss Denby's blithe assumption that since he already had a reputation as a rake, the scandal wouldn't affect him at all. He'd been on the point of explaining that, even for a rake, there were limits to acceptable behaviour and ruining a young lady of quality went rather beyond them.

But if the danger to her own reputation wasn't enough to convince her, he wasn't about to whine to her about the damage not wedding her would do to his own.

There might be some small benefit to be squeezed from disaster: if he were thought to be a heartless seducer, he'd no longer be a target for the schemes of matchmaking mamas and their devious daughters. However, for someone about to go hat in hand looking for a government posting, the timing couldn't be worse. Being branded as a man unable to regulate his behaviour around women certainly wouldn't help his chances of finding a sponsor…or winning back Wellington's favour.

He seized his empty glass and threw it into the fireplace.

He was still brooding over what to do when Alastair came in.

'Devil's teeth, Max, what fandango occurred while I was

out today? Even the grooms are buzzing with it—some crazy tale of you trying to ravish some chit in the conservatory?'

Max debated telling Alastair the truth, but his hot-headed cousin would probably head out straight away to track down Henshaw and challenge him to a duel, pressing the issue until the man was forced to face him or leave the country in disgrace.

Of course, being an excellent shot as well as a superior swordsman, if Alastair prevailed upon Henshaw to meet him, his cousin would kill the weasel for certain—and then *he*'d be forced to leave England.

He'd complicated his own life sufficiently; he didn't intend to ruin Alastair's as well.

'I…got a bit carried away. Lady Melross and her crony came running in before I could set the young lady to rights.'

Alastair studied his face. 'I heard the chit's bodice was torn to her bosom, the buttons of her pelisse scattered all over the floor. Devil take it, Max, don't try to gammon me. You've infinitely more finesse than that…and if you wanted a woman, you wouldn't have to rip her out of her gown—in a public place, no less!'

Wishing he hadn't tossed away his perfectly good glass, Max rummaged for one on the sideboard and poured himself another brandy. 'I'm really not at liberty to say any more.'

'Damn and blast, you can't think I'd believe that Banbury tale! Did the Denby chit deliberately try to trap you? Dammit, I *liked* her! Surely you're not going to let her get away with this!'

'If by "getting away with it", you mean forcing me to marry her, you're out there. I made her an offer, as any gentleman of honour would in such a situation, but thus far, she's refused it.'

Alastair stared at him for a long moment, then poured himself a brandy. 'This whole story,' he said, downing a large swallow, 'makes no sense at all.'

'With that, I can agree,' Max said.

Suddenly, Alastair threw back his head and laughed. 'Won't need to worry about the Melross hag blackening your character in town. After bringing her party to such a scandalous conclusion, *Jane*'s going to murder you.'

'Maybe I'll hand her the pistol,' Max muttered.

'To women!' Alastair held up his glass before tossing down the rest of the brandy. 'One of the greatest scourges on the face of the earth. I don't know what in hell happened today in the conservatory and, if you don't want to tell me, that's an end to it. But I do know you'd never do anything to harm a female and I'll stand beside you, no matter what lies that dragon Melross and her pack of seditious gossips spread.'

Suddenly a wave of weariness come over Max…as it had in the wake of the Vienna disaster, when he'd wandered back to his rooms, numbed by shock, disbelief and a sense of incredulity that things could possibly have turned out so badly when he'd done nothing wrong. 'Thank you,' he said, setting down his glass.

Alastair poured them both another. 'Ransleigh Rogues,' he said, touching his glass to Max's.

Before Max could take another sip, a footman entered, handing him a note written on Barton Abbey stationery. A flash of foreboding filled him—had Miss Denby already reconsidered?

But when he broke the seal, he discovered the note came from Lady Denby.

After thanking him for his offer to apologise and his assurance that he stood by his proposal to marry her stepdaughter, since Miss Denby informed her she had no intention of accepting him, there was really nothing else to be said. As both Miss Denby and her own daughter were most anxious to depart as soon as possible, she intended to leave immediately, but reserved the privilege of writing to him again when she'd had more opportunity to Sort Matters Out, at which time she trusted he would still be willing, as a Man of Honour, to Do The Right Thing.

An almost euphoric sense of relief filled Max. Apparently Lady Denby hadn't managed to convince her *stepdaughter* to 'Do the Right Thing' before leaving Barton Abbey. With Miss Denby about to get everything she wanted—a return to her beloved Denby Lodge and a ruination that would allow her to wait in peace for the return of her Harry—Max was nearly certain no amount of Sorting Things Out later would convince Miss Denby to reconsider.

He'd remain a free man after all.

The misery of the day lightened just a trifle. Now he must concentrate on trying to limit the damage to his prospects of a career.

'Good news?' Alastair asked.

Max grinned at him. 'The best. It appears I will not have to get leg-shackled after all. Amazingly, Miss Denby has resisted her stepmother's attempts to convince her to marry me.'

Alastair whistled. 'Amazing indeed! She must be dicked in the nob to discard a foolproof hand for forcing the Magnificent Max Ransleigh into marriage, but no matter.'

'There's an army sweetheart she's waiting to marry.'

'Better him than you,' Alastair said as he refilled their glasses. 'Here's to Miss Denby's resistance and remaining unwed!'

'Add a government position to that and I'll be a happy man.'

Max knew the worst wasn't over yet. Whispers about the scandal in the conservatory would doubtless have raced through the rest of the company like a wildfire through parched grass. At some point, Aunt Grace would summon him in response to the note he'd sent her, wanting to know why he'd created such an uproar at her house party.

The two cousins remained barricaded in the library, from which stronghold they occasionally heard the thumps and bangs of footmen descending the stairs with the baggage of departing guests. But as the hour grew later without his aunt summoning him, Max guessed that some guests had chosen to remain another night, doubtless eager to grill their hostess for every detail over dinner, embarrassing Felicity, making Jane simmer and contemplate murder.

Alastair, ever loyal, kept him company, playing a few desultory hands of cards after he'd declined the offer of billiards. He wasn't sure he'd trust himself with a cue in hand without trying to break it over someone's head.

Probably his own.

So it was nearly midnight when a footman bowed himself in to tell him Mrs Ransleigh begged the indulgence of a few words with him in her sitting room.

Max swallowed hard. Now he must face the lady who'd stood by him, disparaging his father's conduct and insisting he deserved better. And just like Vienna, though all he had done was assist a woman in distress, this time he'd ended up miring not just himself, but also his aunt, in embarrassment and scandal.

He'd not whined to Miss Denby about the black mark that would be left on his character by her refusal to wed; he wasn't going to make excuses to his aunt, either. Girding himself to endure anger and recriminations, he crossed the room.

Alastair, who knew only too well what he'd face, gave him an encouraging slap on the shoulder as he walked by.

He found his aunt reclining on her couch in a dressing gown, eyes closed. She sat up with a start as the footman announced him, her eyes shadowed with fatigue, filling with tears as he approached.

His chest tightening, he felt about as miserable as he'd ever felt in his life. Rather than cause his aunt pain, he almost wished he'd fallen with the valiant at Hougoumont.

'Aunt Grace,' he murmured, kissing her outstretched fingers. 'I am so sorry.'

But instead of the reproaches he'd steeled himself to endure, she pushed herself from her seat and enveloped him in a hug. 'Oh, my poor Max, under which unlucky star were you born that such trouble has come into your life?'

Hugging her back, he muttered. 'Lord knows. If I were one of the ancients, I'd think I'd somehow offended Aphrodite.'

'Come, sit by me,' she said, patting the sofa beside her.

Heartened by her unexpectedly sympathetic reception, he took a seat. 'I'd been prepared to have you abuse my character and order me from the house. I cannot imagine why you have not, after I've unleashed such a sordid scandal at your house party.'

'I imagine Anita Melross was delighted,' she said drily. 'She will doubtless dine out for weeks on the story of how she found you in the conservatory. Dreadful woman! How infuriating that she is so well connected, one cannot simply cut her. But enough about Anita. Oh, Max, what are we to do now?'

'There isn't much that can be done. Lady Melross and her minions will have already set the gossip mill in motion, thoroughly shredding my character. Frankly, I expected you to take part in the process.'

'Frankly, I might have,' his aunt retorted, 'had Miss Denby not insisted upon speaking with me before she left.'

Surprise rendered him momentarily speechless. 'Miss Denby spoke with you?' he echoed an instant later.

'I must admit, I was so angry with both of you, I had no desire whatsoever to listen to any excuses she wished to offer. But she was quite adamant.' His aunt laughed. 'Indeed, she told Wendell she would not quit the passage outside my chamber until she was permitted to see me. I'm so glad now that she persisted, for she confessed the whole to me—something I expect that you, my dear Max, would not have done.'

'She...told you everything?' Max asked, that news surprising him even more than his aunt's unexpected sympathy.

His aunt nodded. 'How Mr Henshaw made her an offer, so insistent upon her acceptance he was ready to attack her to force it! I was never so distressed!' she cried, putting a hand on her chest. 'Is there truly no way to lay the blame for that shocking attack where it belongs, at Henshaw's feet?'

'If Miss Denby disclosed the whole of what happened, you must see that there is virtually no chance we could fix the responsibility on him.'

'Poor child! I feel wretched that someone I invited into my home would take such unspeakable liberties! With her shyness and lack of polish, she would never have found much success in the Marriage Mart, but to have her ruined by that... that infamous blackguard! And then, to have *you* wrongfully accused for her disgrace! 'Tis monstrous, all of it!'

Max sat back, his emotions in turmoil. Though he hadn't truly blamed Miss Denby for what had happened, he'd resented the fact that, at the end of it all, *she* had got what she wanted, while *he* was left a position that made obtaining his goal much more difficult.

Still, he could work relentlessly until he achieved what he wanted; her ruination couldn't be undone. It had taken courage to insist on braving the contempt of her hostess so she might explain what had really transpired, thereby exonerating him to a woman whose good opinion she must know he treasured.

In refusing to allow herself to be forced into something she did not want, regardless of the personal cost, and in remaining steadfastly loyal to her childhood love, she'd displayed a sense of honour as unshakeable as his own. He couldn't help admiring that.

'I hardly expected her to tell you the truth…but I'm glad she did,' he said at last.

'Oh, Max, you would have said nothing and simply shouldered all the blame, would you not?' she asked, seizing his hands.

He shrugged. 'With Henshaw showing himself too dishonourable to admit to his actions, I don't see how I could avoid it. There was no point making accusations we have no way of proving.'

'Are you certain that's the right course? It seems monstrous that you both must suffer, while the guilty party escapes all blame!'

'We'll have to endure it, at least for the present. I intend to quietly search for evidence that might incriminate Henshaw, but I'm not hopeful anything useful will turn up. In the interim, I'd rather Alastair not learn the truth. He's already suspicious of Lady Melross's story. If he were to find out what really happened, he might go after Henshaw and—'

'—tear him limb from limb, or something equally rash,' Mrs Ransleigh finished for him. 'Although it will chafe him to be kept in the dark, I appreciate your doing it. Ever since… That Woman, he's been so reckless and bitter. Even after all those years in the army, he's still spoiling for a fight, still heedless of the consequences.'

'It shall remain our secret, then.'

She sighed. 'If there is any way I might be of assistance, let me know. I can think of little that would give me more pleasure than being able to show up Anita Melross for the idle, malicious gossip she is.'

'If the opportunity arises, I will certainly call on your help.

By the way…did Miss Denby also tell you I'd asked for her hand and she'd refused me?'

'She did. Bless the child, she even said that after you had been everything that was gentlemanly, preventing Henshaw from ravishing her and comforting her afterwards, she simply could not repay your kindness by shackling you to a girl you didn't want. She insisted you must remain free to take a wife of your own choosing, who would be the suitable hostess and companion to a man in high position that she could never be.'

Max smiled, his spirits lightened by the first glimmer of amusement he'd felt since Lady Melross burst into the conservatory. 'Difficult to be angry with someone who rejects you with such glowing compliments.'

'And such absolute sincerity! It was the longest and most eloquent speech I've got from her since her arrival. Perhaps she isn't quite as hopeless as I'd thought.'

Max resisted the impulse to defend Miss Denby. How well she'd cultivated the image of an awkward, ill-spoken spinster! If only his aunt could have seen her, fierce determination in her eyes as she'd vividly described her world at Denby Lodge.

She'd been quite magnificent. Even had he wished to wed her, he would have felt compelled to let her go.

'I must say, I was relieved to discover she has an army beau who will marry her when he returns,' Mrs Ransleigh continued. 'Having been the unwitting instrument of her disgrace, it makes me feel a bit better to know she won't be condemned for ever to live without the care and protection of a good man.'

Max nodded. 'That's the only reason I didn't push her harder to marry me. Not that I'd ever force myself on a woman.'

'Of course you would not. Well, I'm off to bed. Calamities such as the events that transpired today exhaust me! But I did not wish to sleep before telling you I knew everything, lest you take it in your head to lope off somewhere in the night, still believing I thought ill of you.'

'I'm so glad you do not. And I've no plans to take myself off as yet.'

'Stay as long as you like,' his aunt said as she offered him her cheek to kiss. 'By the way, I should like to reveal the truth to Jane. She is perfectly discreet and, as she is now quite an influential hostess in London, she might find the means to be of some help.'

'Miss Denby already mentioned that Lady Denby hoped to enlist you and Jane in defending her stepsister; I'd appreciate anything you might do to assist Miss Denby as well. Of all the unwilling participants in this débâcle, she is the one who loses the most.'

Mrs Ransleigh nodded. 'We will certainly give it our best efforts.'

'I'll leave you to your slumber, then. Thank you, Aunt Grace. For still believing in me.'

'You're quite welcome,' she replied with a smile. 'You might want to thank Miss Denby, too, for believing in you as well.'

Bidding her goodnight, Max walked out. Though he hadn't yet worked out how he was going to work around this check to his governmental aspirations, he felt immeasurably better to know that he had not, after all, disappointed and alienated his aunt.

That happy outcome he owed to Miss Denby. He found her courage in risking censure to defend him to his family as amazing as her fortitude in refusing a convenient marriage.

Aunt Grace was right. He did owe her thanks. But given the disastrous events that seemed to happen when she came near him, he didn't think he'd risk delivering it in person any time soon.

Chapter Ten

In the late afternoon a month later, Caroline Denby turned the last gelding over to the stable boy and walked out of the barn. After returning from the disaster at Barton Abbey, she'd thrown herself into working with the horses, readying them for the upcoming autumn sale. But as she'd suspected, though she'd left the scandal behind, its repercussions continued to follow her.

In the last two weeks, several gentlemen who'd not previously purchased mounts from the stud had journeyed into Kent, claiming they wished to view and evaluate the stock. Since the gentlemen had spent more time gawking at her than at the horses, she suspected their real interest had been to inspect for themselves the subject of Lady Melross's most titillating gossip—the hoyden who'd been discovered half-naked with Max Ransleigh.

If they'd been expecting some seductive siren, she'd doubtless sent them away disappointed, Caro thought with a sigh.

At least there was no question of her returning to London for another Season, and after a week of fruitless attempts, Lady Denby had given up trying to convince her to marry Max Ransleigh as well. Though Eugenia still hadn't entirely forgiven her for the débâcle which had put such an unpleasant end to the house party, when Caro had explained during the drive home what had really happened, her stepsister had been first shocked, then indignant, then had wept at the outrage she had suffered.

So it now appeared, Caro thought with satisfaction as she paced up the steps into the manor and tossed her gloves and crop to the butler, that she'd gained what she'd wanted all along: to be left in peace to run her farm.

She was hopeful that Eugenia would also get what she wanted, the successful Season she'd dreamed of for so long. While Caro worked with her horses, Lady Denby had been busy with correspondence, consulting with Lady Gilford and Mrs Ransleigh and writing to her many friends to ensure enough support for Eugenia's début that her prospects would not suffer because of Caro's scandal.

Grateful for that, Caroline refused to regret what had happened. And if she sometimes woke in the night, her soul awash with yearning as she recalled being cradled against a broad chest, while a strong finger gently caressed her cheek and a deep masculine voice murmured soothingly against her hair, she would, in time, get over it.

Garbed in her usual working attire of breeches and boots, she intended to tiptoe quietly up to her chamber and change into more conventional clothing before dinner. But as she crept past the parlour, Lady Denby called out, 'Caroline, is that you? I must speak to you at once!'

Wondering what she could have done now to distress Lady Denby, she changed course and proceeded into the room. 'Yes, Stepmama?'

In her agitation, Lady Denby didn't so much as frown at Caro's breeches. 'Oh, my dear, I fear I may have inadvertently done you a grave disservice!'

Foreboding slammed like a fist into her chest. 'What are you talking about?'

Lady Denby gave her a guilty look. 'Well, you see, after the events at Barton Abbey, I wrote to the trustees of your father's estate, informing them you were to be married and asking that the solicitors begin working on marriage settlements.' Before Caroline could protest, she rushed on, 'I was so very sure you would, in the end, be convinced to marry! Then last week, after finally conceding there would be no wedding, I wrote back to them, telling them you had refused Mr Ransleigh's offer. In today's post, I received a reply from Lord Woodbury.'

'Woodbury?' Caro gave a contemptuous snort. 'I can only imagine what *he* had to say about it. How I wish Papa had not made him head of the trustees!'

'Well, dear, he was one of your papa's closest friends and his estate at Mendinhall is very prosperous, so it's not unreasonable that Papa thought Woodbury would take equal care of yours.'

'I won't deny that he's a good steward,' Caro replied, 'but Woodbury never approved of my working the stud. The last time they met, he told Papa he thought it well past time for me to put on proper dress and start behaving like a woman of my rank, instead of racketing about the stables, hobnobbing with grooms and coachmen.'

When Lady Denby remained tactfully silent—probably more in agreement with Lord Woodbury's views than with her own—Caroline said, 'What did Lord Woodbury write, then?'

Her stepmother sighed. 'You're not going to like it. Apparently he heard about the events at Barton Abbey. He claims the shock of it must have unbalanced your mind for, he wrote, no young lady of breeding in her right senses, caught in such a dire situation, would ever turn down a respectable offer of marriage. He's convinced your, um, "unnatural preoccupation" with running the stud has made you unable to realise how badly the scandal reflects upon you and the entire family. So, to protect you and the Denby name, he's convinced the other trustees to agree to something he's long been urging: the sale of the stud.'

Shock froze her in place, while her heart stood still and blood seemed to drain from her head and limbs. Dizzy, she grabbed the back of a wing chair to steady herself. 'The sale of the stud?' she repeated, stunned. 'He wants to sell *my horses*?'

'Y-yes, my dear.'

It was impossible. It was outrageous. Aside from Lady Denby's generous widow's portion, the rest of the estate, including Denby Lodge, the Denby Stud and the income to operate it, had been willed to her. Papa had always promised the farm and the land would remain hers, for her use and then as part of her dowry.

She shook her head to clear the faintness. 'Can they do that?' she demanded, her voice trembling.

'I don't know. Oh, my dear, I'm so sorry! I know how much the stud means to you.'

'How much… Why, it means *everything*,' Caro said, feeling returning to her limbs in a rush of fury. 'Everything I've worked for these last ten years! Has it been done yet? May I see the note?'

Silently, her stepmother held it out. Caroline snatched and read it through rapidly.

'It does not appear the sale has gone through yet,' she said, when she had finished it. 'There must be some way to stop it. The stud belongs to me!'

But even as she made the bold declaration, doubt and dread rose up to check her like a ten-foot gate before a novice jumper.

Did she have control of the stud? Numb, shocked and trying to cope with the immensity of her father's sudden death, she'd sat silent and vacant-headed during the reading of his will. Thinking back, she knew the assets of the estate had been turned over to trustees to manage for her, but no details about how the trust was to be administered, or the extent of the powers granted the trustees, had penetrated her pall of grief and pain.

'What will you do?' Lady Denby asked.

'I shall leave for London tomorrow at first light and consult Papa's solicitor. Mr Henderson will know if anything can be done.'

Lady Denby shook her head. 'I'm so sorry, Caroline. I would never have written if I'd had any suspicion Lord Woodbury would do such a thing.'

Absently Caroline patted her hand. 'It's not your fault. According to the note, Woodbury has been trying to convince the other trustees to sell the stud for some time.'

Anguish twisted in her gut as the scene played out in her head: some stranger arriving to lead away Sultan, whom she'd eased from his mother's body the night he was born. She'd put on him his first halter, his first saddle. Turning over Sultan, or Sheik's Ransom or Arabian Lady or Cleveland's Hope or any of the horses she'd worked with from foal to weaning to training, would be like having someone confiscate her brothers and sisters.

'Thank you for telling me at once,' she said, brisk purpose submerging her anxiety—at least for the moment. 'Now, you will please excuse me. I must confer with Newman in the stables, so he may continue the training while I'm gone.' She dismissed the flare of panic in her belly at the thought that when she came back, she might no longer be giving the orders. 'Would you ring Dulcie for me and ask her to pack some things?'

'While you're at the stables, be sure to tell John Coachman to ready the travelling barouche.'

Already pacing towards the door, Caro shook her head impatiently. 'No, I'll go by mail coach; it will be faster.'

'By mail coach!' Lady Denby gasped. 'But…that will not be at all proper! If you don't wish to take the barouche, at least hire a carriage.'

'My dear Stepmama, I don't wish to make the journey in the easy stages required if I'm forced to hire horses along the way! I'll take Dulcie to lend me some countenance,' she added. Despite her agitation, she had to grin at the dismay the maid would doubtless feel upon being informed she would be rattling around in a public vehicle, probably stuffed full of other travellers, that broke its journey at the inns along the route only for the few minutes required to change the horses.

'Where will you stay in London?' Lady Denby cried, following her out into the passage.

'With Cousin Elizabeth. Or at a hotel, if she's not in town. If necessary, Mr Henderson will find me something suitable. Now I must go. I have a hundred things to do before the Royal Mail leaves tomorrow.'

Giving her stepmother's hand a quick squeeze, Caro strode through the entry, trotted down the steps and, once out of her stepmother's sight, set off at a run for the stables.

It was long past dark by the time she'd concluded her rounds of the stalls with Newman, her head trainer, reviewing with him the regimen she wished him to follow with each horse.

'Don't you worry, Miss Caroline,' he told her when they'd finished. 'Your late father, God rest 'im, trained me and every groom at Denby Stables. We'll do whatever's needful to carry on. You go up to London and do what you must. And, miss…' he added gruffly, giving her arm an awkward pat, 'best of luck to you.'

With a wisp of a smile, Caro watched him go. Even after

so many years of living in a large household, it never ceased to amaze her how quickly news travelled through invisible servants' networks. Although she'd told Newman nothing beyond the fact that urgent business called her away to London, somehow he must have discovered the true reason behind her journey.

Her final stop before returning to the house was Sultan's box. 'No, my handsome boy, I'll not take you with me this time,' she told him as she stroked the velvet nose. 'You're too fine a horse to risk having you turn an ankle in some pothole, racing through the dark to London. Though you would fly to take me there, if I asked you.'

The gelding nosed her hand and nickered his agreement.

The darkness seemed to close around her, magnifying the fear and anxiety she'd been struggling to hold at bay. Sensing her distress, Sultan nosed her again and rubbed his neck against her hand. Trying to give her comfort, it seemed.

What comfort would she have, if she lost him, lost them all? She had no siblings, no close neighbours other than Harry, and he was off in India. All her life, her horses had been her friends and playmates. She'd poured out her problems and told them her secrets, while they listened, nickering encouragement and sympathy.

Denby Lodge was a vast holding, its wealth derived from farms, cattle and fields planted in corn and other crops. Like her father, she'd been content to let the estate manager— and then the trustees in London—concern themselves with the other businesses, as she let the housekeeper manage the manor itself and its servants, while she focused solely on managing the stud.

She'd not been dissembling when she told Henshaw she possessed no feminine talents. She didn't sew or embroider, paint, sing, or play an instrument. What was she to do with herself without her horses to birth, raise and train?

It was all she knew. All she had ever done. All she had ever wanted to do. What could she find to replace the long hours spent in these immaculately kept barns with their rows of box stalls, where every breath brought the familiar scents of hay and bran and horse, saddle leather and polished brass? What could replace the thrill of feeling a thousand pounds of stallion thundering under her as he galloped across a meadow, responding to signals she'd ingrained in him after hours and hours of patient, careful training?

After all she had done to keep the stud, it was intolerable that some self-important peer, who wished to dictate to her what a woman's place should be, might have the power to strip it all from her.

What was to become of her if Woodbury succeeded?

Weary, anxious, desperate, she wrapped her arms around Sultan's neck and wept.

Chapter Eleven

Little more than thirty hours later, Caroline climbed down from the hackney that had brought her back from the solicitor's office and walked slowly up the stairs into her cousin Elizabeth's modest town house. A house that been part of her cousin's marriage settlements, fortunately, Caro thought, making it one of the few assets her profligate husband hadn't been able to squander.

Oh, fortunate Elizabeth.

A dull ache in her head, she felt the weariness of every sleepless hour she'd endured, from her last night at Denby Lodge, briefing the trainer and preparing for the journey, to the long dusty, uncomfortable transit into London. She'd barely taken the time to greet Elizabeth and inform her about her urgent mission before leaving for Mr Henderson's office.

Where she was met by the chilling news that her trustees, approved by the Court of Chancery under her father's will to care for her inheritance, definitely had the legal right to sell off any land or assets they saw fit, for the good of the estate.

Lady Elizabeth was out, the butler told her as he let her in. Her chest so tight with pain and outrage she could barely breathe, too exhausted to sleep, Caroline went to the small study, took paper and scrawled a letter to Harry, pouring into it all her anguished desperation.

Not that it would make any difference; she probably wouldn't even post it. By the time the letter reached Harry, even if he wrote back immediately, agreeing to marry her by proxy, it would be too late. The sale, Mr Henderson had advised her this afternoon, was already near to being concluded.

She was going to lose the stud.

That awful fact echoed in hollowness of her belly like a shot ricocheting inside a stone building, chipping off pieces that could wound and maim. She felt her heart's blood oozing out even now.

She might as well shoot herself and get it over with, she thought bleakly.

A rustling in the passageway announced her cousin Elizabeth's return. Not wishing to leave the letter there, where some curious servant might read her ramblings, she quickly sanded and folded it and scrawled Harry's name on the top. Setting it to the side of the desk, she rose to meet her cousin.

Elizabeth took one look at her face and gathered her into a hug.

'Men!' she said bitterly, releasing Caro before linking arms and leading her to the sofa. 'They shape our world, write its laws and pretend we are helpless creatures who cannot be trusted to manage our own lives. So they can take it all.'

'At least you have your house. Maybe I can come and reside with you, once…once it's gone. I don't think I can bear to live at Denby Lodge, afterwards.'

'You'd certainly be welcome. I don't have nearly the income I once did, but it's enough for us to manage.'

'Oh, I should have wealth aplenty for us both, especially after the sale. My kind trustees are managing the estate so brilliantly, I should be awash in guineas. Lord Woodbury would doubtless approve my buying every feminine frippery under the sun…as long as I don't do the only thing in life I care about.'

Elizabeth poured them wine and handed Caro a glass. 'Come and live with me, then. We'll be two eccentric blue-stockings, keeping pugs, reading scientific tracts and nattering on about the rights of working women and prostitutes, like that Mary Wollstonecraft creature.'

Caro attempted a smile, but with her whole world disintegrating around her, she didn't have the heart to appreciate her cousin's attempt at humour. 'You should think twice before making such an offer. I'm a social pariah now, remember.'

Her cousin merely laughed. 'Oh, yes, I've heard the fantastical tale Lady Melross has been spreading. You, baring your bosom to snag a gentleman? Max Ransleigh, rake though he be, mauling a gently born girl in his own aunt's conservatory? No one who knows either of you could possibly believe it.'

In no mood to recount the story again, despite the curiosity in her cousin's eyes, Caro merely shrugged.

Tacitly accepting her reluctance, Elizabeth sighed. 'Is there no way to get around Lord Woodbury?'

'Only if I could find a fortune hunter desperate enough to escort me to Gretna Green tonight.'

Elizabeth shuddered. 'Don't even joke of such a thing! Besides, wouldn't Woodbury put a stop to that, too?'

'He couldn't; I'm of age. And, once married, my new husband would take ownership of everything from the trustees, with the power to cancel the sale.'

'I trust you are only jesting,' Elizabeth said, looking at her with concern. 'Gaining a husband would give you no more control over your wealth than your trustees do, as I learned to my sorrow. Oh, if only Harry were not so far away in India!'

'I know,' Caro said, feeling tears again prick her eyes. She'd never expected that at the most desperate hour of her life her closest childhood friend would be too far away to help her. 'I wrote to him tonight, useless as that was. But the plain fact is he's not here, nor could he possibly return before the sale goes through…and then the stud is lost to me for ever.'

Merely saying the words sent a knife-like pain slashing through her. Lips trembling, she pushed the image of Sultan from her mind.

'That soon?' Elizabeth was saying. 'I'm almost willing to draw up a list of eligible gentlemen.'

'He could have all my money, as long as he left me enough to maintain the stud. If only I knew someone besides Harry who'd be honourable enough to make such a bargain and keep—' Caroline broke off abruptly as Max Ransleigh's words echoed in her ears: *You could run the stud with my blessing…*

A near-hysterical excitement blazing new energy into her, she seized her cousin's arm. 'Elizabeth, you are acquainted with the Ransleighs, aren't you?'

'I haven't moved in their circles since my début Season, but I still count Jane Ransleigh as a friend. She's Lady Gilford now, one of society's most important—'

'Yes, yes, I know her,' Caroline interrupted. 'Is she in town? Could you get a message to her?'

'I suppose so. What is it, Caro? You're as white as if you were about to faint—and you're hurting my arm.'

'Sorry,' she mumbled, releasing it at once. Lightheaded, desperate, feeling every hour she'd gone without food and sleep and rest, she said, 'I must get a message to her cousin, Max Ransleigh. Tonight, if possible.'

'Max Ransleigh? Ah, the man who…' Comprehension dawned in Elizabeth's eyes. 'Are you sure?'

'I am. Though I'm not at all sure, after the scandal I dragged him into, that Lady Gilford would agree to give me his direction.'

'You don't have to ask her. Max is here now, in London.

Jane told me at tea last week that he'd come to town to meet with the colonel who used to command his regiment.'

'Do you know where he is staying?

'No, but Tilly, my maid, could find out. A friend of hers is the housekeeper's assistant for Lady Gilford.'

'Could you ask her to go to Lady Gilford's at once?'

Elizabeth studied her. 'Are you sure you want to do this?'

'No,' Caro replied, panic and hope coursing through her in equal measure. 'Nor have I any assurance he would even agree to see me, if I can locate him. But it's the only chance I've got. The sale will be final before the month's end.'

'What about the Curse? Your mother, aunt, cousin, grandmother—every female on your mother's side, for the last two generations has died in childbed. I thought you intended never to risk that.'

Putting out of her mind the heat that had flared between them in the glasshouse, Caro said, 'Mr Ransleigh's only seen me in atrocious gowns and in breeches, so maybe he won't want that from me. By all accounts, he prefers beautiful, sophisticated women and I'm hardly that. I'd give him free rein, with my blessing, to pursue and bed any other woman he wished.'

Elizabeth's eyes shadowed; Caro knew her husband had availed himself of that privilege without his wife's blessing. And despite her passionate love for him.

Maybe there was something to be said for wedding with cool calculation, with no emotions involved.

'Even if he took his pleasure elsewhere, he'd want to couple with his wife. Like every other man, he'll want an heir.'

'Perhaps. I'll worry about that later, after I save the stud.'

'What about Harry?' Elizabeth persisted.

A bittersweet pang went through her. She'd never imagined a future that did not include working the stud with Harry, the two of them linked by the same companionable affection they'd shared since childhood.

Pushing away the doubts, she said, 'What good would it be to have Harry, with no stud to run? Once the horses are sold and scattered, it would be nearly impossible to reassemble the breeding stock. As for the Curse, what good is hanging on to life if I've already lost what I love the most? No, Elizabeth, if there is a single chance of saving my horses, I simply must take it.'

Elizabeth hesitated another moment, frowning. 'I'm not at all sure this is wise, but...very well, I'll send Tilly to Lady Gilford's.'

Caroline crushed her cousin in a hug, hope and fear and desperation racing through her with the speed of a thoroughbred galloping towards the finish line at Newmarket. 'I'm not sure it's wise either. But ask her to hurry.'

On the other side of Mayfair, Max Ransleigh was sharing a brandy with the colonel of his former regiment at his lodgings at Albany.

'I appreciate your support, sir,' Max told him.

Colonel Brandon nodded brusquely. 'Can't trust these civilians not to muck things up. Foreign Office!' He snorted. 'If any of them had ever faced down fire in the heat of battle, they'd know the mettle of the men who fought beside them beyond any doubt. The very idea that you could have anything to do with that attempt against Wellington would be considered insulting and ridiculous by any soldier who ever served with you. As the scurvy diplomats should have realised.'

'If my own father wasn't willing to go to my defence, I don't suppose I can complain about the Foreign Office's lack of support,' Max countered, trying to keep the bitterness from his tone.

'Your father's a political type and they are even worse than the Foreign Office. I suppose policy making requires compromise, but hell's teeth, give me a battlefield any day! No wrangling over this clause or that provision, just the enemy before you, your men around you, and duty, clear and simple.'

'After my brief time in Vienna, I must agree,' Max said.

'I've no doubt we can find you some position where you belong, in the War Department. Though I must warn you, Ransleigh, you've certainly muddied the waters with this heiress business. Not that I credit any of the wild stories floating about, but the fact that you are believed to have compromised a well-born girl and then refused to marry her won't make finding a post any easier. Especially not coming on the heels of that Vienna affair.'

So, just as he'd feared, he was being blamed for the fiasco. The anger, resentment and frustration with his situation—and Caroline Denby—that simmered just beneath the surface fired hotter and Max had to rein in the strong desire to explain what had happened and defend himself.

But the colonel wasn't interested in excuses. 'I'm well aware of that,' he said shortly.

'I cannot help but advise that it would improve your prospects if you'd just marry the chit. Or you might try to locate that damned female who tried to cozen up to you in Vienna.'

'I intended to do so right after I returned from Waterloo. But the Foreign Office gave me to understand it wouldn't make any difference.

'The Foreign Office prefers concealing dirty linen to laundering it,' the colonel said acidly. 'No, I'm convinced that if you could get her to confess to the plot, it would go a long way towards redeeming your reputation. I might even be able to talk Wellington around.'

'Do you think so?' Max tried to stifle the hope that flared within him. 'It would mean a lot to know I'd regained his trust.'

'Old Hookey is notoriously intolerant of error, but he has a soft spot for the ladies. He might be induced to see there was no other course that you, as a gentleman, could have taken but to help a female in distress.'

Max tried to curb a rising excitement. 'Then perhaps, while you look around for a posting, I'll head back to Vienna and see what I can turn up.'

'Couldn't hurt,' the colonel said. 'Those lackwits in the Foreign Office bungled their chance to have you, the fools. The War Office's a better place for the man who led the counter-charge and saved the colours at Hougoumont! Had the chateau fallen, we might have lost the whole damn battle, and now be watching Bonaparte march through Europe again. Report back to me in a month and I'll see what I can do.'

'Thank you, Colonel. I'm much in your debt.'

Brandon waved off Max's thanks. 'It's a commander's job to watch out for his men. Only wish I'd returned to London sooner, so you'd not have been left twisting in the wind for so long. Drinking and wenching is all good and well, eh?' he said, giving Max a wink. 'But a man of your talents should occupy his time with something more challenging.'

Max grinned. 'Amen to that, sir.'

After an exchange of courtesies, Max bowed and took his leave, fired with more purpose than he'd felt since leaving his unit after Waterloo. The colonel's optimism provided him the first real glimmer of hope he'd had since that awful day in Vienna, when the world as he'd known it had shattered around him like the windows of Hougoumont under French artillery fire.

After nearly a year of drifting idly about—drinking and wenching, as the colonel had said—he might finally be on the threshold of the new career for which he longed.

He might even win back Wellington's approval.

That happy thought cheered him as the hackney he'd hailed

carried him towards the lodgings in Upper Brook Street that, being barred from his own family's home in London, he'd borrowed from Alastair.

With a respectable position, he'd be able to hold his head up again when he visited his mother.

He wasn't sure when, or if, he'd seek out his father. The earl had made clear during their one meeting that his son was no longer of any use to him in the Lords and a person of no use to the earl was no longer of any importance either. The truth of that fact stung less now than it had when he'd first had to face it, after Vienna.

A short time later, the hackney halted in front of Alastair's town house. Paying off the driver, Max paced to the entry, the cold sharp night air as invigorating as the renewed hope within him.

He was about to mount the steps when, in the darkness beside the entry stairs, something stirred. Reflexes honed by years on a battlefield had him instantly whipping out the blade hidden in his boot. Half-crouched and prepared to strike, he called out, 'Who's there? Come out where I can see you!'

While he poised, knife extended, a shadow straightened and walked toward him. In the dim illumination of the streetlamp, she pulled off the hood of her cloak.

For a shocked moment he thought he must be hallucinating. 'Miss *Denby*?' he said incredulously.

'Mr Ransleigh,' she acknowledged with a nod. 'Although I may be the last person in England you wish to see, may I beg a moment of your time?'

Max blinked, still not quite believing she was standing beside his doorstep. What could have possessed her to come alone to his lodgings and wait for him in the fair middle of night?

A strong protective instinct surfaced, warning whatever brought her would likely mean yet more scandal and he'd had enough already.

'You shouldn't be here,' he said flatly, his eyes sweeping the street, which mercifully appeared to be deserted. 'Where are you staying? Give me your direction and I'll call on you tomorrow.'

'I know it's highly irregular to come here, but it's not as if I have any reputation left to lose. The matter about which I must consult you is so pressing I don't want to wait until tomorrow. That is, if…if you will consent to speak with me.'

Whatever it was, his first imperative was to get her away from his front door and out of sight of the neighbours or any passers-by returning home from some *ton* party.

'Very well. Please, do come in,' he urged, hurrying her up the stairs and through the doorway.

The sleepy footman within snapped to attention, closing his gaping mouth at Max's warning frown when he perceived Max was accompanied by a female. At Max's pointed glance, he stepped out of the way and handed over his candle.

Just what he needed, Max thought, his anger and frustration surfacing again, Miss Denby turning up to cause more problems just when Colonel Brandon was about to begin delicate negotiations to secure his future.

Max hustled her past the servant down the hall and into the back sitting room, where the glow of the light wouldn't be visible to any neighbours on the other side of Upper Brook Street. Now to discover her mission and hustle her back out again before she caused any more damage.

Chapter Twelve

Torn between irritation and curiosity over Miss Denby's audacity in sitting beside his steps like a forgotten parcel, Max tried to muster up a cordial tone. 'Perhaps you'd better explain and be on your way.'

She took a deep breath. 'When I refused your offer at Barton Abbey, you assured me that if I should ever change my mind, I should let you know.'

Max swallowed hard, her words like a noose tightening around his neck. Now, when it finally looked like he might work out the future he wanted, was she suddenly going to hold him to that honour-coerced offer?

Grasping at something to deflect her, he said, 'I seem to remember that you were quite adamant about refusing it. You insisted you would marry no one but your Harry.'

'So I was, but I've just encountered circumstances that force me to revise those plans. Upon my father's death, trustees were appointed to oversee the management of the estate he bequeathed to me. As long as they did not interfere in the running of the stables, I was perfectly content with the arrangement.'

He recalled the great lengths she had gone to, willing to sacrifice her reputation—and sully his—to maintain control over the stud. 'And now they are interfering?' he guessed.

'Worse than interfering. I've just learned they intend to sell it. A buyer has been found and, unless something happens to prevent it, in about two weeks' time the estate will no longer own the stud.'

'And you can do nothing to stop this?' he asked, appalled despite himself and keenly aware of what the loss of Denby stables would mean to her.

'Lord Woodbury, the head trustee, has never approved of my involvement with the stud. When he learned that, despite becoming embroiled in a scandal that threatened my reputation, I refused to marry, he convinced the other trustees that my unnatural position running the stud had so corrupted my feminine nature, they should sell it to "protect" me and the good name of the family from further harm. Believing that, he's unlikely to listen to any plea I might make begging him to halt the sale. The only way—'

'—is to marry and have control over your assets pass to a husband,' Max finished, understanding now why she had come to him.

'I'm desperate, or I would never be going back on my promise to leave you free to wed a woman of your choice. But you did once tell me you thought we might rub along well together, so if you would consider renewing your very kind offer, wedding me could offer you a few advantages.'

Her words tumbled over each other, as if she'd stood there in the dark rehearsing the speech over and over. Pausing only to drag in a ragged breath, she continued, 'I know you are already comfortably circumstanced, but I am a very wealthy woman. As long as you guarantee me sufficient funds to maintain the stud, you are welcome to the rest. Buy a higher rank in the army, purchase an estate, make investments on the 'Change. Travel to Vienna and hunt down the conspirators who engineered the attack on Lord Wellington. Whatever you wish that coin can buy, it can be yours.'

As if she didn't dare give him the opportunity to utter a syllable, she rushed on, 'Wedding me would also help to re-establish your reputation since, as you asserted from the first and I now recognise, my refusal to marry has most unfairly layered blame upon you. Indeed, if you truly wish to spike the guns of Lady Melross's malicious gossip, you might have Lady Gilford put it about that we've been acquainted for some time and the wedding long planned. No one would think it remarkable that the son of the Earl of Swynford, discovered caressing his almost-betrothed in a secluded conservatory, would feel no need to justify his actions or explain the nature of his relationship to a mere Lady Melross.'

The idea was so ingenious that, despite the turmoil of thoughts whirling in his brain, Max had to laugh. 'Brilliant! An audacious lie—but plausible.'

'We'd have to wed by special license, but many prominent individuals do so, to avoid the vulgar publicity of having the banns called. If Lady Gilford and her friends seemed to find nothing exceptional about it, society would accept it as well.'

'You mis-spoke, Miss Denby,' Max said, shaking his head with rueful admiration. 'You are quite diabolical. I begin to believe you'd make a master politician.'

That earned him a wisp of a smile before, clutching her hands together, she dropped her eyes, avoiding his gaze. 'As for intimacy,' she continued, her cheeks colouring, 'I should prefer a marriage in name only, for reasons I would rather not discuss. Since you aren't the eldest son, there's no title to pass along. Having already asked so huge a favour, I should make no other claim upon your time or your affections. Although, obviously, you would not be free to marry, I will neither interfere in nor protest at any other relationship you choose to enter. Although if…if you felt for some reason that you *must* exercise your marital rights…well, I realise I would have no grounds to refuse you.'

Taking another deep breath, she raised her chin and faced him squarely. 'So that is the bargain. I don't expect you to give me an answer tonight, but I will need your reply within a few days. I know I have no right to intrude upon you with my dilemma…but the stud is my life. With everything I am and everything I love about to be stripped away, I simply had to seize any possible chance to prevent it.'

She fell silent, watching him, her dark eyes huge and imploring in a face lined with weariness. Tears had gathered at the corners of her eyes, he noted, sparkling like brilliants in the candlelight.

A host of questions crowded to his lips, even as his startled wits tried to sort out the preposterous new scheme she'd just laid in front of him. But before he had a chance to ask any of them, she sighed and hoisted herself unsteadily to her feet.

'I'll go now, through the kitchen if the footman will lead me out, so it's less likely any of your neighbours might see me and make matters worse. If such a thing is possible.'

But as she took a step, she stumbled and fell forwards. Max jumped up to catch her before she tumbled to the floor, her slight frame swaying in his hands.

'You're not well,' he exclaimed, all the questions swirling in his mind slamming to a halt at that observation. 'Here, sit back down.'

He eased her into the chair, sure she would have collapsed had he not supported her weight. 'Where is Lady Denby? When did you arrive in London?'

She gave her head a small shake, as if the answer to so simple a question was a profound mystery. 'I arrived…this afternoon? Yes, it was this afternoon. Just myself and my maid. Stepmother got Lord Woodbury's letter two days ago; I travelled post yesterday and last night, arriving today to consult with Papa's solicitor and see if anything could be done.'

'You travelled post yesterday?' he repeated with a frown. 'When did you last sleep? Two nights ago? Three?'

'I don't recall.' She scrubbed a hand over her eyes, as if trying to clear the exhaustion from them. 'Something like that.'

'When did you last eat?'

'I'm not sure. The Royal Mail stops only to change horses, you know, not long enough to order a meal. Upon reaching London, I went directly to the solicitor's office, then back to my cousin Elizabeth's. And when I thought maybe you could help me, I came here.'

'Sit back in that chair before you fall out of it,' he ordered, pacing over to throw open the door. The footman he'd intended to call stood just beyond the threshold; from the flush on the man's face and his half-bending stance, Max suspected he'd been listening through the keyhole.

'Fetch some bread, cheese and ham,' he instructed. 'Brandy for me and some water.'

'No, you needn't entertain me,' Miss Denby protested as he closed the door. 'I've already trespassed enough on your time. I will await your reply at my cousin's house. Lady Elizabeth Russell, in Laura Place.'

She made another wobbly attempt to rise; gently he pushed her back into her chair. 'Miss Denby, there is no way I am sending you out of the kitchen door like some Whitechapel purse-snatcher to creep home through the midnight streets. By the way, please assure me you didn't walk here alone in the dark.'

'No, I did not.'

'Thank heavens for that!'

'I took a hackney to Hyde Park and walked from there. I didn't want the neighbours to see a carriage pull up and a female alight from it before your front door.'

Which meant she had traversed quite a distance through

the London night. Though Mayfair was one of its more prosperous sections, no area of the city was entirely safe after dark for a young woman alone.

Max uttered an exasperated oath. 'Are you always this much trouble?'

'I'm afraid so,' she replied, with an apologetic look that almost made him chuckle.

'Well, your nocturnal wanderings are over,' he pronounced, curbing his humour. 'You will sit by that fire and warm yourself, then take some nourishment while I consider what is to be done.'

A ghost of a smile touched her weary lips. 'So masterful, Mr Ransleigh. Spoken like an earl's son indeed.'

Despite himself, he had to grin—was there any situation into which he'd got with this girl that didn't become absurd? 'It's the army officer in me,' he corrected.

'I knew it couldn't be the diplomat. Never make up their minds about anything without debating it for weeks.'

But, too distressed and weary, he suspected, to give more than token protest, she settled into the wing chair with a sigh, leaning her head back and closing her eyes.

Wilson returned a moment later with the refreshments, nearly goggle-eyed with curiosity. Instructing the footman to venture out into the night and find a hackey, Max closed the door in his face. Probably not even Wilson's scandalous employer Alastair had ever escorted an obviously gently bred female into the house after midnight.

'So, let me see if I understand you correctly,' he said after she'd begun dutifully nibbling on some ham and a biscuit. 'You propose that we wed immediately so that I may take charge of your assets before Lord Woodbury can sell off the stud. I would agree to allow you sufficient funds to run it and go my own way, with the rest of your dowry to invest as I see fit.'

'Correct.'

'In addition, I am free to engage in such…relationships as I choose, with your full approval.'

'Yes,' she confirmed, meeting his eyes steadily, though a hint of a blush coloured her cheeks.

He turned away, considering. Though he found her unusual and quite attractive in an unconventional way, he had no more inclination to marry now than when honour had forced him to make her an offer at Barton Abbey. Sympathetic though he was to her dire situation, his first impulse was to refuse.

But then he recalled Brandon's advice that the most helpful thing he could do to speed the colonel's efforts would be to redress the scandalous situation with the heiress.

Wedding her would rub out the tarnish on his honour, especially if he prevailed upon Jane to circulate the myth of their prior relationship that Miss Denby had just invented. His lips twitched again with appreciation at that blatant falsehood. Oh, how satisfying it would be to rout the noxious Lady Melross!

More importantly, wedding Miss Denby was the only way she could salvage *her* reputation. Though he wanted to remain angry with her for embroiling him in this mess to begin with, in truth, she was as much an innocent victim of the scandal Henshaw had unleashed upon them as he was.

As a gentleman of honour, he didn't see how he could refuse her plea that they marry now, any more than he could have avoided making her an offer after the escapade in the glasshouse at Barton Abbey.

Dismayed by that conclusion, he stared into the fire, his mind furiously casting about for any feasible way out…and finding none. It seemed he might have to marry her after all. Could he make himself do it?

If he did, he vowed the relationship would have to be more than the cold-blooded alliance of convenience his parents had made. He already knew that even if they had nothing else in common, there was passion between them.

He stole a covert look at Miss Denby, who had, after presenting her first proposition, having laid out all her arguments, left him alone to ponder his decision, with no further effort to entreat or cajole.

Though she was certainly far lovelier than she gave herself credit for being, there was no getting around the fact that she was nothing like well-connected society beauty Lady Mary Langton, whom he'd vaguely imagined marrying back when he was thought to have a brilliant political future.

But there might be advantages to that. Since Miss Denby wanted to remain in the country, he would not have to torture himself escorting his wife through endless rounds of society amusements, when he'd much prefer being at the nearby political gatherings from which he was now barred.

But she would never bore him. Unless he was much mistaken about her character, she'd never beg him for trifles, demand that he dance attendance upon her, sulk or pout or importune him to get her way over some matter upon which they disagreed. Like a man, she'd discuss and reason and agree to compromise.

He'd be passing up his only chance to marry for love, but he wasn't sure he really believed in that poetic nonsense anyway. Of his closest friends, only Alastair had experienced it, and all that had got him was a desire to blow himself up on the nearest battlefield.

By now, Miss Denby had stopped eating and sat gazing glassy-eyed into the distance. Since she appeared too weary to notice, he indulged himself by openly inspecting her.

He'd thought it angular, but in fact her face was all soft curves and planes crowned by high cheekbones and finished with a determined little chin below full, soft lips he remembered all too well. Above that graceful arch of neck, another stray auburn curl caressed the edge of a delicious little shell of an ear.

How far down her back and breasts would that thick mass of curls tumble when he removed it from its pins? His fingers tingled and desire stirred, thick and molten in his blood.

She wore another of her dreadful, over-trimmed dresses. He imagined the kind of gown he might buy for her, that would show off to perfection her slender form...and luscious bosom.

His mouth grew dry as he remembered that, too.

This current appraisal confirmed his previous assessment that she was far lovelier than anyone at Barton Abbey had realised. Having gone about all her life thinking of herself almost as her father's son, she treated her womanly attractions as negligible. She seemed to have no inkling whatsoever of their potent power.

He could teach her that. Awaken her.

The zeal with which she pleaded for her horses, the fire he'd seen in her as she rode, the energy and determination that had driven her to travel halfway across England by coach and halfway across London by night all bespoke a passionate nature.

That passion and loveliness could be his, to arouse and enjoy. But, no, hadn't she also requested a marriage in name only?

Why would a woman of such obvious fire wish to enter a marriage without any? he wondered. Had one of her father's buyers cornered her in a stall one night, frightened her, manhandled her, as Henshaw had?

Anger boiled up at the thought. If she had been attacked, she'd not been violated; forthright as she was, she would have told him if she were not a virgin. He would certainly never force himself on her, but he had no right whatsoever to his reputation as Magnificent Max, able to charm any woman and persuade any man, if he couldn't manage to seduce his own bride. The fiery young woman who, he recalled with satisfaction, had already admitted in the conservatory at Barton Abbey that he tempted her.

A more unpleasant explanation occurred, chilling his ardour like the splash of a North Sea wave. Did she spurn fulfillment because she wanted to 'save herself' for the absent Harry? He was willing to risk many things, but not the possibility of being cuckolded.

'Despite our marriage vows, you offered me freedom of conduct if I agree to wed you, did you not, Miss Denby?' he asked, breaking the long silence.

Startled out of her abstraction, she looked up. As the meaning of his words penetrated, surprise widened her eyes. 'You might actually…consider doing this?'

'If I do, I'm afraid I'm not prepared to be as generous about your conduct. I require unquestioned faithfulness in my wife. What of Harry, when he eventually returns?'

'I promise you, upon my most solemn honour, that if you agree to marry me, I will pledge you my loyalty as well as my hand. I would never betray you with anyone else. Not even Harry.'

Another woman, seeing what she most desired within grasp, might dissemble at such a moment, but Miss Denby had never told him less than the absolute truth. Even when it didn't flatter her, he recalled ruefully.

He remembered her soldier's bearing as she straightened her shoulders and marched off with no tears or pleading after he refused her first offer. How she'd backed away, apologising for intruding upon his peace, when they'd met by accident in the conservatory the second time. How she'd stationed herself outside his aunt's door at Barton Abbey, refusing to leave until she had spoken with Mrs Ransleigh and exonerated him.

He knew in his bones she meant every word of her promise and intended to keep it.

That fact sealed his fate. Perhaps on some level he'd known, ever since they'd been caught by Lady Melross in the glasshouse, that eventually it would come to this, for his initial fury had subsided to a calm resignation.

Never one to put off what must be done, once he'd truly decided to do it, Max dropped to one knee before her. 'Miss Denby, would you do me the honour of accepting my hand in marriage?'

Her eyes widened further. 'Don't you want to consider this further?'

'I have considered it. I'm quite willing to proceed at once.'

A look of befuddled wonder came over her face. 'You'll really marry me, Mr Ransleigh?'

'If you will have me, Miss Denby,' he replied, amused and a little touched by the enormity of her surprise. It seemed she hadn't truly believed her last-minute, desperate appeal would succeed.

Did she count the wealth she brought him, her intriguing personality, that ferocious honour and sense of loyalty…that luscious body, of such little worth?

Max would have to show her differently. Marriage to Caroline Denby might even be…fun.

If she'd been so unprepared for his acceptance, though, maybe she hadn't considered the consequences very carefully. 'Are you sure *you* don't need to think it over further?'

'Absolutely!' she cried, one of the tears still lingering at the corners of her eyes spilling down her cheek. Tentatively, as if she couldn't quite believe she now had the right, she laid her hand on his. 'I should be honoured to accept your offer, Mr Ransleigh.'

'Please, my friends call me Max.'

'Yes, friends. I believe we can be very good friends…Max.'

Friendship was a beginning, he thought. But with any luck and a full measure of his celebrated charm, he hoped to become a good deal more. If he must wed, by heavens, he intended his union to be a passionate one.

'If you've finished, let me escort you back to your cousin's house—by way of the front door, if you please. Now that we are to marry, I'll have no more skulking alone about the back streets of London.'

She nodded, 'And if we're to wed without delay, there is much to be done.'

'I'll set about obtaining a special licence, but there doesn't need to be unseemly haste.'

'But we only have—'

'I'll speak with Lord Woodbury and the trustees, telling them I don't wish the stud to be sold. Once they know we are to wed, I'm sure they will respect that choice.'

Her lips twisted in distaste. 'I expect you're right. *My* desires mean nothing, but the trustees will bow to the wishes of my intended husband.'

'Who also happens to be the son of a powerful member of government, someone they would not want to offend. Might as well use Papa's position to our benefit.' *Since it has done me little other good of late*, Max thought cynically. 'Besides, I suspect Lady Denby would be hurt were we to rush off and marry without even informing her.'

To his satisfaction, her eyes lit at that observation. 'You are right again, of course. She's harangued and cajoled me toward matrimony so frequently, I know she would be disappointed not to be present when her fondest wish is finally realised.'

'Exactly. Once I obtain the licence, we can be married at Denby Lodge, if you prefer.'

'I'd rather do so here, as soon as Stepmama and Eugenia can get to London. I don't trust Lord Woodbury.'

'Would you like to accompany me when I call on him?'

'Only if you intend to make him grovel,' she retorted.

He grinned at her. 'That could probably be arranged.'

Her eyes scanned his face, weighing the seriousness of his offer. Finally realising he meant every word, she said, 'That, I would very much like to witness—galling as it will be to watch him treat you with every solicitude, when he has always dismissed my opinions out of hand.'

'He will never do so again,' Max promised. Having a female, especially a young female, run a horse farm might be unusual, but since it was Lord Woodbury's interference that had forced this situation upon them, Max was not inclined to be forgiving.

She smiled with genuine gratitude. 'Though I sorely wish I might be able to do it on my own, watching you vanquish Lord Woodbury will still be satisfying. Thank you for being so considerate. And waiting until I can have my family present for the wedding. It will make it seem more…real.'

'Legally, it's absolutely real, wherever it takes place.' Pushing away the faceless image of an army lieutenant serving in far-off India, he continued, 'You must be very certain this is what you want; there'll be no going back later.'

'No going back for you, either,' she countered soberly. 'I only hope you won't hate me one day…as you might well, should you ever fall in love with a woman you then can't marry.'

'I think I will be quite satisfied with our bargain,' he assured her…and, to his surprise, realised that if wedding her made obtaining a posting easier, he might actually mean those gallant words.

'I shall do my best to make sure you never regret it.'

Max brought the hand she'd given him to his lips. As he brushed them against her knuckles, he heard her quick intake of breath, felt the shiver that moved through her.

Desire rose in him, sharp, sudden. He wanted to taste her

skin, take her mouth, trace his thumb over the outline of her breasts, sure he would find the nipples taut and pebbled.

But not yet, not now, while fatigue clouded her eyes and worry over the loss of her home and her horses consumed her thoughts.

She tugged at her hand, confirming that caution. At once he released her.

At that moment, there was a knock at the door. Wilson peeked in to inform Max that a hackney awaited them.

'I'll return you to your cousin's, then,' Max said, helping her to her feet. 'You need your rest. Can't have my bride looking haggard, letting Lady Melross claim she had to be coerced into marrying me.'

'No, I must be radiant—if only to confound Lady Melross.'

Max escorted her out, reflecting that over his time as a privileged son, he'd had women from Diamonds of the *ton* to experienced courtesans try to entice him. None of them had sparked in him the combination of curiosity and desire inspired by the plain-spoken Caroline Denby—who'd made no attempt at all to entice him.

He had a sudden, lowering thought that he was about to marry a woman who might well fascinate him for the rest of his life…and she was marrying *him* to save her horses.

He'd just have to be up to the challenge of fascinating her, then. He might not be able to coerce an apology from the Foreign Office, but surely he could make one slip of a girl never regret marrying him.

Chapter Thirteen

Two days later, Max collected Caro at Laura Place and escorted her to the offices of Mr Henderson in the City, where Lord Woodbury, as spokesman for her father's trustees, was to meet them.

The solicitor, to whom Caro had already sent a note apprising him of her new status, greeted her warmly and treated Max, she thought, with just the right amount of deference, respectful of his status as an earl's son, but not fawning over him. After offering congratulations on their imminent nuptials, he said, 'I'm assuming you wanted to consult Lord Woodbury about transferring control over Miss Denby's inheritance?'

'Yes. Most urgently, though, I want to inform him that I do not wish for Denby Stud to be sold.'

'I'm so very glad to hear it!' Mr Henderson exclaimed. 'Having Miss Denby assume so active a role in the business might have been uncommon, but knowing how well she discharged those duties, I very much regretted the trustees' decision, an action I had no authority to countermand. I'm delighted you intend to retain ownership.'

'Anything that pleases my intended, pleases me as well,' Max said. 'I've been impressed by how highly Miss Denby has spoken of your services, Mr Henderson. If you will, I'd like you to work with my solicitors in drawing up the wedding settlements. We're both anxious to be wed as soon as possible,' he added, giving Caro a warm, lover-like look so believable that her face heated…and her body hummed.

Observing that glance, the lawyer smiled. 'So I see. I'm honoured by your confidence and will begin the necessary paperwork at once. Now, if I may show you into my private office? Lord Woodbury awaits you.'

Max offered his arm; Caro took it and together they walked into the office.

Lord Woodbury rose from his chair as they entered. After looking at Caro with some surprise, he recovered to say, 'Ah, the affianced couple! Allow me to wish you both every happiness.'

'Thank you,' Max said. 'As I mentioned in my note, I wish to briefly review the status of Miss Denby's estate.'

'Of course. Miss Denby, I'm sure Mr Henderson will make you comfortable elsewhere whilst Mr Ransleigh and I discuss these matters.'

'No, I wish her to be present,' Max said. 'The first item under review is halting the sale of the Denby Stud and Miss Denby knows the details of its operation much better than I.'

Woodbury looked as if he'd like to assert she knew them far too well—but after viewing Max's expression, swallowed those words and said instead, 'You wish the estate to retain ownership?'

'I don't want any major changes made to the estate's assets before my man of business and I have the opportunity to review the whole.'

To Caro's mingled outrage and chagrin, without a syllable of protest, Woodbury replied, 'Quite understandable, Mr Ransleigh. I must confess some surprise, however, that you have an interest in running the stud. I assumed you would prefer to return to a government post.'

'I probably shall accept another position. Since my bride has overseen the stud's operation with great competence for years, I see no reason to make any changes in its management.'

Though the approving light in Woodbury's eyes dimmed, to Caro's added irritation, whether out of respect for the Earl of Swynford's son or because a *man* made the statement, Woodbury did not argue. After a moment, he said only, 'I suppose you may order things as you like in your own household.'

'Indeed I shall. I shall also see that my bride is never again slighted or insulted by those into whose safekeeping her inheritance was entrusted.'

Woodbury had the grace to look a bit uncomfortable. 'Certainly not.'

'I regret to say I am most disappointed in your stewardship, my lord. Nay—' Max held up a hand when Woodbury, eyes widening in surprise, began to sputter a protest. 'I appreciate that, in the main, the estate has prospered. But I must wonder at the character of a man who would so carelessly injure the delicate sensibilities of a female under his protection.'

Woodbury stared at him. 'Delicate sensibilities of a female...you mean *Caro*?'

After a warning glance from Max, Caro stifled the protest automatically rising to her lips. Following his lead, she sighed heavily and dropped her gaze, trying her best to look like a fragile maiden in distress.

'I understand you were a close friend of Sir Martin. I cannot imagine he would have been happy to learn you intended to strip away from his poor orphaned daughter the great project upon which the two of them had worked closely for so many years, the sole reminder she possessed of the father for whom she still grieves.'

'Well, I certainly—' Woodbury sputtered.

'Then there's the matter of the letter you wrote to Lady Denby, making rather…regrettable remarks about my be-trothed. I'm shocked that a gentleman of your standing would have given so much heed to scurrilous rumour, rather than discreetly enquiring of the families involved. Surely you don't expect the Earl of Swynford to post details about private family matters on a handbill in every print-shop window! Or that he would stoop to correct common gossip.'

'But Lady Denby herself wrote me that you were not to wed!' Woodbury protested.

Max shook his head pityingly. 'Perhaps you did not read her letter aright. She merely meant to inform you that, at the time of her missive, we were not planning an immediate wedding. We subsequently decided to advance the date of our nuptials. In any event, I was quite disappointed by the unnecessary haste with which you set about disposing of a major component of my betrothed's estate without even the courtesy of consulting me. As was my father, the earl.'

'Your father, the earl?' Woodbury echoed, his indignation visibly wilting at Max's mention of his father's disapproval.

'I suppose you were only doing what you thought best—'

'Indeed, I was!' Woodbury inserted hastily.

'Still, I think you owe Miss Denby an apology.'

Woodbury opened and closed his lips several times, in-dignation seeming to vie with prudence as he attempted to dredge up the appropriate words.

'My father, the earl, would think it a handsome gesture,' Max added softly.

The expression on his face as sour as if he had just swal-lowed a large bite of green apple, Woodbury turned to Caro.

'My apologies, Miss Denby, if I have given offence,' he said woodenly. 'It was certainly unintended.'

She nodded. 'Apology accepted, Lord Woodbury. We may have had our...disagreements, but I know you tried to serve the best interests of the estate.'

'Since your trusteeship will end within days anyway, you may consider yourself relieved of your duties now,' Max announced. 'Mr Henderson can oversee whatever needs to be done until our marriage. Thank you for your efforts on Miss Denby's behalf, Lord Woodbury, and a good day to you.' Gesturing towards the door, Max gave him a regal wave of farewell.

Caro doubted the Prince Regent himself could have sounded more dismissive. Stifling any reply he might have wished to make, Woodbury bowed and departed, looking like a resentful schoolboy who'd just been caned by the headmaster.

After he'd exited, Max turned to Caro. 'Satisfied?'

Caro jumped up and sank before him into a curtsy deep enough to do justice to the Queen's Drawing Room. 'Completely, my lord. How perfectly you play the "earl's son" when you wish! I was nearly intimidated myself.'

'I did study at the feet of a master,' Max said drily.

'You tell a falsehood with as much skill as I do.' She chuckled. 'I can only imagine the outrage of your father, could he have heard you invoking his name in this case! To give Lord Woodbury his due, he did manage the *other* assets of the estate quite competently.'

'Yes, but while doing so, he deeply wounded the delicate sensibility of the female under his protection. Made her desperate enough to travel through the night to reach London and then endanger herself crossing the city alone in darkness. She even offered herself in a marriage she did not want, to undo the damage he had done. That's not an injury I will easily forgive.'

She was about to protest the 'delicate sensibility' description…but, in truth, she *had* been desperate. Looking up to admit that, she met his gaze, so full of concern that it sent a shock through her.

The rout he'd just made of Lord Woodbury was more than a clever demonstration of his rhetorical power; it showed he was indeed prepared to defend what mattered to her. That he took seriously his promise to protect it, and her.

For the first time since her father's death, Caro felt…safe. A wave of affection and gratitude swept through her, brought the sting of tears to her eyes, made her want to throw her arms around his neck.

'Thank you for standing behind me to save the stud.' The last part of his comment suddenly registering, she added softly, 'As for that marriage, I'm daily coming to believe proposing to you was the wisest decision I've ever made.'

He took her hand and kissed it. 'I hope so. You are mine to protect now, Caro. I intend to do that to the very best of my abilities.'

As soon as he touched her, the clarity of her thoughts muddied, her mind disturbed by a rush of sensation, like the clash when the foam of a receding breaker meets the thrust of an incoming wave. Staring down at the hand he still held, distracted by the feelings coursing through her, she stuttered, 'I—I will t-try to prove myself worthy of that care.'

Then she looked up from her tingling fingers, became caught by his ardent gaze…and was lost.

She couldn't seem to either speak or look away. The attraction between them intensified, throbbing in her veins, humming in her ears, drowning out sound, paralysing thought.

That same strange, powerful compulsion she had felt in the conservatory at Barton Abbey welled up again, pulling her towards him. As if hypnotised, she found herself lifting her chin, stripped of everything but the need to feel his lips against hers.

He placed his warm, strong hand under her chin, drawing a murmur from her as she angled her head to feel the slide of his fingers against her skin. A maelstrom of desire began churning in her belly, tightening in her chest, as she raised her lips towards his.

Just as her eyelids fluttered shut, the door swung open. The sound acting upon her taut nerves like the crack of a whip, she pushed away from Max with a gasp, her heart pounding.

Henderson walked in, a stack of documents in his hands. 'I've begun the preliminary paperwork, Mr Ransleigh. If you'll have your solicitors contact me, I'm sure we can sort everything out quickly. If you have no further business here, may I offer you some refreshment before you leave?'

'Thank you, but we must be going. Let me again express my gratitude for the advice and support you have given my fiancée.'

Henderson bowed. 'Having known and esteemed Miss Denby since she was a child, I'm pleased to find that you intend to honour her wishes…and her.' Surprising Caro, he added, 'You might just be worthy of her.'

Grinning, Max returned the bow, the earl's son seeming not at all offended to have his conduct judged by a mere solicitor. Her nerves still jangled, Caro let him lead her back to the carriage, trying to stifle the yearning of a body that stubbornly regretted not getting that kiss.

Max had been not nearly as affected by it, she scolded herself. He'd probably kissed a score of girls, many of them prettier, every one of them more skilled in allurement than she. A simple little kiss was not for him the soul-shattering experience it promised to be for her.

Oh, this would never do. She simply had to wrestle this

unruly attraction under control. Certainly before the wedding…after which she would suddenly be cast into significantly closer proximity to him for a much longer interval.

She really was getting married. A *frisson* of alarm, underscored by a deeper, hot liquid excitement licked through her. Once she truly belonged to him, body and soul, how was she to resist the force driving her to yield to him?

By recalling that the power of the Curse loomed a mesmerised moment of forgetfulness away.

Caro sighed. If she had any hope of resisting him, she must concentrate more on that real danger and learn to deal better with his maddening, bewitching allure. And with the wedding a mere few days away, she'd better learn quickly.

Chapter Fourteen

A little over a week later, Caro stood before the glass in a guest bedchamber of Lady Gilford's London town house. Lady Denby stood behind her, instructing the maid who was adjusting the skirts of her pale-green wedding gown.

Wishing she could soothe away the anxiety in her stomach as easily as the maid smoothed down the soft silken skirts, Caro studied her reflection critically. She couldn't remember ever owning so flattering a garment. At home, she'd ordered a few gowns each year from the village seamstress, but they had been adequate rather than stylish, and during her aborted Season, she'd taken care to choose cuts and colours as unsuited to her as possible.

For her wedding, she'd wanted to wear something that at least wouldn't make Max regret his decision the minute he saw her at the altar.

Would he find her appealing? Anticipation and unease skittered across her skin. In the few rushed days since their trip to Mr Henderson's office, she'd not made any progress in bringing her response to him under control. She felt attraction curl in the pit of her stomach every time he handed her into a carriage or took her arm up the stairs. Each time, she longed to extend and lengthen the contact.

In fact, the more time she spent with him, the more powerful his allure seemed to become, to the point that she feared if he made any move to make their marriage a real one, even the threat of the Curse might not be enough to armour her against him.

Which made it all the more imperative for her to get this marriage business finished as soon as possible and leave him in London to tend his career while she returned to Denby Lodge.

'Enough, Dulcie, you may go,' Lady Denby was saying. As the maid departed, Lady Denby gave her a reproving look. 'How lovely you are! I can't believe you hoodwinked me into wearing those atrocious dresses!'

'You have forgiven me, I hope.'

'With you mending matters by marrying Mr Ransleigh after all, of course I have. I do hope you'll be very happy.'

'I hope to make him so,' Caro said, thinking guiltily how robbing him of the chance to marry a lady he truly loved would make that goal more difficult. With society holding him responsible for her ruin, honour had given him little choice but to agree to her bargain.

'You mustn't worry about tonight,' Lady Denby said, obviously noticing Caro's nervousness. 'You may know everything about breeding horses, but the human animal is quite different. I'm sure Mr Ransleigh will be gentle and careful with you.'

Would he? They'd said nothing more since the first night about that part of their agreement. Legally, she couldn't deny him if he decided to ignore her request that theirs be a marriage in name only. Would he choose to do so...or not?

She came back from her reverie to find Lady Denby staring at her. 'I'm not worried,' she said a bit too heartily.

'You must put out of your mind that silly business about "the Curse",' Lady Denby said, patting her hand soothingly.

'I admit, the experience of some of your relations was unfortunate, but your mama, Sir Martin told me, had always been delicate. You are young and in robust health; there's no reason not to believe your own experience won't be much happier. Indeed, when the midwife places that first babe in your arms, you'll know it was worth all the discomfort and danger.'

Not if the hands receiving the babe were dead and cold, Caro thought.

'In any event, Mr Ransleigh will hope for an heir, as all men do, and you can't mean to deny him,' Lady Denby concluded, with a sharp glance at Caro.

Having no intention of confessing her bargain to her stepmother, Caro said meekly, 'No, of course not.'

Blessing again the fact that Max bore no responsibility for passing on his father's title, Caro hoped, for the present at least, that he'd be content to dally with the ladies sure to flock about such a dynamic, handsome, charismatic man—especially once he'd been restored to some important government position. She squelched a little niggle of jealousy at the thought.

It was ridiculous for her to be jealous that he would doubtless share with other women the intimacy she needed to avoid—and had actively *encouraged* him to pursue elsewhere.

She had about as much luck banishing the emotion as she had at controlling her responses to Max. Sighing, she shook her head at her own idiocy. Her inability to think coolly and logically about this matter was yet another indication that the sooner they parted after the wedding, the better.

Before they could walk out, a beaming Eugenia hurried in. 'Caro, how lovely you look! Oh, Mama, I've just had the most wonderful talk with Lady Gilford and Miss Ransleigh. Lady Gilford said she was going to speak with you about having us stay with her for the whole Season, so Felicity and I can share the experience! How kind she is, inviting us and allowing Caro and Mr Ransleigh to have their wedding breakfast at her house.'

As well as quietly putting out the taradiddle Caro had constructed about a previous attachment between herself and Max Ransleigh. 'We owe her a great deal,' Caro said. 'I'm glad everything is going to work out for your Season.'

'How much better everything looks now than when we left Barton Abbey! Though…I am sorry about Harry, Caro. I hope you are not too unhappy about marrying Mr Ransleigh instead. Not that I can imagine any girl being unhappy to marry someone so handsome, charming and well connected! But I know Harry was your best and dearest childhood friend.'

'I am quite content to marry Mr Ransleigh,' Caro answered, trying to keep her voice even and mask the frantic agitation the mere thought set fluttering in her veins.

The busyness of the last week had made it possible for her to put out of mind the fact that she'd traded away the ease, long friendship and wordless understanding she'd always shared with Harry for the edgy uncertainty of marriage to a man whose mere presence in a room made her pulse race.

But though she might refuse to *think* about it, the fierce attraction continued to simmer between them, driving her at once to try to stay near him and to flee his hold over her. With her nerves constantly on edge, she'd barely slept and, despite Lady Denby's assurances, could scarcely contemplate the wedding night without a panicky feeling in her gut. Would he come to claim her? Could she make herself resist him if he did?

Oh, how much easier this would have been had Harry been the bridegroom with the right to enter her chamber tonight! A vision of his dear face rose up before her and she felt tears prick her eyes.

But it wouldn't be Harry tonight. It would never be Harry.

Facing the dilemma before her, she'd made the only choice she could. There was no use looking back; she could only go forwards.

As she reaffirmed that conclusion, Lady Gilford opened the door and beckoned to them.

'How charming you look, Miss Denby! Shall we go? Max and the clergyman will be awaiting us at the church.'

In the nave of St. George's, Hanover Square, Max paced, trying to settle down a few nerves of his own. Once the decision to wed Caro Denby had been finalised, he'd experienced surprisingly few qualms and only one minor regret. Despite his vaunted charm, he hadn't made much headway in seducing his bride; if anything, she seemed more skittish than ever.

Perhaps it was only maidenly nerves and inevitable; knowing nothing about virgins, Max couldn't tell. An experienced man did have the advantage; he knew what to expect of intimacy, where his innocent bride could only speculate. The stories reaching her ears must be lurid indeed, Max reflected, for as the day of their wedding grew nearer, Caro had grown as unsettled as a green-broke colt sidling in a paddock, eyeing the saddle about to be placed on its back. Each time he took her arm to assist her into a carriage or walk her into a room, she jumped as if scalded by his touch.

He shook his head ruefully and laughed. Bless her, did she think he was going to drag her into the bedchamber tonight and mount her with no regard for her fears or her comfort, like a stallion covering a mare?

The door to the sanctuary opened and his senses sprang to the alert. But instead of the priest leading in the bridal party, the figure striding in was his father, the Earl of Swynford.

Max sent a swift prayer of thanks that he had the space of several rows between them to collect his thoughts before he must greet the man with whom he'd had no contact since the morning he'd been dismissed from Ransleigh House. He'd taken Caro to call briefly on his mother—after making sure his father would be out. He'd left his sire only a terse note to inform him of his upcoming nuptials.

The man whose approval he'd once sought to win before all else halted before him. 'My lord,' Max said, bowing. 'I didn't expect you'd have the time to attend.'

'I shan't stay for the wedding breakfast, but I thought it wise to appear for this, so society would know I approved your choice. Despite the recent scandal over this girl, it seems you managed to land on your feet after all. "A previous attachment", indeed,' the earl said with a snort. 'I hope you thanked your aunt and Jane Gilford for their assistance in promoting that falsehood.'

'Yes, I've much appreciated all the efforts they expended on my behalf,' he said drily.

That barb hit home; his father frowned. 'You mean to imply that I have done nothing? You must remember, my son, at the time of your ill-advised liaison in Vienna, I was in the midst of very delicate negations to—'

Max held up a hand. 'I understand, Father.' The hell of it was, he *did* understand, though he still couldn't help resenting the fact that his father had not tried harder to find a way to intervene on his behalf.

'Well, however odd the path you followed to settle on this girl, it's a good choice. Better to have had a bride from a political family, but after Vienna, there's not much chance of that. At least you found yourself an heiress. Being rich will go a long way toward reconciling society to your lapses in judgement.'

Angry words rushed to his lips, but arguing with his father wouldn't set the proper tone for his wedding day. Restraining himself with effort, he said instead, 'I'm glad you approve my choice.'

'I expect you'll get her breeding and leave her in the country. I don't recall meeting her last Season, but Maria Selfridge told me she wasn't up to snuff, with little to recommend her beyond a good pedigree and a better dowry.'

'Indeed?' Max said, annoyed by this cavalier dismissal of Caro, even though he knew she'd taken great pains during her brief Season to create exactly that impression. 'I find her both intelligent and lovely. But, yes, I expect we will settle at her property in Kent, to which she is very attached.'

His father nodded. 'Probably a wise move. Live retired for a year or two, breed some sons, let the memory of the scandals die down. By that time, when you come back to London, I'll probably be able to find a position for you.'

A cold anger rose in him, surprising in its intensity. 'There's no need, Father. I'm sure whichever flunky with whom you're now working is performing quite adequately, else you'd have turned him off, too. In any event, Colonel Brandon is soliciting a post for me in the War Department. If you'll excuse me, I must see what is keeping the priest.'

With a nod to his father, Max strode across the room and out into the foyer.

He closed the door, his hands still shaking with the force of his fury and, acknowledging that, his lips curved in a wry smile. Apparently the resentment and hurt over his father's abandonment ran far deeper than he'd thought.

Taking a shaky breath, he was wondering if he should hide out in the gardens until the priest summoned him for the ceremony when the bridal party appeared at the entry door.

Then he saw Caro and his anger at his father was swept away by wonder.

He'd known since first discovering her 'disguise' that she was attractive. He'd been anticipating seeing her garbed in a more flattering gown—and taking her out of it. Still, he was not prepared for the enchanting vision that now met his appreciative eyes.

Vanished with the ugly gowns was any chance her unusual activities could lead one to find her mannish or unfeminine. Sunlight shining through the open doorway haloed her in gold, while its beams burnished to copper the artful arrangement of her auburn curls. The soft sage colour of her gown set off the cream of her shoulders and the rounded tops of her breasts that swelled up from beneath the fashionably low neckline. The long skirt and demi-train, mercifully unadorned, draped and flowed about her waist and hips, showing off her shapely, slender figure to perfection.

While he drank in the sight of her, she must have seen him, for she froze in mid-step on the threshold, her hand clutching at her stepmother's arm. With her dark eyes staring at him, she looked as uncertain and wary as a startled doe poised to flee.

This was no creature of salons and ballrooms, skilled in meaningless chat and empty flattery, but a pure, untamed soul whose words mirrored her actions and showed her to be exactly what she claimed: a woman who emanated a fierce independence and a feral energy that triggered a primitive response in him.

He wanted to devour her in one gulp.

But that would be for later…if the time was right. Max sighed. Nervous as she'd been this last week and still looked, that time probably wouldn't be tonight.

The priest entered and nodded at them both. 'Are you ready to proceed?'

Max walked over to claim her hand. He wasn't surprised to find it cold. 'Shall we do this?' he murmured, half-expecting her to say 'no'.

Taking a deep breath, she seemed to gather her composure. 'Yes. I'm ready.'

'Let us begin, then, Father Denton,' Max told him.

Within moments, they had taken their places before the altar. For Max, unable to wrench his wondering gaze from Caro, the ceremony afterwards was a blur. He barely registered his father watching sombrely, Lady Denby dabbing at her eyes, the delight on Felicity and Caro's stepsister's faces, the pleasure on Jane's and Aunt Grace's.

In some miraculous transformation, the nervous bride had disappeared, replaced by a serene lady lovelier than he could have imagined, who repeated her vows in a calm voice. From time to time, she glanced up at him shyly, golden motes dancing in huge dark eyes he could lose himself in.

Then the priest clasped hands together, pronouncing them husband and wife, and led them off to sign the parish register.

'Well, it's done,' she said quietly as she wrote her name in a firm hand.

'You look enchanting.'

She angled her head at him, apparently assessing the genuineness of his compliment. 'You truly think so?'

'I do.'

She smiled. 'Then thank you. Was that your father, glowering at us? I would think he'd approve of your marrying a fortune, at least. Will he be at the wedding breakfast?'

'No, thankfully. Mother should be and a handful of Jane's friends. I hadn't expected him here, either, or I would have warned you.'

She shrugged. 'I'm more nervous about your mother. Shock doubtless limited her conversation during the brief call we made on her; I fear she will want to corner me for a proper grilling this time, trying to discover how some country nobody made off with her son.'

'You needn't fear that. Aunt Grace has already told her what happened at Barton Abbey. She wants only to see me happy. Since you are now my wife, that means she wants you to be happy too.'

Caro gave him a dubious look, but had no time to reply before Lady Gilford came over to give them each a hug. 'A splendid wedding! Shall we return to the house? I expect guests will be arriving for the wedding breakfast soon.'

Looking a bit alarmed, Miss Denby—no, *Mrs Ransleigh*, a title it was going to take Max some time to adjust to, he admitted—said, 'There won't be many, will there? Stepmama said it was to be just a small reception.'

'Of course. In keeping with the story already circulating—which, Max tells me, was your invention, and very clever!—I thought it best to keep it very select, just immediate family and a few close friends.'

Caro nodded. 'Fewer people to gossip.'

Lady Gilford gave a peal of laughter. 'Oh, no, quite the opposite! With only the *crème de la crème* in attendance, those who weren't present will envy those who were and want to know everything about it...so they can discuss it as if they, too, had been invited. It will be quite the talk of the town.'

'Approving talk?' Caro asked.

'Definitely. Without wishing to sound arrogant, I do have a fair amount of influence. Where I and my friends approve, others follow...especially now that Max has done the sensible thing and got himself wed to a lady of intelligence and breeding.'

'And beauty,' Max said, pulling Caro's hand up for a kiss that set his lips—and other parts—tingling.

Blushing a bit, she pulled her hand free. 'And large dowry,' she added. 'How much more sensible could any gentleman be?'

So completely had Max concentrated on Caro's flustered reaction—and the brief moment when her hand had tightened on his before pulling away—the sound of his father's voice startled him.

'Congratulations, Mrs Ransleigh, and welcome to the family,' the earl was saying.

'It was good of you to attend, my lord,' Caro said, dipping him a curtsy.

'I wanted all of London to know I approve of my son's choice.'

'This time, you mean?'

In the sudden hush, Max could almost hear the gasp of indrawn breath; no one who knew the Earl dared risk inciting his famous temper. Max tensed, mentally scrambling for words to deflect what would probably be a stinging rejoinder.

It must be bridal luck, for the earl merely gave a thin smile. 'This choice, no one could dispute.'

'I'm glad you think so and I'm sure he appreciates your taking the time to attend the service. I'm sorry we shall not see you at Lady Gilford's breakfast, but as I understand your duties keep you excessively busy I shall bid you farewell here. Thank you again for attending, my lord.' She made the earl another graceful curtsy.

It was almost a...*dismissal*! Max thought, shocked. He'd assumed her initial, rather confrontational greeting to his sire was perhaps an awkward choice of words due to nervousness.

But she didn't appear nervous—quite the opposite. Her poised figure and cool manner seemed to indicate she neither feared, nor desired to impress, the powerful earl whose behaviour, her tone suggested, she disapproved of. Astounded, Max had to conclude she'd said exactly what she had wanted to say.

Since he wasn't sure how he might deflect a tongue-lashing from his father, thankfully the earl chose to be forbearing. With only a surprised lift of his eyebrow in Max's direction, he bowed and kissed Caro's hand. 'Let me wish you both happy.'

Max watched his father walk away. Still somewhat awed, he offered Caro his arm and led her to their waiting coach. As she settled into her seat, he said, 'I should warn you not to tweak my father. Few who do so emerge unbloodied.'

Caro merely shrugged. 'Unless the earl can sell off my stud, I've nothing to fear from him. His approval means nothing to me—nor are your future prospects held hostage to his patronage any longer. Which is fortunate, since it's certainly done you little enough good so far. I'm sorry if I sounded... ungracious; I do appreciate his recognition of you, however belated.'

A flush of gratitude warmed Max at this unexpected avowal of support. Before he could summon a reply, Caro continued, 'But how could he not approve? He'd look rather foolish if he refused to bless his son's marriage to a girl of impeccable birth who brought a fortune into the family. As I possess no ties of childhood affection that make me anxious for his favour, I'll not easily forgive him for refusing to assist you when you needed him most.'

She halted the protest he'd been about to utter with a lift of her hand. 'Oh, I understand he is a busy man with heavy responsibilities. But to my mind, there is no responsibility more important than helping your own kin.'

'Being his son has brought me many advantages,' Max replied, finding himself in the odd position of defending the man who'd hurt and angered him so deeply.

'He gave you the advantages of birth and his approval when it cost him nothing...but didn't lift a finger when assisting you might have made his own position more difficult,' she retorted. 'That is not what I call "affection" or "loyalty". One deserves better from one's family.'

Like watching a stable mongrel run out to bite a pure-bred hunting dog twice its size, Max couldn't quite get his mind around the audacity of little Caro Denby nipping at the mighty Earl of Swynford with her disapproval.

'You intend to offer me better,' he asked, bemused.

Looking up at him, her face still fierce, she said, 'Of course. I told you I would when you agreed to wed me. I just promised it again before God and those witnesses.'

'My little warrior,' he said. But her unexpected loyalty penetrated deep within him, soothing a place still raw and aching. He'd thought to protect and defend her from his father; he'd never expected *her* to defend *him*.

'I know you must still want his approval; he is your father, after all. But you are no longer a puppet dancing as he pulls the strings, forced to settle for whatever he decrees. You have wealth of your own, a patron in Colonel Brandon who is independent of his influence. You can meet him on *your* terms now.'

He'd never before considered it, but she was right. The idea of being truly out of his father's shadow was…liberating. 'You really are ferocious,' he said, half-amused, half-serious. 'Remind me never to cross you.'

Her fierceness vanished in a grin. 'That's probably wise. I suppose I am passionate about those things I believe in.'

'Like your horses.'

'And your future. But I can't disapprove of the earl completely. If he *had* supported you as he should, you wouldn't have been exiled and at Barton Abbey to rescue me.'

'I've become more thankful by the hour that I was.'

As the coach bowled along, a gallery of the ladies he'd squired on one occasion or another suddenly ran through Max's mind. All had been practically quivering with eagerness when he introduced them to the earl, echoing his father's opinions, anxious to win his favour. His bride not only had made no such effort, she'd practically tweaked his father's nose.

Because the mighty earl had not stooped to stand by him.

Max shook his head anew. He'd known from the moment they'd met that Caro was unique; how she continued to surprise him!

Having traversed the short distance between parish church and his cousin's house, the coach halted and a footman ran up to let down the steps.

Caro took a deep breath. 'Well, here we are. I hope Lady Gilford spoke the truth when she promised there would be only a few close family and friends at the reception.'

'If you can face down my father,' Max said as the footman helped her out, 'you can face down anyone.'

She gave him a rueful smile. 'I'm better at facing people down when I'm angry. Unless your family and friends incite my hostility by criticising you or the quality of the Denby Stud, I'd rather avoid conversation. I communicate much better with horses.'

'Tell them to neigh,' he suggested, eliciting a giggle as he led her in.

Chapter Fifteen

Caro paused uncertainly beside Max on the threshold of Lady Gilford's reception room as the butler announced the bride and groom, to the applause of the assembled guests. Lady Gilford had told the truth; probably not more than thirty people stood within a spacious room that could have easily had many more.

Their hostess immediately took Caro's arm and led them along, introducing friends and relations. Caro tried to do her part, nodding, smiling, dredging up names to match faces from her vague memories of her brief London Season. She didn't want to embarrass her hostess or Max by appearing to be the gauche, country bumpkin she truly was.

She even managed to do tolerably well, she thought, when meeting again Max's mother and his aunt, Mrs Grace Ransleigh, two ladies who had little reason to like her.

Hiding whatever chagrin she must be feeling to find her splendid son married to a woman so lacking in all the society graces, Lady Swynford congratulated her and pronounced her charming. The hostess of Barton Abbey, whose house party she'd marred with scandal and whose private rooms she'd invaded, was equally forbearing when she begged that lady's forgiveness.

'I may have initially resented your actions, but your insistence on revealing the truth about you and Max won my gratitude in a moment,' Mrs Ransleigh told her. 'I'm delighted to wish you both very happy.'

Thinking guiltily how disappointed both his mother and aunt would be if they knew the true terms of the bargain she'd made with Max, she said, 'I hope to make him so.'

Mrs Ransleigh gave her a shrewd glance. 'I think he's luckier than he knows.'

'Indeed I am,' Max agreed, reclaiming her arm, which set little shivers vibrating deep within her. 'I can't wait to discover just how much,' he added in a murmur meant for her ears only, accompanying the words with a look that whispered of warm sheets and intimate caresses.

The vibrations magnified, making her hands and lips tremble as a surge of both desire and panic washed through her. Her cheeks heating, she mumbled an incoherent reply to Mrs Ransleigh.

Turning away from Max, who continued chatting with his mother, she found herself face to face with Alastair Ransleigh.

After all the good will and compliments, his sardonic expression was a reviving slap, for which she uttered a silent thanks. Seductive innuendo confounded her, but the patent disapproval on his face she could deal with.

'Mr Ransleigh,' she acknowledged him with a curtsy. 'I'm sure Max is happy you journeyed to London to celebrate with him.'

'But you are not?' he shot back.

Shrugging, she raised her chin. 'Whether or not you approve of my wedding him is a circumstance over which I have no control. I could assure you I meant the best for your cousin, but only time will prove the truth of that.'

He inclined his head. 'A clever response and correct on

both counts, *Mrs Ransleigh*. I must warn you, there are four of us who have guarded each other's backs since we were children. Play my cousin false, and you will have not just me, but three other Ransleighs to deal with.'

Caro laughed. 'Do you think to frighten me? I realise your opinion of ladies is very low, Mr Ransleigh, but not all women are cut from the same cloth. Just as appearances in Vienna are not proof your cousin bears any blame in the attempt made on Lord Wellington.'

'We agree on one point, then,' Alastair replied.

At that moment, Max turned back to her and discovered Alastair's presence. After exchanging greetings, the two cousins shared a few moments of handshaking and hearty, man-to-man congratulations.

Watching them, Caro had to smile. Their deep mutual affection was so obvious that, knowing Alastair Ransleigh's sad history, she supposed she could forgive him his suspicions.

But it had been a long, exhausting week; so weary was Caro that she silently rejoiced as the guests paid their respects to their hostess and began drifting out. For a short, cowardly moment, she wished she could go back upstairs to the chamber she'd shared last night with Eugenia and listen to her stepsister's eager chatter until they both fell asleep.

But she'd made a bargain and it was now time to begin fulfilling it. Instead of sleeping upstairs, she'd spend the night in a suite at the Pultney Hotel...with her new husband.

She swallowed hard. Max had shown her nothing but kindness, had suffered scandal on her behalf, had been the instrument of saving her beloved horses. He'd given her much; now she must respond by doing the hardest thing that had ever been required of her: placing control of herself and her body in his hands.

She wasn't going to do it trembling like a coward.

So she nodded with an appearance of cool self-possession

as they took their leave of the party. Tried not to flinch when Max took her arm, too acutely conscious of his presence beside her to make any sense of the thanks he offered Lady Gilford.

Then they were out of the door, down the steps and he was handing her into the hackney. As he climbed in after her, she tried to think of some polite and amusing topic of conversation. But the courage necessary to keep herself from trembling sapped all the strength she had left, leaving her mind an utter blank.

Embarrassed, she hoped her nervousness was not as apparent to Max as it was to her. But since she jumped every time he touched her and he was not a stupid man, she figured miserably that he was probably only too aware of it.

When his voice came out of the darkness, she braced herself for some reproof about her timidity. Instead, he said, 'I must admit, in all the rush to finish up the details necessary for the wedding, I've not thought much beyond today. We could take a bridal trip, if you like. I'm ashamed to admit, I have no idea where you might wish to go. Do the wonders of ancient Rome appeal to you? The mountains of Switzerland?'

Seizing on that safe topic, she said, 'Have you visited them?'

'Rome, yes, and some other parts of Europe during my travels to and from Vienna.'

'What did you find most interesting about Rome?'

Fortunately, he'd found the city fascinating and was quite willing to describe it. Caro needed only to insert an enquiry here and there to prompt him to elaborate on his observations.

After a few minutes during which nothing more was required of her than to listen, Max said, 'But enough of my travels. Would you like to visit the city?'

'Perhaps some day. For now, I wish to return to Denby Lodge as soon as possible. As you may recall, the winter sale takes place—'

Before she could finish her remarks, the carriage braked and slowed to a halt. Max hopped out and waited by the steps for her to alight. A mix of dread and anticipation accelerating her heartbeat, she put a cold hand on his arm and followed him into the hotel.

Chapter Sixteen

Acutely conscious of the powerful, virile man beside her, Caro responded with mechanical civility to the manager's greeting. Her nerves tightened as if turned upon a vice with each step up the stairway as a servant led the way and ushered them into an elegantly appointed sitting room. In her super-sensitised ears, the soft snick of the door as he exited echoed as if he'd slammed it.

Numbly Caro noted the trunk Dulcie had packed for her sitting inside the adjoining dressing room. Opposite that, beyond a partially opened door, was a bedchamber dominated by an enormous, four-poster bed.

Images danced through her mind…Max's warm, strong hands stroking her skin as he removed her gown…his hard lean body, naked in the candlelight.

A wash of heat coursed through her. Jerking her gaze away from the bed, she tried to shut the thoughts out of her mind.

She turned to find Max, with an amused smile that said it must not have been his first request, asking if she'd like a glass of wine.

Seizing upon anything that might calm her nerves, Caro accepted gratefully. Beneath the anxiety, eddies of excitement were building. Her body whispered its hope that tonight

Max would ignore their bargain and claim his marital rights. Lead her into the bedchamber, press her against the softness of the mattress, caress and kiss her as he removed her gown and bared his own body to her touch and admiration.

Her hands tingled at the thought of running the pads of her fingers over his arms, his legs, the flat nipples of his chest.

In another part of her brain, a near-panicked awareness shouted she must avoid that outcome at all costs…or she was lost.

Hoping he would make that decision soon and remove her from this agony of speculation, she walked to the sofa and perched on the edge, her back to the bedchamber door.

He brought her the wine and took a seat beside her.

'Before we arrived, you were saying you wished to go home?'

'Y-yes,' she said distractedly. Heavens, how was she to think when he sat so close beside her she could feel the heat emanating from his body, his soft exhales of breath?

'As you may remember,' she forced herself to begin again, 'the winter sale will take place in less than a month. There's much work that must be done.'

'I can well imagine.'

She looked down, unwilling to meet his gaze as she continued, 'It's not…necessary that you come to Denby, too. You've lived all your life in a hectic political household, took part as diplomats from every nation met to decide the future of Europe, then fought against Napoleon at Waterloo in the greatest army ever assembled. I wouldn't expect you to be content rattling about a horse farm in Kent.'

Even as she uttered the words, she felt a completely illogical pang of regret. She'd come to hope they might pursue the friendship begun these last few days, she suddenly realised. In the moments when his imposing physical presence was not setting her nerve endings afire and turning her mind to mush, she'd enjoyed his companionship. Life without his intoxicating presence would seem somehow...tamer, less vital and exciting.

'Would you miss me if I don't accompany you?' he murmured. Before she could decide how to reply, he distracted her by placing one warm, strong hand on the back of her neck.

Though she jumped at first contact, she soon found the gentle massage of his fingers on the tightly corded muscles wonderfully soothing. Oh, how she wanted to lean in and give herself up to the pleasure of his touch!

Soon, she might have to give up everything...perhaps even her very life. The tension retightening, she leaned away from his hand.

'I will miss you,' she answered honestly. 'But I gave you my pledge not to interfere in your life and I meant it.'

'I see. I could escort you home, at least. Unless...you don't want me to meet your neighbours?'

That question was so absurd she had to laugh. 'Nonsense—I shall be proud to introduce you in the neighbourhood!' Envisioning the probable reaction, she added with a grin, 'I'm sure many in the county will be astonished to discover that mannish scapegrace Caro Denby, who could scarcely make it to church with her skirts unmuddied and her gloves clean, managed to land an earl's son. I'm afraid there are several matrons whose opinions of my running the stud matched Lord Woodbury's.'

'In my guise as the elevated son of an earl, would you like me to snub them?'

'I think you'd find them difficult to snub! Even the prospect of having to be pleasant to me wouldn't be distasteful enough to discourage those with marriageable daughters from seizing the opportunity to have their girls flirt with you, so they may claim acquaintance with your family when they go to London.'

To her dismay, at the prospect of having the lovely, blue-eyed Misses Deversham or the curvaceous brunette Miss Cecelia Woodard make eyes at Max, she felt a sharp pang of what could only be jealousy.

The ambitious mothers of local maidens were not the only ladies who would be happy to claim Max's acquaintance in London. Now that he once again had the promise of high position, all sorts of women would be throwing out lures, hoping to entice a handsome earl's son with a conveniently absent wife.

Was letting him go a mistake?

She shook her head. This was ridiculous. Max was not hers to hold. Even if he cared for her, under the terms of the bargain they'd made, she had promised him the freedom to pursue any women he wanted.

She looked up from that disagreeable fact to find him watching her, a slight smile on his face. 'If I can't discourage them from flirting with a snub,' he murmured, that heated, caressing tone in his voice again, 'then I shall just have to play the besotted bridegroom.'

Her mouth dried and panic jockeyed with attraction in the pit of her stomach. She stared at him, unable to tear her eyes from the intensity of his gaze, feeling the looming presence of the wide bed in the room behind them as if it were branded upon her shoulders.

The moment of surrender or resistance was imminent, the knowledge of its nearness pulsing a warning in her blood.

Her body craved surrender with every rapid heartbeat. Her mind, grimly conscious of the danger of the Curse, screamed at her to resist.

Sure she would go mad, pulled between two such diametrically opposing demands, a sudden, frantic desire to put off the decision filled her. She opened her lips, but her brain had gone blank and she could think of nothing else to delay the moment any further.

Would he take her now? In the next few minutes, she would finally find out.

Chapter Seventeen

Torn between wanting him to bed her and dreading that he would, when Max took Caro's hand again, she jumped.

Instead of tightening his grip and leading her into the bedchamber, Max released her. 'Caro, Caro,' he murmured. 'I'm sure you know all about encounters between a stallion and a mare, which don't appear very pleasant.'

She felt her face heat, but better to address the matter head-on, as it were. 'Not for the mare, at any rate.'

'I'm not so sure she doesn't enjoy it, but I'll bow to your superior knowledge of the equine species. I don't suppose you have any experience about mating of the human kind?'

'None,' she admitted. 'I thought gentlemen didn't want brides who had such experience.'

'That may be true, but it does create a drawback. You have nothing but my assurance that coupling between a man and a woman is nothing like what you've observed. It can be gentle, tender, cherishing.'

She nodded, every image his words conjured up stringing her already taut nerves tighter. Oh, how she wanted to experience it! If only she dared let him touch her, boldly and unafraid of the consequences. Still torn in opposing directions, she wished desperately he would make the decision for her and get on with it.

Distracted by those chaotic thoughts, when he touched a thumb to her cheek and stroked it, again she flinched.

He shook his head and chuckled. 'That's what I thought. Relax, sweeting. I promise I will never hurt you. You believe that, don't you, Caro?'

To her dismay, a tear pooled at the corner of her eye, then ran down to wet his thumb. She was acting as dithering and missish as the sheltered *ton* maidens she despised, she thought, disgusted with herself, the battle between his powerful attraction and her need to resist it making her uncharacteristically indecisive.

Before now, she'd always made up her mind quickly and acted upon it. But until now, she'd never imagined there could be something that appealed to her so powerfully that she was tempted to risk the Curse.

He'd just given her a perfect opportunity to tell him about it, she realised. Why not reveal the true reason for her fear and reluctance?

She was about to confess it…until she remembered Lady Denby's advice. Even the stepmother devoted to her well-being discounted the seriousness of the Curse. Max, who had no experience at all with childbirth, would probably dismiss her concern as laughable.

Or, even worse, pity her cowardice.

Lady Denby was doubtless right about the other, too. Max might not have yet expressed a desire for a son, but, eventually, he would want one. They both knew the promise she'd extracted from him not to consummate their marriage was unenforceable. The best she could hope for would be to delay that consummation long enough to achieve for the stud what her father had dreamed, before Max's desire for a son led to its probable result.

'Caro!' he called softly, telling her that she'd been silent too long, debating how best to answer his question. 'You can't truly believe I would hurt you!'

'No, no, of course not.'

'Good,' he said, relief in his tone. 'Then believe this, too. I respect you and care for you. Yes, I also desire you, as a lovely woman who is much more attractive than she knows. But regardless of my rights as your husband, I will never force intimacy upon you. Never take from you anything you are not willing to give, that you do not hunger for as fiercely as I do.'

Oh, if only she did not hunger for it so fiercely, she thought, suppressing a sigh. 'I understand. And thank you.'

'A kiss to seal the bargain, then?'

Caro eyed Max uncertainly. Was a kiss simply a kiss, or a prelude to more? But he'd just said he wouldn't force her. And surely she was sensible enough to resist letting a simple kiss turn into something else.

Besides, she had burned to kiss him since that interrupted moment in the solicitor's office. Why not stop worrying about what might happen next and simply enjoy claiming what she'd been denied?

Giddy anticipation thrumming through her, she gave in to the force that, since their first meeting in the conservatory at Barton Abbey, had impelled her towards him. 'A kiss,' she agreed.

She angled her chin up and closed her eyes, waiting, a breathless excitement feathering through her veins. Through closed lids, she could sense his face descending toward hers, feel the warmth of his breath on her cheek. Anticipation coiled tighter and tighter within her, impatience mounting to at last feel the brush of his mouth against hers.

But after a moment, when he had moved no further, she opened her eyes and looked up at him, puzzled.

He was gazing at her intently, the energy emanating from

the molten blue of his eyes like the crackle in the air before a lightning strike. 'I promised never to take from you, Caro,' he murmured. 'To give you only what you desire. So…show me what you want.'

Somewhat dismayed, she stared back at him. She'd never kissed a man in her life besides Harry and that hardly counted. They'd both been twelve when he surprised her by bussing her on the lips. She'd punched him afterwards.

Max had probably kissed dozens of women. Maybe hundreds.

Struggling with that daunting observation, her cheeks heating with embarrassment and thwarted desire, she said, 'I don't know…what to do.'

She feared he'd laugh at that humiliating confession, but instead he smiled. 'Don't think, just feel. Do what you want.'

What did she want? To touch him. The thick, wavy dark hair that always brushed his forehead. The smooth skin of his forehead and cheeks, the chin that in the late evening showed a dark shadow of stubble.

Uncertain, tentative, she reached up and ran her hand through his hair, to find it thick, luxurious, silky-coarse. Its soft slide against her fingers was arousing, making her want more. Emboldened, she traced the faint lines of his forehead, brushed a fingertip across his eyebrows, drew her nails lightly across the stubble of his chin. Traced her thumb across the surface of his lips, the skin firm, but softer than she expected.

He'd watched her expectantly as she explored his face, but as she traced her finger across his lips, his eyes drifted shut. 'Yes,' he murmured against her finger. 'Yes.'

Suddenly, she wanted to know if the stubble that clicked against her nails would sound the same, brushed against her teeth. Urging his head down, she leaned up and opened her lips, raking her teeth across his chin, catching the taste of him on her tongue.

Heat and pleasure jolted through her. She added tongue to teeth, her finger twining in his hair as she licked and nibbled the short, wiry stubble that carried the taste and scent of male and shaving soap.

A sharp imperative began thrumming in her blood. Though she'd not yet had her fill of his chin and the strong underside of his jaw begged to be explored, she simply had to taste his mouth.

Rather than joining her lips to his, at first she licked them, tracing them from corner to crest to corner. A deep groan sounded, echoing in her chest—his or hers, she wasn't certain.

Fevered impatience building tighter within her, she licked his lips again, then pressed hers against their wet surface. But that didn't seem to be close enough, deep enough. Her tongue teased at the corners of his mouth and, before she could realise what she wanted, he opened for her.

She slid her tongue inside to discover a new world of wonder. Another wave of shocked, fevered excitement swept through her as her tongue collided with his.

And then his hands came up to cradle her face, gentle but urgent, and he was kissing her back. The rasp of his hot, wet tongue as he stroked it back and forth, back and forth against hers sent a heated excitement pulsing to the very core of her.

Her whole body seemed to be throbbing, melting. Her breasts felt heavy, turgid, the nipples tingling, while warmth and wetness pooled between her thighs.

He teased her with his tongue, tracing the edge of hers, then withdrawing, while, frantic, she pursued his. When he suddenly clamped his lips around her tongue, sucking it deep into his mouth, the pleasure crested until she thought she might faint.

Her breath came in short, fevered pants and she couldn't seem to draw in enough air. A sharp need built in her, driving her towards something she didn't recognize, but wanted desperately. Her nails biting into his back, she clung to him, kissing him urgently, suckling his tongue and lips, trying to get closer, deeper, as if she might penetrate to the very core of him.

And then he broke the kiss, pushing her away before tucking her under his chin and holding her close. Against her ear, she could feel the hammering of his heart, the rapid rise and fall of his chest as he drew in breaths as ragged as hers.

'Well,' he said unsteadily a few moments later, 'that was certainly worth the bargain.'

Her mind was still so fuzzy, she could barely understand his words, much less produce a reply. While she fumbled, trying to recover, he pushed away and slid to the far side of the sofa.

Was that his hardness she saw, straining against his trouser front? A sudden desire filled her to touch him.

Before she could act upon the urge, he said, 'With all you've had to do these last few weeks, you must be exhausted. If we're to leave for Denby Lodge early tomorrow, you must rest. Take the bed; I'll be quite comfortable on the couch here in the sitting room.'

Bringing her hands to his lips, he kissed each fingertip, stirring the fire still not banked within her. 'Rest well, dear wife. I shall see you in the morning.'

So…he didn't mean to claim her. An incoherent protest formed in her still-foggy brain. Suppressing it, her aroused nerves sparking and sizzling with frustrated need, she nodded blankly, struggled to her feet and stumbled into the bedchamber.

Only to return to the sitting room a moment later. 'I'm sorry, but since it was our wedding night, I…I told Dulcie I wouldn't be needing her. I can't unfasten the bodice of this gown without assistance. If you wouldn't mind…?'

'Of course.'

She turned her back to him, still in that half-aroused state where relief that he would not be bedding her battled with frustration.

Her sensitised nerves felt every small tug and touch of his fingers as he loosened the ties of her gown, then the laces of her stays. There were too many layers of clothing, she thought, yearning for just one touch of his hands against her bare skin.

Then, when she thought he'd complete the process without it, he smoothed his hands from the nape of her neck to the edge of her bodice, loosened the material of gown, stays and shift, and pulled it away from her skin. As if he, too, could not end the night without making a small beginning on exploring her body, he slipped his fingers under the loosened garments and slowly stroked the flesh beneath.

She froze, closing her eyes, every bit of awareness focused upon the delicious friction between the slightly rough pads of his fingers and her bare skin. Oh, that he might continue stroking her, working from the back of her gown to the front, where his questing fingers might explore the swell of her breasts, discover the nipples peaked and aching!

For a few thrilling moments, it seemed he might, as he caressed his fingers slowly from the back of the gown around to her shoulders. But he halted there, thumbs resting on her bared collarbones as he pulled her against him and nestled his chin in her hair.

After cradling her a moment, he released her and stepped away. 'I'd better stop now,' he said, his voice sounding strained. 'Can you manage from here?'

'Y-yes, I think so,' she stuttered.

'Goodnight, then. Sleep well.'

He gave her a little push towards the bedchamber, then closed the door behind her.

In a gradually fading sensual haze, she removed her gown, shift and stays, drew on the night rail and climbed into the mammoth bed. The chill of the linens against her body finally extinguished the last of her fevered tension.

'Sleep well,' Max had advised. As Caro pondered the power of her response to him this night, she wasn't sure she'd be able to sleep at all.

Even now, thinking about kissing him brought her senses simmering back to life. When she reviewed her behaviour since arriving at the hotel, she had to suppress an hysterical laugh. After dithering in a missish quandary between desire and dismay, she'd fallen into his hands like a ripe fruit after one simple kiss.

She'd been right to fear the potent effect he had on her. They'd been wed barely half a day, and if he'd made any move to join her in the big bed she'd not have repulsed him. Indeed, before stumbling into the room, she'd come very close to inviting him.

It didn't do any good to remind herself that though he liked her, he wasn't in love with her; that she'd given him full freedom to pursue other women, a freedom he would almost certainly exercise at some point.

She still wanted him and burned for his touch.

Even reminding herself that giving in to the craving he elicited so easily would surely lead to her conceiving a child and testing the power of the Curse didn't lessen his hold over her—at least, not while he was touching her.

And he was so clever, drat him. If he'd cajoled or tried to coerce her, it would have been much easier to resist him. Instead, he'd promised never to hurt her...and let her desires set the pace of their intimacy.

She remembered the thrill of exploring his face, his lips, the wicked taste of his mouth, and groaned. At this rate, she was going to be dragging him to bed within a week of their return to Denby.

The danger was not just his physical appeal, devastating though that was. Their outings together this week as they prepared for the wedding had shown him to be not just kind and thoughtful, but clever, insightful and amusing. She *liked* being with him and could all too easily imagine coming to depend on his presence. Missing him when he went away, as he surely must.

She didn't want to end up like her cousin Elizabeth, pining away for the husband who'd beguiled and then abandoned her. Not that Max would treat her so shabbily, but it would never do to let herself grow too fond of a man who would probably never see her as more than a pleasant companion.

Sighing, she punched the pillow and turned over. There was still so much work left to achieve the dreams she and her father had had for the stud. War had put a temporary end to negotiations with the Italian owners from whom they had purchased Arabians in the past, but with matters on the Continent stabilising after the final defeat and exile of Napoleon, she could renew the correspondence. Visit Ireland to choose the necessary mares, then begin the complicated and delicate process of breeding the right dams to the correct sires and cross-breeding the offspring into the bloodlines they'd already established.

By that point, the stud would be established enough to turn over to another manager, if necessary. Her father had estimated it would take several years to reach that stage.

How was she going to resist Max long enough?

Despite her need to resolve that dilemma, the exhaustion of the last few weeks began to gather her in its grip. But before sleep pulled her under, she concluded her best hope was to allow Max to escort her to Denby Lodge and introduce him to the neighbourhood, as he seemed to want. Then, before her senses triumphed over good sense, she must persuade him to leave.

Chapter Eighteen

Three weeks later, Max stood at the rails of a paddock at Denby Lodge, watching Caro work with a young gelding. Though he came here every day, he didn't think he'd ever tire of observing the expertise and finesse with which she coaxed, enticed and commanded the young animal to do as she bid.

As soon as she had finished working the gelding, they were to take their daily ride, during which she showed him around the estate and he encouraged her to talk about her horses. Having spent most of his boyhood away at school, he was discovering he genuinely enjoyed the simple routines of country life and learning how she had helped Sir Martin establish the stud.

She stretched a hand out, coaxing the horse—a movement that pulled the fabric of her jacket taut enough to outline her breasts. His breath hitched and his body tightened.

He'd always thought her lovely, even in the breeches and boots, which, with a semi-defiant glance at him, she'd resumed wearing after arriving home. But here on her own land, among the horses she loved, she positively glowed with determination and purpose.

She was driving him crazy. A lithe, unconsciously sensual grace filled her every move. The enthusiasm and passion with which she attacked every aspect of her work, which brought a becoming flush to her face and a dynamic energy to her actions, kept him continually aroused. So far, he hadn't broken his promise to take only what she was willing to give, but keeping it was about to kill him.

Just thinking about that kiss on their wedding night made his pulse jump and his member harden. He'd suspected from the first that she possessed a highly passionate nature; he'd been looking forward to awakening it. But all the passion he could wish for had been present in her very first kiss which, making up in ingenuity and enthusiasm what it lacked in expertise, had nearly brought him to his knees with frustrated desire.

After closing the door to her bedchamber on their wedding night, he'd damn near had to warn her to lock it, fearing he might lose the battle to keep himself from slipping in later. Caressing her, while she was compliant and drowsy with sleep, into the acquiescence he sensed waited just below the surface.

With so promising a beginning, he'd hoped that after returning home to her beloved stables and familiar routine, she might come to him within a day or so. But though he believed she no longer feared him, he still hadn't managed to beguile her into crossing that final barrier and inviting him to her bed.

And so, although he had initially intended to remain at Denby Lodge only long enough to see her settled and meet her friends and neighbours, he found himself lingering, hoping each day might bring the moment when she finally gave herself up to the passion that always simmered between them. How he longed to show her the richness and joy physical union could add to the growing friendship they already shared!

She seemed more relaxed and approachable on their daily rides, sometimes giving him kisses or permitting touches she shied away from at the manor. Innocent that she was, perhaps she believed the possibility of being discovered by some farmer or woodsman and the lack of a proper bed kept her safer from seduction.

His lips curved in a grin. He'd love to demonstrate what could be accomplished with the aid of a saddle blanket under the concealing canopy of an accommodating stand of oak.

Maybe today?

At that moment, a groom trotted over to her. After turning the gelding's reins over to him, Caro walked to the fence.

'I'm sorry to have kept you waiting,' she said with an apologetic smile as she climbed over the rails to join him. 'I'm making such rapid progress now with Sherehadeen, I'm afraid I lose track of time.'

'I enjoy watching you. It's a true gift, the knack you have for working with horses.'

She shrugged. 'It's more experience than gift,' she replied modestly—which Max didn't believe for an instant. 'Anyone could do so, with the proper training.'

'Maybe you could show me, then.'

Surprise widened her eyes. 'It's such a slow process, I didn't think you would be interested. But if you'd like to learn, I'd be happy to show you.'

'I would like it,' he said, catching up her hand and kissing her fingers. *How I wish I might learn the right touch to use with you*, he thought, watching her eyelashes flicker briefly, as if savouring the contact. How he burned to make her feel more intensely, so intensely she'd be propelled beyond caution into a passion that would not be denied.

'Where are we to ride today?' he asked as he gave her a leg up, letting his hands linger as long as he dared.

'Another place that's very special to me. I used to visit there almost daily, but I…I haven't been back for a while.'

'Then it shall be special to me, too.'

She raised her eyebrows, as if she didn't trust his words. But though he'd never been above making pretty speeches to gratify a lady, he found he didn't even attempt to flatter Caro. She was so straightforward herself, it seemed…dishonest, somehow, to offer her Spanish coin. Somewhat to his own surprise, he found that whatever avowals of interest, support or affection he offered were absolutely sincere.

As they walked the horses side by side, Caro said, 'I did appreciate your treating me as "special" at Squire Johnson's dinner party last night. In fact, I must commend you for playing "the devoted husband" on all our neighbourhood visits with the same perfection you bring to the role of "haughty earl's son".' She chuckled. 'Thereby astounding several matrons who were certain you could never have seen anything appealing about Caro Denby beyond her enormous dowry.'

He found himself irritated with her. 'That's not true, Caro, and you know it. Why do you so underrate your many excellent qualities?'

'Oh, I don't underrate my talents. But you must allow even Stepmama despaired of me and she holds me in great affection! The skills I do have are not those generally possessed by females or esteemed by such arbiters of behaviour as Lady Winston and Mrs Johnson. Who were both astounded, I'm sure, when you repulsed Lady Millicent's attempts to partner you at cards.'

'With my bride garbed in a gown as lovely as that golden dress you wore last night, why would I wish to look at anyone else?'

'Perhaps because she was so intent on trying to seduce you?'

Max groaned, feeling almost…guilty that Caro had noticed the widow's none-too-subtle efforts. He'd been saddled with Lady Millicent, the highest-ranking female in the neighbourhood, as a dinner partner, and she'd taken every opportunity during the meal to brush his elbow, touch his hand or bend low over the table to give him a good view of her assets.

'Was it that obvious?'

'Probably. To me, anyway.'

'In my younger days, I might have found her attentions flattering.' *And in his frustration right after Waterloo, he might have taken her up on her offer.* 'But though she's handsome enough, I thought her casting out lures right under the nose of my wife to be quite distasteful. I didn't wish to cause ill feeling in the neighbourhood, but I had a difficult time rebuffing her advances with even a show of courtesy.'

Caro looked down at her hands on the reins. 'I'm glad you rebuffed her,' she said gruffly, 'even though I have no right to ask it.'

'You have every right, Caro. You're my wife. It would be shockingly bad conduct for me to embarrass you in front of your neighbours by loping off like a hound on a scent after a woman whose pedigree is far more elevated than her morals.' He grinned. 'I far prefer loping off after you.'

She looked back up, her eyes mischievous. 'Should I interpret that as a challenge?'

'Do you want it to be?'

'Very well, race you to the fence at the end of the meadow.'

Before the last of her words reached his ear, she'd kicked her mount to a gallop. He set off after her, loving the rush of wind in his face, the thrill of the chase surging in his blood.

It had been like this since their wedding night, she leading him, he pursuing. Like every day and night since, she reached the end of meadow just ahead of him. But soon, they would reach it together, he vowed.

He was about to applaud her victory, but as they rounded the crest of a small hill near a stone-walled enclosure, she suddenly dismounted, her face solemn. Above the wall, its edges draped by the forlorn, still-leafless branches of a rambling rose, he saw the tops of several gravestones.

Her gaze already focused on the graveyard, she paced slowly forwards. Unwilling to break the silence, Max reined in and jumped down, walking beside her to the gate, where they turned the horses free to graze. He followed her to a pair of marble tombstones whose carvings read Sir Martin Denby, dead the previous year, and Lady Denby, beloved wife, deceased some twenty-five years previous.

When Caro knelt by her father's gravestone, he went to his knees beside her. To his surprise, she reached over to take his hand. He wrapped it tightly in his own.

'I used to come here often when I was a girl,' she said softly. 'Mama died giving birth to me, so I always wondered what she'd been like. A portrait of her hung in Papa's room, but he never visited her here. Not until after his death did I understand why. Riding the farm, working with the horses, sometimes it seems like he's just away on a trip, maybe in Ireland looking at breeding stock. But coming here, seeing the date on that stone, I can't escape the fact that he is really gone.'

Tears tracked down her cheeks. Knowing how rarely she wept, sadness filled him for her grief. 'I'm so sorry, Caro. Lady Denby told me how close you were. Losing him must have been so difficult.'

'Stepmama is wonderful, but we're as different as…as these old boots and a pair of satin slippers. Papa and I understood each other, knew what the other was thinking and feeling without a need for words. He was…everything to me. Father. Teacher. Adviser. Friend.'

She looked over at him. 'This is the first time I've been able to bring myself to visit since…since he joined Mama here. Thank you for coming with me.'

He raised the hand she'd given him and kissed it. 'You're not alone any more, Caro. You have me now.'

Two new tears welled up, sheening her eyes. 'Do I?'

She did, he thought, suddenly recognising that truth. He'd pledged his faith to her the day they had exchanged their wedding vows, but after sharing her life every day for almost a month, he felt that commitment to her on some deeper level. Before he could assure her of that, she rose and turned to walk out.

As he followed, she asked, 'Were you ever close to your father? Even if you were not, it must have been difficult to face his disapproval.'

Mention of his father called up that familiar acid blend of anger, bitterness, pain and regret. 'Yes, it's hard to accept he considers me a disappointment when, my whole life it seems, I wanted only to earn his attention and approval. I was the second son, not the heir, not the one who received whatever interest he could spare from his public life.'

Remembering, Max smiled faintly. 'I used to wait for his occasional visits at home or school with as much fear and anticipation as if he were the king himself. When I left the army, I was thrilled and honoured that my contribution in the diplomatic corps might assist his work in the Lords. But after Vienna, when I became the subject of rumour and speculation he considered damaging to his efforts, I was banished.'

'What…what did happen in Vienna?' When he looked up sharply, she said, 'I don't mean to pry! But I cannot believe you would do anything dishonourable.'

Warmth filled him at her avowal. 'Thank you. Even without knowing the circumstances, you've shown more faith in me than my father.'

She smiled. 'We've already established his conduct left much to be desired. But you needn't tell me if you don't wish to.'

'I don't mind.' Somewhat to his surprise, he realised that was the truth. He'd fobbed off the curious who'd enquired after he'd been sent home, sharing the facts only with Alastair and his aunt, but he knew Caro would listen carefully and return an honest opinion, rather than mouth useless platitudes.

Leaning against the stone wall, watching their mounts grazing in the distance, he said, 'Going to Vienna as aide-de-camp to Lord Wellington was a great opportunity. Even beyond the chance to assist a great man and do some small bit for my country, it was fascinating to be part of such a brilliant assembly of statesmen and diplomats.'

'I can well imagine!'

'Shortly after we arrived, I made the acquaintance of Madame Lefevre, widowed cousin of one of the French diplomats, whom she served as a sort of housekeeper and hostess. Many of the delegates, after Napoleon's devastation of Europe, despised the French and would have nothing to do with them. But I had to sympathise with the difficult task faced by Prince Talleyrand and his staff, trying to keep the country they loved from being dismembered and punished after all those years of war.'

She nodded. 'As we would wish to safeguard our beloved land.'

'Exactly. At any rate, unlike most of the females present, Madame preferred not to call attention to herself. At the many social events, she kept apart, observing rather than participating. It was that aloofness, as much as her beauty, that first caught my eye and, on a whim, I asked her to dance. Impressed by the keenness of her observations, I sought her out at other functions and we struck up a friendship. Unlike nearly every other woman I'd been associated with—until you—she demanded very little from me.'

Caro made a rueful grimace. 'No, *I* only demanded that you marry me.'

A demand to which he was daily becoming more reconciled, he thought, smiling at her. 'Like you, she never sought compliments or presents or commanded my slavish attention. Quite the contrary—she always appreciated even the most trifling assistance. I soon noticed, however, that she often had bruises on her wrists, sometimes even on her face. When she finally admitted her cousin abused her, I was outraged, but there was nothing I could do about it; despite the rumours later, she was never my mistress, nor had I any legal pretext to intervene on her behalf. Frustrated that I could not improve her circumstances, I did what little I could. She never asked more of me.'

Max laughed bitterly. 'Or so I thought. In the months since Vienna, I've gone over every action and conversation. I truly cannot recall her ever expressing any political opinions. Perhaps she was no more than an unwilling pawn, forced by her cousin's threats of violence to participate in the plot. But the plan worked masterfully; in using her as bait, someone must have known I might resist seduction, but I would never refuse to assist a lady in distress.'

He sighed, gazing sightlessly into the distance as he continued, 'The night of the incident, she sent an urgent note summoning me from the room where I waited to accompany Lord Wellington to an important meeting. After asking my help on a small matter, she deliberately delayed my return; meanwhile, a hired gunman burst into the room where Wellington awaited me and fired at him. Thank the Lord, he escaped unharmed. Madame Lefevre and her cousin disappeared from Vienna that same night.'

'I've combed my memory, trying to find some sign, some indication I'd missed, that a plot was afoot...' He shook his head. 'I just don't recall any. But if I had not allowed myself to be lured into assisting her, the conspirators could not have found such an ideal opportunity to attack England's most skilful general.'

'You can't know that for sure,' Caro objected. 'Had that opportunity not occurred, Wellington's enemies would have searched out others. No one of sense could fault you for responding with chivalry and compassion to what appeared to be a lady's unfortunate circumstances! Did the authorities not pursue Madame and her cousin?'

'I'm not sure. My relationship with her was well known enough that I was…detained that same night, while an inquiry was launched into my involvement. Otherwise, I would have set off to look for her immediately.'

She must have noticed the constraint in his voice. 'You were…confined?' she asked.

He grimaced. 'Not in prison. Just transferred to rooms far from Lord Wellington's and forced to remain there. Under guard. Watched over,' he added, feeling his face flush at the words, 'by soldiers of the unit I'd lately led in battle.'

'How awful for you,' Caro said softly, compassion in her eyes. 'But surely no one believed *you* would have had anything to do with an attack on your commander!'

'Before any official determination could be made, Napoleon escaped from Elba. The Congress quickly adjourned and the principals scurried home to their respective capitals. Then came Waterloo and here we are now.'

'Is there nothing else you can do to finally clear your name?'

'The Foreign Office implied that, with the whole matter having been overcome by events, it wasn't worth attempting. However, Colonel Brandon, my former commander who's now searching for a new post for me, believes that if I could locate Madame Lefevre and obtain testimony corroborating my behaviour during the affair, it would be quite helpful.'

'Then you must go to Vienna,' Caro said. 'Surely the truth will absolve you.'

'Thank you,' he said quietly, glad to have had his intuition confirmed. Somehow, he'd known she would believe in him and urge him to seek vindication. 'I'm inclined to go to Vienna after leaving Denby, while Colonel Brandon explores his connections. Though I'm not certain, even if I can find Madame and compel her to testify, that it will change my father's opinion.'

'Oh, Max, I'm so sorry,' she said, reaching over to run a finger down his cheek.

He caught her hand and held it there, thrilling to her touch.

'The earl may be a great man in the affairs of the nation,' she continued, 'but he isn't half the father Sir Martin, simple country squire, was to me. Though I shall *try* to keep my disapproval to myself when I meet your father again, I cannot help feeling he is a selfish, foolish man to carelessly throw away his son's affection.'

Once again, the idea of Caro Denby utterly unimpressed with the man whose voice still rang in the halls of Parliament and whose approval was sought by most of his peers made Max smile. 'You did make your opinion rather clear at the wedding. I was quaking in my boots, waiting for him to deliver one of his famous set-downs. As one who's received quite a few, I assure you, he can deliver a jobation that will rattle the teeth in your head.'

Caroline merely sniffed. 'He could try. I shouldn't have chastised him, I know. Since I certainly don't wish to make matters worse between you, I shall attempt to be more conciliating in future.'

'My sweet defender,' he murmured, squeezing her fingers.

'Your defender, yes. You have me, too, now, you know.'

Max felt an odd little pang in his chest at that avowal. She would stand by him, care about him, support him…as none but his fellow Rogues ever had.

It seemed that she didn't find him valuable only as Max-the-earl's-son or Max-the-rising-diplomat or even Max-the-soldier. Simply being Max was enough. A strong surge of tenderness and gratitude tightened his chest.

Uncomfortable with the intensity of the emotion, he pushed it away and turned his mind instead to enticing sensual connotation of her words.

Oh, how he wanted to have her! Under his intense gaze, she blushed and looked away, telling him she'd just realised the double meaning of her words. But in this instance, her protective assumptions about the countryside were correct; he could hardly seduce her with the shades of her parents looking on.

At that moment, a sudden gust of wind nearly sailed the hat off his head and a large cold drop of rain lashed his cheek.

'The weather is looking to turn,' he said, gazing up at the scudding dark clouds. 'We'd better head back.'

'Thank you for coming with me. I knew I must return some time, but I'd been dreading it. Having you here made it…better. Not so lonely.'

To his surprise, he realised that for much of his life, despite the accolades of the sycophants and admirers who'd always wanted something from him, except when in the company of the Rogues, he'd been lonely, too. Until now.

'I'm glad,' he said and led her back to the horses.

He had returned to the house, while, despite the rain that began to fall steadily, Caro headed back to the paddock to work, telling him she'd see him at dinner. Max wandered to the library, thinking to choose a book. Instead, he found himself staring out of the window, thinking about Caro.

He recalled their conversation at the graveyard today. He'd

never shared with anyone the conflicting feelings he felt for his father. He'd never before realised how alone he'd often felt in the midst of his own family. Perhaps it was because being with Caro felt so different. Where she was, he felt a sense of warmth, affection and serenity, as if he...belonged.

A stab of unease rose at that conclusion. It would be vastly deflating for Magnificent Max to fall in love with a female who, thus far, gave little evidence that his hopes of fascinating *her* would ever be realised.

Maybe he ought to give up both that and his attempts at seduction—for the present, at least—and head to Vienna. The longer he waited, the less likely he'd find any trace of Madame Lefevre.

He'd not yet decided what he meant to do when Caro burst into the library, excitement shining in her dark eyes. 'I've just received a letter from Mr Wentworth! It seems the breeder in Italy to whom Papa wrote long ago, hoping to obtain another of his excellent Arabians, actually received his offer! Even better, he accepted Papa's terms.'

'That's wonderful news,' Max said, pleased for her. She'd just been telling him of her father's plans to introduce new Arabians into the stud's bloodlines. 'How soon will you be able to get the horse?'

'Almost immediately, it turns out. Signor Aliante had to wait for cessation of hostilities on the Continent to transport the animal, but, Mr Wentworth writes, the stallion has just arrived in London. Mr Wentworth is having him sent down to Denby; he should arrive in a few days. Papa would be so proud! This is the first step toward achieving everything he wanted the stud to become!'

Max smiled, charmed by her enthusiasm and the look of pure happiness on her face. 'We should celebrate, then.'

'We should! I'll have Manners see if there is any champagne in the cellar.'

Max stepped over to give her a hug, but she waved him off. 'Don't; I'm all over mud. I shall see you soon at dinner!'

When they met later in the dining room, the vision Caro presented was worthy of celebration. Her auburn hair was arranged in a delightful tumble of curls and the flattering gown she wore showed her magnificent bosom to full advantage.

She was unusually animated throughout dinner, plying him with questions about the army, everyday life on campaign and his impressions of Spain and Portugal. Normally as soon as they finished eating, she left the table, giving him a hurried excuse for a kiss before going—alas, alone—to bed so she might rise at dawn to begin her workday in the stables.

But this night, she stayed at the table, as if as reluctant as he to end the splendid camaraderie of the evening. She laughed as he told her about the night of pouring rain when he'd bivouacked in a Portuguese stable, wrapped up in his cloak on a thick layer of hay. And been awakened repeatedly through the night by the cows attempting to eat his mattress.

Eyes glowing, she touched his hand, let her fingers linger on his arm. She seemed more relaxed—and less guarded—than at any time since the kiss on their wedding night. All his instincts telling him capitulation was near, Max exerted himself to be at his most charming, teasing her, trying everything he knew to beguile and entice her.

Finally, noticing the long-suffering look on the face of the footmen standing at his post by the sideboard, Max said, 'Shall we withdraw and let Joseph clear the table?'

Caro glanced at the mantel clock and straightened with a start. 'Heavens, it's much later than I realised! Excuse me, Joseph, for keeping you well past the time you should be putting your feet up.'

'Thank you, mistress,' the footman responded. 'Shall I have Mr Manners bring the tea tray to the study?'

'No, it's too late for tea. Tell the kitchen staff to bank the fires and go to bed.'

As the footman bowed himself out, Max claimed the decanter and led her to the study. 'Shall we finish the last of the wine? It will help you sleep.'

'It's been such a marvellous day!' With a slow grin as she sank on to the sofa, she gave him a naughty look that sent heat all the way down to his toes. 'Maybe I don't want to sleep.'

Max tried to tell himself not to read too much into that statement. But a wild hope blazed through him, like lightning in advance of a storm.

Seating himself close beside her, breathing in her enticing scent, a sharp desire filled him to bend down and cover with kisses that delectable swathe of bare skin from her throat to the tops of her breasts. He ought to put up his glass and take himself off to bed before he lost control and broke his promise, but he couldn't bring himself to end this enchanted spell of an evening.

'We should go to bed now, I suppose,' Caro said as she drained her glass. From beneath her lashes, she gave him a look that was part enticement, part hesitation.

Beguiled by her loveliness, hard and nearly mad with repressed desire, Max found it increasingly difficult to hear the little voice urging caution. 'Let me escort you up.'

His heart leapt and his member stiffened further when she replied, 'That would be…lovely.'

She offered her arm. Trying to restrain the excitement racing through him, he took it and walked her out, thinking she must surely be able to hear the thundering beat of his heart.

A few moments later, they reached her room. After he

opened the door and walked her inside, his heart seemed to stop altogether.

Would she invite him to stay…or bid him goodnight?

Chapter Nineteen

Standing inside her bedchamber door, Caro smiled back at Max. It *had* been an excellent day, the best she could remember since Papa's death.

She had all the horses for this year's sale, including the gelding she'd been working today, nearly ready. With Max's steady presence beside her, she'd finally had the courage to visit the graveyard and acknowledge that Papa was truly gone. She'd never stop grieving for him, but today, she'd finally allowed herself to lay him to rest.

Best of all, the Arabian stallion, the animal her father had considered the key to bringing the stud's bloodstock to a new level of quality, would be arriving any day.

Max had been the perfect companion, seeming to understand how much the achievement of Papa's goals meant to her. In truth, he'd encouraged her almost since their first meeting to talk about her horses and her plans for stud. And he'd even finally told her something of his own life, his difficulties with his father, his hopes of clearing his name.

Tonight, she would put out of mind the truth that the partnership that buoyed her today could only be temporary, for Max must soon leave, either to Vienna, or back to his life in London.

'Thank you for a wonderful day. A wonderful evening.'

'I'm so glad you'll soon begin realising your father's dream, Caro.'

Wishing she dared ask him to stay, she waited for him to bid her goodnight. Instead, his intent gaze locked on her face, he lingered.

She wanted him to linger. To admit the truth, she burned for another kiss like the one they'd shared on their wedding night.

There would be very few more nights when he would be near enough to kiss. If she were careful, maybe she could chance allowing herself something more intimate than the quick peck on the cheek that had been all she'd dared offer him since they returned to Denby.

Her heart commencing to beat a rapid tattoo against her ribs, she said, 'Won't you kiss me goodnight before you go?'

'With pleasure, my lovely wife,' he said, his deep voice sending a thrill of anticipation through her.

The kiss was delightful—a long, unhurried brush of his lips against hers, ending with a sweep of his tongue across their sensitive surface.

Excitement shot to every nerve, tingling in her nipples, pulsing between her thighs. Without quite intending to, she found herself kissing him back, deepening the pressure of her lips on his. She wasn't sure whether she opened to him or he to her, but suddenly their tongues were tangling, twining, licking, sucking.

She pulled his head down, wrapped her arms around him, plumbed his mouth with her tongue until she was breathless and dizzy. Until her breasts felt swollen and aching for his touch. As she arched her neck, he trailed tiny kisses from her mouth over her chin, down her neck, to the top of her low-cut bodice, then licked the skin beneath the gown's edge.

Suddenly, more than she'd ever wanted anything, she

wanted to have the gown and stays removed and feel his mouth against her bared skin.

Papa was gone; she'd never get him back. But the man who'd helped her accept that loss was vital and alive beside her. Before he left her, too, fiercely grateful and pulsing with need, she simply must have a touch and taste of him.

Ignoring the little voice shouting of danger, she caught his chin and tipped it up to face her.

'I want you to unlace me.'

'Whatever my lady wishes,' he replied, the hard glitter of desire in his eyes making her pulse leap.

Don't think, he'd told her on their wedding night. *Do what you feel.*

Insistent, driven, shutting her mind to everything but the sensations he aroused in her, she directed his hands to the tapes of her gown, the ribbons of her stays. Kissing him still, she let him loosen and pull them away, then guided his head down to her bared breasts.

She cried out at the first touch of his tongue on their sensitive surface, marvellous, exquisite, beyond anything she could have imagined. She threw her head back, gasping, as with fingers and tongue, he explored each breast, from the plump fullness beneath around to the top and finally, thrillingly, suckling the hardened nipples.

Heat and need consumed her. She pulled at his shirt, clawing at the cravat as he unwound it and tossed it aside. Jerking the shirt open, she slid her hands inside, her fingers seeking his nipples as his mouth laved, caressed and pleasured hers.

Emboldened by an urgent imperative that would not be denied, she slid her hands down his chest to his trouser flap and plucked open the straining buttons. His manhood sprang forth and she filled her hands with it, wrenching a cry from him.

While he suckled her, gasping, she fingered his length, from the hot, velvety tip to the coarse sacs beneath. Without realising how she'd got there, she felt the edge of the bed behind her. Her wobbly knees gave way and she sank back upon it.

Max tugged off her skirts while she kicked at them to help him, until she was clad only in the thin linen chemise. His eyes were a fierce blue in the candlelight that played over his powerful shoulders, his chest rising and falling rapidly in time to his ragged breathing. She leaned forwards to yank down his breeches, then paused to admire him, jutting proudly erect before her. He groaned and shuddered when she grasped him again and traced his length, then laid her cheek against it. 'Beautiful,' she murmured, 'Beautiful.'

With a growl, he kicked off his breeches and pulled her up against the pillows. Kissing her, he smoothed his hands down the thin fabric still covering her belly, then dragged the linen upwards and parted her legs to his view, his fingers tracing the most intimate part of her as he gazed at her. 'Beautiful,' he murmured in return.

When he touched the small nub at her centre, intense sensation rocketed outwards, making her cry out and leap beneath his hand. Murmuring, caressing her again and again while she thrashed her head against the pillows and the intensity built and built and built. His fingers dipped within her wet passage, massaging her in a maddening, delectable, slow liquid slide, in and then out again.

Suddenly she simply had to have him there, the firm hard length of him filling the place his fingers were stroking. With an incoherent murmur, she urged him above her, widened her legs and guided him to that pulsing, aching, spot.

She let out a sob of relief as he entered her, then stiffened with a little gasp at the stretching, tearing pain. Immediately he stilled, soothing her with kisses until her body relaxed and the pulsing within her began again, impelling her to thrust her hips and pull him deeper.

But holding himself above her, his elbows locked and arms corded with effort, only slowly did he increase the penetration. Wanting him deeper, wanting *something* she craved desperately, but which seemed to dance just beyond reach, she thrust up to meet him as he drove downwards, until she felt him fully encased within her.

He began to increase the rhythm now, faster and faster, seeming as driven as she. Suddenly she reached the precipice and sailed over, while starbursts of delicious sensation exploded within her.

Gasping, spent, she sagged back against the pillows, head whirling from wine and sensation. Murmuring her name, Max cried out. Moments later, he collapsed beside her and drew her close, cradling her against his chest.

Smiling, sated, satisfied, Caro fell asleep.

The warm tickle of a sunbeam on his face woke Max the following morning. As his mind rose slowly to consciousness, he reflected that he must have drunk more wine than he'd thought to have slept so late, when memories of the previous night came flooding back.

Grinning, he stretched languorously, an expansive feeling of contentment filling him. He'd always suspected Caro would be deeply passionate. The reality had proved better than his imaginings.

He couldn't wait to test that fact again. Though judging by the sun, the morning was rather far advanced, maybe he could do so even now.

But as he prepared to rise, he realised he was not in the bedchamber he'd occupied since coming to Denby Lodge, but in hers. The linens on the bed beside him were cold. Where had she gone?

Knowing his Caro, she'd probably tiptoed out at dawn, leaving him to sleep while she went off to work with her horses. With only a few weeks remaining before her sale, he advised his disappointed body, he'd probably not be able to lure her back to bed again this morning.

Would she meet him boldly this morning or blush to face him in the light of day, after giving herself wholly and urgently into his hands? Handling him in return. A hot flush of desire rushed through him as he recalled how she'd stroked him, fitted him to her, linked her legs behind his back to urge him deeper.

Despite her midnight display of passion, by daylight she'd probably be shy, he predicted. Suddenly he couldn't wait to discover which Caro he'd meet today, the practical, pragmatic horsewoman in her breeches and boots, or the wicked siren who'd stroked him in her bed.

Pulling on enough clothing to be decent, he jogged back to his chamber, changed into fresh attire and headed downstairs. Stopping in the breakfast room for some nourishment, he learned from Manners that the mistress had eaten early and gone to the stables. Tossing down his last sip of ale, he gave the butler a broad wink that had the servant hastily biting his lip to keep from smiling as Max walked out.

Max chuckled. The fact that the mistress had slept with her husband last night would be all over the manor by now.

As he neared the barns, Max picked up his pace. From a distance, he could just make out Caro standing by the fence of the first paddock, where she'd been working the gelding on a lunge line yesterday.

Joy, effervescent as the bubbles in last night's champagne, rose in his chest. He couldn't wait to see her, kiss her again. Though he'd been forced to enter this marriage, the reality of it was turning out to be better than he'd ever dared hope. With the passionate relationship he'd needed to seal his satisfaction with the bargain finally developing, he couldn't help but congratulate himself.

After spending every day with Caro for nearly a month, he found her as interesting, intelligent and amusing as he had the day she'd propositioned him for the first time in the greenhouse at Barton Abbey. He'd come to admire her expertise with horses and appreciate the firm grasp of business affairs that allowed her to run the stud with such efficiency. The scope of her interests and depth of her knowledge of the world, on display each evening as they talked over dinner and tea, continued to surprise and delight him.

To have ended up wedding a lady who combined the straightforward demeanor of a man with the passionate response of a vixen was a stroke of good fortune. To have found all that in a lovely woman who was also a substantial heiress made him the luckiest man in England.

All that remained to make his life complete would be to find Madame Lefevre and have her testimony clear his name.

Her back to him as she spoke with the head trainer, Caro didn't see him approach. After pausing until the conversation had concluded and the groom turned away, Max seized her by the shoulders, twirled her around and pulled her into his arms, then leaned down to place a kiss on her forehead.

'How is my lovely wife this morning?'

'Max!' she protested, her face colouring.

Shy, just as he'd predicted, Max thought, grinning.

'Walk with me?' he asked, his hands resting on her shoulders. 'I wish you'd awakened me before you left. I would have liked to demonstrate my appreciation for last night in a most *tangible* way.'

His fingertips first warned him that something was wrong, as he felt her shoulders stiffen under his touch. But his giddy mind still hadn't quite accepted the fact as she pulled free.

'I'm glad you were…satisfied.'

Her cool tone and averted face were so shockingly different from the joyous, passionate woman he'd made love to just a few hours ago, he felt her withdrawal as sharply as a slap. His delight and anticipation swiftly faded.

As he searched her averted face, trying to figure out what had happened, the happiness he'd felt upon waking this morning leached away, as water held in the hand seeps through clenched fingers.

'What is it, Caro? What's happened?'

'There's nothing wrong,' she said quickly, even as she took another step back, as if she couldn't tolerate his nearness. Avoiding his gaze, she added, 'I'm just…tense, with the sale so close upon us and so much left to do.'

He wouldn't let her retreat. Catching her chin, he forced it up, so she had to look him in the eye. 'Don't go all missish on me! Where's the straightforward woman I married? *Something* is distressing you. Why not just tell me what it is?'

To his dismay, her forehead creased and her lips began to tremble, while tears gathered at the corners of her eyes.

'Come on, Caro,' he coaxed, her reaction sparking real concern in him now. 'You know I don't bite.' Trying to distract her, he put a bit of wickedness in his smile as he added, 'At least, not so that it hurts.'

'It may hurt more than you can possibly imagine.'

Before he could ask her what she meant, she gave him a short nod. 'You're right; I have to tell you. Let's walk.'

A shock of alarmed disbelief ripped through him when he went to take her elbow—and she brushed his hand away.

Crossing her arms protectively in front of her chest, she said, 'You know how strongly I resisted getting married. Though it's true that I never wanted to wed anyone but Harry, there was another reason for my resistance. An even more serious one.'

While he listened in disbelief, she briefly told him about a condition which had afflicted nearly every female of her mother's family, a condition that had resulted in those women dying in childbed with their first child.

'Obviously, I know nothing of childbirth other than that it can be dangerous for the mother. But…you are saying there is some sort of—of flaw of the body that afflicts all women of your blood?'

She smiled without humour. 'I call it "the Curse".'

He shook his head. 'You truly believe in this? Isn't it more probable it is just unhappy coincidence?'

She hugged herself more tightly. 'Lady Denby said you'd probably think that. She doesn't believe it either. But I do. I've seen it. Not in my own mother's case, of course, but with my cousins. Four of them, dying as young women in birthing their first child.'

While he struggled to wrap his mind around those facts, she finally looked up at him. 'So you see, I haven't been trying to tease or bedevil you. As drawn as I am to you—and you cannot help but have noticed how much—I was…afraid,' she finished, two tears tracking down her cheeks. 'Afraid of what might happen, if I let you make love to me.'

Knowing how difficult it must have been for his strong, fierce Caro to admit that, appalled by what he'd just heard, Max could think of nothing to say.

'I thought, since you could have any woman you fancied, maybe you wouldn't desire me. I thought I could resist you. But last night…I wanted you more than my next breath. And it was wonderful beyond anything I could have imagined! But this morning, all I could see in the dull orange of the rising sun was the face of my cousin Anne as she died at dawn, holding my hand. And blood, everywhere blood.'

'Oh, Caro,' he murmured, and pulled her into his arms. This time, she did not resist.

For a long moment, he simply held her, her muffled sobs

resonating against his chest, while disbelief, horror and concern for her chased each other around his head.

Finally, she calmed and pushed away. He let her go.

'Why didn't you tell me this before we were wed?' he asked, anger beginning to merge into his tangle of emotions. 'Don't you think I had a right to know that ours could never be a normal marriage, without—without putting your life at risk?'

'I did tell you I wanted a marriage in name only,' she reminded him. 'And you did agree…though we both knew such a condition was not enforceable.' She shrugged. 'I didn't wish to show myself to be the coward I am. Besides, it is *my* risk.'

'Devil take it, Caro, I'm not such a monster as to heedlessly put your life in danger to satisfy my own lust!'

'What's done is done,' Caro said. 'I'm afraid you are saddled with me now. After last night, I shall just have to accept the risk. There are compensations, after all.' She gave him a wan smile. 'I shall no longer have to try to resist you.'

Even knowing the danger he placed her in, having to resist her would be difficult for *him* as well. A few moments ago, despite being shocked and appalled by what she'd revealed, just the feel of her breasts pressed against his chest, her flat belly rubbing against him, had been enough to make his member stir. Knowing the power of passion, he realised how insidiously his body could lure him into ignoring the risk.

Like standing near a burning building as fire consumed it, he felt falling around him the charred bits of this morning's illusion that with Caro, the marriage he hadn't wanted could turn into a close, fulfilling union.

Once again, not her fault. She *had* asked for a marriage of convenience. One like his parents'. Only he, arrogant bastard that he was, had thought to turn it into something more.

'Maybe it would be best if I made sure we both resisted temptation,' he said at last. 'I'm not sure I really believe in this "Curse" of yours, but it's enough that you do. Damn it, Caro, I don't want you risking your life. And frankly, I have even less desire to be a father than I did to be a husband. Heaven help me, with the example I had, what would I know about fathering?'

She flinched and he realised his reminder about his reluctance to wed must have hurt. But right now, hurting too, he couldn't make himself utter words of comfort.

'Why don't I leave for Vienna, as I've long planned? You've got your horses to train and the sale coming up; I'm sure you don't need me here complicating your work.'

'Distracting me,' she amended, making him feel a tad better. But then, taking an unsteady breath, she nodded her assent. 'Yes, that would probably be best. I've a thousand things to do and you will want to get on with your life.'

On with his life…leaving behind the inconvenience of a wife who cringed at his touch. How easily, Max thought, sorrow twisting like a knife in his gut, Caro seemed able to dismiss him.

Whereas, after their month together, *he* was now linked by affection as well as law to a wife he could not bed. Anger flared hotter. Once again, he was trapped in an impossible situation.

Maybe he could at least right the one in Vienna.

'Very well. I'll make arrangements to leave immediately. Today, if possible.'

She nodded vigorously. 'That would be best. As I shall be very busy all day, I may not be able to see you off, so I'll bid you farewell now. Good luck, Max. I hope you find the evidence you need.'

She stepped towards him, kissed his cheek briefly and stepped back. He made no attempt this time to pull her into his arms.

'Goodbye, Max. May you have a safe and successful journey.'

At that, she turned away and set off at a near-run towards the barn, as if she couldn't escape his presence quickly enough.

Max stood and watched her retreat, the idyll of their country life retreating with her. Joy had already drained away; now even his anger dissolved, leaving in its place a sense of loss that wounded him more sorely than he could have ever anticipated.

If his being gone was what she wanted, he'd oblige. He had a deal of experience in being sent away, too.

Turning on his heel, wildly contradictory emotions churning in his chest, Max set off for the house.

From the safety of the barn, Caro watched Max walk away. She pressed her lips together, her nails biting into the stable rail as she resisted the temptation to run after him, ask at least for a parting kiss to remember him by.

Ask him to stay.

But he'd been angry as well as appalled when he walked off. Would he ever kiss her again? Would she even see him again?

A throb of emotion made up of strong relief and a deep agony pulsed through her. The tears she'd been suppressing began to drip down her cheeks as she gave in to the memories warring within her.

She'd awakened in his arms, filled with a bone-deep peace and sense of wicked delight as she remembered each delicious kiss, touch and caress from the night before. She'd snuggled closer, trying to decide whether to awaken his quiescent member with strokes and kisses, or begin at his toes and explore every inch of his strong, perfect body.

Until her muzzy, sleep-dulled brain had cleared enough

for her to realise the full implications of what she'd permitted—nay, *encouraged*—Max to do. Dismay and horror rushed through her, bringing her fully awake in an instant.

He'd only spilled his seed within her once. Perhaps she hadn't conceived…yet.

But despite her dismay, merely thinking about him buried deep inside her body, moving within her, setting off such exquisite and powerful sensations, sent a rush of arousal through her.

Loving him had been quite simply the most marvellous, incredible, amazingly powerful experience of her life. Even knowing the danger, thinking about it reignited within her the desire to entice him to love her again and again and again. Aware now of its potential for delight, her body hungered for his caress, eager to repeat the journey towards that precipice, wanting to reach it with him and soar over together into ecstasy.

Watching him disappear around the bend leading to the house, fighting to keep herself from trying to recall him, she now understood why her mother and aunt and cousins had been willing to risk the Curse. It had little to do with a wife's duty to bear a son and everything to do with the euphoria of completion and the sense of union with another human soul that forged a bond even deeper than the one she'd shared with her father.

Could she let him go?

After her father's years of preparation, with the arrival of the Arabian, the dream of having the stud fulfil its full promise was within reach. The horse would be here within days. All that remained then would be to visit the breeders in Ireland for suitable mares and the last step of the cross-breeding process could begin.

Papa had estimated several years would be required to evaluate the foals and determine the final, best mix. But if she had at least one full year, she might get the process far enough under way that, if necessary, she could turn it over to someone else. With the stud books kept carefully and with continuous consultation, Newman might be able to carry on the programme without her.

If she worked diligently all that time, perhaps, when all was in place, she could seek out her husband. Ask to start over. Accept the risk of the Curse in exchange for the joy of being fully his wife.

If he would take her back. She tried to put out of her mind all the legions of beautiful, talented, enticing women waiting to amuse, seduce and pleasure a man like Max Ransleigh. Women she'd promised him complete freedom to enjoy.

What a fool she'd been, giving her blessing to that! Doubly foolish, for she'd let herself become attached to Max Ransleigh.

He didn't belong to her. Since it was inevitable that he return to his world, better for her that he leave now.

That bitter truth burning in her gut, she turned away from the door and forced her mind back to the horses. She'd work here until late tonight, hoping he completed his preparations and left today. She wasn't sure she could stand another scene like the one they'd just played.

Another painful stab of emotion seared her chest, shaking loose a few more tears. Angrily she swiped them from her cheeks. She'd felt bereft when Harry first left to go to university, too. But eventually the rhythm of life on the farm, bearing her along its stream of endlessly repeated tasks, had soothed the ache.

It would again.

But somehow, the prospect of accomplishing Papa's dream no longer filled her with the same thrill as before.

Chapter Twenty

Nearly two months later, Max waited impatiently in an anteroom of the British Ambassador's suite in Vienna. After a month of travelling by horse, carriage and mail coach from one inn or boarding house or manor to another, he was tired, gritty and not happy to be kept waiting by the men whose subtle condemnation had propelled him into the position he was in today.

As the door swung open, Max looked up to see Lord Bannerman, the undersecretary to the ambassador, walking in. Immediately Max's spirits rose; Bannerman was a gifted and discerning diplomat whose talents he had come to appreciate during his days on Wellington's staff. Thank heavens this time the embassy had seen fit to send in someone of authority, rather than the clerk who'd met him when he arrived in Vienna six weeks ago.

'Ransleigh, good to see you again,' Lord Bannerman said, shaking Max's hand. 'I understand congratulations are in order? You're recently married, I hear, and to a considerable heiress.'

'I am and thank you,' Max replied, an ache tightening his chest. Long, weary days of travel and fruitless searching had helped him avoid pondering the unresolved matter of what to do about Caro and their marriage…most of the time. But it remained ever just outside his thoughts, a lingering wound that refused to heal.

'Jennings told me he'd given you as much information as we had on Madame Lefevre. Were you able to turn up anything more?'

'No,' Max said, a month of frustration in his voice. 'What Jennings gave me was damned little. If I may be frank, my lord, I don't think the Foreign Office has much interest in my turning up anything.'

Bannerman smiled. 'You have to admit, Ransleigh, the whole situation was awkward. An attempt on Wellington's life, you claiming one of Prince Talleyrand's own aides was involved, Bonaparte's escape from Elba, every delegation in turmoil. Talleyrand insisting he had no knowledge of any plot and offended by the accusation that someone on his staff would stoop to assassination, neither one of the principals available for questioning… I'm afraid no one is very interested in dredging up that old problem.'

'Except me, whose reputation and career were tarnished.'

'Which was most unfortunate,' Bannerman said, genuine regret in his voice. 'You're a man of great talent, Ransleigh. You would have made a fine diplomat.'

A shock ran through Max. Through all the weeks of tiresome and ultimately futile investigation, he'd stubbornly kept alive the hope that he might somehow find vindication. But in the finality of Lord Bannerman's tones, he realised the trail had gone cold and the only authority with the reach to rake up the ashes had no intention of doing so.

He might truly never be able to clear his name.

Before he accepted that, he'd make Bannerman spell it out completely. 'So, as far as the Foreign Office is concerned, that's an end to it? That's why I was fobbed off with a mere

clerk when I arrived and sent tromping through half the posting towns of Austria and Italy?'

Bannerman shrugged…and suddenly Max understood
why the highly ranked Bannerman had been dispatched to
interview him this time. 'Ah, now I see. The ambassador
wanted you to find out if I *had* uncovered new evidence,
then evaluate anything I might have discovered, so it could
be suppressed if the Foreign Office deemed that prudent.'

'Yes,' Bannerman replied without apology. 'Very astute,
Ransleigh. You truly would have made a superior diplomat.'

'No chance of that now, when I'm being officially prevented from clearing my name,' Max retorted bitterly.

Bannerman shrugged. 'Which means you must be destined
to play some other role. I do understand your eagerness to
wipe that blemish from your record. But, speaking as friend
now, I strongly advise you to proceed no further with this.
Prince Talleyrand has proved himself very helpful in restoring King Louis to his throne in France. The Foreign Office
would find it most indelicate for someone to try to prove
evidence of Bonapartist plotting amongst the prince's staff,
perhaps upsetting the new balance we are trying to achieve.'

'So my good name is to be sacrificed in the cause of maintaining that balance.'

'Talleyrand holds the key to delivering France. We'll not
do anything to undermine him. While you were fighting at
Waterloo, would you not have sacrificed your life to keep
Hougoumont from falling to the French, perhaps giving
Napoleon the victory and unleashing a whole new wave of
conquest upon the Continent? Of course you would have,'
Bannerman answered for him. 'What is happening now in
France may not involve cannons firing, but the outcome is
no less important.'

Swallowing hard, Max nodded. 'You are right; one man's

reputation is not more valuable than the peace of Europe. So I'm wasting my time here.'

'A visit to a city as lovely as Vienna could never be considered a waste,' Bannerman returned blandly.

For a year, Max had been driven by the burning need for vindication. Pain and despair twisted in his chest as that hope died.

He'd never be seen as redeemed by his father. Never regain the trust of Wellington.

'I assure you, the Foreign Office does appreciate what you are sacrificing. I understand Colonel Brandon is looking for a War Department posting for you? We'll certainly assist in whatever way we can.'

'Thank you for that. And for your candour.'

'The business of diplomacy sometimes involves compromises we wish we didn't have to make. Good luck, Ransleigh. Best wishes to your bride.'

Max shook the hand Bannerman offered and, his spirits as weary as his body, walked from the room. As he passed the clerk manning the desk just inside the embassy entrance, the functionary called out, 'Mr Ransleigh! I have a letter for you.'

Only a few people knew he'd gone to Vienna. Since Alastair, the former poet, now seldom put pen to paper, the missive was most likely from his mother or aunt, Max thought. Thanking the clerk, Max took the letter.

With a shock of surprise, he noted the address was written in a feminine hand he didn't recognise. Might it be from Caro?

The unhappy terms upon which they'd parted had remained a hard, indigestible lump in his gut since that morning by the paddock at Denby Lodge.

After his departure, he'd deliberately thrust the problem from his mind, so that over the intervening weeks, he'd resolved none of those emotions. But now he found himself hoping it *was* Caro who had written—and was eager to see what she might have to say.

Restraining his impatience until he reached the privacy of his hotel suite several streets away, he unsealed the letter and rapidly scanned the lines.

My dear Max, I've directed this letter to the embassy, knowing they most likely will be able to pass it along to you. The sale at Denby went quite well, all the horses being placed with suitable owners and a number of new clients leaving preliminary orders for next year.

Immediately after the sale, she continued, her tone friendly, conversational, as if they'd never parted so bitter and abruptly, *I departed for Ireland, where I'm now visiting breeders with whom my father always worked. There are several very promising mares; after making my final choices tomorrow, I'll be travelling back to Denby.'*

He turned the note over. The words that met his eyes there sent such a shock through him, he sat upright in his chair.

I must apologize for the abrupt and hasty manner in which we parted. I hope, in time, you will forgive me for not revealing everything about my condition before we were wed, and we can start anew. I remain your affectionate wife, Caro.

Max re-read the last paragraph three times, the phrase 'I hope…we can start anew' resonating deep within him. He shook his head and sighed. The truth was, despite his anger and frustration the day they'd parted, he'd missed her. After barely a month of marriage, she'd inveigled her way into his consciousness and his everyday life so quietly but effectively that for these two months apart, he felt some vital element was missing, even as he tried to convince himself there wasn't.

With Caro around, almost every day had brought some new insight, some perspective he'd never envisioned, born out of a life experience so different from his own. Some new bit of knowledge about horses or breeding, or a clever flash of humour that delighted him.

She was different from any woman he'd ever spent time with. He found her at once maddening, intriguing, impossible…and enchanting. As he read the letter one more time, the hard lump of anger began to soften and melt away. In its place grew an eagerness to see her again and heal the breach between them.

He let her image, which had been dancing at the edges of his mind the whole time they'd been apart, play again on the centre stage of his mind. Caro, in boots and breeches, coaxing the gelding on a lunge line, or putting one of the sale horses through his steps. Sitting at the dining table, tickling his mind with her observations while her bared shoulders and handsome bosom tantalised his senses. Caro, in those ridiculous spectacles and hideous dress, the first day he'd met her at Barton Abbey.

An expansive sense of hope rose in him, filling in the cold despair left by the wreckage of his quest to find Madame Lefevre. Lord Bannerman was correct; if vindication was not to be had in Vienna, his future must lie elsewhere. And his wife would play a part in it.

He was re-reading the letter when a knock sounded on the door. The hotel servant delegated to serve as his valet appeared, announcing, 'A lady calling on you, sir.' He held out an engraved card.

Max didn't need the raised eyebrows of the servant to know a 'lady' would never visit a gentleman at his hotel. Glancing at the card, he noted the caller was Juliana von Stenhoff, a very expensive courtesan with whom he'd had an on-again, off-again liaison throughout the months of Congress last year.

'Did the lady give her direction?'

'She's waiting in the lobby, sir, and asked if it would be convenient for you to receive her now.'

Whatever did Juliana want with him? Curious, he said, 'Send her up, then.'

Though he'd not spent much time in the city itself, he was not surprised that Juliana had discovered he was back; she was impeccably well connected to the upper echelon of official Vienna. Doubtless, she also knew *why* he'd returned.

Perhaps Juliana, like Lord Bannerman, wanted to discover if he'd had any success. Max flattered himself that she'd developed an affection for him during their relationship and had been distressed by the disastrous end of his mission in Vienna.

Too bad he would not be able to tell her he'd found a way to rectify that finale.

A few moments later, Madame von Stenhoff swept into the room in a cloud of expensive perfume.

'Max! It's wonderful to see you again!' she exclaimed, offering him her powdered cheek to kiss before settling in the chair he showed her to. 'I'd heard you'd come back to Vienna. I called earlier, but was told you'd gone off into the countryside.'

'Yes, I've done a good bit of travelling.'

'Trying to find the Lefevre woman?'

'Yes. And frankly, having no luck. Bannerman at the Embassy just advised me to give up the search altogether. It's in the past and all those officially involved want to keep it that way.'

'I'm so sorry! I'd offer to corroborate your story, asserting that, being otherwise occupied by *me*, you couldn't have been bewitched by the French widow. But I'm afraid that wouldn't serve.' She laughed—a tinkling, musical sound that suddenly seemed studied and artificial to Max's ear. 'You men are such awful creatures! None of you would believe that possessing one mistress would stop a man from attempting to entice another.'

Letting that comment pass, Max said, 'I do appreciate your willingness to help.'

'I've always been willing to help...you.' She laid a soft white hand on his arm. 'I'm very fond of you, Max. I've missed you. Perhaps, now that you're back, we could...rekindle old memories?'

Gently he removed her hand from his sleeve. 'There's a small impediment. I have a wife now.'

She shrugged. 'Back in England—and running a horse farm, of all things, I hear! Quite wealthy, though. A clever match, under the circumstances. One that certainly doesn't create any impediments for me.'

The truth was, the fact that he was now married would not be considered an impediment by most of his peers. Nor had he entered marriage promising fidelity. Indeed, the wife in question had already given him permission to indulge himself.

As he knew well, Juliana von Stenhoff was quite a delicious indulgence.

But the fact that Caro had stood by him, believing in him to the point of confronting his father, made taking advantage of that permission smack too much of a betrayal he couldn't stomach. Despite the fact that, unless he was willing to put her at dire risk, they could never again be intimate. No matter how much his frustrated body clamoured for release and his mind whispered there was no harm in it, as Caro would never even know.

But *he* would. Nonsensical or not, tempted though he was by Juliana's sophisticated loveliness, he just couldn't do it.

'I'm afraid this business of having a wife does make a difference to me,' he said, catching up her fingers and giving them a brief kiss before releasing them. 'I appreciate your visit. But you should probably leave now.'

She stared at him for a moment in disbelief. 'Then everything we shared meant nothing to you?'

'Like the Congress itself, momentous and exciting as it was, now it's…over.'

Juliana made a moue of distaste. 'Well, if that's how you wish to look at it… I've never had to beg and don't intend to start now. Enjoy your time in Vienna, Max…alone.'

She rose in a swish of skirts. He could tell she was angry, not really understanding his reluctance to play the game as it had always been played in their world. As he himself had once played it.

Max couldn't blame her. He didn't fully understand what had changed in him either.

As she reached the doorway, she paused to look back over her shoulder. 'She must be special…this wife who runs a horse farm.'

A vision of Caro filled his mind: dark eyes glowing with concentration, auburn hair copper in the sun, as she soothed and gentled and guided a new foal. Spangled by candlelight, stroking and caressing and arousing him.

'She is,' he murmured.

'May she lead you a merry chase!'

Max laughed ruefully. 'She already has.'

Watching the slender, impeccably groomed, seductively dressed figure of the courtesan retreating through his doorway, Max thought that she could hardly be more different from his wife in dress, appearance, background and manner. Yet both women possessed a deep sensuality, cultivated and calculated in Julianna, natural, genuine, unstudied in Caro.

He felt a wave of longing for his wife, her presence, her conversation, her touch. He wanted her back in his life.

Besides, even if full intimacy was denied them, there were any number of other ways to pleasure her—and for her to pleasure him—that would bring them satisfaction without any risk of her conceiving a child.

Suddenly, he couldn't wait to teach her.

Nothing further could be done in Vienna, hard as it still was to concede that fact. Time to accept that and move on.

He probably ought to travel by way of London and call on Colonel Brandon. But then, as soon as possible, he would go back to Denby Lodge.

Caro was a challenge he'd yet to master. But if in spite of her permission, he was giving up all other women—and it appeared he was—he'd better go home and figure her out.

Chapter Twenty-One

Back at Denby Lodge, Caro stood by the barn door, supervising the installing of the new mares brought back from Ireland. The horses had made the transit in very good condition; she could begin working with them tomorrow.

She sighed, fighting fatigue and a vague depression. The day Max left, she'd felt relief that she'd no longer have to struggle with the impossible task of trying to resist him. But once he was gone, she'd missed him terribly. Missed his stimulating conversation over dinner, the interest he showed in the stud and his encouragement to realise her goals; missed their rides around the estate, during which she'd been acquainting him with the fields and woods she loved so deeply.

With her newly awakened senses clamouring for satisfaction, she drove herself hard each day so she might fall into bed too exhausted to yearn for his touch.

And there was something more. At first, she tried to tell herself her abrupt swings of mood and sudden desire to burst into tears were simply nervousness about the sale, even though, under her father's supervision, she'd conducted such sales many times. But by the time she finished her travels in Ireland, she could no longer deny that something more had changed than simply the loss of Max's presence.

For the last month, she'd awakened every morning with her stomach in turmoil, frequently finding herself forced to cast up her accounts before even rising from her bed. The smell and taste of food remained vaguely nauseating; she tired far too easily and her breasts had grown swollen and tender.

Then, for the second consecutive month, she'd missed her courses that were usually regular enough to set a clock by. Much as she tried to resist the conclusion, she knew she must be with child.

After the first flurry of panic, she'd come to a calm acceptance. Unfair as it seemed to have succumbed after only one interlude, if she had conceived, no amount of wishing otherwise could undo the condition. Instead, knowing the time she had left to work the stud might be even more limited than she'd imagined, she'd pledged to devote all her flagging energy and effort towards training horses for next year's sale and beginning the breeding process with her new acquisitions.

She'd written to Max from Ireland, once she'd been fairly sure about her condition. She'd debated telling him her suspicions, but ended by not doing so. If he chose to come back to Denby, she'd tell him then, but she didn't want the fact that she might be carrying his heir to force his hand, if he preferred not to return.

Sadness whispered through her. She could hardly blame him if he didn't come back. She'd already given him her blessing to conduct a life apart from her, in the London that was as dear and familiar to him as the barns and fields of Denby Lodge were to her.

Why should he visit a horse farm, when he had important work in the city…and his cares could be eased by some beautiful Cyprian skilled in the arts of pleasing a man?

She'd thought surely when she returned from Ireland, she

would be able to shake off her melancholy, that beginning to work the new horses would revive her energy and enthusiasm.

But for the first time in memory, returning to Denby Lodge hadn't filled her with excitement and unmuted joy. Instead, as she rode about the estate today, she'd found herself thinking about Max.

The wide sweep of meadow by the river reminded her of the day they'd picnicked there, him regaling her with stories about incidents from the Congress of Vienna. Reining in near the dense wood across from the manor brought back the afternoon they'd stopped there, walking the horses while she answered his questions about managing timber. In her desire to show him all her favourite places, she'd somehow managed to imprint his presence all over Denby land.

Now, everywhere she looked, she saw Max.

Perhaps it was because she carried his child. Now that she'd got beyond her initial terror, she was fiercely protective of the baby. Max Ransleigh was like the prince who visits the peasant girl in a fable: fascinating, exciting, larger than life, but a figure who would touch her life only briefly. All-too-ordinary horseman's daughter Caro Denby would never hold him here with her agricultural pursuits, but if she survived the birth of his child, she would have something of him to treasure always.

She put a protective hand over the slight round of her belly. And if he did, for some reason, return?

She couldn't expect him ever to spend much time at Denby, especially since he'd emphatically stated he had no desire to be a father. Sorrow filled her at all he had missed, having so distant a relationship with his own sire. Oh, that he might discover through their child the depth and richness of the love she'd known with her father!

But if he should come back, she'd made up her mind that, for as long as he remained at Denby, she would cast aside all inhibitions and do everything in her power to seduce him as often as possible. She'd revel in exploring the potent desire that drew them together, until he left for London again or her thickening body made her no longer attractive to him.

If he came back... Sighing, she released the rail and walked towards the groom who held out the new mare's lead.

Two weeks later, Caro was schooling one of the new mares in the paddock when she noticed someone at the bend of the lane walking toward the stables from the direction of the manor. Concentrating on her task, at first she paid little attention, until a familiar *something* about the stance and gait of the approaching figure seized her attention.

It couldn't be...yet she was almost certain the man walking down her lane was Max.

Disbelief turned to surprise and then an upsurge of excitement as the gentleman drew nearer and she identified him with certainty.

Why he had returned, she had no idea, but, dropping the mare's lead, she ran to the fence and scrambled through it. 'Max!' she cried, sprinting toward him. 'Is it really you?'

'Did you miss me, then?' he asked, studying her face as he halted before her.

Too happy to dissemble, she said, 'More than I ever believed possible.'

'Good,' he said, grinning. 'Why don't you show me how much?'

Caro threw her arms around his neck and pulled his face down, her lips assaulting his with two months of pent-up hunger. He opened to her, kissing her back just as fervently, until they were both breathless.

Finally, Max broke the kiss. 'Now, that's what I call a welcome! But I'm all-over dirt from riding; let me get back to the house and make myself presentable. Perhaps we could have tea? There's so much we have to discuss.'

'I should like that. Just give me some time to turn over the rest of today's training to Newman.'

'Shall I meet you in the salon in an hour?'

'Yes, an hour.'

He kissed the tip of her nose. 'I'll see you again soon, then.'

Her heart thudding in her chest with anticipation, Caro watched him walk with long, confident strides back down the lane to the manor, unwilling to let go of the sight of him until the curve of the lane took him from view. Joy filled her heart and mind to overflowing, washing away, at least for the present, all the fears, disappointments and worries that had plagued her.

He had come back. Whatever happened after, she would have him for tea and dinner and through the night.

Recognising the immensity of the joy and gratitude suffusing her at seeing him again, she finally had to admit another truth she'd long suspected, but had avoided acknowledging. Despite her counsel and caution and knowledge of the dire consequences, she'd fallen in love with her husband.

Just as it was too late to avoid the power of the Curse, there was little she could do now to protect her heart. Though she knew he was fond of her, he would probably never return the intensity of the affection she felt for him. But though he might not love her, she was certain she could seduce him into making love to her.

For however long he remained at Denby, she intended to fully enjoy his presence…and his touch.

Calling out for Newman, she hurried into the barn.

After reviewing the training schedule in record time, Caro raced back to her chamber and had Dulcie help her into her most attractive gown, scandalising the maid by leaving off her undergarments. One good thing about increasing, she thought as she regarded her reflection critically in the glass— her breasts looked even more voluptuous than usual.

She hoped he wouldn't be able to take his eyes off them.

When the maid finally finished, she nearly ran down the stairs to the parlour. She slipped quietly in, feasting her eyes upon Max, who stood facing the hearth. 'Hello again, Max,' she said, walking toward him. 'Welcome home.'

'Hello, Caro,' he said, and pivoted to face her. To her satisfaction, after greeting her, his eyes dropped immediately to her neckline. The thought of his eyes—and soon, his lips— lingering there made her nipples tighten and sent a spiral of desire through her. *My dear Max*, she thought, excited anticipation filling her, *you're about to get a welcome I hope you will never forget.*

Caro was even lovelier than he remembered, Max thought as his wife poured tea. She wore that gown of soft green he liked so much—not the least because it showed off her figure to perfection. Indeed, that taunting glimpse of her full breasts in that scandalously low-cut gown—he must remember to have her order a dozen more just like it—had his mouth watering and his whole body throbbing with desire.

He tried to summon enough wit to ask her about the sale and her trip to Ireland, and to respond to her questions about Vienna. But having not availed himself of the delights offered there, all he could think of was how long he would have to wait before he could coax Caro up to bed and begin leading her down all the many paths to delight.

'How goes Colonel Brandon's quest to find you a post?' she asked as she handed him a cup. 'I imagine you talked with him in London before returning here.'

'Actually, I didn't stop in London,' he replied, seating himself beside her on the sofa. *After two months away, he'd been too impatient to see Caro again.* 'Now that the sale has concluded, I thought perhaps I could wait for news here.'

'Of course you can, as long as you like.' She looked down at her teacup, her cheeks colouring. 'I'm…so sorry about what happened before you left. As I told you in my letter—'

'Apology accepted, Caro. You don't need to explain. I would have preferred knowing the whole truth at the beginning, but there was no deception; you made your preferences plain from the first. I was the one who wilfully misunderstood.'

She looked up, a film of tears in her eyes. 'I should have made myself tell you the whole. After I had not I…I wasn't sure you'd ever forgive me enough to come back.'

'I had to come back. I missed my wife.'

She smiled tremulously. 'You did?'

'Yes. You did say you missed me, too, didn't you?'

Nodding, she put down her cup. 'And promised to show you how much. Shall I do so again?' she asked, a hot glow in her eyes that sent an answering blaze of heat through him.

'By all means,' he replied, setting aside his own cup, his fingers trembling with eagerness.

She put her hands on his shoulders and kissed him again, then placed little nibbling bites over his chin and lips.

He responded avidly, opening his mouth to her. Another blast of desire roared through him when he felt her hands under his coat, tugging at the buttons of his waistcoat, scratching aside the linen of his shirt to find bare skin beneath. With her fingertips, she kneaded and massaged the muscles of his chest, all the while licking his lips, sucking and nipping at his tongue.

Dizzy, his pulse hammering in his temples, Max could scarcely catch his breath. Though he finally broke the kiss, he clamped his hands over hers to trap them under his shirt, craving the feel of them against his bare skin. 'I love the way you welcome me, dear wife,' he said unsteadily, 'but if you don't stop, I won't be able to wait until dinner, much less tonight, without trying to woo you into bed.'

'I don't want to wait, either,' she said, taking his hands and moving them down to her breasts. 'Touch me, please. Oh, I've burned for your touch!'

'And I've burned to touch you,' he murmured. With Caro so eager—and himself beyond eager—the idea of waiting hours, through dinner and conversation and the tea tray, was simply unacceptable. But he didn't wish to ruin what was promising to be a spectacular reunion by having some footman or housemaid stumble into the parlour and discover her sitting on his lap with her bosom bared and her skirts about her waist.

Mind made up, he leapt up from the couch.

'Where are you going?' Caro gasped, dismay on her face.

'Nowhere, sweeting,' he said, smiling at her distress. 'And neither are you.' Striding over to the hearth, he snatched the key from its place on the mantel, swiftly locked the door and returned to the sofa. Dropping the key beside his cup, he said, 'And where were we, wife?'

'Ah, my clever husband,' she said, raising her smoky gaze to his. 'We were right—' she placed his hands over her breasts '—*here*.'

'I love *here*,' he murmured before leaning to take her mouth hungrily while he cupped her breasts and rubbed his thumbs over the prominent nipples. With a little cry, she yanked down her bodice and suddenly his hands were filled with warm, bare flesh. She must have left off both chemise and stays, he realised, before turning his attention to laving and sucking first one nipple, then the other.

While he suckled her, she moved her hands in a sensuous slide down his bare chest. When the constriction at his trouser front suddenly eased, he realised she was unbuttoning the flap. He felt cool air as she freed him; an instant later, the coolness was replaced by the warmth of her hand. His member leapt and he cried out as she gripped him lightly, stroked him, rubbed her thumb over the tip.

'Not yet, or I'll never last,' he gasped. Gently plucking her hands away, he said, 'First, let me show you how much I like being back.'

'I give myself into your hands,' she said, angling her head back upon the sofa cushions and arching her back, displaying her bare breasts to him. 'What of these, my lord?' She guided his hands under their ripe fullness. 'Do you like these?'

'I love them.'

'Then show me…with a kiss.'

Eagerly Max leaned forwards, cupping and caressing one breast, his thumb working the nipple, while he sucked the other into his mouth.

He felt her nails bite into the skin of his back, through his shirt. 'Ah, I like that, too,' she panted.

His mouth still at her breasts, he reached down with one hand, tugged up her skirts and slid his fingers beneath them. Grasping her leg, while he suckled her, he smoothed and caressed the back of her knee, the satin expanse of one thigh.

Moaning, she let her legs fall apart, giving him the access he needed. While he lightly nipped first one nipple, then the other, he slowly moved his hand higher, to the velvety inside of her thighs. Teasing the tight curls apart, finding her moist and ready, he rubbed the nub at their centre.

She gasped and bucked against his hand. Soothing her with a murmur, he pressed her back against the cushions and stroked her again, matching the rhythm of his fingers to that of his tongue against her nipple. Her breath sobbing in and out, she began moving her hips against his ministering hand.

He followed her frantic motions, increasing the pace. Her breathing turned to short panting gasps, her nails cutting into the flesh of his neck. He slid one finger, then another, into her slick depths while massaging the tender nub above with his thumb. Seconds later, she reached her peak and came apart in his hands.

For a few moments, she lay limp against the cushions. Then she opened dazed eyes and smiled at him.

'That was amazing.'

He felt like a strutting peacock, full of self-satisfied masculine pride at the compliment. 'Thank you. I found it rather amazing, too.'

'Did you? But I do think it was unfair of me to find pleasure, while you had none.'

'Watching you is a pleasure.'

'I should like to return the favour…if you will let me. Though I'm not perfectly sure just what to do, I expect you can guide me.' She reached to slide a finger down his still-rigid length.

Gasping as pleasure pulsed through him, he caught her hand. 'I think you have a natural talent.'

'And does that…not please you?' she asked, her tone anxious.

He wondered if she'd been told that wives were to lie still during their husbands' efforts, enduring with silent decorum. 'It pleases me immensely.'

'Good. I was never brought up to behave like a decorous lady. And with you, I fear I can't make myself behave like a lady at all. So won't you let me please you…more?' Extracting her fingers from his restraining hand, once again she traced his length.

His manhood leapt beneath her stroking fingers and he gasped for breath. He'd wanted only to give her a taste of passion, intending to wait for the privacy of a bedchamber and the lazy uninterrupted hours of the night to show her more.

But the exquisite feel of her stroking him, the idea of her

exploring his body not in the dimness of a candle's faint glow, but boldly, in the full light of day where he could see her every expression, was so enormously arousing he couldn't make himself tell her to stop.

'Do you like that?' she asked softly.

'Yes,' he said on a groan.

'Good,' she said and kissed him. And as he had done for her, in rhythm to the stroking of her tongue within his mouth, she slid her hand up and down his length, fondling the taut sides and creamy tip, until he shattered in her hands as she had shattered in his.

After a few moments, when strength returned to his bone-less arms, he gathered her close. For a long quiet moment, they simply held each other.

With her head cradled on his chest, listening to the sigh of her breathing as it steadied, Max felt a surge of new hope for the success of their union.

Finally, he moved her back to arm's length. 'I'm afraid we must now tidy ourselves and prepare for dinner before the household is scandalised.'

'Why should they be? We're respectably married, and you've been gone a long time. A *very* long time.'

Max thought of the many occasions when his father had been gone for months. But he couldn't imagine his reserved mother or the rigidly formal earl enacting a scene at Swynford Court such as the one they'd just played out in this parlour, no matter how long his father had been absent.

While he smiled at the very notion, Caro said, 'I suppose we must tidy up. I'm afraid I've quite ruined your neckcloth.'

'To say nothing of the silk of your bodice and skirts.'

'I'll order a tub. Will you come and help me bathe?'

Despite their recent activity and his fatigue, desire stirred in him again. Was she inviting him to what he thought she was inviting him? Even if just to watch, he was ready.

'I wouldn't miss it.'

With a sigh, she levered away from him. She gave his spent member a loving stroke before doing up his trouser flap. While he in turn tried to restore her ruined bodice, she helped him tuck in his shirt and button his waistcoat.

'There. We're not quite respectable,' she said, 'but at least we are clothed.' She linked her hand in his. 'Walk with me, won't you? It's shameless of me, I suppose, but I can't get enough of touching you. Does that displease you?'

'Not a bit. I can't get enough of touching you.'

They had repaired to their separate chambers while water was fetched. A few minutes later, she responded to his knock, bidding him to enter. He found her wrapped in a dressing gown, standing beside a steaming tub.

'I was waiting for you to help me in.' She surveyed his coat and breeches with a frown. 'But you're not ready.'

'Did you plan to wash me, too?'

'If you like.'

He imagined warm, wet silky skin, with her touching him all over. Hardening immediately, he said, 'I should like it very much.'

'Let me act as your valet, then.'

And so she did…nearly driving him mad in the process. After peeling off his coat and waistcoat she took her time removing the remaining clothing, rubbing and stroking each new area of skin uncovered. His wrists and forearms, biceps and shoulders, chest and flat nipples that puckered under her touch as she removed his shirt. She pulled his breeches down over his bottom, opened her dressing gown and wrapped it around the two of them, hugging him close, rubbing her belly against his erection and the soft rounds of her breasts against his chest.

After pulling his head down for an urgent kiss, she said, 'We must climb in before the water gets too cold.'

He helped her in and followed, sinking into the blessed heat. But before she could turn to face him, he lifted her to sit on his lap, facing away from him. Pulling her against him, he kissed and licked her neck, cupping her breasts to hold her against him in the gentle ebb and flow of the water.

He found it delicious, exciting, and soon they were both panting with arousal. He lifted her, guided himself between her legs and anchored her against him with one hand cupping her mound, the other parting her curls to caress the little nub.

'Please,' she gasped. 'This time, I want to feel you inside me.'

'No, sweeting, we don't need to take the risk. I can show you other ways to pleasure that will not endanger you.'

In one swift motion, she levered herself off his lap, turned to straddle him and, before he realised what she was doing, thrust down hard, taking him deep within. He cried out as a wave of heated sensation engulfed him—the warmth of her body, her scent, the hot sweet tightness of her passage embracing him, rocking against him in the semi-weightlessness of the water. Taking his hand, she touched it to where their bodies joined.

'See,' she gasped. 'Is this not…better still?'

In the tiny part of his brain not overwhelmed with sensation, he knew he should push away and withdraw. But then she kissed him, her tongue ravishing his mouth as she wrapped her legs around his back and thrust against him again and again, rocking into him with the ebb and flow of the heated water.

And then there was nothing but wetness and heat and ever-higher waves of sensation as the tension built and built until all he could do was kiss her back and clutch her to him and ride out the pleasure. Finally, she cried out and writhed against him while he pulsed and emptied himself deep within her.

She sank back against him limply. Cradling her to his chest, he leaned back against the side of the tub, resting his head on the edge, his soul filled with a deep sense of peace.

He *had* come home, he realised. There was nowhere else he'd rather be than right here, a wonderfully passionate Caro naked in his arms, his member sheathed in her.

But no…he should not be sheathed in her! Conscious thought returning in a rush, he sat up straight. 'Caro, sweeting, we mustn't do this. I didn't come back to place you at risk, but to—'

'Hush,' she said, putting a finger to his lips. 'You don't have to worry about that any more.'

His nascent guilt subsiding, he relaxed back into the tub. 'You've discovered the Curse is an illusion?'

'No, I still believe it. But there's no longer any reason for me to fear intimacy because…because I'm already with child.'

His sleepy languor dispelling as effectively as if the bathwater had suddenly turned to ice, he cried, 'With child! Caro, are you sure?'

'Almost positive. I have all the signs and I've twice missed my courses.'

Consternation displaced the sense of peace and wellbeing. 'Devil take it, Caro, what are we to do?'

'Nothing. There's nothing that can be done now. Except, I hope, more of this.' She rocked against him.

Despite his dismay, a pulse of sensation throbbed through him, stiffening his member. Before he could form some response, she pressed a long soft kiss on his lips.

'My dear Max, what happens now is in God's hands. But if something untoward should transpire—'

'Don't even think it!' he interrupted.

'—then I should like to know that I had tasted all the sweetness life can offer. And nothing I have ever tasted is sweeter than this. Did you not find it wonderful, too?'

'Yes,' he affirmed. 'It is indeed wonderful. But, Caro, shouldn't you see a doctor? Let me take you to London with me when I go to meet with Colonel Brandon. Surely there's a specialist there who could examine you and determine—'

'No, Max. My cousin Anne consulted the best physician in London. He checked her carefully, laughed at her fears and told her there was absolutely nothing wrong with her. But there is some good news in all this; those few who do not succumb to the Curse seem to have no difficulty with subsequent births.'

A *frisson* of hope lightened the weight of guilt and apprehension. 'That is good news. We shall just assume that you will fall in that group.' *And so he would maintain, to ease her fears, if nothing else.*

She nodded. 'I'm not going to spend the next few months looking over my shoulder for the Grim Reaper, but savouring every bit of enjoyment life has to offer. Won't you help me?'

What else could he do, but try to make these next months happy for her? Though he would never have knowingly put her at risk, if he had not called up every charm and trick he knew to seduce her that long-ago night at Denby, she might have resisted him…and not now be facing this test. 'Of course.'

'And, Max…I know you have no desire to be a father. I'll try to make sure that the child isn't a burden to you.'

Another little shock zinged him. In his concern for Caro's health, it hadn't really registered that, at the end of it all, he would be a father. He could hardly think of anyone less suited, he thought, his dismay and apprehension deepening.

Those emotions must have been writ clear on his face, for Caro laughed softly. 'It won't be as bad as all that. The farm is a wonderful place for a child to grow up. Don't worry; on your visits, he will only be presented to you when he's on his best behaviour, his face freshly washed and his nankeens clean.'

Her eyes glowed as she spoke about the child…his *son*. 'You are happy about the prospect?'

'I love it,' she said simply.

He wished he could avow some excitement of his own… but his tongue seemed stuck to his teeth. He realised it probably hurt Caro that he was unable to respond with enthusiasm about the child she now seemed eager to bear, but he'd never dissembled to her.

He'd concentrate on handling one challenge at a time. While he tried to dredge up some anticipation for being a father, he'd work to keep Caro's spirits cheerful…and try to persuade her to see that London physician.

Suddenly he was conscious of how cold the bathwater had become. 'Come, we'd better get you out before you catch a chill.'

She let him help her out. After they'd both wrapped up in thick robes, she said, her tone wistful, 'Could I ask a favour?'

Ignoring a stab of alarm, he said, 'What would my lady have of me?'

'Sleep in my bed tonight. Let me touch you, taste you… everywhere.'

Max blew out a relieved breath. 'Willingly. Though I suppose we must dress and dine first.'

'I'll order a tray. I want to dine with you clad only in your dressing gown, knowing there is nothing beneath it but skin, every inch of which you are going to allow me to explore.'

Amazingly, he felt desire rising again at the thought of Caro touching him, tasting him.

'Then I am at your service.'

So, wrapped in dressing gowns—he imagining as eagerly as Caro her dining with nothing but bare skin beneath the soft covering of her robe—they huddled together on the sofa in her sitting room. Once the food arrived, Max discovered he was starving and fell upon the cold ham, cheese, biscuits and ale with enthusiasm.

They talked of the investigation in Vienna, the success of Caro's sale at Denby Lodge, the pedigrees of the new mares she'd just purchased and the prospects for the foaling season to come.

Finally, replete, he took Caro's hand and kissed the fingertips. 'Now, my dear wife, to bed.'

'Finished at last, my lord glutton?' she teased. 'I hope your appetite for other pleasures is equally robust.'

'I shall be delighted to demonstrate just how insatiable I can be,' he promised.

'Good.' Taking his hand, she led him through the door into the bedchamber. Slipping beside him on the bed, she guided him back against the pillows and tugged his robe open. 'Now, it is *my* turn to gorge myself.'

And she did, beginning at his toes, stroking, nipping, suckling and tasting, in a long slow assault that had him breathing hard by the time she reached his ankles and gasping by the time she reached his knees. His fingers clutched the linens as she worked his thighs, parting them, stroking, kneading them with her fingers. His aching member jutted up proudly when she reached it, his body already dewed in perspiration at the thought of what she might do there.

She rubbed her face against him, wrapped his hardness in the silk of her hair up to the smooth tip, then traced the tiny opening with her fingertip and her tongue, caressing the sacs beneath with a silken brush of strands, before taking him in her mouth.

His hands splayed on the bed, his back arched, he moaned and cried out as she explored him, tasted him, devoured him. Just when he felt he couldn't hold on another second, she climbed up and straddled him, thrust him deep inside and rode him, her beautiful full breasts jutting above him.

Afterward, he pulled up the bed linens and wrapped her in his arms, too full of awe to speak. What a wonder she was, shy yet brazen, calm and patient with her horses, yet sensual and demanding. Intelligent, inquisitive, thoughtful, an expert in her realm, though she focused on pursuits unlike those of any woman he'd ever known.

Uniquely Caro. *His* Caro.

Max woke several times in the night, to find Caro touching him—her lips to his, or her hands tracing the muscles of his chest, or her fingers exploring the contours of his manhood, nuzzling his chest as it swelled at her caress. He showed her how he could pleasure her as she lay on her side with him behind her, stroking into her while her tender nub and breasts lay open to his touch. In the dark of early morning, he kissed her from sleep and cradled her beneath him, her legs wrapped around his back as he thrust deep and hard, driving her into the softness of the mattress.

Finally, one last time as dawn began to light the sky, he insisted it was his turn to taste and explore her. He began at her temples, licking and sampling, moving down to her chin, the hollow of her throat, the tender skin beneath her ears. While he kissed her, he slid his hand down to cup her mound, parted her moist folds to caress the plump nub within, slipped a finger inside and back out, massaging mound and nub and passage. Continuing his gentle efforts there, while she gasped and murmured, he moved lower to lick her shoulders, her collarbone, her elbows, her wrists. After tasting her breasts again, he proceeded to her belly, nibbling on her hip bones, licking the deep recess of her belly button until she shattered against his fingers.

Giving her a few moments for her ragged breath to steady,

he set off again, this time to the silk of her inner thigh. He revelled in the warmth and scent of her, his goal almost within reach. Finally finding what he craved, he circled her nub with his tongue, suckled it, raked his teeth over it.

By now, she was gasping and straining against him, but he refused to hurry. Wanting to inflame her by gradual degrees, he slowed the rhythm as he licked and stroked her passage, intoxicated by the taste of her, almost painfully aroused by the thought of being embraced within her heat as she reached her climax.

But before he could tease her over the edge, she pushed at his shoulders, urging him back. 'Go with me,' she pleaded.

Drawing himself up, he entered her as she wrapped her legs around him to hold him deep. For sweet exquisite moments, they moved together, one flesh, one purpose, one goal. At last, she cried out, her hands gripping his shoulders, as his seed burst within her.

Exhausted now, they lay spent in each other's arms and slept.

It was nearly noon when they finally woke. Looking out of the window at the full daylight, Caro groaned. 'I must do some work, I fear. Though with you here, I wish never to leave my bed!'

'It will still be here later…and so will I,' he assured her.

To his delight, she asked him shyly if he'd like to accompany her to the stables. He quickly agreed, marvelling how she could be so reticent about that when she seemed not at all embarrassed to descend the stairs with him at nearly noon and demand a plate of bread and cheese from servants who must know what they'd been doing abed all those hours.

Content to stand at the rail and observe Caro's expertise, he found the routine of training as fascinating as ever. When he complimented her on her skill in soothing the skittish young mare she'd been working, she said, 'It's easy, really. You just have to observe what she's telling you with her neck and ears and haunches, and move at her pace. Would you like to try?'

'I'm a rank novice,' he replied. 'I don't want to make a mistake and set back her training.'

'You won't. Horses are very forgiving, if they sense you mean them well. I'll show you what to do.'

And so he proceeded to the centre of the paddock, where she taught him how to hold the lead rein, how much pressure to apply from it to the mare's halter, what verbal commands to use.

Then she had him stand behind her, his hands on the reins along with hers, while he tested and mastered the touch. After several circuits around the ring, she removed her hands, letting him do it on his own.

The mare continued to circle on command, just as she had for Caro.

'Excellent,' she told him. 'See, you do have the touch.'

He felt a glow of pride at her praise, even though, with her standing before him, her warm round bottom rubbing against his legs, he was finding it increasingly difficult to concentrate on technique.

Finally he abandoned the attempt altogether, dropping the reins and wrapping her in his arms. Murmuring, she leaned into him and pulled one of his hands down to cup her breeches.

Amused and tantalised by her boldness, he caressed her, his member leaping when she shivered under his touch. Whirling her around, he gave her an open-mouthed kiss, his heart exulting.

Who could have imagined he would find Venus in an old pair of breeches and her father's worn riding boots? The angle of her cheekbones, the contour of her lips, the sleek curve of her hips and roundness of bosom; the scent of her hair and skin, the taste of her mouth; everything about her intoxicated him. He wanted to inhale and devour and savour.

Breaking free with a mischievous glance, she snatched up the lead rein. 'We'll set her free in the meadow and take the tack back to the barn.'

After turning the mare loose, they walked inside to hang up the reins, leads and halter. Caro looked up at him, her eyes heavy-lidded.

'What are you thinking about?' she asked.

'Bed,' he answered promptly. 'Or tea, like yesterday's.'

'Beds are very nice,' she agreed. 'But I've always loved the scent of the barn…all that sweet, fresh hay, forked into mounds as soft as a feather mattress.' Slowly she wet her lower lip with the tip of her tongue.

His body responded instantly. He couldn't banish the threat of what might happen in seven months. But he would willingly give her all the pleasure she wished for now.

'Soft as a feather mattress?' he repeated, pulling her into the nearest box stall, empty now that all the horses had been loosed in the pastures. Turning to face him, she plucked open the buttons of jacket and blouse and bared her breasts. 'Are you thinking of these?' she murmured.

With an incoherent growl, he bent and drew one taut nipple into his mouth, raking it with his teeth, while she arched her neck, gasping. Her fingers fumbled for the buttons of his trouser flap, wrenched them open, found him hard and eager.

His breathing grew ragged and his pulse accelerated as she stroked him while he suckled her. Finally, lifting his head to kiss her lips urgently, he half-walked, half-stumbled with her to the mound of hay in the corner of the box. After pulling off her boots, he settled himself into the fragrant cushion. With hands now trembling with eagerness, he pulled down her breeches while she unbuttoned his trouser flap, then lifted her to straddle him and guided her on to his lap. They both gasped as his hot, hard member touched her moist folds. Seizing his shoulders, she kissed him and thrust down hard, taking him deep.

His breath coming fast and hard, he cradled her soft bottom, pulling her tightly against him as he moved slowly within her. Whimpering, she tried to speed the pace, but he wouldn't let her, maintaining instead a steady, barely quickening rhythm that soon had her crying out with every thrust, until she spasmed around him and he followed her over the brink.

For a few moments, Max lay back, lazy and replete, twining her braids around the fingers of one hand while he trailed the fingers of the other over her breasts, admiring their voluptuous fullness, the nipples cherry-red from his teeth and tongue.

'You continue to amaze me,' he murmured.

'I can't seem to help myself. It's no wonder full knowledge of lovemaking is kept from maidens. If they knew it could be like this, there would never be another virgin bride.'

'It isn't always like this.'

'Isn't it?'

'Well, it's always good. But not…amazing, wonderful. You make it so, Caro.'

She smiled, her expression tender. 'No, I'm quite sure it is you who make it so. Thank you, Max. I never expected to know such happiness. I…thank you.' She kissed him gently.

Just then, Max heard the murmur of voices and the sharp strike of hoofs on the stone floor. 'We'd better get presentable, lest we scandalise the grooms as we have the household staff.'

Grinning, he pulled her up. Kissing and touching delaying their efforts, she managed to button his trouser flap and tuck in his shirt while he retrieved her boots and helped her into her breeches. Hand in hand, nodding to the grooms as they passed them, they walked out of barn.

Max stood in the sunlight, breathing deeply of the soft country air, his senses replete, his mind filled with a sense of peace more profound than he could ever remember experiencing in London or back at Swynford Court.

Here there was no autocratic father to please, no hunting for a suitable position. Only his deeply sensual, straightforward Caro and days filled with the rhythm of challenging work. He had the odd thought that he could almost believe he would be content to stay here for ever, pleasuring and watching over Caro and her horses.

'What next, my fair taskmaster?' he asked, pulling a stray bit of straw from her hair.

Smiling, Caro had opened her kiss-swollen lips to answer, when suddenly her eyes widened at something she must have seen behind him. A look of incredulous delight lifting her face, she cried, 'Harry!'

By the time Max recalled the identity of the person with that name, his wife had run over to throw herself into the arms of the man she'd told him she'd always intended to marry.

Chapter Twenty-Two

A jolt going through him, Max watched as a tall blond man in the uniform of the 33rd Foot caught his wife and swung her around before setting her back on the ground. 'Caro! It's so good to see you again!'

'When did you get back?' she demanded. 'Why didn't you write you were coming?'

Dropping a kiss on her hands before releasing them, the officer stepped back. His smile fading to a frown, he gave Max a hostile glance.

'There wasn't time,' he replied, turning his attention back to Caro. 'When I got your letter, I talked the colonel into letting me come back to take care of some battalion business he was going to entrust to another officer.'

'My letter?' she echoed, looking puzzled.

'The one you wrote telling me that Woodbury had convinced the other trustees to sell the stud. You sounded so desperate, I thought I'd best get back here with all speed. I feared I'd find you distraught, maybe with the horses already gone. Instead,' he said, his tone turning frosty as he inspected her, 'you look like you've just been trysting in the barn. With him?' He transferred his disapproving gaze to Max.

Caro's cheeks flamed a guilty red, turning the lieutenant's

expression even grimmer. But before Max could intervene to tell the man a thing or two, Caro said, 'I have a lot to explain. But first, let me introduce you. Max, as I imagine you have guessed, this is Lieutenant Harry Tremaine, my oldest and dearest friend. Harry, this is Max Ransleigh.'

After the two exchanged stiff bows, Harry said, 'Earl of Swynford's son, aren't you? On a buying trip for him, I expect? Let me wish you well before you depart.'

'Please, Harry…' Caro protested. 'With your permission, Max, I'd like to tell Harry what…has happened since I first discovered Woodbury meant to sell the stud. We'll rejoin you in the house a bit later.'

'Why do you ask for *his* leave?' Tremaine demanded.

'Because he's my husband, Harry,' she said quietly. 'Did you not know?'

The stunned shock on Tremaine's face announced quite clearly that he had not. 'Husband!' he echoed. 'No, I hadn't any idea. What the deuce has been going on?'

'It's…complicated,' she allowed, giving him a strained smile. 'With your leave, Max?'

He would have preferred to order the man off the property. Everything about Lieutenant Harry Tremaine made him bristle with outrage, from the proprietary manner in which he looked at Caro to the way he strutted about the paddock with an unconscious air of authority, as if he had every right to be at Denby Lodge, monopolising its mistress.

Still, though he'd much rather challenge Tremaine to a bout of fisticuffs, Max bowed to Caro's wishes. He supposed her 'oldest friend' did deserve to receive an explanation of the radical change in Caro's life—without an outsider listening in. 'I shall see you later,' he said grudgingly. 'Not much later, though,' he added in a warning tone.

'Thank you,' she said simply. 'Come along to the paddock, Harry. While we talk, you can see the new mares I have just purchased.'

Max walked back towards the manor as his wife led the interloper into the paddock, trying to master the anger, resentment and, yes, jealousy nipping at him.

So this was the man she loved, the one she'd always thought to marry. He hadn't much worried about Lieutenant Harry Tremaine while the soldier was halfway around the world.

Now that he was back in England, was Max playing the fool, letting his wife speak to her old lover in private?

After the last two days, Caro ought to be sated. But she'd shown herself to possess an incredibly sensual appetite.

Might she try satisfying it with Tremaine?

Stop it, he ordered himself. This way lay madness. Caro had made him a solemn promise before God and he knew down to his bones she meant to keep it. He'd talk to her about Tremaine when she came back to the manor, but he'd not insult her honour by going back to fetch her.

He reached the house, went to the library and poured himself a large glass of wine. He only hoped their talk would be of short duration.

Meanwhile, at the paddock, Caro distracted Harry for a short time as, with a true horseman's interest, he inspected the new mares. Soon enough, though, he completed his appraisal and turned back to her.

'Married!' he exclaimed. 'How is that possible?'

'I think I'm offended. It's not *impossible* someone would want to marry me,' she said, trying to lighten Harry's thundercloud expression.

'You know what I meant,' he said impatiently. 'The marriage is final, then? You can't get out of it?'

'No. We wed in church, before God and witnesses. It's fully binding.'

'Why Ransleigh? I didn't even know you were acquainted with the man.'

Omitting that she'd originally requested Max to ruin her, Caro briefly summarised what had happened at Barton Abbey, her refusal of Max's first offer, then the desperation over the sale of the stud that led her to reconsider. Harry listened in grim silence.

'I'm sorry, Harry, if you feel…betrayed,' she said when she'd finished the account, 'but truly, it was the only alternative—'

'I understand,' he interrupted. 'I don't like it, but I understand. As soon slay you where you stand as take away the stud. Damn Woodbury! I just wish I had been here, so you could have turned to me. Or that India wasn't so damned far away, that I could have returned here before it was too late.'

'I wish you'd been here, too. But you weren't. And that's an end to it.'

'An end…to us?' He shook his head disbelievingly. 'I can hardly imagine such a thing. I've never even considered marrying anyone else.'

Caro felt tears welling in her eyes. From the moment she'd decided to marry Max, she'd dreaded having to eventually face Harry and explain why she'd all but jilted him. She'd thought then that he would write her before returning from India, so she'd have time to prepare for the difficult reunion.

Groping to find the right words, she said, 'I never had either, until circumstances forced me into it. But if I had to marry someone else, I'm glad it was Max. You'll like him, Harry; he's a good man—kind, intelligent, sympathetic.' *Whose touch drives me wild*, but she didn't need to tell Harry that. 'Most importantly, he understands how I feel about my horses and supports my continuing to work with them, much as Papa did.'

'You must give me leave not to like him…now that he possesses all I've ever wanted.'

Caro felt another jolt of sadness and stiffened, fighting it. She couldn't weaken; she owed Max more than that. 'No. But some day you'll find someone else worthy of you. Probably a lady better suited than me to be your wife.'

'Forgive me if, at the moment, I don't find your prediction very comforting,' Harry said bitterly.

The pain and sadness of her best and oldest friend slicing her to the quick, Caro wished she could find something more soothing to say. But even in her distress, a subtle awareness distanced her from his pain.

Deep within her glowed the memory of Max's kiss, his fierce possession, the shared passion that bound her to him and made them one. Much as she might regret Harry's heartache and the fact that there could never be a future between them, she belonged to Max now.

'I expect not. I had weeks to reconcile myself; being hit with the news all in an instant, it will take time for you to accept it.'

'Or to persuade you to run away with me.'

She smiled. 'I couldn't and you know it, or you'd never have said such a thing. Well, that's the whole of it. We'd best go back now.'

'I suppose. I wouldn't want your *husband* to get jealous.'

Caro laughed. 'I sincerely doubt he would. But staying out here tête-à-tête is bound to cause gossip. And—' the sudden realisation sent a pang of regret through her '—now that I'm married, I suppose you mustn't run tame here any more.'

She looked up to find Harry watching her, his face bleak. 'On the voyage back, I thought of all the changes I might find when I arrived. The stud sold, the horses scattered. You sunk into despair and depression. Never once did I dream I might have to give up the dearest friendship of my life.'

Not until this moment had it struck her that marrying Max inevitably meant the death of her closeness with Harry. Max could become an even better friend, a little voice said. She pushed aside that probably vain hope.

'I'd never thought it, either. But there's no use repining over facts that cannot be changed. We can only face the situation with honour, and go forwards.'

As she turned to walk towards the manor, Harry grabbed her shoulder. 'Just once more, I want to hold you like you were still to be mine,' he said. Before she could think to resist, he pulled her roughly into his arms and kissed her.

At the shock of his lips brushing hers, she slammed her hands into his chest, shoving him away.

'Last time you tried that, I planted you a facer!' she cried angrily. 'I ought to do so again.'

'I'd deserve it, I suppose. But despite that lapse, I am a man of honour. I'll not cross the line again.'

Reading the sincerity in his eyes, Caro knew he meant it. 'Let us try to salvage something of friendship, then. Come in with me. I'd like you to become better acquainted with Max.'

Harry shook his head. 'I couldn't greet Ransleigh now with any appearance of courtesy. Perhaps later, before I return to India. I'll send a note first…so you can ask your *husband* for permission to receive me.'

She nodded. 'That would be helpful.'

'Helpful. Devil take it!' He closed his eyes, obviously trying to take in the enormous implications of her marriage. 'Goodbye for now, then,' he said when he opened them, his face now shuttered. 'My sincerest wishes for your continued health and happiness.'

'Goodbye, Harry. Give my best to your family.'

He bowed, then walked back to the stable to retrieve his

mount. A moment later, she watched him ride by on the trail through the woods leading back to his father's manor. A chapter in her life now closed for ever.

Sighing, she trudged towards the house. She must get back and reassure Max. Not that she thought he would truly be jealous, but it must be disconcerting to watch one's wife fling herself into the arms of the man she'd once proclaimed she meant to marry. Even though said wife had vowed she'd given up all ties to her former lover and pledged her loyalty to him.

She wondered how long Max would stay...if she could entice him to linger. Sighing, she shook her head at her own idiocy. Two nights and days of delicious lovemaking and she was falling further than ever under the spell of her dynamic, sensual, compelling husband.

She probably ought to urge him to return to London... before she grew to long for his company even more keenly.

The thought struck her then, and unconsciously her hand strayed to her lips. She'd been shocked by Harry's unexpected kiss, filled by an immediate sense, on a level deeper than reason or honour, that having him touch her was *wrong*. Beyond that sensation, though, she'd felt...nothing. No stirrings of desire, no immediate tingle of sensual arousal like that which suffused her whenever Max touched her.

Apparently she now belonged to Max even more completely than she'd known.

Despite that truth, forcing her oldest friend to ride away from the wreckage of their friendship left an aching pain in her breast, as decades of fond memories clashed with honour and commitment, splintering into sabre-sharp shards within her heart.

Her emotions in turmoil, slowly she walked back to the manor.

Where her husband waited.

Chapter Twenty-Three

Max paused in pacing the library to pour himself another glass of brandy. He glanced up at the steadily ticking mantel clock, then out the window again. How long could a simple talk take?

He had to clutch the glass and take another gulp, trying to resist the almost overwhelming urge to pace back to the stables and put his hands in a stranglehold grip around the neck about which his wife had recently clasped her arms. A furious, irrational rage boiled in him at the mere thought of the possessive look Tremaine had cast at Caro, a rage made even more inexplicable since, if he considered the situation rationally, he didn't really doubt that his wife would do nothing more than explain to her childhood friend the tangled trail of events leading to their marriage.

Tremaine had been genuinely shocked to discover Caro wed. Max tried to force himself to dredge up some sympathy for the unhappiness and chagrin her old friend must be feeling.

He wasn't having any luck.

The intensity of his instinctive response to Tremaine and his inability to reason it away disturbed Max. He'd vied for female attention before, and though admittedly he'd seldom had to yield a woman he wanted to another, he'd never experienced anything like this fierce, primal sense of ownership, this desire to maim and destroy any man who dared touch *his* lady. This must be what jealousy felt like and he didn't much enjoy the emotion.

But then he'd never been married before, nor entered into any relationship with a woman meant to last longer than an affair.

For the first time, he began to understand the ferocity of the pain and rage that had driven his cousin Alastair after he'd lost the woman he'd loved.

Not, of course, that he loved Caro like that, he assured himself. He'd told her from the very beginning that he expected fidelity in a wife, though at the time he hadn't dreamt how strongly even a hint of attention from another man would affect him.

He was still wrestling with this unprecedented tangle of emotions when a knock sounded at the door. His spirits leapt, but instead of Caro, the butler stood at the threshold, offering him a letter newly arrived from the post.

Recognising Colonel Brandon's hand, he broke the seal and scanned it. The colonel wrote that he'd found a promising post in the War Department and wished Max to return to London and consult with him about it.

An honourable position where he might do some good, the Colonel described it. What he'd sought ever since returning from Waterloo appeared now within his grasp.

He should leave immediately. But pleased as he was at the prospect of employment, he felt a curious reluctance to leave Denby Lodge. Max didn't want to look too closely at how much Lieutenant Harry Tremaine's unexpected return played in that hesitation.

Before he could examine the matter further, the door opened again and this time Caro herself walked in.

She gave him a tentative smile. Immensely happy to see her in a way he could not explain, Max walked over to kiss her forehead. 'Lieutenant Tremaine is not joining us?'

'No. He's not yet been back to see his family.'

Guiltily aware of how delighted he was she'd returned alone, Max said, 'I hope the interview wasn't too painful.'

'I hope you're not angry I wished to see him alone. But I did feel I owed Harry an explanation.'

'No, I'm not angry.' As long as explanations were all she gave Tremaine, he was satisfied.

'Being totally unprepared to see him, I'm afraid I greeted him with…rather too much enthusiasm, for which I apologise. I'd completely forgotten that I'd written to him the night I returned from the solicitor's office, before I thought of coming to you. Elizabeth's father still franks her letters; one of the servants must have put it into the post.'

'How did he take the explanation?'

'He…wasn't happy, but he's a man of honour, as you are. In any event, I made you a promise of loyalty and fidelity before we were married. I fully intend to keep it. That and my…affection belong to you now.'

He'd known as much, but having her reaffirm it eased the turmoil of emotions churning within him. Reassured on that front, he recalled the colonel's letter.

Holding it up, he said, 'I've just heard from Colonel Brandon. I must return to London to consult with him. Why not come with me? You could see a physician, buy whatever you need…'

Smiling, she shook her head. 'I've already told you there is nothing a physician can do for me. And I have everything I need. It's sweet of you to be concerned, but with the new mares just arrived and the stallion to work, plus all the training to supervise, I must stay here, where I belong. Doing the work that marrying you, dear Max, allowed me to continue.'

A brief shadow flitted across her face. 'With luck, work I can bring to completion before time runs out. But enough of that.'

Max frowned, her words reviving his worry over her health. He still wasn't sure he really accepted the reality of the Curse, but he didn't want to take any chances with Caro's life. 'Are you sure you should continue working the stud?'

'I'm feeling quite well…except for first thing in the morning. And though I suppose after several more months, I may have to give up riding, for the moment I am fine.'

'Can I not coax you to at least consult a physician here, if you will not travel to London? It would make me feel easier.'

Giving him a look of resignation that said she was just humouring him, she replied, 'I suppose I could, if it would ease your mind.'

'It would. Being responsible for your condition, I want to take every possible precaution.'

With a little sigh, she looked away. 'Yes, you would feel responsible, I suppose. Though you shouldn't.'

He caught her hand and kissed it. 'There will really be a child? I confess, I find it hard to accept the truth of that.'

'Sometimes I have trouble believing it, too, even as I feel my body changing.'

An unprecedented sense of awe and tenderness filling him, he gathered her into his arms. She came willingly, laying her head against his chest. For a long moment he held her there, her cheek against the steady beat of his heart while he nestled his chin into the sweet fragrance of her hair. He found he didn't want to let her go.

He wished she'd agree to accompany him to London, but it was only reasonable that she'd want to stay at Denby, training her horses and working with the new breeding stock.

'Do you…think you will return to Denby before the birth?' she asked.

'Of course! In fact, I'll probably return here immediately after I consult with the colonel. I'm going to try to convince you to come to London for your lying-in, where there will be physicians and midwives to attend you.'

'We have those in the country, too, you know,' she said with a chuckle. 'After all the horses I've helped birth, I probably know as much about the process as any midwife. When the time arrives, Lady Denby will come to assist me. I hope to give you a healthy son.'

'Right now, I'm more concerned with having a healthy wife. You are…' He hesitated, his tongue trying to form other words before he made it say, 'Very dear to me, Caro.'

She leaned up to kiss him. It started as a soft slow brush of her mouth against his, but then, as if she just couldn't resist the temptation, suddenly she teased his lips apart and slid her tongue into his mouth.

A rush of desire flooding him, he kissed her back with equal hunger, moving his hands down to cup her bottom and fit her against his arousal.

After a moment, with a sigh, she pulled away. 'Would that we could "take tea" again now, my naughty husband! But there are tasks I must finish before nightfall.'

Stepping away from him, she licked one finger and painted the moisture over his lips. 'Until later, my dear Max,' she promised, chuckling as she danced away from the hand he tried to snag her with before she could exit the room.

Max smiled as he watched her go. He hoped she never stopped surprising him. His disappointment with the outcome of the investigation in Vienna and this afternoon's jealousy of Harry Tremaine faded as an effervescent feeling of hope and well-being buoyed his spirits.

He'd have new, fulfilling work, a tantalising, amorous

Caro for his wife…and, with any luck, a healthy child. With Caro's help, he might even work out how to be a better father than his own.

In London ten days later, Max sat once more in Colonel Brandon's study as his mentor poured some refreshment. He couldn't help recalling that the last time he'd shared a brandy with the colonel here, he'd returned to his rooms to find a frantic Caro, imploring him with a new proposition he hadn't been able to refuse.

Thank heavens he hadn't! He smiled, recalling their last night together before he set out for London. She'd certainly proven her affection, in so many delectable ways that he'd been doubly reluctant to leave for London without her. Indeed, he told her outright that she was spoiling him; he simply couldn't get enough of her.

With a naughty smile, she'd replied that she couldn't get enough of him and tilted her hips to take him deeper.

She'd thought he was teasing, but the words had held more truth even than he wanted to admit. He'd had affairs with women much more practised than Caro; it was her utter lack of artifice that so mesmerised him. He found her uninhibited joy and considerable inventiveness endlessly arousing.

'Here's a brandy to toast the business,' the Colonel said, pulling him from sensual reverie. 'First, congratulations on marrying your heiress. Your wedding, and the earl's blessing on it, helped speed the business of finding a suitable post.'

'What does this posting involve?'

'Logistics and procurement. Requires a man with a talent for organisation, a good head for figures and the ability to, shall we say, persuade sometimes recalcitrant suppliers to deliver contracted goods on time and as specified.'

'I'd work out of London?'

'For the most part, though you would need to visit the suppliers and army units upon occasion. If you accept it, would your bride join you here?'

'Probably not. She's a country girl at heart and very devoted to her farm and her horses.'

'Aye, I'd heard as much.'

Recalling the pains Caro had taken to present an unflattering picture of herself to the *ton*, Max could only imagine what the Colonel had heard. 'You should probably discount anything that's been said about her. She's clever, intelligent… and utterly bewitching.'

'All April-and-May with you, is it?' The colonel chuckled, slapping him on the back. 'I'd heard 'twas a match of convenience, so I'm happy to learn 'tis more than that.'

At the colonel's words, Max suddenly realised that, some time between his first visit to the colonel's lodgings several months ago and tonight, their relationship *had* become more. Just how much more, he wasn't quite sure. 'How soon would you need my answer?'

'Take your time. There's no one else of your ability and lineage who'd be better for the job, so I can persuade the head of department to wait on your answer.'

'I would like to talk it over with my wife. She's increasing, and I don't like leaving her alone.'

'That's wonderful news! Here's to the safe delivery of an heir!'

That being a toast to which Max could drink with enthusiasm, he raised his glass to the colonel. Though he remained for a time longer, chatting with his former commander about the activities of other acquaintances from their regiment, with the business concluded, he found himself eager to be off.

It hadn't been mere politeness when he'd told the colonel he was impatient to return to Caro. Even if the Curse were an illusion, he wanted to be there, so she wouldn't have to carry alone the burden of worrying over it.

If he did accept the colonel's post—and it seemed so ideal, there was no reason he shouldn't—he probably would have to assume it before Caro reached her time. All the more reason to try to persuade her to come to London to deliver the child.

Maybe he could also talk her into having some competent female stay with her at Denby Lodge after his departure. Lady Denby would be occupied with her daughter's Season until summer, but perhaps her cousin Elizabeth might agree?

He didn't intend for the person holding her hand in his absence to be Lieutenant Harry Tremaine. Surely the man would need to return to India before Max had to take up his posting in London.

Perhaps, before he returned to Kent, he'd pay a quick visit to Caro's cousin Elizabeth. And while he was there, he could ask her about the Curse.

Chapter Twenty-Four

Half an hour later, Max knocked on the door of Lady Elizabeth Russell's town house in Laura Place. Learning from the butler who admitted him that his mistress was at home, Max told him to tell her he wished to consult with her about her cousin, Caroline Denby.

After showing him to a parlour and pouring him wine, the servant departed to fetch his mistress. A short time later, Lady Elizabeth entered the room.

'Good evening, Mr Ransleigh. What a pleasure to see you again! Did Caro accompany you to London?'

'No, I'm afraid I couldn't persuade her to leave Denby Lodge. She's just taken delivery of a new Arabian stallion and several mares from Ireland.'

Elizabeth laughed. 'Then I doubt you'll get her to budge from the stables before next spring. All is…well with her, I trust?'

'She is in excellent health at present. I'd like to ensure that she stays that way. Which is why, although I have not yet consulted her about this, I wished to speak with you.'

Elizabeth's smile faded. 'Is something wrong?' Her eyes widening with alarm, she cried, 'Sweet Heaven, please tell me that she's not with child!'

Until that moment, Max hadn't been sure he really credited the existence of the Curse. But as he watched the colour drain from Lady Elizabeth's face, the anxiety that he'd been suppressing since Caro had first told him about her pregnancy boiled to the surface.

Consternation drying his mouth and speeding his pulse, he said, 'She believes she is. So maybe you'd better tell me everything you know about the Curse. How can I help her through it?'

Elizabeth shook her head, tears welling in her eyes. 'I don't know that there is anything you can do.'

Frustration sharpening his tone, he snapped, 'So she seems to believe, but there must be *something*. Does it spring from some weakness of the body? Will she lose the child before term?

'No, it's not until after the birth that the difficulties begin. Bleeding. Fever. Death. It happened that way with her mother, aunt, cousins—nearly every female on her mother's side for the last two generations. When we were little, we used to joke about it…until it claimed cousin after cousin.'

Max had wanted to believe the deaths were coincidence, illusion, tales told to frighten young brides. But this much loss seemed far more than random coincidence.

'The physicians can do nothing to prevent it?'

'Apparently not. Our cousin Anne consulted every prominent practitioner. She was examined several times and each doctor pronounced her perfectly normal. But when her term came, she died anyway, just like the others. Whatever flaw causes this, it must be deep within the body.'

Max's mind raced while he tried to think of something else that might be done to counter the threat. But if physicians could do nothing…

'Is she…in good spirits?' Elizabeth asked.

'She was distressed when she first told me about it, before I went to Vienna.' After what Elizabeth had just revealed, Max wished even more fervently that she'd first told him about it before he'd seduced her, rather than after. 'Since my return, she's seemed quite unconcerned.'

Elizabeth shook her head. 'That's so like Caro. Knowing that if she is with child and nothing can be done, there is no point worrying about it. No wonder, with new horses arrived, she won't leave Denby! She must be desperate to push the training along as quickly as possible in case—' She broke, flushing. 'What can I do to help?'

'I've been offered a posting in the War Department. If I accept it, I may have to leave Denby Lodge before Caro reaches her time. I'll return for the birth, of course, but I shouldn't wish to leave her alone in the interim and Lady Denby will be occupied with her daughter until the end of the Season.'

Elizabeth nodded. 'I'm expecting my grandmother from Ireland for a visit, but I could bring her with me. Just let me know when you'd like me to come to Denby.'

'Thank you.' He grinned ruefully. 'Caro will probably have my head for washing for finding her a companion without consulting her wishes first, but I would feel better if she were not alone these next few months.'

'Of course. You…care about her, don't you?'

'Very much.'

Elizabeth smiled. 'Then go back to her. And tell her I'll be praying for you both.'

Little more than a day later, Caro was about to hand over to the head trainer the lead line of a young horse she was breaking to saddle when the familiar gait of a tall man approaching the paddock made her heart skip a beat.

'Max?' she cried, tossing the reins to Newman and pacing over to the fence. 'I didn't expect you back so soon!'

Delight lightening her spirits and a smoky sexual awareness firing her blood, she reached for the top rail, hungry for the first touch of him.

'Hello, Caro,' he called as he approached.

He looked dusty and tired, as if he'd been travelling swiftly and hard, she thought as she climbed the rails. He held out his hands to steady her as she clambered down the other side.

Then gathered her into his arms. 'I missed you, sweeting.'

Pulling his head down, she kissed him fiercely. With a groan, he wrapped her in his arms and kissed her back just as fiercely.

Some time later, regretfully, she broke the kiss. 'Shall I walk you to the manor? You can tell me everything Colonel Brandon said.'

'Do you have time now? I don't want to interrupt your training.'

Normally, she would be annoyed to have her routine disturbed…but this was Max and she'd missed him acutely. 'Yes, I'm ready to take a break…to see you.'

Linking her arm in his, she said, 'What did you learn about the posting? Do you think you'll accept it?'

'It involves the purchase and shipment of supplies to army units. And I'm inclined to take it. Are you sure you couldn't consider coming to London with me? I'd feel much easier knowing you were nearby, with all the superior resources of the city—the best physicians, midwives, aides, close at hand.'

She shook her head. 'As I told you before, we have doctors here. And I have my work, as you will have yours.'

Much as she hated to ask it, best that she know straight away how much time she had left with him. Trying to keep her tone casual, she said, 'When must you return to London?'

'No particular time. The colonel said he would hold the position until I'm ready to take it. I thought to stay at Denby with you for a while, perhaps until your stepsister finishes her Season and Lady Denby returns.'

'But 'tis only January and she probably won't return until May or June at the earliest.'

'I happened to speak with your cousin. Lady Elizabeth. If I must leave earlier than that, she mentioned she might be able to come for a visit. I don't like to think of you here alone.' He shook his head and sighed. 'I wish there were something more I could do to protect you.'

'There's nothing,' she said, reaching up to stroke his face. 'But as I told you earlier, the handful of Mama's female relations who didn't perish after birthing their first child seemed to go on to bear others without problem. So don't be burying me yet.'

He snaked out a hand to still her lips. 'Don't even joke about that! Perhaps I'll stay until May or June, then. If you'll have me.'

'Then let us enjoy each other to the fullest until May or June…or until I'm too large and cumbersome to be desirable.'

'You will always be desirable to me.'

'That sounds most promising,' she said, a thrill going through her at the welcome news that she might be able to seduce him again and again, right up to the end.

But even as she rejoiced in the news, a little voice warned that the longer he stayed, the more impossible it would be to keep her heart from shattering when he left. But she couldn't make herself lie and tell him she'd prefer him not to remain.

Instead, she said, 'If you will stay for a while, could I ask you a favour?'

'Of course.'

'Would you mind having me show you the stud books and operating records for the farm? Acquaint you with the horses we have and which stage of training they are in, introduce you to the trainers? So if…anything should happen to me, you'd be more knowledgeable about the stud and better able to decide whether you would want to keep it or sell it off.'

He stopped abruptly and turned to cup her face in his hands. 'I would love to learn more about the Denby operations. But not for that reason. You are going to survive and thrive, Caro, and so is our child. I won't accept anything else.'

Once again her heart did that little flip, and for a moment, she considered confessing her love for him. Might he have come to love her in return?

If fondness was all he could muster in response, such a declaration would likely just make him feel uncomfortable, especially since it seemed he felt guilty about getting her with child. Unwilling to spoil the warm intimacy of the moment, she pushed the question from her mind.

'My sweet Max,' she said instead, 'the outcome isn't in your hands, you know. But I do like having you here. I was so lonely after Papa died, some of my joy in being at Denby was lost. You've restored it to me.'

'I'm glad. Strange as it seems, you've made me feel more at home at Denby in the short time I've spent here than I ever did growing up at Swynford Court or in Papa's vast house on Grosvenor Square. Thank you for that.'

He leaned down to kiss her, softly and gently this time. She closed her eyes, savouring his touch. She would savour every moment with him, she thought fiercely. Since she could not know how many—or how few—there might be.

Chapter Twenty-Five

Approaching six months later, Max leaned against the paddock rail, watching Caro work with the young colt on the lead line, coaxing him to follow. Though heavy with child, she still moved gracefully, he thought with affection, watching her smooth, economical gestures.

'The colt looks better today.'

'Yes, he's getting used to my touch. It also helps that he's finally decided the leaves blowing in the trees and the grasses tapping against the railings aren't a danger to him.'

'I wish I could convince you to stop working the lead line.'

'Really, Max, you worry too much. I've already agreed not to ride any more and train only the smallest colts.'

'Even colts are large and powerful enough to do you an injury,' he countered, concern for her sharpening his tone. 'They may be smaller than two-year-olds, but like Balthazaar here, more skittish and less predictable.'

'Skittish, yes, but none of my horses are unpredictable, if one is alert to their signals. It's my own fault if I fail to heed what he means when he stretches his neck or pricks up his ears.'

Concerned about the danger or not, after months of watching Caro with her horses, he still marvelled at her deft touch and the almost mystical way she seemed able to communicate with the steeds, from foals to four-year-olds fully trained and ready for sale.

'If you don't like my working with Balthazaar, why don't you take him?' she said, breaking in on his thoughts.

'Gladly, if it will get you on the rail and me in the ring.'

As she'd taught him, he walked slowly to the centre where she was working the colt, careful to let the horse see him and accept his presence, not taking over the reins until the animal continued his circuit at a steady pace.

For the next half-hour, while Caro watched, Max eased the horse through a series of patterns, exerting more and more pressure as he taught the animal to accept his commands to advance, stand, move right and left. So absorbed had he become in this slow but exacting process, he was surprised when Newman, the head trainer, appeared at the rail.

'I'll take him in now, Mr Ransleigh. Well done, by the way. You're looking to become almost as good a trainer as Miss Caro.'

'Thank you, Newman,' Max replied, a swell of pride and satisfaction lifting his spirits at the man's rare words of praise. 'Still, it seems to take me so long.'

'As long as is necessary, sir. You heed that old horseman's motto: "If you think things are going too slow, go slower." But you've got a real touch; the beasties respond to you.'

'You do have a deft touch,' Caro said, joining him at the rail as Newman led away the colt.

Max's pleasure deepened. Caro was as sparing with her praise as Newman. Growing up an earl's privileged son, for much of his life he'd had fulsome praises heaped upon him, whether or not his performance merited it. He prized Caro's honesty; one never had to question whether her compliments were genuine.

'If I earn your approval, I'm doubly pleased.'

'It's all trust and patience, Max. This isn't a battlefield,' she said, gesturing towards the training paddock, 'with a winner and a loser. Either both win, or both lose.'

'Like in a marriage?'

'Exactly,' she said, then made a face at him as he snagged her elbow, pulling her down before she could clamber up the rails. 'We'll go through the gate, if you please.'

'Honestly, you're fussier than a brood hen with its chicks,' she protested.

'If I were truly fussy, I'd order you to stay in the house.'

'Where I'd go mad within a week, cooped up with nothing useful to do. Besides, if you *ordered* me to remain, I'd feel nearly honour-bound to climb out of a window.'

'Perhaps I'd just order you to stay in my bed.'

Her eyes danced. 'Now, that's a command I might feel inclined to obey.'

Leaning down, he gave her another kiss, his hands cradling the heavy round of her belly. He'd thought, living with her day after day, their passion would mute, or that as her body grew bigger with child, her appetite for the sensual would decline.

But neither had happened. As her expanding belly limited certain romantic encounters, she thought of new and unexpected ways to pleasure him. He found her body, ripe with his growing child, irresistibly erotic.

'You've made great strides as a trainer,' she told him as he walked her out of the gate. 'Not that I should be surprised, since you apply to that endeavour the same intensity of concentration you employed when memorising the blood lines of the stud and the system used to keep the estate books. Though I must admit, I never really expected you to stay long enough to learn it so well.'

'Why should I not stay?'

'After spending your life at court, in the halls of Parliament, and engaged in great battles, I thought you would find living on a small farm deep in the countryside far too boring.'

'I admit, I once thought that might be true. I've come to enjoy being a part of the rhythm of life on a great agricultural property, involving myself in activities I barely noticed when I lived at Swynford Court. There's a deep satisfaction in coaxing horses to follow my lead, as I used to coax men. I think I've come to love it at Denby almost as much as you do.'

'I'm rather surprised, though, that Colonel Brandon hasn't been urging you to take up your position.'

'I've stayed this long, I might as well remain until after the child comes.'

'Truly?' she asked, surprised.

'Truly.'

'I admit, I will feel…easier, knowing you won't be leaving.'

He would too, Max thought. After months with the potential of the Curse simmering at the back of his mind, he was too concerned for her welfare to tolerate the chance of being away when her time came, only if all he could do to help was encourage her. And he truly had found a measure of peace and contentment, working the stud with her, as profound as it was unexpected.

In fact, he was beginning to wonder if he really wanted to accept Colonel Brandon's post at all…particularly as it meant he would have to leave Caro and his child for months at a time.

Suddenly Caro gasped, jerking him from his thoughts. 'Oh, that was a sharp one!' she said, putting a hand to her belly.

'What is it?' Max asked, immediately concerned.

'A contraction, that's all. Mrs Drewry, the housekeeper,

says it's quite common to have these pains off and on as I near my time.'

'Are you sure? Maybe we ought to summon the midwife.'

'Just like a brood hen—' she teased before stopping in mid-sentence. Pain contorting her face, she began breathing rapidly.

'Let me carry you to the house,' Max said, his concern deepening.

'I don't need to be carried,' she said fretfully.

'Take my arm, then. We're sending for the midwife.'

Before she could reply, another pain hit her. She latched on to Max's arm, her fingers biting into his flesh. To his further alarm, she made no further protest about calling the midwife.

Ten hours later, the contractions had not abated. Rather, they had grown steadily stronger and more frequent. The midwife had arrived to assist; Dulcie and the housekeeper scurried in and out with hot water, candles, spiced possets and lavender-scented cloths to mop Caro's sweat-drenched face.

Max alternately paced the room and sat by her side, wishing there was more he could do than rub her back and hold her hands through the worst of the contractions. Looking down at his wrists ruefully, he realised he was going to have bruises.

But as the night wore on towards morning, her suffering intensifying without the labour seeming to progress, the midwife began to exchange worried glances with the housekeeper. The relatively trouble-free months of Caro's pregnancy had lulled Max into an increasing confidence that the uproar over the Curse was just a myth, but at the growing concern on the midwife's face and the deep groans of misery Caro was not able to suppress, he was beginning to lose faith in that theory.

After one particularly painful bout, when Caro lost the

struggle to keep herself from screaming, the midwife examined her, then removed her hands, shaking her head.

'What's wrong?' Max demanded.

'The babe's turned. Most come head first, which is easiest, but I can feel the babe's feet. It's much harder to birth one backwards.'

'Whatever is keeping the damned doctor?' Max barked, looking over at Dulcie, whom he'd charged to dispatch one of the grooms to bring back the local physician.

'I'll check again, master,' Dulcie said, hurrying out.

Caro's eyes, which she'd closed to rest between pains, flickered open. 'Baby…is turned?'

'Yes, missus, I fear so,' the midwife said.

She nodded absently, her face pale, her hair damp with sweat, dark circles of fatigue beneath her eyes. 'Happens… like that sometimes…with horses. Must turn baby.'

'I expect the doctor will try that, when he arrives,' the midwife said.

'Don't wait. Do it now.'

'Mistress, I'm not sure I want to try that.'

'Must. Can't…go on much longer.'

Icy shards of panic sliced through Max's veins. If Caro, who never gave up on anything, felt she couldn't bear much more, things were very bad indeed.

'Do you know what to do?' he asked the midwife.

'Aye, sir, but 'tis difficult. And will be very painful for your lady wife.'

'If you can't get it to turn, the baby is going to kill her,' Max said harshly, putting his worst fear into words for the first time. 'I'll hold her. You turn the child.'

'Oh, sir, I be not sure I want to—'

'Do it,' Caro said again, not opening her eyes. 'Mrs Thorgood, you…know what to do. Do it now.'

The midwife took a deep breath. 'Hold her still as you can, sir.'

Murmuring encouragement, Max slipped his arms around Caro's shoulders, leaning her back against his chest. At his nod, the midwife went to work.

With a wail, Caro bucked in his arms. Ignoring her agony, the midwife pushed and pulled at her belly, while Caro writhed in his arms. Nausea rose in Max's throat, but he choked it down. If Caro could endure this, so could he.

Finally, with a cry of triumph, Mrs Thorgood said, 'Look ye, sir, the babe be turning!'

Max wasn't sure exactly what he was seeing, but the contours of Caro's belly shifted, as if a leviathan inside was flexing and stretching. A few moments later, the midwife said, 'Babe's crowning! Hold on, missis, won't be much longer now!'

The rest of the birth seemed to happen all in a rush. What seemed a very short time later, the midwife had eased the slippery body free, wiped its mouth, given it a slap on the bottom, and as Max heard his child's first cry, wrapped it in soft flannel and handed it to him. 'It's a fine son you've got, Mr Ransleigh.'

Exhausted himself, Max sat back, looking with wonder at the miniature face peering resentfully up at him from within the flannel folds. 'It seems my son isn't any happier about his passage into this world than his mama.'

Despite his light words, Max's heartbeat sped and a sense of awe and humility filled him as he looked at the miracle in his arms. He reached over to grasp Caro's limp hand.

'We have a son, Caro. It's over now, sweeting.'

'Not quite,' the midwife said. 'There's the afterbirth to come.'

Before Max could ask what that meant, Caro groaned. Suddenly the sheets beneath her turned red, as if a swift crimson tide had flooded the shore.

'What's happening now?' he demanded.

The midwife's face blanched. 'She's bleeding, poor lamb. Oh, if it weren't the same thing what killed her poor mama!'

Max had seen blood on the battlefield, severed limbs, men missing arms, hands, bodies missing heads. But this was *Caro*, and a fear he'd never felt when facing the enemy's guns flooded him as the stain on the linen grew wider and wider.

'Can't you stop it? Stanch it somehow?'

'It comes from within her, sir, where the cord attaches. It'll stop on its own…if it does.'

Before the blood loss kills her, his mind filled in the unspoken words.

'What can we do, then?'

'Pray,' the midwife said.

So, tucking her cold hand in his, Max prayed. Surely she'd not suffered all the agonies of birth to slip from him now. He pleaded, bargained, begged the Almighty, promising to do whatever the Lord directed, if only he would spare Caro's life.

She seemed so still, her pale face waxy. But suddenly he realised the red stain was not getting any larger.

'It's stopped,' he whispered to the midwife. 'Is she safe now?'

'Depends on how much blood she lost. And whether fever sets in.'

Max stifled a curse. Each time he thought all the perils had ended, another presented itself. The midwife and Dulcie tried to talk him into leaving the room, bathing and changing out of his stable-grimed clothing, taking some dinner, but Max couldn't bring himself to leave her side. He felt the wholly illogical but none the less overwhelming conviction that if he left the room, he'd lose her for ever.

So he choked down some soup the housekeeper insisted

on bringing him and, as the long hours of the night crept towards morning, he dozed fitfully.

Max came fully awake just before dawn…when he realised the cold hand he'd been holding was now burning hot.

He called for the midwife, who touched her forehead and roused the maid to send for cool water. He was bathing her hands and face with sponges dipped in cool water when at last the doctor arrived.

'Thank heavens you're finally here,' Max cried, overwhelmingly relieved to have someone with medical expertise to buttress his ignorance.

Quickly the midwife related to the doctor what had transpired. After checking the baby and pronouncing him healthy, Dr Sawyer came back to Caro's bed.

'The fever's not breaking,' he observed. 'I should bleed her.'

It was the common medical practice, Max knew. 'But she's already lost so much blood,' he protested.

'Bleeding is the only thing that will remove adverse humours from the body,' the doctor said. 'It may seem harsh, but better harsh remedies than to lose your wife, eh? If you'll move aside, sir, I'll get started.'

Panicked indecision, worsened by fatigue, distress and the horror of having to stand by impotently while Caro suffered, held him motionless, stubbornly clinging to her hand. He was no medical expert…but on some subconscious level, he felt beyond doubt that bleeding Caro now would kill her.

'I can't let you,' he said at last. 'She's too weak.'

'She's too weak to support the contagion in her blood. If I don't remove some of it, I assure you, she *will* die.'

'I can't let you,' he replied desperately.

'You wish to go against my considered medical opinion, Mr Ransleigh?' When Max nodded, the doctor said, 'Then there is nothing else I can do for her. But know this, sir; if the worst happens, her death is on your hands.'

Considerably affronted, the doctor gathered his tools and left the room. Max stared down at Caro, tossing her head restlessly on the pillow.

Had he just condemned her to die? Would she die anyway, no matter what anyone did?

Max had commanded men in battle, ordered troops into positions that had resulted in the death and maiming of many men. But never had he given an order that might have more dire consequences than this one.

His back ached, the stubble on his cheeks itched and he was tired beyond comprehension. But as dawn moved into daylight, he waved away again any suggestion that he leave Caro to the midwife's care and sleep.

He would see her face when she woke…or watch her breathe her last.

He'd thought he'd felt helpless after Vienna, when control over his future had been wrenched from his hands. He'd thought he'd reached the depths of despair after his father had repudiated him and Wellington had refused to have anything further to do with him. But never had he felt as despairing and helpless as he did sitting by Caro's bed, his numb hands bathing her face as Mrs Drewry and Dulcie changed tepid water for fresh.

Unable to bear the thought that he might never talk with her again, he said, 'Newman told Dulcie that Sultan is pacing his stall. It seems he knows you are ill and is concerned for you. He wants his favourite rider back again. The grooms are putting the two-year-olds on lunge lines today and half the four-year-olds began dressage; you should see Scheherazade high-stepping, as if he were born to the knack! But I'll need your help with the colts who aren't yet saddle-broken; I still don't know how to do that. Your son is waiting to become acquainted, too. You do know you have a son, don't you?'

She lay still and silent now. His vision blurring with unshed tears, Max continued, 'He'll need you to sit him on his first pony, teach him to train his horse and read its moods, as his mother can. Caro, you can't l-leave me yet. There's too much left for us to share.'

On and on he talked, as if he could hold her to life by the power of his voice. That slight figure on the bed, now shivering with fever, now burning his fingers with her heat, had been the sole focus of his life for nearly six months now. Every day, she'd come to fascinate him more than she had the first time he'd met her, in that preposterous gown and those ridiculous glasses.

She'd touched his soul as profoundly as she'd pleasured his body. He couldn't envision a future without her. As soon as she was out of danger, he'd write to Colonel Brandon, turning down the post. What need had he to puff himself off with a high government position, trying to persuade his father or anyone else he was important?

He belonged at Denby Lodge with Caro…whose opinion of him was the only one that mattered.

Why had he not realised until this day, when he might lose her for ever, how much he'd come to love her?

Finally, some time after noon, exhaustion claimed him. Slumped over her bed, he fell asleep, his head resting beside hers on the pillow.

It was dark when he woke, the room illumined by a single lamp. He sat up with a start, rubbing sleep from his bleary eyes. Then he clasped Caro's hand.

Which was clammy—cold now, where it had been hot before. His gaze shot to her pale face and colourless lips, the eyelashes collapsed limply against her waxen cheeks.

Alarmed, he squeezed the hand he still held. Then, while he looked on with a relief so deep he thought he might pass out from the force of it, she stirred and opened her eyes.

'Max,' she whispered, a tiny bit of colour returning to her face. 'You stayed.'

'Every minute.'

'I was so tired and I hurt so badly. It felt like I was wandering in a fog, uncertain which way to go. Your voice brought me back.'

Gently, as if she might shatter at a touch, he wrapped his arms around her. 'I was so afraid I was going to lose you.'

She gave him a glimmer of a smile. 'I thought if I died, you could have my money and still marry the woman you wanted. You may be stuck with me now.'

He put his fingers over her lips. 'I don't want any other woman. I don't want any other wife. Only you, Caro. Only the outrageous, passionate, unconventional woman who's turned my whole life upside down.'

Weakly she squeezed his fingers. 'I'm so glad. In fact, over the last few weeks I decided that, if all went well, I didn't want to live the rest of my life apart from you. I've already turned much of the work of the stud over to Newman. I could turn over the rest and go with you to London. If…if you want me.'

Max sucked in a breath, shocked by the enormity of what she was offering him. 'You would give up the stud?'

'Since Papa's death, all I wanted was to realise his dream. But now I have a dream I want even more. To be your wife.'

Humbled, Max kissed her limp hands. 'I love you, Caro Ransleigh. But you needn't make such a sacrifice. I'd like to stay here and run the farm with you, building the stud's bloodlines…and watching our son grow.'

'What of Colonel Brandon's post?'

'I suppose I've known it for some time, but after last night, the truth became perfectly clear. Someone else can have Brandon's post. You and Denby and our new babe are my world now. I don't ever want to leave it again. Do you think you could teach me how to be a proper father, as you've taught me so much else? Could you love me and share Denby with me?'

'Foolish Max,' she murmured. 'Couldn't you tell? I've loved you almost from the first, though I fought accepting it for months. You won't need me to teach you about fatherhood; from the gentleness and patience you show the horses, I know you'll be a wonderful father to our baby. But I must insist that the terms of our bargain change. I withdraw my permission for you to dally with any lady you fancy. I'm a selfish, greedy woman, who wants to keep all your passion for herself. And if you're ever tempted to stray, I warn you, I'm a crack shot.'

Max grinned. 'I don't doubt it. Shall we begin again?'

He dropped to one knee. 'Caro Denby, will you marry me and be my wife, my one and only love, never to be parted, for the rest of our lives?'

Joy lit her weary eyes. 'Now that, my sweet Max, is a bargain I can accept with my whole heart.'

* * * * *

The Rake to Redeem Her

Chapter One

Barton Abbey—late spring, 1816

'I wager *I* could find her.' Smouldering with anger against the woman who had destroyed his cousin Max's diplomatic career, Will Ransleigh accepted a glass of brandy from his host.

'Welcome back to England,' Alastair Ransleigh said, saluting Will with his own glass before motioning him to an armchair. 'Far be it from me to bet against "Wagering Will", who never met a game of chance he couldn't win. But why do you think *you* could find her, when Max, with all his official contacts, could not?'

'I never had much use for *officials*,' Will observed with a grimace. 'Would have transported me for stealing a loaf of bread to feed myself and my starving mates.'

'You've cleaned up so well, I sometimes forget you were once gallows-bait,' Alastair said with a grin. 'But to be fair, where would one expect to look? Madame Lefevre was cousin and hostess to Thierry St Arnaud, one of Prince Talleyrand's top aides in the French delegation at the Congress of Vienna. The family's quite old and well known, even if they did turn out to be Bonapartists.'

'That may be. But it's those in the serving class who really know what goes on: maids, valets, cooks, grooms, hotel employees, servants at the Hoffburg, keepers of public houses. I'll use them to track Madame Lefevre.'

'When I visited Max at his wife's farm, he insisted he was content there.' Alastair laughed. 'He even claimed training horses is rather like diplomacy: one must coax rather than coerce. Except that horses don't lie and their memories are short, so they don't hold your mistakes against you.'

'Just like Max to make light of it. But all of us—you, me, Dom—knew from our youth that Max was destined to be one of England's foremost politicians—Prime Minister, even! Would he choose training horses over a brilliant government career, if he *truly* had a choice? I don't believe it.'

'I was suspicious, too, at first,' Alastair admitted. 'Max, who never showed any interest in a woman who wasn't both beautiful and accomplished, happily wedding a little nobody who prefers rusticating in Kent to London society? But I ended up liking Caro. She rides better than I do—an admission I make most unwillingly—and breeds top-notch horseflesh on that farm in Kent. She's quite impressive—which is saying something, given my generally low opinion of womankind.' He paused, a bleakness passing over his face.

He's still not over her, Will thought, once again consigning to eternal hellfire the woman who'd broken her engagement and Alastair's heart.

His fury reviving against the latest female to harm one of his Ransleigh Rogue cousins, he continued, 'The very idea is ridiculous—Max, involved in a plot to assassinate Wellington? I'd have thought his valour at Waterloo put a stop to that nonsense.'

Alastair sighed. 'The hard truth is that the attempt in Vienna embarrassed both the French, who were negotiating as allies at the time, and our own forces, who didn't winkle out the conspiracy. Now that Bonaparte's put away at St Helena for good, neither side wanted to rake up old scandals.'

'Couldn't his father do anything? He's practically run the Lords for years.'

'The Earl of Swynford preferred not to champion his son and risk further damaging his political standing, already weakened by Max's "lapse in judgement",' Alastair said drily.

'So he abandoned him. Bastard!' Will added a colourful curse from his days on the London streets. 'Just like my dear uncle never to let his family's needs get in the way of his political aspirations. Makes me glad I was born on the wrong side of the blanket.'

Alastair shook his head, his expression bitter. 'Whoever set up the Vienna scheme was clever, I'll give them that. There'd be no approach more likely to elicit Max's response than to dangle before him some helpless woman in need of assistance.'

'He always had a soft spot for the poor and down-trodden,' Will agreed. 'His treatment of me being a prime example. We need to get Madame Lefevre back to England! Let *her* explain how she invented some sad tale to delay Max's rendezvous with Wellington, leaving the commander waiting alone, vulnerable to attack. Surely that would clear Max of blame, since no man who calls himself a gentleman would have refused a lady begging for his help. He found no trace of St Arnaud, either, while in Vienna?'

'It appears he emigrated to the Americas. It's uncertain whether Madame Lefevre accompanied him. If you do mean to search, it won't be easy. It's been more than a year since the attempt.'

Will shrugged. 'An attack on the man who led all of Europe against Napoleon? People will remember that.'

Alastair opened his mouth as if to speak, then hesitated.

'What?' Will asked.

'Don't jump all over me for asking, but can you afford such a mission? The blunt you'll get from selling out will last a while, but rather than haring off to the Continent, don't you need to look for some occupation? Unless...did the earl come through and—?'

Will waved Alastair to silence. 'No, the earl did not. You didn't really expect our uncle to settle an allowance on me, did you?'

'Well, he did promise, after you managed to scrape together the funds to buy your own commission, that if you made good in the army, he'd see you were settled afterward in a style befitting a Ransleigh.'

Will laughed. 'I imagine he expected me to either be killed or cashiered out. And, no, I've no intention of going to him, cap in hand, to remind him of his pledge, so save your breath.'

'Then what will you do?'

'There are some possibilities. Before I pursue them, though, I'll see Max reinstated to his former position. I've got sufficient blunt for the journey with enough extra to gild the right hands, if necessary.'

'I'll come with you. "Ransleigh Rogues for ever", after all.'

'No, you won't. Wait, hear me out,' he said, fore-stalling Alastair's protest. 'If I needed a sabre-wielding Hussar to ride beside me into a fight, there's no man I'd rather have. But for this journey...'

Looking his cousin up and down, he grinned. 'In your voice, your manner, even your walk, there's no hiding that you're Alastair Ransleigh of Barton Abbey, nephew of an earl, wealthy owner of vast property. I'll need to travel as a man nobody notices and the alley rats would sniff you out in an instant.'

'You're the nephew of an earl yourself,' Alastair pointed out.

'Perhaps, but thanks to my dear father abandoning my mother, unwed and increasing, in the back streets of London, I had the benefit of six years' education in survival. I know how thieves, Captain Sharps and cut-throats operate.'

'But these will be Austrian thieves, Captain Sharps and cutthroats. And you don't speak German.'

Will shrugged. 'Thievery is thievery and you'd be surprised at my many talents. The army had more uses for me after Waterloo than simply letting me hang about the hospital, watching over Dom's recovery.'

'He's healed now, hasn't he?' Alastair asked, diverted by Will's mention of the fourth cousin in their Ransleigh Rogues' gallery. 'Has he…recovered?'

Will recalled the desolate look in Dom's one remaining eye. 'Dandy Dominick', he'd been called, the handsomest man in the regiment. Besting them all at riding, hunting, shooting—and charming the ladies.

His face scarred, one arm gone, his physical prowess diminished, Dom would have to come to terms with much more than his injuries, Will knew. 'Not yet. Once I got him safely back to England, he told me I'd wet-nursed him long enough and kicked me out. So I might as well go to Vienna.'

Alastair frowned. 'I still don't like you going there alone. Max said the authorities in Vienna strongly discouraged him from investigating the matter. You'll get no help from them. It could even be dangerous.'

'Dangerous?' Will rose and made a circuit of the room. 'Do you remember the first summer we were all together at Swynford Court?' he asked abruptly, looking back at Alastair. 'The lawyer who found me in Seven Dials had just turned me over to the earl, who, assured I was truly his brother's child, dumped me in the country. Telling you, Max and Dom to make something of me, or else. I was…rather unlikeable.'

Alastair laughed. 'An understatement! Surly, filthy, cursing everyone you encountered in barely comprehensible cant!'

'After two weeks, you and Dom were ready to drown me in the lake. But Max wouldn't give up. One night he caught me alone in the stables. I tried every dirty trick I knew, but he still beat the stuffing out of me. Then, cool as you please, he told me my behaviour had to change. That I was his cousin and a Ransleigh, and he was counting on me to learn to act like one. I didn't make it easy, but he kept goading, coaxing, working on me, like water dripping on stone, until he finally convinced me there could be advantages to becoming more than the leader of thieves in a rookery. Max knew that if I didn't change, when the earl returned at the end of the summer, blood kin or not, he would toss me back into the streets.'

Will stared past Alastair out the library window, seeing not the verdant pastures of Barton Abbey, but the narrow, noisome alleys of Seven Dials. 'If he had, I'd probably be dead now. So I owe Max. For my life. For giving me the closest, most loyal friends and cousins any man could wish for. I swear on whatever honour I possess that I won't take up my own life again until I see his name cleared. Until he has the choice, if he truly wishes, to become the great political leader we all know he should be.'

After studying him for a moment, Alastair nodded. 'Very well. If there's anything I can do, you'll let me know, won't you? If Max hadn't led you and Dom after me into the army, I might not have survived, either. For months after Di—' he halted, having almost said the forbidden name. 'Well, I didn't much care whether I lived or died.'

Will wondered if sometimes, Alastair still didn't much care.

'I might need some help on the official front when it comes time to get the wench into England.'

'She may balk at returning. After all, if she proves herself a spy, the gallows await.'

'I can be…persuasive.'

Alastair chuckled. 'I don't want to know. When do you propose to leave?'

'Tomorrow.'

'But you have just got back! Mama expects you to stay at least a week and Max will want to see you.'

Will shook his head. 'Your mama's being kind and Max would only try to dissuade me. Better I don't see him until…after. If he asks, tell him the army still has business for me on the Continent. Besides, you were right; it's been more than a year. No sense waiting for memories to fade any more than they already have.'

'Do keep me posted. It might take some time to ride to your rescue.'

'Tonight, all I'll need rescue from is too much brandy. Unlikely, as you're being entirely too stingy with it.'

Laughing, Alastair retrieved the bottle and refilled their glasses. 'Ransleigh Rogues for ever!'

'Ransleigh Rogues,' Will replied, clinking his glass with Alastair's.

Chapter Two

Vienna, Austria—six weeks later

Elodie Lefevre shifted her chair into the beam of afternoon sunlight spilling through the window. Taking up her needlework again, she breathed in the soft scent of the late-blooming daffodils she'd planted last autumn in the tiny courtyard garden below. Nodding violas added their sweet fragrance as well.

She paused a moment, letting the calm and beauty seep into her soul, soothing the restless anxiety that lurked always just below the surface. By this evening, she would have this consignment of embroidery finished. Clara would come by with dinner, bringing a new load of embroidery and payment for completing the last.

Against all the odds, she had survived. Despite the constant imperative gnawing within her to get back to Paris, she must remain patient and continue working, hoarding her slowly increasing store of coins. Perhaps late this year, she would finally have enough saved to return…and search for Philippe.

A wave of longing gripped her as her mind caressed his beloved image—the black curls falling over his brow, the dark, ever-curious, intelligent eyes, the driving energy that propelled him. Was he still in Paris? How had he changed in the nearly eighteen months since she'd left?

Would he recognise her? She glanced at herself in the mirror opposite. She was thinner, of course, after her long recovery, but except for her crooked fingers, most of the injuries didn't show. Her blue eyes were shadowed, perhaps, and long hours indoors had dulled the gold highlights the sun had once burnished in her soft brown hair, but otherwise, she thought she looked much the same.

Suddenly, something—a faint stir of the air, a flicker of light—seized her attention. Instantly alert, moving only her eyes, she discovered the source: a barely perceptible movement in the uppermost corner of the mirror, which reflected both her image and the adjacent window that also overlooked the courtyard.

Scarcely breathing, she shifted her head a tiny bit to the right. Yes, someone was there—a man, perched soundlessly on the narrow balcony beside the window, watching her, all but the top of his tawny head and his eyes hidden behind the wall and the vines crawling up it. Had she not chanced to look into the mirror at that precise instant, she would never have seen him move into position.

From the elevation of his head, he must be tall, and agile, to have scaled the wall so soundlessly. The minuscule amount of him she could see gave her no hint whether he was thin or powerfully built. Whether he was armed, and if so, with what.

Not that the knowledge would do her much good. All she had to defend herself was her sewing scissors; her small pistol was hidden in her reticule in the wardrobe and her knife, in the drawer of the bedside table.

But as seconds passed and he remained motionless, she let out the breath she'd been holding. The afternoon light was bright; he could clearly see she was alone. If he'd meant to attack her, surely he would have made a move by now.

Who was he, then? Not one of the men who'd been watching the apartment from the corner ever since Clara brought her here. No one had bothered her since the foiled attack; so small and damaged a fish as herself, she thought, was of little interest, especially after Napoleon's exile at St Helena put an end once and for all to dreams of a French empire.

Elodie kept her gaze riveted on the mirror as several more seconds dragged on. Despite her near-certainty the stranger did not mean her any immediate harm, her nerves—and a rising anger—finally prompted her to speak.

'*Monsieur*, if you are not going to shoot me, why not come inside and tell me what you want?'

The watching eyes widened with surprise, then in one fluid motion the stranger swung himself through the window to land lightly before her. With a flourish, he swept her a bow. 'Madame Lefevre, I presume?'

Elodie caught her breath, overwhelmed by the sheer masculine power of the man now straightening to his full height. If he meant to harm her, she was in very bad trouble indeed.

He must be English. No other men moved with such arrogance, as if they owned the earth by right. He loomed over her, tall and whipcord-lean. There was no mistaking the hard strength of the arms and shoulders that had levered him so effortlessly up to the balcony and swung him practically into her lap.

His clothes were unremarkable: loose-fitting coat, trousers and scuffed boots that might have been worn by any tradesman or clerk toiling away in the vast city.

But his face—angular jaw, chiselled cheekbones, slightly crooked nose, sensual mouth and the arresting turquoise blue of his eyes—would capture the attention of any woman who chanced to look at him. Certainly it captured hers, so completely that she momentarily forgot the potential danger he posed.

He smiled at her scrutiny, which might have embarrassed her, had she not been suddenly jolted by a sense of *déjà vu*. 'Do I know you?' she asked, struggling to work out why he seemed so familiar. 'Have we met?'

The smile faded and his eyes went cold. 'No, *madame*. You don't know me, but I believe you knew my kinsman all too well. Max Ransleigh.'

Max. His image flashed into her mind: same height and build, thick, wavy golden hair, crystal-blue eyes.

An air of command tempered by a kindness and courtesy that had warmed her heart then—and made it twist again now with regret as she recalled him.

The afternoon sun touched this man's tawny hair with tints of auburn; rather than clear blue, his eyes were the hue of the Mediterranean off St Tropez. But beyond that, the two men were remarkably similar. 'You are Max's brother?'

'His cousin. Will Ransleigh.'

'He is well, I trust? I was sorry to have done him…a disservice. I hoped, with Napoleon escaping from Elba so soon after the event in Vienna, that his position had not been too adversely affected.'

He raised one eyebrow, his expression sardonic. Her momentary bedazzlement abruptly vanished as her senses returned to full alert. This man did not mean her well.

'I regret to inform you that your tender hopes were not realised. As you, the cousin of a diplomat, surely know, the "event" that embroiled him in the near-assassination of his commander ruined his career. He was recalled in disgrace and only the outbreak of war allowed him a chance to redeem himself on the field of battle.'

'I understand the carnage was terrible at Waterloo.'

'It was. But even his valour there was not enough to restore his career, which was destroyed by his association with you.'

'I am sorry for it.' And she was. But given the stakes, if she had it all to do over again, she would do nothing differently.

'You are *sorry*? How charming!' he replied, his tone as sardonic as his expression.

Her anger flared again. At men, who used women as pawns to their own purposes. At a woman's always-powerless position in their games. What matter if this man did not believe her? She would not give him the satisfaction of protesting.

As she remained silent, he said, 'Then you will be delighted to know I intend to offer you a chance to make amends. Since you don't appear to be prospering here…' he swept a hand around to indicate the small room, with its worn carpet and shabby furnishing '…I see no reason why you shouldn't agree to leave for England immediately.'

'England?' she echoed, surprised. 'Why should I do that?'

'I'm going to escort you back to London, where we will call on the Foreign Office. There you will explain exactly how you entrapped my cousin in this scheme, manoeuvring him into doing no more than any other gentleman would have done. Demonstrating that he was blameless in not anticipating the assassination attempt, and any fault should be assigned to the intelligence services whose job it was to sniff out such things.'

Her mind racing, Elodie weighed the options. Her hopes rose crazily as she recognised that travelling to London, as this man apparently had the means to do, would get her a deal closer to France, and immediately—not next autumn or in another year, which was as soon as she'd dared hope her slowly accumulating resources would allow.

But even with King Louis on France's throne and the two nations officially at peace, as a French citizen she was still vulnerable. If she testified to involvement in an attempt on the life of the great English hero Lord Wellington, saviour of Europe and victor of Waterloo, she could well be imprisoned. Maybe even executed.

Unless she escaped on the way. Ransleigh would likely want to journey by sea, which would make the chances of eluding him before arrival in England very difficult. Unless...

'I will go with you, but only if we stop first in Paris.' Paris, a city she knew like the lines on her palm. Paris, where only a moment's inattention would allow her to slip away into a warren of medieval alleyways so dense and winding, he would never be able to trail her.

Where, after waiting a safe interval, she could hunt for Philippe.

He made a show of looking about the room, which lacked the presence of a footman or even a maid to lend her assistance. 'I don't think you're in much of a position to dictate terms. And I have no interest in visiting Paris.'

'A mistake, Monsieur Ransleigh. It is a beautiful city.'

'So it is, but unimportant to me at present.'

She shrugged. 'To you, perhaps, but not to me. Unless we go first to Paris, I will not go with you.'

His eyes darkened, unmistakable menace in their depths. 'I can compel you.'

She nodded. 'You could drug me, I suppose. Gag, bind and smuggle me aboard a ship in Trieste. But nothing can compel me to deliver to the London authorities the sort of testimony you wish, unless I myself choose to do so.'

Fury flashed in those blue eyes and his jaw clenched. If his cousin's career had truly been ruined by her actions, he had cause to be angry.

Just as she'd had no choice about involving Max in the plot.

'I could simply kill you now,' he murmured, stepping closer. 'Your life for the life you ruined.' He placed his hands around her neck.

She froze, her heartbeat stampeding. Had she survived so much, only for it all to end now? His hands, warm against the chill of her neck, were large and undoubtedly strong. One quick twist and it would be over.

But despite the hostility of his action, as the seconds ticked away with his fingers encircling her neck, some instinct told her that he didn't truly mean to hurt her.

As her fear subsided to a manageable level, she grasped his hands with a calm she was far from feeling. To her great relief, he let her pull them away from her neck, confirming her assessment.

'Paris first, then London. I will wait in the garden for your decision.'

Though her heart pounded so hard that she was dizzy, Elodie made herself rise and walk with unhurried steps from the room. Not for her life would she let him see how vulnerable she felt. Never again would any man make her afraid.

Why should they? She had nothing left to lose.

Out of his sight, she clutched the stair rail to keep from falling as she descended, then stumbled out the back door to the bench at the centre of the garden. She grabbed the edge with trembling fingers and sat down hard, gulping in a shuddering breath of jonquil-scented air.

Eyes narrowed, Will watched Elodie Lefevre cross the room with quiet elegance and disappear down the stairwell.

Devil's teeth! She was nothing like what he'd expected.

He'd come to Vienna prepared to find a seductive siren, who traded upon her beauty to entice while at the same time playing the frightened innocent. Luring in Max, for whom protecting a woman was a duty engraved upon his very soul.

Elodie Lefevre was attractive, certainly, but hers was a quiet beauty. Sombrely dressed and keeping herself in the background, as he'd learned she always did, she'd have attracted little notice among the crowd of fashionable, aristocratic lovelies who'd fluttered like exotic butterflies through the balls and salons of the Congress of Vienna.

She had courage, too. After her first indrawn breath of alarm, she'd not flinched when he clamped his fingers around her throat.

Not that he'd had any intention of actually harming her, of course. But he'd hoped that his display of anger and a threat of violence might make her panic and capitulate before reinforcements could arrive.

If she had any.

He frowned. It had taken a month of thorough, patient tracking to find her, but the closer he got, the more puzzled and curious he became about the woman who'd just coolly descended to the garden. As if strange men vaulted into her rooms and threatened her life every day.

Maybe they did. For, until she'd confirmed her identity, he'd been nearly convinced the woman he'd located couldn't be the Elodie Lefevre he sought.

Why was the cousin of a wealthy diplomat living in shabby rooms in a decaying, unfashionable section of Vienna?

Why did she inhabit those rooms alone—lacking, from the information he'd charmed out of the landlady, even a maid?

Why did it appear she eked out a living doing embroidery work for a fashionable dressmaker whom Madame Lefevre, as hostess to one of the Congress of Vienna's most well-placed diplomats, would have visited as a customer?

But neither could he deny the facts that had led him, piecing together each small bit of testimony gathered from maids, porters, hotel managers, street vendors, seamstresses, merchants and dry-good dealers, from the elegant hotel suite she'd presided over for St Arnaud to these modest rooms off a Vienna back alley.

St Arnaud himself had disappeared the night of the failed assassination. Will didn't understand why someone clever enough to have concocted such a scheme would have been so careless about ensuring his cousin's safety.

And how had she sensed Will's presence on the balcony? He knew for certain he'd made no sound as he carefully scaled the wall from the courtyard to the ledge outside her window. Either she was incredibly prescient, or he'd badly lost his touch, and he didn't think it was the latter.

Her awareness impressed him even more than her courage, sparking an admiration he had no wish to feel.

Any more than he'd wanted the reaction triggered when he'd placed his hands around her neck. The softness of her skin, the faint scent of lavender teasing his nostrils, sent a fierce desire surging through him, as abrupt and immediate as the leap of her pulse under his thumbs.

Finding himself attracted to Elodie Lefevre was a complication he didn't need. What he did need were answers to all the questions he had about her.

Such as why it was so important for her to get to Paris.

A quick examination of her room told him nothing; the hired furniture, sewing supplies and few basic necessities could have been anyone's. She seemed to possess nothing that gave any clue to the character of the woman who'd lived here, as he'd learned, for more than a year, alone but for the daily visits of her former maid.

He'd just have to go question the woman herself. He suspected she would be as vigilant at keeping her secrets as she was at catching out uninvited visitors to her rooms.

To achieve his aims, he needed to master both those secrets—and her. Turning on his heel, he headed for the garden.

Chapter Three

Will found Madame Lefevre picking spent blooms from the border of lavender surrounding a central planting of tall yellow flowers.

Hearing him approach, she looked back over her shoulder. 'Well?'

He waited, but she added nothing to that single word—neither pleading nor explanation nor entreaty. Once again, he was struck by her calm, an odd quality of stillness overlaid with a touch of melancholy.

Men awaiting battle would envy that sangfroid. Or did she not truly realise how vulnerable she was?

'For a woman who's just had her life threatened, you seem remarkably tranquil.'

She shrugged. 'Nothing I say or do will change what you have decided. If it is to kill me, I am not strong or skilled enough to prevent you. Struggling and pleading are so…undignified. And if I am to die, I would rather spend my last moments enjoying the beauty of my garden.'

So she did understand the gravity of her position. Yet the calm remained.

As a man who'd earned much of his blunt by his wits, Will had played cards with masters of the game, men who didn't show by the twitch of an eyelid whether they held a winning or losing hand. Madame Lefevre could hold her own with the best of them. He'd never met a woman so difficult to read.

She was like a puzzle spread out in a jumble of pieces. The more he learned about her, the stronger his desire to fit them all together.

Delaying answering her question so he might examine that puzzle further, he said, 'The garden is lovely. So serene, and those yellow flowers are so fragrant. Did you plant it?'

She lifted a brow, as if wondering why he'd abruptly veered from threatening her to talking about plants. 'The daffodils, you mean.' Her lips barely curved in amusement, she looked at him quizzically. 'You grew up in the city, Monsieur Ransleigh, no?'

'Commonplace, are they?' A reluctant, answering smile tugged at his lips. 'Yes, I'm a city lad. But you, obviously, were country bred.'

'Lovely flowers can be found in either place,' she countered.

'Your English is very good, with only a trace of an accent. Where did you learn it?'

She waved a careless hand. 'These last few years, English has been spoken everywhere.'

She'd grown up in the country, then, he surmised

from her evasions, probably at an estate with a knowledgeable gardener—and an English governess.

'How did you come to be your cousin's hostess in Vienna?'

'He never married. A diplomat at his level has many social duties.'

Surprised at getting a direct answer this time, he pressed, 'He did not need you to perform those "duties" after Vienna?'

'Men's needs change. So, *monsieur*, do you accept my bargain or not?'

Aha, he thought, gratified. Though she gave no outward sign of anxiety—trembling fingers, fidgeting hands, restless movement—the abrupt return to the topic at hand showed she wasn't as calm as she was trying to appear.

'Yes,' he replied, deciding upon the moment. At least seeming to agree to her demand was essential. It would be a good deal easier to spirit her out of Vienna if she went willingly.

He was still somewhat surprised she would consent to accompany him upon any terms. Unless...

'Don't think you can escape me in Paris,' he warned. 'I'll be with you every moment, like crust on bread.'

'Ah, warm French bread! I cannot wait to taste some.'

She licked her lips. The gesture sent a bolt of lust straight to his loins. Something of his reaction must have showed in his face, for her eyes widened and she smiled knowingly.

He might not be able to prevent his body's response,

but he could certainly control his actions, he thought, disgruntled. If anyone was going to play the seduction card in this little game, it would be him—if and when he wished to.

'How did you, cousin to Thierry St Arnaud, come to be here alone?' he asked, steering the discussion back where he wanted it. 'Why did he not take you with him when he fled Vienna?'

'Nothing—and no one—mattered to my cousin but restoring Napoleon to the throne of France. When the attempt failed, his only thought was to escape before the Austrian authorities discovered his connection to the plot, so he might plot anew. Since I was no longer of any use to him, he was done with me.'

It seemed St Arnaud had about as much family loyalty as Will's uncle. But still, self-absorbed as the earl might be, Will knew if anyone bearing Ransleigh blood were in difficulties, the earl would send assistance.

What sort of man would not do that for his own cousin?

Putting aside that question for the moment, Will said, 'Were you equally fervent to see Napoleon restored as emperor?'

'To wash France free of the stain of aristocracy, Napoleon spilled the blood of his own people…and then created an aristocracy of his own. All I know of politics is the guillotine's blade was followed by the emperor's wars. I doubt the fields of Europe will dry in our lifetime.'

'So why did you help St Arnaud?'

'You think he gave me a choice?'

Surprised, he stared at her, assessing. She met his gaze squarely, faint colour stirring in her cheeks at his scrutiny.

A man who would abandon his own cousin probably hadn't been too dainty in coercing her co-operation. Had he hurt her?

Even as the question formed, as if guessing his thoughts, she lowered her gaze and tucked her left hand under her skirt.

An unpleasant suspicion coalescing in his head, Will stepped closer and seized her hand. She resisted, then gasped as he jerked it into the waning sunlight.

Two of the fingers were slightly bent, the knuckles still swollen, as if the bones had been broken and healed badly. 'An example of your cousin's persuasion?' he asked roughly, shocked and disgusted. A man who would attack a woman was beneath contempt.

She pulled her hand back, rubbing the wrist. 'An accident, *monsieur.*'

Will didn't understand why she would protect St Arnaud, if he truly had coerced her participation, then abandoned her. He didn't want to feel the niggle of sympathy stirring within him, had that really been her predicament.

Whatever her reasons, she was still the woman who'd ruined Max's career.

'You'd have me believe you were an innocent pawn, forced by St Arnaud to do his bidding, then discarded when you were no longer of use?'

She smiled sweetly. 'Used, just as you plan to use me, you mean?'

Stung, his anger flared hotter. Plague take her, *he* wasn't her bloody relation, responsible for her safety and well-being. If he used her, it was only what she deserved for entrapping Max.

'Why is it so important for you to go to Paris?' he asked instead.

'It's a family matter. You, who have come all this way and worked so diligently on your cousin's behalf, should appreciate that. Take me to Paris and I will go with you to England. I'll not go otherwise—no matter what...persuasion you employ.'

He stared into her eyes, assessing the strength of her conviction. She'd rightly said he couldn't force or threaten her into testifying. Indeed, even the appearance of coercion would discredit what she said.

He hoped upon the journey to somehow charm or trick her out of going to Paris. But unless he came up with a way to do so, he might end up having to stop there first.

Although one should always have a long-term strategy, all that mattered at the moment was playing the next card. First, he must get her out of Vienna.

'It doesn't appear you have much to pack. I should like to leave in two days' time.'

'How do you mean to spirit me away? Though the watchers have not yet interfered with my movements, I've not attempted to leave the city.'

Having drunk a tankard with the keeper of the public house on the corner, Will had already discovered the house was being watched, but he hadn't expected a woman, diplomat's cousin or no, to have noticed. Once again, surprise and reluctant admiration rippled through him. 'You're aware of the guard, then?'

She gave him an exasperated look, as if he were treating her like an idiot. '*Bien sûr* I'm aware! Although as I said, rightfully judging that I pose no threat, they've done nothing but observe. But since I have recovered enough to—' She halted a moment, then continued, 'There have always been watchers.'

Recovered enough. He wasn't sure he wanted to know from what. Shaking off the thought, he said, 'Do you know who they are?'

'Austrians, I expect. Clara has flirted with some of them, and from their speech they appear to be local lads. Not English. Nor French. Talleyrand has enough agents in keeping, he can learn, I expect, whatever he wishes from the Austrians.'

Will nodded. That judgement confirmed what the publican had told him. Local men, hired out of the army by government officials, would be easier for him to evade than Foreign Office professionals. During the two days he was allotting *madame* to settle her things, he'd observe the guard's routine, then choose the best time and manner in which to make off with her—in case the authorities should object to her departure.

'Are you thinking to have me pay off the landlady and simply stroll out the front door, valise in hand?' *madame* asked, interrupting his thoughts.

'You'd prefer to escape out a window at midnight?' he asked, amused.

'The balcony worked well enough for you,' she retorted. 'It might be wise to anticipate opposition. I should probably go in disguise, so that neither the landlady nor the guards at the corner immediately realise I've departed.'

Though by now he shouldn't be surprised by anything she said, Will found himself raising an eyebrow. 'Leave in disguise? Interesting education the French give their diplomatic hostesses.'

'France has been at war for longer than we both have been alive, *monsieur*,' she shot back. 'People from every level of society have learned tricks to survive.'

It appeared she had, at any rate. If being abandoned by her cousin in a foreign capital were any indication, she had needed to.

'What do you suggest?'

'That we leave in mid-afternoon, when streets busy with vehicles, vendors and pedestrians will distract the guards and make them less vigilant. You could meet my friend, Clara, at a posting inn not far from these rooms. Bring men's clothing that she can conceal beneath the embroidery in her basket. She will escort you up, telling the landlady, if you encounter her, that you are her brother. You will then exit by the balcony while I, wearing the clothing you provide, will walk out with Clara.'

Her suggestion was so outrageous, Will was hard put not to laugh. 'I've no problem exiting by way of the balcony, but do you really think you could pass as a man?'

'I'm tall for a woman. As long as I don't encounter Frau Gruener, who knows me well, it should work. She almost always takes her rest of an afternoon between two and four, by the way. Those watching at the corner, if they notice us at all, will merely see Clara leaving the building, as she went in, with a man. Once we are away from the watchers, I leave it to you—who did so good a job locating me—to manage the rest.'

Intrigued by *madame*'s unexpected talent for subterfuge, he had to admit that the plan had merit. 'It might work. As long as you can walk in men's clothing without it being immediately obvious that you're a woman.'

She smiled grimly. 'You might be surprised at my talents. I'm more concerned about you remaining for more than a few hours in this vicinity without attracting attention. You are…rather distinctive.'

'You don't think *I* can pass unnoticed, if I choose?'

'Your clothing is unremarkable, but you, *monsieur*, are not.' She looked him up and down, her gaze coming to rest on his face. 'Both that golden hair—and your features—are far too striking.'

He couldn't help feeling a purely male satisfaction that she found him so notable. As he held her gaze, smiling faintly, a surge of sensual energy pulsed between them, as powerful as if she'd actually touched him. From the gasp she uttered and her widened eyes, Will knew she'd felt it, too.

Hell and damn. Bad enough that he'd been immediately attracted to her. If he excited her lust as well…

It would complicate things, certainly. On the other

hand, as long as he kept his head, if not his body, focused on his objective, he might be able to use that attraction later. Seducing her to achieve his aims would be much more pleasant for them both than outright coercion.

Filing that possibility away, he forced himself to look away, breaking the connection.

'I'm a dab hand at disguises myself. I'll not accompany your friend as her brother, but as her old uncle, who wears spectacles and has something of a limp. The gout, you know.'

Tilting her head, she studied him. 'Truly, you are Max Ransleigh's cousin?'

He couldn't fault her scepticism; no more than she could Will imagine Max sneaking on to a balcony, breaking into a woman's rooms, threatening her, or disguising himself as an old man.

'I'm from the wrong side of the blanket, so I come by my disreputable ways honestly.'

'Ah, I see. Very well, Clara will meet you at three of the afternoon, two days from now at the Lark and Plough, on Dusseldorfer Strasse. She'll look for a bent old man with spectacles and a cane.' She offered her hand.

'Honour among thieves?' Amused anew, he took her hand to shake it…and a zing of connection flowed immediately through her fingers to his.

Her face colouring, she snatched her hand back. No longer annoyed by the hardening of his loins, Will was beginning to find the possibility of seduction more enticing than regrettable.

'Three o'clock, then.' As she nodded and turned to go back into the house, he said, 'By the way, *madame*, I will be watching. If any tall young man with a feminine air exits your lodgings in the interim, I will notice.'

She lifted her chin. 'Why should I try to elude you? I *want* to return to Paris and you will help me do so. Until then, *monsieur*.'

Before she could walk away, a woman's voice emanating from the second floor called out, '*Madame*, where are you?'

'Get back!' she whispered, pushing him into the shadows beneath the balcony.

'That's Clara, isn't it? The maid who helped you?' Will asked in an undertone as footsteps sounded on the balcony overhead.

'Ah, there you are, in the garden,' came the voice. 'Shall I bring your dinner down there?'

'No, I'll be right up,' *madame* called back.

She pivoted to face Will. 'As soon as you hear me above, go back over the wall the way you came. I will do as you ask; there's no need for you to harass Clara.'

'What makes you think I haven't already…harassed her?'

Her eyes widened with alarm before she steadied herself, no doubt realising that if he *had* accosted the maid, she would have probably arrived frightened and frantic, rather than calmly calling her mistress to supper. Still, even now it might be worth following the maid home and seeing if he could dredge out of her any additional information about her mistress.

As if she could read his thoughts, *madame* said fiercely, 'If any harm comes to Clara, I will *kill* you.'

Amused at her audacity in daring to threaten him—this slender woman who must weigh barely more than a child and possessed neither strength nor any weapon—Will grinned. 'You could try.'

Her gaze hardened. 'You have no idea what I am capable of, *monsieur*.' Showing him her back, she paced into her lodgings, a wisp of lavender scent lingering in her wake.

Chapter Four

Her heart beating hard, feeling as weak as if she'd run a mile through the twisting Vienna streets, Elodie hurried up the stairway to her rooms. Having placed her basket on a table, Clara was looking at the embroidery Elodie had just completed.

'Ah, *madame*, this is the prettiest yet! The colour's lovely, and the bird so vivid, one almost thinks it will fly off the gown.' Looking up at Elodie, the maid nodded approvingly. 'You've got some colour back in your face. A stroll in the fresh air agreed with you. You must do it more often.'

Elodie wasn't about to reveal that it wasn't the garden air that had brought a flush to her cheeks, but an infuriating, dictatorial, dangerous man.

His touch had almost scalded her. It had been many years since she'd sought or experienced such a physical response. The sensation carried her back to the early days of her love for her late husband, when a mere glance from him could set her body afire.

She shook the memory away before sadness could follow in its wake. Given her reaction to him, travelling in Will Ransleigh's company might be more hazardous to her well-being than she'd first thought. But she could worry about that later; now, she had more immediate matters to address.

'I've brought you a good dinner,' the maid said as she bustled about, putting plates and silverware on the table and lighting candles. 'Frau Luvens made meat pie and some of her apple strudel. You will do it justice now, won't you?'

To her surprise, for the first time in a long time, Elodie found the idea of food appealing. The knowledge that at last, at last, she would be able to stop marking time and get back to Paris, was reviving her vanished appetite. 'You won't have to coax me tonight; it sounds delicious. You are joining me, aren't you? You can tell me all the news.'

While Clara rambled on about her day and her work at the grand hotel where she'd taken employment after her mistress had recovered enough to be left on her own, Elodie edged to the window. Though from this angle, she couldn't see all the way under the balcony, her surreptitious inspection of the garden indicated that Monsieur Ransleigh had indeed departed.

By now, Clara had the covers off the dishes and was waving her to the small table. 'Come, eat before the meat pies get cold. Gruber gave me some extra bread from the hotel kitchen. I'm so glad to see your appetite returning! Just in time, as we'll be able to afford meat more often. Madame Lebruge was so complimentary about your work on the last consignment of embroidery, I told her the next lot would be ten schillings more the piece. She didn't even protest! I should have asked for twenty.'

Elodie seated herself and waited while the maid attacked her meat pie. 'I won't be doing another lot. I'm leaving Vienna.'

Clara's hands stilled and she looked up, wiping savoury juice from her chin. 'Leaving? How? I thought you said it would be months before you could save enough to travel.'

'My plans have changed.' Omitting any mention of threats or the edgy undercurrent between herself and the man, Elodie told Clara about Will Ransleigh's visit and offer to escort her to Paris.

She should have known the maid would be suspicious. 'But can you trust this man, *madame*? How do you know he truly is Monsieur Max Ransleigh's cousin?'

'When you see him, you'll understand; the resemblance between the two men is striking.'

'Why would he wish to do you the favour of taking you to Paris?'

'Because I am to do him a favour in return. I promised I would go to England and testify about how I embroiled his cousin in St Arnaud's plot.'

'*Gott im Himmel, madame!* Is that wise? Is it safe?'

Though she was nearly certain Ransleigh was gone, a well-developed instinct for caution impelled her to lean close and drop her voice to a whisper. 'I have no intention of actually going to London. Once we get to Paris, I shall elude him.'

Clara clapped her hands. 'Ah, yes, and I am sure you shall, now that you've finally recovered your strength! But…should I not go with you as far as Paris? I do not like the idea of you travelling alone with this man about whom we know so little.'

'Thank you, dear friend, but you should stay here. Vienna is your home. You've already done more for me than I ever expected, more than I can ever repay.'

The maid waved a hand dismissively. 'How could I do less, when you were so kind to me? Taking on an untried girl as your dresser, you who had to appear with the cream of society before all Vienna! Nor could I have obtained my present position without all I learned serving you.'

'You've returned many times over any favour I did you.'

'In any case, my lady, you shouldn't travel alone.'

'That might be true…if I were travelling as a "lady". But I shall not be, nor is the journey likely to be comfortable. Perhaps not even safe. I don't know if the watchers will be pleased when they discover I've left Vienna and you've already faced enough danger for me. I must go alone.'

'You are certain?' the maid asked, studying her face.

'Yes,' she replied, clasping Clara's hand. Even if she'd planned to travel as a lady of substance, she wouldn't have allowed Clara to accompany her. Escaping swiftly, drawing out of Vienna whatever forces still kept surveillance over her, was the best way to ensure the safety of the woman who had taken her in and nursed her back to health after she'd been brutalised and abandoned.

'So, no more embroidery,' Elodie said. 'But I'm not completely without resources yet.' Rising, she went to the linen press and extracted two bundles neatly wrapped in muslin. Bringing them to Clara, she said, 'The first is a ball gown I never had a chance to wear; it should fetch a good price. The other is the fanciest of my dinner gowns; I've already re-embroidered it and changed the trimming, so Madame Lebruge should be able easily to resell that as well.'

'Shouldn't you have the money, *madame*? Especially if you mean to travel. I could take these to her tomorrow. She's been so pleased with all the other gowns you've done, I'm sure I could press her for a truly handsome sum.'

'Press her as hard as you like, but keep the money for yourself. It's little enough beside my debt to you. I've something else, too.'

Reaching down to flip up the bottom of her sewing apron, Elodie picked the seam open and extracted a pair of ear-rings. Small diamonds twinkled in the light of the candles. 'Take these. Sell them if you like, or keep them…as a remembrance of our friendship.'

'*Madame*, you mustn't! They're too fine! Besides, you might need to sell them yourself, once you get to Paris.'

'I have a few other pieces left.' Elodie smiled. 'One

can't say much good of St Arnaud, but he never begrudged me the funds to dress the part of his hostess. I can't imagine how I would have survived this year without the jewels and finery we were able to sell.'

The maid spat out a German curse on St Arnaud's head. 'If he'd not been in such a rush to leave Vienna and save his own neck, he would probably have taken them.'

Elodie shrugged. 'Well, I am thankful to have had them, whatever the reason. Now, let me tell you how my departure has been arranged.'

Half an hour later, fully apprised of who she was to meet, when and where, Clara hugged her and walked out. An unnerving silence settled in the rooms after her footsteps faded.

Though she supposed there was no need to work on the gowns the maid had left, from force of habit, Elodie took the top one from the basket and fetched her embroidery silks.

Along with the sale of some gems, the gowns she'd worn as St Arnaud's hostess, re-embroidered and sold back to the shop from which she'd originally purchased them, had supported her for six months. At that point Madame Lebruge, pleased with the elegance and inventiveness of her work, sent new gowns from her shop for Elodie to embellish.

Letting her fingers form the familiar stitches calmed her as she reviewed what had transpired in the last few hours. Clara was right to be suspicious; she had no way of knowing for sure that Will Ransleigh would actually take her to Paris, rather than murdering her in some alley.

But if he'd wanted to dispose of her, he could have already done so. Nor could one fail to note the fervour in his eyes when he talked of righting the wrong she'd done his cousin. She believed he meant to take her to London—and that she'd convinced him she'd not go there unless they went to Paris first.

She smiled; he'd immediately suspected she meant to escape him there. Just because he was Max Ransleigh's cousin, and therefore nephew to an earl, it would not do to underestimate his resourcefulness, or think him hopelessly out of his element in the meaner streets of Paris. He'd tracked her down here, most certainly without assistance from any of the authorities. He'd not been shocked or appalled by her idea of escaping in disguise, only concerned that she couldn't carry off the deception. He'd then proposed an even cleverer disguise, suggesting he was as familiar as she was with subterfuge.

Perhaps he worked for the Foreign Office, as Max had, only in a more clandestine role. Or maybe he was just a rogue, as the unpredictability and sense of danger that hung about him seemed to suggest.

He'd been born on the wrong side of the blanket, he'd said. Perhaps, instead of growing up in the ease of an earl's establishment, he'd had to scrabble for a living, moving from place to place, much as she had. That would explain his housebreaker's skill at scaling balconies and invading rooms.

The notion struck her that they might have much in common.

Swiftly she dismissed that ridiculous thought. She sincerely doubted that *he* had ever had his very life depend on the success of the disguise he employed. Nor should she forget that he'd sought her out for a single purpose, one that left no room for any concern about *her* well-being. Still, depending on what happened in Paris, she might consider going to London as she'd promised.

She would give much to right the wrong she'd been forced to do Max Ransleigh. After studying the background of all of the Duke of Wellington's aides, St Arnaud had determined Max's well-documented weakness for and courtesy towards women made him the best prospect among those with immediate access to Wellington to be of use in his plot. He'd ordered her to establish a relationship with Max, gain his sympathy and learn his movements, so he might be used as a decoy when the time was right.

She'd been instructed to offer him her body if necessary, but it hadn't been. Not that she found Max unappealing as a lover, but having learned he'd already taken one of the most elegant courtesans in Vienna as his mistress, she judged him unlikely to be tempted by a tall, brown-haired woman of no outstanding beauty.

His attentions to her had been initially just the courtesies any diplomat would offer his occasional hostess. Until one day, when she'd been sporting a bruised face and shoulder, and he'd figured out that St Arnaud must have abused her.

She'd told him nothing, of course, but from that moment, his attitude had grown fiercely protective. Rather ironic, she thought, that it had been St Arnaud's foul temper and vindictive spirit, rather than her charms, that had drawn Max closer to her.

In fact, she'd be willing to bet, had the moment not occurred for St Arnaud to spring his plot, Max would have tried to work out an honourable way for her to escape her cousin.

But the moment did occur. As little choice as she'd had in the matter, it still pained her to recall it.

The night of the attack had begun with an afternoon like any other at the Congress, until Max had casually mentioned that he might be late arriving to the Austrian ambassador's ball that evening, since he was to confer briefly in private with the Duke before accompanying him to the festivities. It was the work of a moment for Elodie to inveigle from him in which anteroom that meeting was to take place, the work of another that night to intercept Max in the hallway before he went in.

She waylaid him with a plea that he assist her on some trumped-up matter that would call down on her the wrath of her cousin, should she fail to speedily accomplish it. Despite his concern for her welfare, so great was his impatience to meet his commander, who had a well-known intolerance for tardiness, that she was able to delay him only a few minutes.

It was long enough. St Arnaud's assassin found his target alone, unguarded, and only Wellington's own battle-won sixth sense in dodging away an instant before the stranger bursting into the room fired his weapon, had averted tragedy.

To the Duke, anyway. Captured almost immediately, the failed assassin withstood questioning only briefly before revealing St Arnaud's, and therefore her own, connection to the plot. Assuming the worst, St Arnaud had dealt with her and fled. She'd been in no condition afterwards to discover what had happened to Max; she assumed that, disgraced and reprimanded, he'd been sent back to England.

Dear, courteous Max. Perhaps the kindest man she'd ever known, she thought, conjuring up with a sigh the image of his face. Odd, though, that while he was certainly handsome, she hadn't felt for him the same immediate, powerful surge of desire inspired by his cousin Will.

An attraction so strong it had dazzled her into forgetting, for the first few moments, that he'd invaded her rooms. So strong that, though he'd coerced and threatened her, she felt it still.

It had also been evident, even in his ill-fitting breeches, that the lust he inspired in her was mutual. Elodie felt another flush of heat, just thinking of that sleek hardness, pressing against his trouser front.

Such a response, she suddenly realised, might be useful later, when she needed to escape him. A well-pleasured man would be languid, less than vigilant. And pleasuring Will Ransleigh would be no hardship.

Eluding him in Paris, however, would be another challenge entirely.

Chapter Five

Loitering at the corner, hidden from view by the shadow of an overhanging balcony, and cap well down over the golden hair Madame Lefevre had found so distinctive, Will watched the guard posted at the opposite end of the alley. He'd grab some dinner and return to remain here through the night, noting how many kept watch and when they changed. Although he'd agreed with *madame*'s suggestion that she leave in full daylight, it would be wise to know how many men had been employed to observe her—and might be sent in pursuit when they discovered she'd fled.

He shook his head again over her unexpected talent for intrigue.

Before seeking his dinner, he would question *madame*'s friend Clara. He'd not bothered the girl before, having worked out where *madame* had gone to ground without having to accost the maid. Although the person who'd protected *madame* would likely be the most reluctant to give him any information, after an interview that had given rise to more questions than it answered, it was worth the attempt to extract from the girl anything that might shed more light on the mystery that was Madame Lefevre.

A woman who thus far hadn't behaved as he would have expected of an aristocratic Frenchwoman who'd served as hostess to the most important leaders of European society.

Now that he'd confirmed that the woman he'd found was in fact Madame Lefevre, it was time to re-examine his initial assumptions about her.

The speed with which she'd come up with the suggestion that she escape in disguise—masculine disguise, at that—seemed to indicate she'd donned such a costume before. Recalling the grim expression on her face, Will thought it hadn't been in some amateur theatrical performance for amusement of friends.

'France has been at war longer than we've been alive...' Had her family been caught up in the slaughter leading from monarchy to republic to empire and back? It seemed likely.

He wished now he'd paused in London to plumb for more detail about the St Arnaud family. Thierry St Arnaud's employer, Prince Talleyrand, possessed an exceptional skill for survival, having served as Foreign Minister of France during the Republic, Consulate, Empire and now the Restoration. At the Congress of Vienna, the Prince had even managed the unlikely feat of persuading Britain and Austria that France, a country those two allies had fought for more than twenty years, should become their partner against Russia and Prussia.

What remarkable tricks of invention had the St Arnaud clan performed to retain lands and titles through the bloodbath of revolution and empire?

Perhaps, rather than spending her girlhood tucked away at some genteel country estate, *madame*'s aristocratic family, like so many others, had been forced to escape the guillotine's blade. They might even have fled to England; the British crown had supported a large *émigré* community. That would explain her excellent, almost accentless speech.

Or perhaps she was such a mistress of invention because she was one of Talleyrand's agents. His gut churned at that unpleasant possibility.

But though Will wouldn't totally discount the idea, Talleyrand was known to be an exacting master. It wouldn't be like the prince to leave a loose end—like a former agent—flapping alone in the Viennese breeze for over a year; Madame Lefevre would likely have been eliminated or spirited away long since.

Still, it wouldn't be amiss to behave around her as if she had a professional's expertise.

He smiled. That would make the matching of wits all the sweeter. And if the opportunity arose to intertwine bodies as well, that would be the sweetest yet.

But enough of carnal thoughts. He couldn't afford to let lust and curiosity make him forget his goal, or lure him into being less than vigilant. He was certain she intended to try to escape him during their journey, and he'd need to be on his best game to ensure she did not.

As he reached that conclusion, Clara exited *madame*'s lodgings. Keeping into the shadow of the buildings, Will followed her.

To his good fortune, since the onset of evening and the thinning crowds would make it harder to trail her unobserved, the maid headed for the neighbouring market. He shadowed her as she snapped up the last of the day's bread, cheese and apples at bargain prices from vendors eager to close up for the night.

The Viennese were a prosperous lot, he noted as he trailed a few stalls behind her, and remarkably careless with their purses. Had he a mind to, he could have snatched half a dozen as he strolled along.

Unable to resist the temptation to test his skill and thinking it might make a good introduction, Will nipped from behind the maid to snag her coin purse while she lingered by the last stall, bidding farewell to the vendor and rearranging the purchases in her market basket.

He followed her from the market until she reached a mostly deserted stretch of street, where the buildings' overhanging second storeys created a shadowy recess. Picking up his pace, Will strode past her and then turned, herding her towards the wall. With a deep bow, he held out the coin purse.

'Excuse me, miss, I believe you dropped this.'

With a gasp, she shrank back, then halted. 'Why… it is my purse! I was sure I put it back into my reticule!

How can I thank you, Herr…' Belatedly looking up, she got a glimpse of his face. 'You!'

Will bowed again. 'Will Ransleigh, at your service, miss.'

Alarm battled anger in her face. 'I should call the authorities and have you arrested for theft!'

He raised an eyebrow. 'How could you do that, when I've just returned your purse? If officials in Vienna arrest every fellow who follows a pretty girl, the jails would be full to overflowing. I mean you no harm.'

She sniffed. 'I note you don't deny you took it! But seeing as how you could have just as easily knocked me over the head as given it back, I suppose I'll not scream the houses down—for the moment. What do you want?'

'I intend to help your mistress leave the city.'

She looked him up and down, her expression wary. 'I warned her not to trust you. Oh, I don't doubt you'll help her, all right—to do what *you* want her to. Just like that worthless cousin of hers.'

Remembering *madame*'s bent and swollen fingers, Will felt a surge of dislike. If he ever encountered Thierry St Arnaud, he'd force the man to test his strength against a more fitting adversary. 'He intimidated her, didn't he?'

'Bastard.' The maid spat on cobblestones. 'I only saw him strike her twice, but she almost always had bruises. I'll not hurt her more by telling you anything.'

'I appreciate your loyalty. But whatever you can tell me—about her relationship with St Arnaud or my cousin—will help me protect her on the journey. I can do a better job if I'm aware of potential threats before they happen. If I know who's been watching her, and why.'

Her expression clouded, telling Will she worried about her mistress, too. 'Herr Ransleigh, your cousin, was an honourable man,' she said after a moment. 'You promise to keep her safe?'

'I promise.' To his surprise, Will found he meant it.

Clara studied him, obviously still reluctant.

'You want her to stay safe, too, don't you?' he coaxed. 'How about I tell you what I know and you just confirm it?'

After considering another moment, the maid nodded.

'You've been with your mistress more than a year. She engaged you when she first arrived in Vienna— September 1814, wasn't it?'

Clara nodded.

'That last night, before her cousin fled the city, he… hurt her.'

Tears came to the girl's eyes. 'Yes,' she whispered.

'Badly?' Will pressed, keeping a tight rein over his rising temper, almost certain now he knew what she would tell him.

'She was unconscious when I found her. Her ribs broken for sure, and her arm and hand bent and twisted. Didn't come back to herself for more than a day, and for the first month, I wasn't sure she would survive. Bastard!' the maid burst out again. 'Blaming her for the failure of his foolish plan! Or maybe just taking it out on her that it failed. He was that kind.'

'You took her from the hotel to rooms at a boarding house and nursed her. Then, once she'd recovered sufficiently, you moved her to the lodgings here,' Will summed up the trail his search had taken him on.

'By then, she said she was recovered enough to work. I'd sold jewels for her those first few months, until her bad hand healed enough for her to use the fingers. She started doing embroidery then.'

'And there were watchers, each place you stayed with her?'

'I guess there were, though I didn't notice them until she pointed them out after she got better. I was frightened, but what could they want with her? After a few months, I got used to them hanging about.'

'Viennese lads, they were.'

'Yes. I spoke to some of them, trying to see if I could find out anything, but they seemed to know only that a local man hired them. I'm certain someone more important was behind it, but I don't know who.'

Will filed that observation away. 'Why is she so insistent on returning to Paris?'

'Her family's there, I expect. She never spoke about herself, nor was she the sort who thought only of her own comfort. Waiting for her at the dressmakers or at those grand balls, I heard other maids talking about their ladies. *Madame* wasn't like most of them, always difficult and demanding. She was kind. She noticed people and their troubles.'

Her eyes far away, Clara smiled. 'One night, Klaus the footman had a terrible head cold, hardly able to breathe, poor man. *Madame* only passed by him in the hall on her way to a reception, but first thing the next morning, she had me fetch herbs and made him a tisane. Not that she made a great fuss about doing so, playing Lady Bountiful. No, she just turned it over to the butler and told him to make sure Klaus drank it.'

'Did you ever wonder why she'd not brought her own maid to Vienna?'

Clara shrugged. 'Maybe the woman didn't want to travel so far. Maybe she couldn't afford to bring her. I don't think she had any coin of her own. St Arnaud paid my wages, all the bills for jewels, gowns and the household expenses, but he gave her no pin money at all. She didn't have even a few schillings to buy ices when we were out.'

So, as she'd claimed, Will noted, *madame had* been entirely dependent on St Arnaud. 'She never spoke of any other relations?'

'No. But if they were all like St Arnaud, I understand why she wouldn't.' The maid stopped abruptly, wrinkling her brow. 'There was one person she mentioned. Several times, when I'd given her laudanum for the pain after St Arnaud had struck her, she murmured a name as she dozed. Philippe.'

Surprise and something barbed and sharp stung him in the gut. Impatiently he dismissed it. 'Husband... brother...lover?'

'Not her husband—St Arnaud said he'd died in the wars. I did once ask her who "Philippe" was, but she just smiled and made no answer, and I didn't want to press. She sounded…longing. Maybe he's someone she wanted to marry, that her cousin had refused; I can see him sending away anyone he didn't think grand enough for the St Arnauds. Maybe St Arnaud promised if she helped him in Vienna, he would let her marry the man. I know he had some sort of power to force her to do his will.'

For some reason he'd rather not examine, Will didn't like the idea of Madame Lefevre pining for a Parisian lover. Shaking his head to rid himself of the image, he said, '*Madame*'s dependence on St Arnaud for food, clothing, housing and position would have been enough to coerce her co-operation.'

'No, it was more than that,' Clara insisted. 'Not that she didn't appreciate fine silks and pretty gems—who would not? But when she had to, she sold them without any sign of regret. She seemed quite content to live simply, not missing in the least the grand society for whom she used to play hostess. All she spoke about was earning enough coin to return to Paris.'

Not wishing to hear any more speculation about the mysterious "Philippe", Will changed direction. 'She's had no contact with St Arnaud since the night of the attack, then?'

The maid shuddered. 'Better that he believe she died of her injuries. She came close enough.'

'St Arnaud emigrated to the Caribbean afterwards.'

'That, I can't say. I only know he left Vienna that night. If there's any justice in the world, someone somewhere caught him and he's rotting in prison.'

Clara looked up, meeting his gaze squarely. 'If God has any mercy, once she's done what you want, you'll let her go back to Paris. To this Philippe, whoever he is. After all she's suffered, losing her husband, enduring St Arnaud's abuse, she deserves some happiness.'

Will wasn't about to assure the maid he'd send *madame* back—to Paris or her 'Philippe'—until he'd finished with her. And resolved what had already flared between them.

Instead, he pulled out a coin. 'Thank you, Clara. I appreciate—'

'No need for that,' the maid interrupted, waving the money away. 'Use it to keep her safe. You will watch out for her, won't you? I know if someone wished her ill, they could have moved against her any time this last year. But still…I worry. She's such a gentle soul, too innocent for this world, perhaps.'

Will remembered the woman in the garden, quietly picking spent blooms from her flowers while a stranger decided whether or not to wring her neck. She was more *resigned* than gentle or innocent, he thought. As if life had treated her so harshly, she simply accepted evil and injustice, feeling there was little she could do to protect herself from it.

Since his earliest days on the streets, Will had faced down bullies and fought to right wrongs when he found them. Picturing that calm face bent over the blooms and the brutal hand St Arnaud had raised against it, Will felt a surge of protectiveness he didn't want to feel.

No point getting all worked up over her little tragedy;

if she'd ended up abused, she'd played her role with full knowledge of the possible consequences, he reminded himself. Unlike Max, who'd been lured in unawares and betrayed by his own nobility.

And of course the maid thought her a heroine. If she could take in Max, who was nobody's fool, it would have been child's play for her to win over a simple, barely educated girl who depended on her for employment.

Suppressing the last of his sympathy towards Madame Lefevre, he nodded a dismissal to her maid. 'I'll meet you at the inn in two days.'

Clara nodded. 'The old man's disguise—you're sure you can carry it off?'

'Can she carry off hers?'

'She can do whatever she must. She already has. Good-night, sir.' With an answering nod, the girl walked into the gathering night.

Will turned back towards the inn where he planned to procure dinner, mulling over what he'd learned from Clara.

According to the maid, *madame* had been brought, without other money or resources, to Vienna and forced to do St Arnaud's bidding. She cared little about wealth or high position. Her sole ambition was to return to Paris…and 'Philippe'.

She can do whatever she must, the maid had said. Apparently, betraying Max Ransleigh had been one of those things. Eluding Will and cheating Max of the vindication due him might be another.

She was surely counting on trying to escape him, if not on the road, then once they arrived in Paris. He'd need to remain vigilant to make sure she did not.

From the maid's reactions, it seemed even she feared the watchers might not be pleased to have her mistress leave Vienna. Madame Lefevre might well have other enemies in addition to the angry cousin of the man she'd ruined.

Her masculine disguise, which he'd first accepted almost as a jest, now looked like a prudent precaution.

For a moment, he envisioned *madame*'s slender body encased in breeches that outlined her legs, curved over thigh and calf, displayed the turn of an ankle. His mouth watered and his body hardened.

But he couldn't allow lustful thoughts to distract him—yet. His sole focus now must be on getting her safely to Paris. Because until they reached London, he meant to ensure no one *else* harmed her.

Chapter Six

Late in the afternoon two days later, garbed in the clothing of an old gentleman, wearing spectacles so thick she could hardly see and leaning heavily on a cane, Elodie let Clara help her into the taproom of a modest inn on the western outskirts of Vienna. As the innkeeper bustled over to welcome them, Will Ransleigh strode in.

'Uncle Fritz, so glad you could join me! The trip from Linz was not too tiring, I trust?'

In a voice pitched as low as she could make it, Elodie replied, 'Tolerable, my boy.'

'Good. Herr Schultz,' he addressed the innkeeper, 'bring some refreshment to our room, please. Josephine, let's help our uncle up.'

With Clara at one arm and Will Ransleigh at the other, Elodie slowly shuffled up the stairs.

Not until she'd entered the sitting room Ransleigh had hired and heard the door shut behind her did she breathe a sigh of relief. The first step of her escape had proceeded without a hitch. Exultation and a rising excitement sent her spirits soaring.

As she sank into a chair and pulled off the distorting spectacles, she looked up to see Will Ransleigh's expression warm with a smile of genuine approval that gratified her even as her stomach fluttered in response. His expression serious, he was arresting, but with that smile—oh, my! How did any woman resist him?

'Bravo, *madame*. I had grave doubts, but I have to admit, you made a wonderfully credible old man.'

'You made a rather fine old gentleman yourself,' she said, smiling back at him. 'I wouldn't have recognised you if you'd not arrived with Clara. You were a wizard with the blacking as well, going from white-powdered hair to brunette faster than I could don the clothing you provided. Now I see you've transformed yourself yet again.'

Though he'd kept his hair darkened with blacking, he'd changed from the modest working-man's attire he'd worn the day he climbed up her balcony into gentleman's garb, well cut and of quality material, but not so elegant or fashionable as to attract undue notice.

Still, the close-fitting jacket emphasised the breadth of shoulders and the snug pantaloons displayed muscled thighs. If he'd appeared powerfully, dangerously masculine in his drab clerk's disguise, the effect was magnified several times over in dress that better revealed his strength and physique.

His potent masculine allure ambushed Elodie anew, intensifying the flutter in her stomach and igniting a heated tremor below. She found herself wondering how it would feel to run her fingers along those muscled arms and thighs, over the taut abdomen…and lower. While her lips explored his jaw and cheekbones, the line of brow over those vivid turquoise eyes…

Realising she was staring, she hastily turned her gaze away.

Not fast enough that he didn't notice her preoccupation, though. A satisfied gleam in his eye, he said, 'I hope you approve of the latest transformation.'

'You're looking very fine, sir, and don't you know it,' Clara interposed tartly. 'Ah, mistress, didn't you make a marvellous old gent! I believe we could have met Frau Gruener herself on the stairs without her being the wiser.'

'It's just as well we didn't. I'm no Mrs Siddons,' Elodie said, arching to stretch out a back cramped from bending over a cane during their long, dawdling transit.

'What do you know of Mrs Siddons?' Will asked, giving her a suspicious look.

Cursing her slip, Elodie said, 'Only that she was much praised by the English during theatrical entertainments at the Congress, who claimed no Viennese actress could compare. With your expertise in disguises, I begin to believe you've trod the boards yourself. Is that how you found this moustache?' Stripping off the length of fuzzy wool, she rubbed her lip. 'It itched terribly, making me sneeze so hard, I feared it would fall off.'

'My apologies for the deficiencies in your costume,' he replied sardonically. 'I shall try to do better next time.'

'See that you do,' she flashed back, relieved to have detoured him from any further probing about her familiarity with the English stage.

'I don't wonder your back is tired,' Clara said. 'I don't know this quarter of Vienna and you could hardly see behind those spectacles. The transit seemed to take so long, once or twice I feared we might be lost.'

'No danger of that; I shadowed you all the way and would have set you straight if you'd strayed,' Ransleigh said. 'I also wanted to make sure you were not followed.'

Reassured by his thoroughness, Elodie said, 'We weren't, were we?'

'No. It was a good plan you came up with.'

Elodie felt a flush of warmth at his avowal and chastised herself. She wasn't a giddy girl, to be gratified by a handsome man's approval. She needed to remember the purpose for which he'd arranged this escape—that hadn't been done for *her* benefit.

Despite that acknowledgment, some of the warmth remained.

A knock sounded at the door and Elodie turned away, averting her now moustache-less face until the servant bringing in the refreshments had deposited the tray and bowed himself back out.

'Shall we dine?' Ransleigh invited. 'The inn is said to set a good table.'

Elodie shook her head wonderingly. 'Just how do you manage to discover such things?'

He gave her an enigmatic smile. 'I'm a man of many talents.'

'So I am discovering.' She wished she could resist being impressed by his mastery of detail, but fairness wouldn't allow it.

'*Fraulein*, will you join us before you leave?'

At the maid's nod, they seated themselves around the table. Since their previous exchanges had been limited to threats on her life and plans for escaping Vienna, Elodie wondered whether—and about what—Ransleigh would talk during the meal.

Somewhat to her surprise, he kept up a flow of conversation, discussing the sights of Vienna and asking Clara about her experiences with the notables she'd encountered during the Congress.

Will Ransleigh truly was a man of many talents. He seemed as comfortable drawing out a lady's maid as he might be entertaining a titled lady in his uncle the earl's drawing room. If he did, in fact, frequent the earl's drawing room.

He claimed he'd been born on the wrong side of the blanket, but his speech and manners were those of the aristocracy. Where was he in his true element? she wondered. Skulking around the modest neighbourhoods of a great city, chatting up maids and innkeepers, or dancing at balls among the wealthy and powerful?

Or in both?

He was still an enigma. And since she was forced to place her safety in his hands, at least until Paris, that troubled her.

Their meal concluded, Clara rose. 'I'd best be getting home. It will be dark soon and I don't know these streets.'

'I'll escort you,' Ransleigh said.

'I'd not put you to the trouble,' Clara protested.

'Of course he will,' Elodie interrupted, relieved by the offer and determined to have him honour it. 'I'd like him to accompany you all the way home…and make sure there's no unexpected company to welcome you,' she added, voicing the uneasiness that had grown since she'd successfully escaped her lodgings.

'Your mistress is right. Though I don't think her flight has yet been discovered, we should take precautions,' Ransleigh said. 'Once whoever has set a guard realises she has left the city, they'll probably come straight to you.'

Dismay flooded her. All her attention consumed by the magnificent prospect of returning to Paris, Elodie hadn't imagined that possibility. Turning to Ransleigh, she said anxiously, 'Should we take Clara with us, for her own safety?'

'I don't think she needs to leave, though she might well be questioned. If we're lucky, not until we're well away. She can then tell them truthfully that a certain Will Ransleigh urged you to accompany him to London and met you at this inn, but how or with whom you left it and in which direction, she has no idea. After all, if they want anyone, it's you, not her.'

'Are you sure? I'd thought my leaving, drawing after me whatever threat might still remain, would keep her safe. But what if I'm wrong?' Elodie turned to Clara, still torn. 'If anyone harmed you—'

'Don't distress yourself, *madame*,' Ransleigh interrupted. 'I've already engaged a man to watch over the *fraulein* until he's sure she's in no further danger. A solid lad, a former Austrian soldier I knew from the army. He's waiting below to help me escort her home.'

'Thank you, sir.' Clara dipped Ransleigh a curtsy— the first sign of respect she'd accorded him. 'I never expected such a thing, but I can't deny it makes me feel easier.'

Surprised, touched and humbled, Elodie felt like curtsying, too. *She* should have realised it was necessary to guarantee Clara's safety after their departure. Instead, this man she'd viewed as concerned only with achieving his own purposes had had the forethought— and compassion—to arrange it.

In her experience, aristocrats such as St Arnaud viewed servants as objects put on earth to provide for their comfort, like horses or linens or furniture. Her cousin would never have seen Clara as a *person*, or concerned himself with her welfare.

Ransleigh had not only anticipated the possible danger, he'd arranged to protect Clara after their departure, when the maid was of no further use to him.

She couldn't prevent her opinion of his character from rising a notch higher.

Still, she mustn't let herself be lured into trusting in his thoroughness, competence and compassion—qualities that attracted her almost as much as his physical allure. They were still a long way from Paris.

Before Elodie could sort out her tangled thoughts, Clara had wrapped herself in her cloak. Elodie's previous high spirits vanished as she faced parting for ever from the last, best friend she possessed.

'I suppose this is farewell, *madame*,' Clara said, a brave smile on her face. 'I wish you a safe journey— and joy, when you get to Paris at last!'

Unable to summon words, Elodie hugged her. The maid hugged her back fiercely, blinking away tears when at last Elodie released her. 'I'll try to send word after I'm settled.'

'Good. I'd like to know that you were home—and *safe*,' she added, that last with a meaningful look at Ransleigh.

'Shall we go, *fraulein*?' Ransleigh asked.

Smiling, Clara gave her a curtsy. 'Goodbye, *madame*. May the blessed angels watch over you.'

'And you, my dear friend,' Elodie replied.

'After you, *fraulein*,' Ransleigh prompted gently as they both stood there, frozen. 'Your soldier awaits.'

Nodding agreement, Clara stepped towards the door, then halted to look at him searchingly. 'Maybe I was wrong. Maybe *madame* should trust you.'

Much as she told herself that after a lifetime of partings and loss, she should be used to it, Elodie felt a painful squeezing in her chest as she listened to their footsteps echo on the stairs. When the last sound faded, she ran to the window.

Peeping around the curtain, so as to be hidden from the view of anyone who might look up from the street, she watched three figures emerge from the inn: Ransleigh, Clara and a burly man who looked like a prizefighter. As they set off through the darkness, the thought struck her that Ransleigh, moving with the fluid, powerful stride of a predator on the prowl, seemed the more dangerous of the two men.

Elodie's spirits sagged even lower as she watched Clara disappear into the darkness. The maid had been her friend, companion and saviour for more than a year.

Now, she'd be alone with Ransleigh. For better or worse.

She got herself this far, she'd make it the rest of the way, she told herself bracingly. And at the end of this journey…was Philippe.

With that rallying thought, she settled in to wait for Ransleigh's return.

Chapter Seven

The maid conveyed safely to her lodging where, fortunately, there had been no one waiting to intercept her, Will left Heinrich on watch and headed back to the inn. Their room above the entry was dark when he glanced up at the window before entering.

He'd already paid the proprietor, explaining he planned an early departure. In truth, he intended for them to leave Vienna during the blackest part of the night. Since it appeared *madame* was already asleep, he'd slip in quietly, letting her get as much rest as she could before what would be an arduous journey.

Taking care to make no sound that might attract the attention of the innkeeper serving customers in the tap-room beyond, he crossed the entry and silently ascended the stairs. As he eased through the door into their room, the dim outline of something by the far wall had him reaching for his knife, until he realised what he'd sensed more than seen in the darkness was Madame Lefevre.

'I thought you'd be resting,' he said, closing the door quietly behind him.

'I couldn't sleep until I knew our plans. And I wanted to thank you for seeing to Clara's safety. That was generous of you…and unexpected. I'm very grateful.'

'She being an innocent in all this, I'd not want to be responsible for causing her any harm.'

Harm coming to *madame* he had less of a problem with, he thought. But if she were threatened, it would be after conviction for crimes committed, her punishment determined by the rule of law, not by an attack in some back alley.

Crossing to the window, he made sure the curtains were securely drawn. Lighting a taper, he said, 'I think we can chance one candle.'

As it flared to life, he saw Elodie Lefevre, still in old man's attire, seated in the corner next to the window—her back to the wall, beside the quickest exit from the inn. The very spot he would have chosen, were he required to wait alone in this room, unsure of what danger might threaten.

While he wondered whether she'd seated herself there by design or accident, she said, 'What have you planned for tomorrow?'

'Actually, I've planned for tonight. As soon as all is quiet downstairs and in the street, we will slip out by the kitchen door into the mews. I checked last night; no one keeps watch there. We'll be out of the city and along the road to Linz well before daylight.'

Madame nodded. 'The sooner we begin, the sooner we arrive.'

'When he travelled from Paris to Vienna for the Congress, Wellington made it in just ten days…but he only slept four hours a night. Though I don't mean to dawdle, I'm allowing a bit longer.'

'I'm ready to travel as quickly as you wish. Much as I enjoyed limping on my cane, though, I think another change of costume would be wise.'

Will had a strong sense that this wasn't the first time Elodie Lefevre had fled from pursuit. Had the Revolution forced her family out of France? She would have been scarcely more than a babe during the Terror.

Quelling for now the urge to question her further, he said, 'What do you have in mind?'

'If anyone interrogates the innkeeper, they'll be looking for a young gentleman accompanied by an older man. If that trail goes cold, they would probably next seek a man and a woman posing as a married couple or lovers or siblings or cousins. Whatever explanation we used, if I travel as a female with no maid and only a single male companion, we'll attract notice, making it much more likely that innkeepers and stable boys and barmaids at taverns and posting inns will remember us.'

'What makes you think we'll be stopping at taverns or posting inns?' he asked, teasing her to cover his surprise about her knowledge of the realities of travel. Had she spent her whole life eluding pursuers?

Ignoring the remark, she continued, 'We could pose as an older woman and her maid, but it's still unusual for women to travel without a male escort, to say nothing of the difficulty of your being convincing in either role for any length of time. So I think our best alternative would be for you to remain as you are, a young gentleman, and I will travel as your valet. Men travel the posting roads all the time; you'd be just one more of many and no one pays attention to servants.'

Her scheme for leaving her lodgings had been good; this one was even better. Trying to suppress the admiration he didn't wish to feel, Will said, 'You think you could play the role of valet better than I could that of an old woman?'

She nodded. 'Much more easily. As I said, a woman of any age travelling would excite curiosity, while a valet would be virtually invisible. Whether we stay at an inn—or under a tree or in a hedgerow,' she added with a quirk of a smile at him. 'And if we need to make a hasty exit, it will be much easier if I'm not encumbered by skirts.'

Will couldn't imagine any of the aristocratic ladies of his acquaintance—Alastair's mother or sisters, for example—inventing so unorthodox a scheme or proposing it in such a straightforward, unemotional manner. 'Why do I have the feeling you've done this before?'

A faraway look came into her eyes, and for a long moment, while he hung on her answer, she remained silent. 'I've had to come up with…contrivances upon occasion,' she said at last.

Which told him nothing. *Where have you been and*

what have you done? Will wondered. 'You're a most unusual woman, Madame Lefevre.'

She gave him a faint smile, but said only, 'These old man's garments will suffice until we can procure others. I've kept two gowns in my portmanteau, in case I might need them before we arrive at Paris. Have you a route in mind?'

Will stifled a pang of disappointment that she'd not responded to his compliment by telling him more about her life. His curiosity fanned ever hotter by each new revelation, he was by now eager to discover what events had shaped her.

Maybe along the way, he'd figure it out, find a way to fit the puzzle pieces together. Or, even better, maybe along the way he'd lure her into trusting him enough to volunteer the information.

It would only be prudent to arm himself with as much knowledge about her as possible. As long as he kept in mind that anything she revealed might contain more craftiness than truth.

'Have *you* a route in mind? Your suggestions thus far have been excellent.'

She dropped her gaze and, though he couldn't tell for sure in the dim candlelight, he thought she flushed. 'Thank you,' she said gruffly. 'I've only travelled this way once, when I accompanied St Arnaud, so I don't know the road. It would be wise, I think, to keep as much as possible to the larger cities, where one gentleman will hardly be noticed among the host of travellers. Have you the means to hire horses? It would make the journey faster.'

'A gentleman travelling with his valet would more likely travel by coach.'

'Not if the valet were a bruising rider. The further and faster from Vienna we travel, the safer we'll be from pursuit.'

Will wasn't so sure. If Talleyrand were keeping tabs on *madame*, they would be more vulnerable the closer they got to Paris. But he didn't want to voice that fact, adding more anxiety to what must already be a difficult situation, with her poised to assume yet another false identity. Despite the maid's assertion that she could do 'whatever she had to', he didn't want to push her too hard and risk having her fall apart.

'Very well; I'll travel as a young gentleman. "Monsieur LeClair", shall we say? And you will be my valet, "Pierre".'

'"LeClair"?' she repeated, a slow smile lighting her face. 'Very good, considering nothing about this journey is "clear" or straightforward!'

The honest delight on her face, so strikingly different from the expressionless calm with which she usually concealed her feelings, struck Will near his breastbone with the force of a blow. Warmth blossomed in its wake. Damn and blast, he didn't want to start…liking her!

While he wrestled with his reaction, she continued, 'I'm pleased you approve my plan.'

'For the time being, subject to change as I feel necessary,' he cautioned, pulling himself back together.

'I've got horses waiting at an inn on the edge of Vienna. With hard travel, we may reach the outskirts of Linz by late tomorrow.'

'Excellent. You are very thorough, *monsieur*,' she said approvingly. 'Anything else I should know?'

'No, Pierre; we'd better get a few hours' sleep. I'll rouse you when it's time. You use the bed.'

'Oh, no, *monsieur*, that would never do. Your valet should occupy a pallet at the foot of the bed. I've left the wig and cane over there—' she indicated the dining table '—for you to return to your store of trickeries.'

Flinging the blanket she'd held in her lap over her shoulders, she crossed to the bed and settled herself on the floor by the footboard—back to the wall, with a clear view of both the window and the door, he noted. '*Bonsoir*, Monsieur LeClair.'

'*Bonsoir*, Pierre.'

She closed her eyes. Within a few moments, the even sound of her breathing indicated she must have fallen asleep.

Will should sleep, too. He had only a few hours before he needed to be up, all his wits about him, ready to spirit them out of the inn unobserved or to improvise some sleight of hand, should that be necessary for them to escape pursuit. But as he blew out the candle and lay down on the bed, Will found slumber elusive.

Partly, it was his ever-deepening curiosity about Elodie Lefevre. What remarkable experiences had shaped this woman who noticed watchers at her corner, came up with plans for escape and evasion and talked of disguises as casually as another woman might discuss attending the theatre or purchasing a bonnet?

When he compared her reactions to the emotion-driven behaviour of the women he'd known, he was struck again by her calm. After leaving the only friend she knew, about to creep away with a virtual stranger in the middle of the night, she'd displayed no more than a natural sadness at parting from the maid. There'd been no panic, no fretting over whether she was doing the right thing. No worrying over her ability to carry out her part in the deception, no endless questioning over what was to happen next and—praise Heaven!—no tears. She hadn't even called down evil upon his head for forcing her into this.

Instead, she'd made a single terse compliment about his thoroughness.

'You truly are an amazing woman, Elodie Lefevre,' he told her sleeping form. *But I'd be an idiot to trust you.*

She had paid him one other compliment in their short acquaintance—she'd called him 'striking'.

For the last few hours, the urgency of getting her out of her lodgings and the necessity of planning their escape had helped him dam up his strong physical response to her. But in the darkness, safe for the moment and all plans in place, that one memory was enough to send desire flooding over the barriers.

Despite the contrivance of having her travel as his

'valet', with her bundled at his feet, her soft breaths filling the silence and the subtle scent of lavender beguiling his nose, it was impossible for him to think of Elodie Lefevre as anything other than a woman. A woman made even more alluring by her unique, exceptional abilities.

A woman he wanted.

He stifled a groan as, despite his fatigue, his body hardened. His mind might be urging him to review each detail of their upcoming journey, but his body was recalling the softness of her neck under his fingers, the surge of connection between them when she took his hand.

Damn and blast, what had begun as a grim mission to vindicate Max had become a challenge that filled him with unanticipated excitement. He relished the idea of being on the road with her, overcoming whatever dangers arose, discovering bit by bit more pieces to the puzzle that was Elodie. At the same time, he must maintain a delicate balance between his growing fascination and the necessity to stay vigilant, lest she lull him into complacency and play him for a fool.

And then there was lust. With an anticipation so intense it ought to alarm him, he looked forward to sharing a room with her at the posting inns—and all the enticing possibilities for seduction that offered.

But when he recalled the disguises they'd agreed upon, he had to stifle a laugh. She could have contrived no better way to keep his amorous impulses at bay. They could hardly travel unnoticed if he was seen to be openly lusting after his valet!

He'd just have to get her back into maiden's attire as soon as possible.

Chapter Eight

Five days later, in a small inn south of Stuttgart along the road to Paris, Elodie loitered in a dim, smoky corner of the taproom, mug of ale in hand. Will sat at a table in the centre, gaming with a disparate group of fellow travellers.

Wearing gentleman's attire, the only disguise he employed was hair-blacking, there being nothing he could do beyond keeping his face downcast to camouflage those remarkable eyes. He lounged with cravat askew, long legs outstretched in an indolent pose, as he held the cards before him.

To a casual observer, he appeared to be just another young man who'd decided to go adventuring now that Napoleon's wars no longer threatened the Continent. A younger son of good family, probably, well born but not important or wealthy enough to require an entourage. A young man seemingly indifferent to his comfort—and that of his humble valet, since he'd chosen to ride on this journey, rather than spend the additional blunt necessary to hire a carriage.

It was an image he'd calculated with care. But Elodie, now better attuned, knew that despite his lazy stance, Will keenly observed every detail of the men in the room and the inn itself, always assessing possible threats, ready to make a quick exit in case of danger. Much as she herself did.

From the beginning of their odyssey, she'd watched him intently, at first apprehensive, since she'd had to commit her safety into his hands. By now she'd relaxed a bit, appreciating the high level of alertness he maintained—with remarkably little sleep—and the care he took to evaluate their surroundings and the people with whom they came into contact.

For as long as she could remember, *she'd* been the one who had to be vigilant to protect herself and those she loved. How much easier it was for a man, who could interact with innkeepers and barmaids and grooms and tradesmen virtually unnoticed, as a woman could not. She'd even allowed—if only to herself—that his skill at disguise, invention and evasion equalled her own.

She was beginning to believe that Will Ransleigh would get her safely to Paris after all.

Though she must never forget he was expending all that effort for his own purposes.

Over the last few days, they'd worked out a routine, riding hard by day, not choosing an inn for the night until well after dark, by which time she was so weary she almost fell out of the saddle. In the early dawn,

Will would arrange fresh horses and buy food to carry with them for the next day, and they'd take their meals by the roadside.

She smiled into the darkness. Breaking their fast in the open might have been a dreary, rushed affair, but in Ransleigh's company, the meals had assumed almost a picnic atmosphere. She had to admit she was intrigued by him. Though she herself said little, with a bit of prompting, she'd persuaded him to regale her with tales of his many adventures.

He was a marvellous storyteller, his vivid descriptions making her feel she was reliving the episodes with him. He had her laughing at his account of dismal billets and narrow escapes from marauders on the Peninsula, the comic ballet of Brussels packed to the gills with foreigners. Unknowing, he fed her starved soul with details of the Paris he'd explored before Napoleon slipped his leash at Elba and plunged France back into war.

Notably missing among his tales, however, was any mention of his origins. Which was only fair, since she'd divulged absolutely nothing about herself. But she'd grown increasingly curious to know more about the man, as the relationship of captor and—though willing—captive subtly began to alter, until it now verged dangerously close to camaraderie.

Which was perhaps the point of his tall tales. Perhaps he was trying to earn her trust, beguile her into thinking of him as a friend, a companion…a lover?

Tightness coiled in her belly and she blessed again the disguise that required them to stay at arm's length during the day, the arduous long rides that made her fall asleep almost instantly when she could finally rest for the night.

Otherwise, the two of them alone in the secret darkness… She didn't think she could have resisted the temptation to taste those sculpted lips that she watched, fascinated, as he spun his tales, acutely conscious of his sheer masculine power and the fierce pull of attraction between them. Resisted the desire to run her fingers down the muscled thighs she watched day after day control his mount with effortless precision. Denied herself the chance to explore the naked torso of which she caught only teasing glimpses when he pulled off his shirt to wash in the early mornings.

Did he wait to do that until he knew she was awake, deliberately tempting her?

Over the years, she'd used her body when necessary and, more often, had it used without her consent. It had been a very long time since she'd *wanted* a man.

But she wanted Will Ransleigh. In his smoky gaze when no one was watching them, in the lingering caress of fingers on her arm or hand the few times touching her had been necessary, she knew he wanted her, too.

The day of reckoning was coming when that mutual desire would no longer have to be denied. Heaven help her, how she *burned* for it!

But that time wasn't here…yet. They were still too far from Paris. And she was still too far from deciding just how—and when—she would seduce Will Ransleigh.

Tonight, announcing he needed to replenish their

funds with a little gaming, Will had insisted, despite her fatigue, that she remain in the taproom and linger in the shadows. So she would be close at hand, in case they needed to leave the inn in a hurry.

She'd forced herself to stay awake by watching the game, counting cards and points. She'd been annoyed to discover she must admire Will Ransleigh's prowess at cards, too.

With the same precision he analysed rooms and roads, he surveyed his opponents with that deceptively disinterested, downcast gaze. Having watched the game for several hours, Elodie was convinced he'd worked out just how much he could win from each opponent without straining their purses enough to provoke a belligerent response and just how much overall so as not to have his skill excite comment. He bolstered her belief by deliberately losing a hand from time to time and by his occasional crows of triumph when he won, as if winning were a surprise. Whereas, she was certain he could have fleeced all his opponents, had he chosen to.

Clara had told her how he'd lifted her purse at the market.

Would he have the skill to fleece her, when the time came? Smiling faintly, she thought of Will removing the rough, scratchy man's garb, covering her mouth with his, her body with his, parting her legs to bare to his touch and possession that hottest, most needy place...

The cold splash of ale on her knee jerked her back to awareness. Lost in sensual imagining, she'd drifted off and nearly dropped her mug. Alarmed to have come close to creating a commotion that would have attracted unwelcome attention, she looked up to find Will staring at her.

Elodie froze; not wishing to bring her to anyone's notice, Will never looked directly at her when in company.

'Pierre, take yourself up to the room before you shatter the mug—or spill any more of that good ale! I can wash up and remove my own coat tonight.'

A quick nod punctuated the command. Too weary to object, Elodie walked quietly out, hearing as she closed the door Will tell the others, 'Doesn't have the stamina of youth, poor Pierre. Old family retainer, you know.'

A murmur of commiseration followed her up the stairs. Old family retainer indeed, she thought indignantly, recognising the subtle taunt. The day was coming, Monsieur Ransleigh would soon discover, when she would be neither 'old' nor slavishly obedient.

Their room tonight was on the top floor. She paused after climbing to the first-floor landing, which boasted a window overlooking the street. Weary though she was, the star-spangled sky called out for admiration.

Just a few days' journey ahead, Paris beckoned. And somewhere within that teeming city, she urgently hoped, was Philippe.

Longing for him swelled within her, the ache sharper than usual. She'd been away so long, she was as apprehensive as she was excited to arrive at last and discover whether the long months of hope were justified. Whether she could find him and make him hers again.

She immediately banished a soul-chilling fear that

she might fail. Of course she would succeed, she reassured herself. They belonged together. No amount of time or separation could change that.

With a sigh, she trudged up the final set of stairs, the starlight from the window below fading as she ascended. Five steps down into the darkness of the hallway, she was grabbed roughly from behind. The hard chill of a blade pressed against her neck.

'Come with me quietly, madam,' a voice murmured, 'or your next move will be your last.'

Elodie tensed, her heartbeat skyrocketing. After an instant, though, she forced back the panic, emptying herself of everything but the need to calculate the physical advantage of the man detaining her and the meaning of his words.

Though he'd spoken in French, his accent was English; he knew she was not Ransleigh's valet, which meant he must have tracked them from Vienna. Would he kill her, or just threaten her to force her co-operation?

'Don't hurt me, sir!' she said, putting some of the alarm she'd suppressed into a voice pitched as low as she could make it. 'You're mistaken; I'm Monsieur LeClair's valet, Pierre.'

'No, you are Elodie Lefevre, implicated in the plot to assassinate Lord Wellington in Vienna last year,' the voice replied. 'You're going to descend these stairs with me to the back entrance. Now.'

Her mind tumbling over itself, looking for some means to escape, Elodie let the man push her ahead of him to the landing, stumbling as much as she dared to delay their progress. 'You are wrong, *monsieur*!' she whispered urgently. 'Speak to my master, he can straighten this out!'

A short laugh huffed against her ear. 'I mean to speak to him. After I take care of you.'

'Take care of me? What do you—?'

'Silence!' the man hissed in her ear. 'Speak again and I'll shut you up permanently.'

The assailant knew what he was doing; he kept her arms pinned behind her as he shuffled her forwards, and the blade at her throat never wavered. Could she stumble, catch her foot under his boot and use his own weight to knock him down the stairs, ducking out of the way before he cut her throat?

Probably not. Dragging her feet from step to step, muscles tensed and body poised to flee at the first opportunity, Elodie let her captor push her down the stairs and turn her towards the back exit leading to the stables.

Once outside, she would have more room to manoeuvre. Her assailant knew she was a woman; perhaps she could pretend to faint. Just a moment's opportunity and, thankfully free of encumbering skirts, she could take to her heels.

Her assailant unlatched the door and thrust her into the deserted stable yard. Knowing this would probably be her best chance, she'd gathered herself to make a break when, out of the stillness, came the unmistakable metallic click of a pistol being cocked.

Her assailant heard it, too, and halted. From deep within the shadows by the wall, Will said, 'Put down the knife, or I'll blow your head off. At this distance, I can't miss.'

'I can cut her throat before you can fire.'

'Perhaps.' A glimmer of humour coloured his voice. 'But you would still be dead, so what would it matter? *Monsieur*, you will oblige me by giving over the knife and keeping your hands well in front of you. Then you will accompany me and my much-maligned valet up to our room.'

When the man holding her hesitated, Will sighed. 'Do not try me, sirrah. I'm not at all averse to decorating this wall with your brains.'

With a reluctant laugh, the man surrendered his knife. Taking it, Will said, 'Pierre, search his pockets.'

Weak-kneed with relief, Elodie turned to face her attacker. She had no idea how Will had discovered them, but she'd never in her life been so relieved to see anyone.

While Will kept his pistol trained on the man, Elodie hurriedly rifled the man's greatcoat, removing a pistol from each pocket and holding them up. 'That's all.'

'Good. Pierre, you go first and make sure no one else is about. Sound an all clear and we'll follow you.'

A few moments later, Will herded her erstwhile attacker into their top-floor bedchamber. After pushing him into a chair, he quickly bound the man's wrists behind him, then motioned her to light a candle.

As soon as he held it close enough to make out the attacker's features, his expression turned from angry to incredulous. 'George Armitage! What the deuce are you doing here?'

'Trying to keep you from catching a bullet or being fitted for the hangman's necktie,' Armitage replied.

While Elodie tried to figure out what was going on, Will said drily, 'Your concern would overwhelm me... if you hadn't been trying to carve up my valet. If I unbind you, do I have your word as an officer you'll not threaten him again or try to escape?'

'You do,' Armitage said.

'Pierre, pour some wine,' Will directed as he set about removing the ropes.

'No need to maintain the fiction; I know he's no lad,' Armitage said.

'But the rest of the inn doesn't need to know. What are you doing here, skulking about and attacking harmless servants? Last time we talked, you were about to leave Paris with your regiment, bound for London.'

'So I was, and did. Sold out and went back to the estate, but as Papa has no intention of turning over the reins any time soon, it was bloody boring. I took myself off to London and lounged about the club, losing at cards and vying for the favours of various actresses until Locksley—you remember him, lieutenant in the 95th—talked me into joining the Foreign Office. Thought it might provide some of the excitement I'd missed since leaving the army.'

'But how did you end up here?'

'You were seen leaving England, bound for Vienna, barely two weeks after returning from Brussels. Knowing what had happened to your cousin Max, it wasn't difficult to figure out what you meant to do.'

'And the Foreign Office was so displeased by that, they sent a bloodhound after me?'

'Though the officials weren't too concerned when Max tried to track down Madame Lefevre, some who knew you felt you might be better at ferreting her out. I can't believe you weren't aware that no one, neither the English, nor the French, nor the Austrians, *wished* her to be found. So when I discovered they meant to send someone to stop you, I volunteered. Fellow officer and all—didn't want to see you come to harm.'

'I suppose I owe you thanks, then. I must say, though your tracking skills are acceptable, if tonight was an example of how you plan an ambush, your Foreign Office career is likely to come to a quick and violent end.'

Ignoring that jibe, Armitage continued, 'The Foreign Office just wants you back in England, out of this, but there are others with less charitable intentions. Once *madame* scarpered, according to my superiors in Vienna, several agents set out after her.'

Will's amused expression sobered. 'Who?'

'They didn't say. Could be French agents, or maybe the same Bonapartists who embroiled St Arnaud, angry the plot didn't succeed and eager to punish those who failed. I don't suppose I could persuade you to abandon plans of bringing the lady back to England?'

As Will shook his head, George sighed. 'Knowing your aim was to restore Max's reputation, I didn't think so. Now that I've warned you, if you're not prepared to listen to reason, you're on your own.'

'What will you do now? Honour among old soldiers

notwithstanding, I don't imagine your superiors would be pleased to learn we had a pleasant chat and you let me go.'

'No, I'll tell them I tracked you to the inn, but you'd left before I arrived.'

'You think they'll believe that?' Will laughed. 'I repeat my advice about seeking another career.'

Armitage waved a careless hand. 'If they do give me the sack, I'll find something else to do. I can always retire in disgrace on Papa's land and die of boredom. What of you? Not knowing who else may be trailing you or how close they are, you'll leave at once, I expect?'

Will frowned—his expression mirroring Elodie's concern as she followed the conversation, too alarmed by Armitage's news to object to being treated as if she were a piece of the furniture.

As the months after the assassination attempt had passed without incident, her worry that someone besides St Arnaud wished her dead had slowly dissipated. In time, she'd even found the presence of the guards keeping watch over her lodgings comforting. Discovering that she was being followed by some anonymous someone had just shattered that peace of mind.

'As soon as it's light enough to see,' Will was saying.

'Let's drink a bottle, then, to friendship and the regiment. Who knows when we'll meet again?'

Will nodded. 'I considered knocking you out before we left, to give you a more believable excuse for not apprehending me, but you could say instead that I drugged you. Much less painful.'

Armitage grinned. 'Much more civilised.'

Will gestured to Elodie. 'Fetch more wine from the saddlebags, Pierre. Then get some rest.'

Chapter Nine

They had left Armitage, who imbibed the majority of the wine, sleeping off his efforts at conviviality. During their hurried preparations to depart and the hard ride that followed, they had not had—or made—time to discuss the events of the previous night.

Not until after mid-afternoon the next day did Ransleigh signal them to a stop. As he led their mounts into the shade of some tall trees, within sight of the main road, but far enough away that they'd not eat the dust of passing carriages with their bread, Elodie wondered if he would speak of it now.

She shivered, still feeling the sting at her neck where the blade had nicked her.

What would George Armitage have done with her, if Will Ransleigh hadn't come to her rescue? He'd wanted to save his army comrade from Foreign Office scrutiny, possible danger—and from her. She warranted no such protection.

No one, neither the English, nor the French, nor the Austrians, wished her to be found, he'd said.

Unease clenched in her belly. Who was tracking her? Not since the earliest days after the attack in Vienna had she felt so vulnerable.

After extracting bread, cheese and wine from the saddlebags, Will parcelled out portions and they settled to eat, making stools and a table out of a fallen log.

Setting down his wine, Will turned to her, his eyes sparkling as they always did when he was about to spin another tale. But whatever he saw on her face made the gleam fade.

'You're wondering who else is out there and if last night's attack is only the first,' he said abruptly.

She nodded, then felt a tingle of shock that he had read so much in her face. Had she been that unguarded? Or had he just learned her expressions too well?

Pushing back that alarming thought, she replied simply, 'Yes. And I should thank you for rescuing me. How did you know I was in danger, by the way?'

'I heard the two of you on the stairs as I left the taproom. Since there was only one logical way for your attacker to smuggle you out and you were very cleverly delaying him, it was easy enough to slip out the front and await you in the stable yard.'

Despite his dismissive words, Elodie knew the successful intervention had required skill and timing. Putting a hand to the scratch at her throat, she said, 'Anyway, thank you. I don't know what he would have done, if you'd not intercepted us.'

Will shrugged. 'Since it was George, probably just tied you up while he tried to talk me into turning you over to the local authorities and heading back to England.'

Elodie had a sudden, terrifying vision of being cast off penniless and friendless, under very real threat of imprisonment. Thank heaven Will Ransleigh was so dedicated to his cousin! 'I'm grateful for your help. But what of those who might be more dangerous?'

'From what George told us, everyone from the Austrians to the British Foreign Office knows we're headed for Paris. After failing to stop us, George will have to report where he discovered us and the identities under which we were travelling.'

'Time for a new disguise, then?' She sighed. 'They'll still be looking for two lone travellers, whatever new appearance we assume. If we could somehow merge with a group, it would be easier to continue unremarked.'

'I'm thinking it might be better to head south and take a less direct route. They'll be watching for us on the major posting roads now.'

'They'll be watching for us to arrive in Paris, too, however long it takes,' she pointed out.

'True, but after another week, when they could reasonably expect us to turn up on our present course, they'll be less vigilant. There must be hundreds of people entering Paris every day. The guards can't scrutinise every one of them…especially if we enter in the early morning, with the rush of farmers bringing goods to market.'

She smiled, trying to envision Will Ransleigh in a farmer's smock, driving a herd of pigs. He'd probably do it expertly and look dashing. 'After we travel south, should we purchase some livestock?'

'Yes, valet Pierre should probably become farmwife Paulette.' From the saddlebag, he extracted a map and consulted it. 'If we turn due south towards Bavaria, skirt around the edges of Switzerland and proceed from Strasbourg towards Nancy, we could head west straight to Paris.'

She shook her head. A map! She tapped the saddlebag. 'Hair-blacking, spectacles, canes, wigs—I almost expect there's a flock of chickens hidden in there, too. Is there anything you do not carry in that bag of deception?'

He grinned. 'I like to be prepared.' The smile fading, he continued, 'We shouldn't underestimate the pursuers. The other parties to the affair seem to want to forget it happened, so the most serious threat might be posed by St Arnaud's confederates. He can't have been working alone; if his partners discovered that, contrary to what St Arnaud assured them, you'd not been silenced, they might want to correct his lapse.'

'Quite possibly,' she agreed. The thought was dismaying, but it was useless to panic. It was hardly the first time her life had been in danger. If they *were* being trailed by forces who wanted to eliminate her, there was nothing she could do but take all reasonable precautions—and keep going.

'Well, today seems the very breath of early summer,

with wildflowers blooming under a gentle sun and the sky blue as the Mediterranean. This bread is fresh and crusty, the cheese piquant, the ham savoury, and the wine delicious. I don't intend to allow whoever might be out there to steal my enjoyment of it. So, tell me another story.'

Instead of obliging, Ransleigh remained silent, studying her. 'You are remarkable, you know,' he said after a moment.

'Remarkable?' she echoed, raising an eyebrow.

'You've been threatened by me, forced to leave your only friend, hauled out of Vienna, attacked at midnight at knifepoint and acknowledged that everyone from the British Foreign Office to Bonapartist agents may be looking to snuff you out. Yet all you ask of life, of me, is a story.'

She shook her head, a little mystified by his intensity. 'All we can ever ask of life is the joy of this moment. There are no promises about the next.'

'The joy of this moment,' he repeated. 'Ah, *yes*.' Before she could imagine what he meant to do, he reached over, tipped back her hat and kissed her.

Elodie couldn't have stopped him if Talleyrand himself were holding a pistol on them. For days, she'd been unable to tear her eyes from the play of those lips as he spun his tales…from imagining how they'd feel and taste pressed against hers.

Their touch was hard, demanding, flavored of the wine he'd drunk. The taste of him intoxicated her, as if she'd drained the whole of the wineskin. She heard small mewing noises of encouragement and was shocked to realise they came from her, while, driven by a hunger long denied, she wrapped her arms around his shoulders and plastered herself against him.

His tongue probed her lips, opening her, and plunged deep. It chased hers in fiery dance, then encircled and suckled, pulling her deeper, unleashing a maelstrom of desire so intense her sole imperative was to have all of him.

She fumbled at the waistband of her trousers, desperate to open herself to the sleek hardness pressed against her, to feel it invade her body as his tongue had conquered her mouth.

Suddenly, in a shock of cold air, he pushed her away. In a tumult of clashing sensations—desperate need, impatience to continue, dismay that he had stopped—she finally heard it: the clatter of jangling harness, a murmur of voices as travellers approached down the road.

At least she had the solace of knowing he felt the same desire and disappointment. As he backed away, he grabbed her chin and, one last time, his mouth captured hers. Then, before refastening the single button she'd managed to unloose in her trouser flap, he slid a hand through the opening and stroked his fingers swiftly across the hot waiting flesh.

Just that glancing touch to the sensitive nub jolted through her like a lightning bolt, the sensation so powerful that, had it lasted a touch longer, she would have reached her release.

When had she last felt that joy? Had she ever felt it so intensely?

Gasping, disoriented, Elodie tried to settle her agitated senses as travellers came into view on the road beyond. Soon, a group of friars with cart and cattle slowly lumbered past.

'Would that I could get away with kissing my soon-to-be-former valet one last time,' Ransleigh murmured against her ear, the warmth of his breath setting her still-acutely sensitive body pulsing again. 'But you wished for a group to travel with and I think the Lord just answered that prayer. Given how we were engaged as they arrived, you can't say the Almighty doesn't have a sense of humour.'

Trying to quell the desire still raging through him, Will concentrated on regulating his breathing as he and Madame Lefevre watched the monks plod past.

As soon as the dust settled, she turned back to him. 'Travelling under the protection of the good friars is tempting, but we'd be rather conspicuous, don't you think? Unless you have robes, hoods, sandals and rope belts hidden in that bag.'

'Not yet, but I will. By the quantity of cattle and the amount of goods in the wagon, this group must have been to the farmers' market at Sonnenburg. Moving as slowly as they are, they probably spent the night at the religious guesthouse we passed at mid-morning. You stay here; I'll ride back and obtain what we need to become "Brother Pierre" and "Brother LeClair".'

'That's outrageous!'

'What, you don't think you can pass as a monk?'

'No! Well, yes, but lying to a priest? A whole group of priests?'

She looked so aghast, he had to laugh. 'Ah, so you do possess some scruples! I, alas, have none. Come now, think of it as…divine intervention sent to protect you. It would be a wonderful disguise, you must admit. We could travel south to wherever they are going, spend a few days at their monastery and then head for Paris. Absolutely no one would think to look for us dressed as monks.'

She nodded reluctantly. 'That's true enough.'

'If it chafes your conscience so badly to dissemble to the holy brothers, you could confess the deception before we leave. Besides, even if we admit we are in disguise, have not religious houses for millennia offered sanctuary to those in danger?'

Since she didn't immediately lodge another protest, Will knew she was weakening. Though he thought it a brilliant plan, her concession was all he needed.

'I suppose so,' she admitted at last. 'But how do you plan to obtain the supplies? The guesthouse isn't a clothing shop.'

'I'm sure the friars have a few robes and vestments they can spare. I'll tell the abbot there was a fire at my monastery that destroyed some of the brothers' robes and, as penance for some misdeed, I pledged to replace them. If I let him charge twice what they are worth, I'm sure I can persuade him to sell me a few.'

Frowning, *madame* wrapped her arms around her head. At Will's raised eyebrow, she said, 'I shield myself from the lightning bolt the *bon Dieu* will surely send to punish your sacrilege.'

Will chuckled. 'Never mind the good Lord, just protect yourself from view by passing travellers. It shouldn't take me more than an hour to reach the guesthouse. I'll have us outfitted and on our way to catch up with the friars before nightfall.'

As promised, after a glib explanation and a generous donation, Will returned to *madame*'s hiding place two hours later with the necessary robes, hoods, belts and shoes. After giving her some privacy to change into the latest disguise—and trying very hard to avoid the further sacrilege of imagining her naked—he stowed the rest of their provisions and clothing in the saddlebags.

A few moments later, she returned, face lowered beneath the shadowing hood, hands clasped together in her sleeves in a prayerful attitude, looking the very picture of a humble friar.

'What an excellent Brother Pierre you make!' he marvelled. 'If I didn't know your identity, I would absolutely believe you a man of God.'

She shuddered. 'Please, don't tempt the Lord's wrath again by claiming that! Since Armitage knows our current aliases, we should complete the blasphemy by changing names. Shall I be "Brother Innocent" and you, "Brother Francis"?'

'Of Assisi?' he asked with a grin, following her thoughts.

'Yes. A sinner and voluptuary before he came to the Lord. Perhaps the so-divine aura of the name will stick,' she replied tartly. 'I intend to protect what's left of my immortal soul by swearing a vow of silence. You will have to spin this web of lies by yourself.'

Throwing herself up on to her mount, she rode off. He was still chuckling when he caught up to her. But, true to her declaration, she ignored his attempt to converse. After a few snubs, he left her to her chosen silence.

Watching her, bent humble and prayerful over the saddle, Will had to shake his head. Madame Lefevre adopted the role of holy brother as quickly and unquestioningly as she had transformed herself from a gentlewoman into an old man into a valet. Will wished his subordinates on his army missions had understood their roles and mastered them as quickly and completely.

Not that she was merely a follower. Had she not astutely observed that travelling in a group offered them the best chance to evade their pursuers and reach Paris undetected, he might never have recognised the potential in that passing group of monks.

He had to appreciate the good Lord's sense of irony. How much better a rebuke to the raging desire that had nearly made him take her by the roadside in the full daylight, where anyone might have discovered them, than to send a band of friars?

But, as that same good Lord knew, even in men's

garb, Elodie Lefevre posed enough temptation to break the will of a saint and he was nothing close to that.

All those days telling stories, his gaze continually straying to her soft lips and generous mouth, while eyes blue as the lake at Swynford Court in June focused on him with complete concentration, as if he were the only being in the universe. Wisps of brown hair escaping from under the homespun cap made him itch to slide their silkiness through his fingertips, while his hands ached to cup the softness of those pale, freckled cheeks. Mesmerised by her, he rambled on, recounting by rote stories with which he'd regaled fellow soldiers at camps and billets and dinners from the barren heights of Badajoz to the ballrooms of Brussels, all his will needed to resist the ravaging hunger to taste those lips, invade that soft mouth, pull the essence of her into him, possess her and all her secrets.

It had been worth it, worth everything, to begin the process with that kiss. She tasted of the bread and wine she'd praised, of lavender and woman. He'd hardly begun to penetrate her mystery, to discover the source of that amazing ability to block out all the world's dangers and embrace the joy of a single moment, but he'd learned she was no sensual innocent.

She'd kissed him back with fire and expertise, fanning his passion to an intensity he couldn't remember ever reaching so quickly before. If not for the inextinguishable instinct for survival born of six years living on the streets, he would never have heard the travellers approach—or been able to force himself away from her.

Just then, he spotted the dust cloud in the distance that marked the progress of the monks who'd passed them earlier. Gesturing towards it, he said, 'Time for Act Two to begin.' He checked a smile at the scowl 'Brother Innocent' threw him as he spurred his mount forwards.

Reining in beside the group, Will slid from the saddle and greeted the monks with a nod and the sign of the cross. 'God's peace, good brothers! Where are you bound?'

'His peace to you as well,' replied a monk mounted on a donkey, to whom the others deferred. 'We travel to our abbey at Leonenburg, which we should reach just after nightfall. And you?'

'Returning from Vienna on a mission for our abbot. I'm Brother Francis and this is Brother Innocent—who pledged a vow of silence towards the success of our journey. May we join you?'

'Of course. Anyone doing God's work is welcome.'

As they fell in behind the slow-moving cortège, *madame* gave him a reproachful look from beneath her hood—doubtless again fearing the imminent lightning strike.

But in a sense, they were doing God's work, he reasoned with her silently. Righting the wrong done Max and restoring to the nation the talents of a man who could do great good was a worthy endeavour.

Hauling into danger a woman who he was—grudgingly and much against his will—beginning to think might have been almost as much an innocent victim of the plot as his cousin might not, though, a stab of conscience replied.

Was that the reason, rather than a desire to wash her hands of his blasphemous deception, she'd chosen her name? he wondered.

Maybe the influence of *his* name was affecting his views. Though he'd never been a voluptuary, he'd committed sins enough to stay alive on the streets and to survive years of war.

A little humility and some genuine penance wouldn't come amiss. As they travelled in this herd like docile holy sheep, he appreciated having a divine ally in resisting her allure. As last night's attack chillingly demonstrated, he couldn't afford to let the attraction between them diminish his vigilance.

He didn't even want to think what might have happened, had her assailant been someone other than George. Someone who would have cut her throat without a qualm in the darkness of the hallway while he sat gaming in the taproom.

When he'd slipped from the common room up the stairs, the vision of her seized by an unknown assailant, moonlight glinting off the knife at her throat, had punched all the air from his lungs. Savage rage against her attacker and the urgent imperative to rescue her had refilled them.

George confirmed that the danger her maid feared was very real. The hasty, casual promise he'd given Clara to keep her safe was going to require all his wits and every artifice he'd learned as a young thief and perfected as a soldier. For now, he'd just have to keep a tight rein over his increasingly intense need to possess her.

But once they were safely in Paris… If she thought he'd stand aside and turn her over to some no-surname-Philippe before they settled what raged between them, she knew nothing of the iron resolve of Will Ransleigh.

As predicted, Will and Madame Lefevre had reached the monastery just after dark, were greeted by the abbot and invited to rest from their journey for as long as they liked. Billeted in a common room and eating with the group, he had little opportunity to speak privately with *madame*, stealing just a moment to recommend they remain several days at the monastery, and receiving her nod of agreement in reply.

Madame had mimed her willingness to work in the vegetable garden, while Will joined the monks cutting wood in the forest. Outside the walls of the monastery, he could relax a little; within them, unused to the traditions of a monastic order, he needed all his skill at mimicry to carry off the deception.

Madame, however, must have been raised a good Catholic, or was a better mimic than he, for she followed the order of worship and the prayers as if born to them. Or had she learned them after the fall of the Republic, when Napoleon made his Covenant with the Pope and religion returned to a France which for years had functioned without a church?

After five days with the brethren, who accepted their presence, respected their privacy and asked them no questions, Will approached *madame* to suggest they could move on. Silently she gathered her belongings, Will leaving a handsome gift with the abbot before they left the friendly gates of the abbey and made their way west through the foothills towards Switzerland.

Once they could no longer see the sheltering walls of the abbey in the distance, *madame* pulled down her hood and turned to Will. 'Perhaps we should continue this disguise for the rest of the journey. It's served us well enough thus far.'

Will clapped a hand to his chest theatrically. 'Behold, she speaks! Does this mean you've forgiven me for the deception? Or did you ease your conscience by receiving absolution from the abbot?'

She grinned at him. 'I confessed the truth the very first night. Did you never wonder why the brothers were so discreet?'

'Because they are holy men, above the sin of gossip?'

'They are still human and curious. Besides, that tale of being on a mission wouldn't wash; your ignorance of the ways of holy orders would have shown the moment the abbot questioned you about it, if your performance at Compline the night of our arrival hadn't already made everyone suspicious.'

After a moment's annoyance, Will grinned back. 'And here I thought they'd accepted me as an exemplary monk.'

'They admired how hard you worked, if several had

to keep from smiling at your ignorance of the most basic prayers.'

'You broke that vow of silence to discuss me?'

'No, I overheard them talking about you in the refractory. I confessed to the abbot only that I was female, fleeing in disguise under threat of my life, and that you were helping me to reach my family in France.'

'Had you no other sins to confess?' Will teased.

The playful look faded from her face as she stared at him. He felt her gaze roam his face, his mouth, his body and return to focus on his lips. 'Not yet,' she replied.

Her meaning hit him like a punch to the belly, the always-simmering need he worked hard to contain bursting free in a blast of heat that hardened his body and roared through his veins. For a moment he saw only her, felt only the pulse of desire pulling them together.

His mouth dry, his brain scrambled, he couldn't come up with a witty reply. She broke the connection, turning away from him.

'We're still a long way from Paris.' To underscore the point, she urged her mount to a trot.

He didn't dare trust her, but there was no question about the strength of his desire for her. He urged his horse after her, wishing they could gallop all the way.

Chapter Ten

Following their former pattern of hard-riding days and short nights, for almost two weeks Will had led Madame Lefevre around the foothills of the Alps, finally descending to Nancy. Once past that city, they joined a growing stream of travellers headed north-west through the vineyards and fields of the Lorraine towards Paris.

Although in its anti-clerical zeal the Revolution had destroyed or sold off most of France's great abbeys and monasteries, in their guise as monks, they were still able to claim shelter for the night at the re-established churches along their route. Will continued to negotiate for food and fresh horses, joking, to *madame*'s repeated warning about hellfire, that he was fast becoming a model priest.

Allies and collaborators by necessity, they were now an experienced team, able to communicate silently through looks and gestures. Though they'd not encountered any further need for stealth, they maintained their roles diligently. As he'd learned in Seven

Dials, one never knew when rats might come pouring out of some unseen hole.

They still took their meals in the open, and Will still spun the tales, *madame* listening with every appearance of fascination. But she never volunteered anything about herself.

He no longer wanted to ask. Instead, foolish as it might be, Will wanted her to open to him willingly, without his having to trick or pry the information from her.

Though this woman had betrayed his cousin and brought scandal upon his name, he was having a harder and harder time reminding himself of the fact. Much as he tried to resist it, the slender sprig of camaraderie that had sprouted in Vienna had grown stouter and stronger through the intrigue and dangers of the road, entwining itself around him until it now threatened to bind him to her as powerfully as the sensual attraction that tempted him with every breath.

Each day, he'd slip into his stories some comment or observation that invited her to reciprocate with a similar experience of her own. At first, he'd wanted to tempt her into talking about herself, eager to use his wits to separate fact from deliberate falsehood.

Each day, as she had remained silent, disappointment grew sharper. He'd long since given up the suspicion that she had any intentions of feeding him false information to gain some advantage; her behaviour upon the road had been absolutely upright and above-board, just as he would have expected of a comrade-in-arms. Increasingly, it pained him that after their shared adventures, he knew nothing more about Madame Lefevre's past than he'd learned before they left Vienna.

In many ways, he felt closer to her than to anyone else in his life save his Ransleigh cousins. He could sense he was nearing the essence of her, the soul of her that danced always just beyond his reach. But she continued to withhold herself from him, in body and in spirit.

Was that a ploy, too? To disarm him by holding herself apart?

Tactic or not, he hungered for both. He wanted her to hunger for him, too. To yield her secrets.

Before he seduced her. For in a day or so, they'd be in Paris and the game would begin again in earnest. Some time before they passed through the city gates, he intended to bind her to him with the silken ties of physical possession. Before she could try to run, or set off to search for the mysterious Philippe.

Before he took her back to England.

Despite their growing closeness, he still meant to carry her there. He just wasn't so sure now, he admitted with a sigh, what he meant to do with her once they arrived.

Having spotted a likely resting spot under a stand of trees near a small river, he motioned her to turn her mount off the road. While she watered the horses, Will removed his saddlebag and extracted their simple meal, his thoughts returning to the conundrum of England.

Maybe he could stash *madame* at some quiet place

in the country; he owned several such properties. He'd journey to London alone, feel out some contacts in the Foreign Office. Maybe there was a way to clear Max's name without incriminating Madame Lefevre.

The idea of giving her up to the gallows was growing more and more unacceptable.

By the time she finished with the horses, he had bread, ham, cheese and wine set out on a saddle blanket on the sun-dappled grass under the trees. This time, hoping to lure her into speaking, as they sat to consume their meal, he did not immediately launch into a story.

It seemed she was content to eat in silence. Just as Will was about to judge his experiment a failure, she said, 'So, are you out of tall tales?'

'Have you not grown tired of my exploits?'

'Not at all. But there is something else I'd like to know about. Won't you describe your childhood? You've spun many stories of your roguish life, but nothing of how you became who you are.'

The whirlpool of the past swirled in memory, threatening to suck him down into its maelstrom of fear, hunger, pain and grief. He shook his head to distance it. 'There's nothing either entertaining or edifying about it.'

'It was…difficult?'

'Yes.'

'I'd still like to know. I've never met a man like you. It's ill bred to be so curious, I realise, but I feel driven to discover how you became who you are.'

He saw an opportunity and grabbed for it. 'I'll tell

you about my youth—if you tell me about yours. Over our travels, I've blathered on at length about my mis-spent life. You've told me nothing.'

After a moment, she nodded. Exultant, he exhaled the breath he'd been holding.

'Very well. But you first. How did you learn all these things you seem to do so instinctively? To move as si-lently as silence itself. To be so aware of everything, everyone, all the time. The ability to be anyone, mingle with anybody, to converse as an English aristocrat or a Viennese workingman.'

'Silence, so as to move and not be seen. Awareness, in order to snatch purses and not get caught. Pickpockets in England are transported or hung. And to be anyone? Perhaps because I have been almost all those things and had to mimic them to survive until I mastered the roles.'

'How did the nephew of an earl, even an illegitimate one, become a thief, a pickpocket and a working man?'

Will thought of the taunts and hazing at Eton that no amount of bloody-knuckle superiority had stopped. Crude drawings of cuckoos left on his chair, muttered obscenities about his mother issuing from within a gag-gle of boys, impossible to identify the speaker. Would this daughter of aristocrats scorn him, too, when she knew the truth?

Somehow, he didn't think so.

'During her come-out in London, my mother, a cler-gyman's daughter, was bedazzled by my father. The younger son of the Earl of Swynford, he was a rogue, gamester and self-centred bastard of epic proportions.

He lured her to his lodgings, a midnight excursion that ruined her reputation. When she refused to slink away to the country in disgrace, her family disowned her. For a time, they lived together at some dismal place just outside Seven Dials, but after losing a fortune at cards one night, he fled to Brussels. His older brother, now the earl, had already warned him he'd pay no more of his debts, and my father wasn't prepared to adapt himself to a debtor's life in Newgate. He left behind my mother, six months gone with child. Mama managed to eke out a few pennies doing needlework, enough for us to survive.'

Though all he remembered was being hungry. Frightened. Alone. And, later, angry.

'And then?' she prompted softly.

'When I was five years old, the local boss made me a runner and the street lads became my family. For the next six years, I learned the finer points of card sharping, lock-picking, house-breaking, knife-fighting and thievery.'

'Did your father never come back for you?'

'No. I heard he died of a bullet wound, courtesy of a man he'd been trying to cheat at cards in some low dive in Calais. But among his papers, later delivered to the earl, were letters written by my mother, begging him to make provision for their child. The earl set his solicitor to investigate and, once paternity was established, he had me brought to Swynford. Although, over the years, I'm sure he's regretted the decision to turn a second-storey boy into a gentry-mort, my cousins did their best to make me into a proper Ransleigh. Especially Max. Now, your turn.'

He caught her chin, making her face him. 'Who are you, Elodie Lefevre? Because if you're St Arnaud's cousin, I'll eat this tree.'

Before she could deny or dissemble, he rushed on, 'Don't you owe me the truth? I've told you about my ill-begotten youth. I've kept you safe and brought you almost to the gates of Paris. I simply can't believe St Arnaud would have left his own cousin in Vienna. Beaten her, perhaps, but not abandoned her; *someone* in the family would have taken him to account. Who are you, really?'

He held her gaze, implacable, willing her to confess, while his heart pounded, frantic with hope and anticipation.

Finally, she said softly, 'I was born Elodie de Montaigu-Clisson, daughter of Guy de Montaigu-Clisson, Comte de Saint-Georges. Our family home was south of the Loire, near Angers.'

He ran a map of France through his head. 'Isn't that in the Vendée?'

'Yes.'

That fact alone could explain so much. 'Was your family involved in the Royalist rising against the Revolution?'

'My papa joined the Comte de La Rochejaquelein, as did almost all the nobility of the Vendée. I don't know much, I was only a babe when the Republic was declared. But I do remember turmoil. Being snatched from the house in the middle of the night. Fire licking through the windows. Living in a garret in Nantes. Mama weeping. More fighting. Then that day…that awful day by the river.'

She'd lived in Nantes. Suddenly he recalled the event that had outraged all of Europe. 'You witnessed The Noyades?'

'The Republican soldiers herded all the townspeople to the quai beside the river. They marched the priests on to a small boat, locked them below and scuttled the vessel.' He could almost see the rippling surface reflected in the bleakness of her eyes. 'They did it again and again, one boatload of priests and nuns after another. All those holy ones, drowned. I was five years old.'

A child so young, watching that. He put a hand on her shoulder, stricken. 'I'm so sorry.'

'It was terrible. But it was also wonderful. There was no screaming, no pleas, no panic. Just…serenity. Mama said they went to a secret place in their hearts, where no evil could touch them.'

Like you do now, he thought. 'And after? If I'm remembering correctly, the Revolutionary government offered amnesty to all Vendéeans who surrendered and took the oath of allegiance. Did your father?'

'He died in the final battle. We left the garret in the middle of the night, our shoes wrapped in rags to muffle the sound, and boarded a ship. I remember wind shrieking, rain lashing, travellers screaming, thinking we would all drown like the priests and have to swim to heaven. Then…calm, green land, Mama weeping on the shore. We travelled north for many days, around a great city, surrounded by people speaking a language I couldn't understand.'

'You sailed to England, then? A number of *émigrés* went to the north, supported by the Crown.'

She nodded. 'Mama, my elder brother and I settled in a cottage on land owned by Lord Somerville.' She smiled. 'He had a wonderful garden. I used to spend hours there.' The smile faded. 'It was *my* secret place when Mama wept, or food supplies ran low. When the children in the village taunted me for my poor English and tattered clothing, for being a foreigner.'

'If you were living in England, how did you come to the attention of St Arnaud?'

'My brother, Maurice, ten years older than me, despised the Republicans who seized our land, killed my father and turned Mama into a grief-stricken old woman. When Napoleon abolished the Directoire and made himself First Consul, instituted the Code Napoleon and promised a new France where merit and talent would be rewarded, Maurice was ecstatic. He hated living as a penniless, landless exile, dependent on charity. He determined to enter Napoleon's army, perform great feats of valour and win back our lands. So we returned to France. On his first army leave, he brought home a friend, Jean-Luc Lefevre.' Her expression turned tender. 'I loved him the first moment we met.'

Instinctive, covetous anger rose in him. He squelched it. Devil take it, he wouldn't be jealous of a dead man! 'Whom you married. He was lost in the war?'

Pain shadowed her face. 'He fell at Lützen. He died the day after I reached the billet to which they'd taken him.'

'Is that when you learned to walk like a man? To disguise yourself on the journey?' At her sharp look, he said, 'I was a soldier, remember. I know what happens in the aftermath of battle. It's…dangerous for women.'

Eyes far away, she nodded. 'There'd been another battle at Bautzen, just after I buried Jean-Luc and left for home. Skirting the battlefield, seeking shelter for the night, I came upon a ruined barn. Inside were several soldiers, deserters probably, with a woman. They were…ravishing her.'

He'd seen enough of war to know what happened to some men when the blood-lust faded. Dismay filling him at what he feared he'd hear next, Will seized her arm.

Caught up in memory, she didn't seem to notice. 'I heard her crying, pleading with them.' Tears welled up, and absently she wiped them away. 'I heard her, but I did nothing to help. I was so ashamed.'

'Thank heaven you did nothing!' Will cried, relieved. 'What could you have done, except invite the same treatment?'

'Nothing, probably,' she admitted. 'But I vowed never to be so helpless again. I went back to the field—the burial teams hadn't covered all of it yet—and "borrowed" a uniform from a dead soldier. It was already bloody, so all I needed was a bandage around my head. I wanted to be ready.'

'In case you encountered renegade soldiers?' Will nodded his approval. 'Ingenious, to use the uniform as protection.'

'As protection, and also to be able to intervene if I encountered a…similar situation.'

'Intervene?' he echoed, appalled. 'I trust you never attempted to! Such men are beyond reason or shame; trying to stop them would have gotten you beaten, or worse.'

'I never had the opportunity. If I had, though, I planned to tell them there were willing women in the next town, and ask that they leave the one they had to me, since I was wounded and lacking my usual vigour.'

Will stared at her a moment, astounded. But foolhardy as such an action would have been, he could believe Elodie would have attempted it—and shuddered to think what might have happened.

'Why did you travel to Lützen alone, anyway? Did your husband have no family to accompany you?'

She shook her head. 'His family were *aristos*, like mine. All but he were killed or scattered during the Terror.'

'Had he no friends, then?' When she shook her head, he burst out, 'But to travel among rival armies after a battle, a woman alone? I can't believe you took such a risk!'

'To save the life of someone you love is worth any risk. You, who have done so much for Monsieur Max, must know that is the truth.'

She had him there. He knew without question he'd face any danger to protect his cousins.

'Soon after I got back to Paris,' she continued, 'Maurice came to me. His mentor, St Arnaud, needed a favour.'

'A hostess for Vienna.'

'Yes. My brother met St Arnaud through the army; he approved of us because we were *ancien régime*, part of the old nobility, like he and *his* mentor, Prince Talleyrand. Maurice had become Arnaud's protégé, so, when he needed a hostess, Maurice suggested me.'

'Did you know about the plot?'

'Not until after we arrived.'

'And St Arnaud used this "Philippe" to compel you to participate? Who is he—your lover?'

Even to his own ears, the question sounded sharp. Elodie merely smiled and shrugged.

'Something like. But enough for now; I've already told you more than you told me and we're losing the light. Besides, as you've said, we will be in Paris soon, perhaps even tomorrow.'

Her eyes on his, she laid her hand on his leg. Every muscle froze.

'In case our pursuers were able to figure out what happened after Karlsruhe, we should refashion ourselves once more. Enter Paris in the early morning with the crowd heading for Les Halles, just another farm couple with something to sell. I still have a simple gown in my pack. I could change here and we could stay at an inn tonight…as man and wife.'

The breath seized in his lungs. There was no question what she offered, with her gaze burning into his and her fingers tracing circles of fire over his thigh.

And no reason not to accept. If this were a trick to impair his vigilance, he'd just have to risk it.

'I thought you would never ask, my dear Brother Innocent. Let me help you change.'

'Not yet. I intend to wash in the river before putting on a clean gown.' She wagged a teasing finger at him. 'You stay here. No peeking!'

But her laughing eyes and caressing fingers told him she wouldn't mind at all if he watched her bathe.

He couldn't have kept himself from following her if the whole of Napoleon's Old Guard stood between him and the river.

Chapter Eleven

The chill of the early summer water shocked her, sending shivers blooming down her skin, but Elodie welcomed its bracing grip. Ah, to be clean, to wear her own clothes again!

Perhaps as soon as late tomorrow, she would find Philippe. As always when she thought of that moment, she felt stirring anew the mingled joy and anxiety that sat like a rock in her belly.

First, she'd have to deal with Will Ransleigh.

She couldn't deny a groundswell of regret that their paths must diverge. He was an amusing companion, a born storyteller, and more skilled at disguise, evasion and subterfuge than anyone she'd ever met.

Dissembling their way across Europe, they'd made good comrades. Despite the danger, this journey from Vienna had been unique and magical, a gift she would remember and savour, something never to be experienced again.

She would miss him, more keenly than she'd like,

but there was no question of a future. Now that Paris loomed and parting was inevitable, best to get on with it as quickly as possible.

She just hoped she'd be able to carry out her plans for that parting without a check, unease fluttering in her gut. Acquainted now with Will's high level of vigilance and excellence of observation, she'd need to be exceptionally careful in order to make her escape.

But before she eluded him, there was one final gift she could give—to him and to herself. Today and tonight, she would send him to the moon and the stars on a farewell journey of pleasure he would never forget.

Steeling herself to the cold, she strode into deeper water, quickly washing herself and her hair with a small bar of soap from the saddlebag. Despite warning him away, she knew he'd be watching from the copse of trees bordering the stream.

She'd start with a show to whet his appetite.

Shivering in the chill, she waded back to knee-deep water. With slow, languorous movements, she smoothed back the wet mane of hair, knowing it would flow sleekly over her shoulders. She leaned her head back, letting sunlight play over her breasts, the nipples peaked and rigid from the cold.

She lathered her skin again, then cupped her breasts in her hands and caressed the slippery nipples between her thumb and forefinger.

Sensation sparked in them, hardening them further, while matching sensation throbbed below. Half-closing her eyes, she imagined Will's hands mimicking the action of her thumbs. Would he bring his tongue to them, or use that hot, raspy wetness to stroke her tender, pulsing cleft?

She wanted him to tease her body to madness, as she'd imagined so many nights when she lay alone, chaste as the church floor they bedded down upon, acutely conscious of him sleeping beside her.

Heat crested and flowed outward from the slippery abrasion at her nipples, the hotter moisture at her centre. The fire building within now insulated her from the water's chill, made her breath uneven, her legs tremble, eager to part and receive him. She couldn't remember the last time she'd been so ready for a man, or ever wanting one as badly.

She opened her eyes to a muted splashing, and found Will, already shed of coat, boots and hose, wading out to her. Need blazed in his eyes.

Desire squeezed her breath out, gave it back to her in short, shallow puffs. The sensations at her breasts, between her legs, spiralled tighter, stronger.

'Shall I wash you?' she asked, her throat so dry she could hardly get the words out.

'If you'd be so kind.'

Oh, she wanted to be kind! She tugged at his shirt, impatient for an unimpeded view of the bare chest he'd teased her with so many nights on the road.

The skin was golden, sculpted over broad, muscled shoulders. His flat nipples were peaked, like hers. She couldn't wait to taste them. Couldn't wait a moment longer to see all of him.

Impatiently she tugged open the buttons of his trouser flap, freeing his member, which sprang up before her, proud and erect. Wobbling a bit in the current, he yanked the breeches further down and stepped out of them, tossing them back to the bank.

Her pulse stopped altogether, then stampeded. She could only stand, gaping at this Greek god of a man who'd come to earth to bathe in the stream and steal her heart. Would loving him transform her into some other being, a cow, a tree, as so often happened to unfortunate maidens who tangled with the Olympians? she wondered disjointedly.

Her admiration must have been obvious, for when she forced her gaze from his magnificent physique back up to his face, he was smiling. 'Soap?' he suggested.

She looked for it, then realised she still held it in her hand. After dousing him with water, she applied it to his neck, shoulders and chest. Breath catching in her throat, she massaged the film into a froth, touching, caressing, memorising the hard curve of muscle, the hollows between sinew and bone.

She thought he might break then, seize her and take his pleasure, but to her surprise and delight, he remained completely still, allowing her to touch him as she wished while standing so close she could feel his heat down the whole length of her body.

Lower she scrubbed, over the taut belly, the smooth curve of hip bone, until finally she took him in her hands.

His breath hissed out and he shuddered as she mas-

saged the lather around his glorious hardness. Unable
to resist temptation any longer, she leaned in and took
one nipple between her teeth.

'Elodie!' he cried with a muffled gasp, then jerked
her chin up to kiss her, one strong arm binding her to
him. His mouth mastered hers, his tongue probing deep,
leaving her senses swimming and giddy.

Still, he did not take her. She knew instinctively that
even now, if she pushed him away, he would let her go.
Awe and gratitude filled her.

And then, suddenly, she had to feel him there, in
that aching, needy place that had been unsatisfied for
so long. Her body had been handled and bullied, but
not since she was very young, falling in love with the
man who'd been so briefly her husband, had she encountered tenderness.

Still revelling in his kiss, she wound her arms around
his neck and pulled herself up, so she could wrap her
legs around his waist. Bringing his rigid erection to the
hot, moist openness only he could fill.

Groaning, he broke the kiss. 'Are you sure?'

'Yes! Please! Now,' she gasped back, then uttered a
long, slow moan of ecstasy as he entered her.

Then, he was walking with her, his hands cupping
her bottom to hold her in place as he took them deeper
and downstream, beneath the tender summer-green
branches of a huge tree that overshadowed the bank.
Kissing her again, he balanced her in his hands, using
the river's current and the water's buoyancy to aug-
ment his thrusts.

It was delicious, floating submerged in coolness yet captured at her very core by urgent, demanding heat. The sensations built and built and built as she rode him, her breath gone to sobbing gasps, her nails digging into the muscles of his shoulders, until finally she shattered and spun apart into dazzling shards of pure delight.

She came to herself, clinging weakly to him, her whole body limp, his hardness still buried deep within her throbbing core. *'Ma petite ange,'* he murmured, kissing her again, light, feathery touches on her eyelids, her brows, her forehead. He licked her throat, the shell of her ear, the edges of her lips, until the spiral within began to rotate again and she rocked her hips against his.

Exquisite sensation shot through her when he put his mouth to her breasts, rolling the tender nipples between his teeth. Desire accelerated, building hotter and faster, making her thrust towards him while the flow of the river magnified every movement. In a rolling, rhythmic motion, they slid together, tugged apart, the liquid friction within and without catapulting her to the waterfall's peak, where this time, they tumbled over together.

Some timeless interval later, Will pulled her with him to the bank. Under the embrace of the overhanging tree's branches, he sat, settling her between his legs, his warmth cradling her from the chill of air and water. 'I really had planned for there to be wooing, fine food and wine, a bed,' he said, planting a kiss on her head.

'I know,' she said on a sigh. 'I just couldn't wait any longer.'

'I'm glad you couldn't. I've wanted that for months.'

'You haven't known me for months,' she pointed out.

'True.' He wrapped his arms around her. 'But I've been looking for you all my life,' he added, so softly she wasn't sure whether she'd heard the words or only imagined them.

So had she been looking, the thought struck deep. Hoping for a lover who would give back rather than demand, who would care about her, rather than simply use her. She'd lived on her own, by her wits, pummelling some small space of existence from a bully prizefighter of a world for so long, she had to go back into the mists of long-ago childhood to remember when she'd trusted anyone else to keep her safe. When she had last felt so protected. So…not alone.

The realisation was both thrilling and terrifying. Will Ransleigh, who would drag her to the gallows to save his cousin, had no part in her future, and the notion that she could depend on him after tomorrow was madness.

Yes, she'd been touched by his tenderness in seeing to her pleasure. Moved by his respect for her abilities and energised by the excitement of the sleight-of-hand they'd pulled off during their journey. But the sweetness of it was simply the rich dessert at the end of a meal—delectable, but not the sort of wholesome fare it took to sustain life.

Her life was with Philippe and that was an end to it.

She struggled, trying to use logic to disentangle her emotions from him, but like pulling at a fraying cloth, ragged threads of connection remained. Giving up, she made herself move away from him, squelching her body's protest at the loss of his warmth.

'It's good you had the foresight to find us a resting place that cannot be observed from the road,' she said, trying for some dispassionate comment.

'I know you trust me to keep us safe.'

She wanted to deny it, but had to admit the statement was true. It should frighten her anew to realise she'd fallen into such an instinctive reliance on him... but that reliance remained, tenacious as the river tugging at her ankles.

Which was illogical and dangerous. If she weren't exceedingly careful, this man could stop before it ever began her hunt for Philippe in Paris and she must never forget that.

Pushing her ungovernable emotions aside in disgust, she said, 'If we don't dress soon, we will freeze.'

'I suppose. But I don't want you dressed.' He skimmed his fingers over her breasts, down between her legs. She sighed and lay back against him, feeling his spent member stir.

'Don't tempt me,' he said with a groan. 'Just the touch of you arouses me and we need to be sensible. We must dress now and ride quickly if we want to reach the village before dark.'

'Yes, sensible,' she agreed. Movement was what she needed. Returning to their travels, like rewinding a stopped clock, would set her emotions back on their proper course and reanimate her purpose, both shocked to a halt by the intensity of this interlude. Remind her that, but for one night of pleasure, their paths *must* diverge.

'We should purchase some livestock, too. Chickens, perhaps? The easier to blend in with the other farmers headed to market.'

'Another good idea. You're quite resourceful.'

She couldn't help feeling warmed by his praise. 'I've had to be.'

He helped her rise, his hands at her waist. 'Posing as man and wife for tonight,' he murmured, bending to kiss her, 'is your best idea yet.'

Ah, yes, she still had tonight, their last night, to savour. Her reward for all her forbearance along the road.

Passion, she could give him, though she could pledge him nothing else. Framing his face in her hands, she murmured, 'Perhaps livestock isn't so essential. All we really need is a room with a bed.'

'I hope that's a promise.'

She skimmed her fingers from his shoulders over his torso and down his body before leaning to snag his breeches and toss them up. 'Count on it.'

Chapter Twelve

Like a man and a maid in love for the first time, they helped each other dress, Will touching, kissing, laughing with Elodie as she donned her simple maid's gown and he changed back into a combination of working man and gentleman's attire that might be worn by a prosperous farmer. He knew that once they reached Paris, she would try to slip away from him, but he felt too light and euphoric to worry about it, happiness fizzing in his chest like a freshly opened bottle of champagne.

He'd had many an adventure, but never one like this. Never with a woman who was as uncomplaining a companion as a man, as resourceful as any of the riding officers with whom he'd crept through the Spanish and Portuguese wilderness, working with partisans and disrupting the French.

Coming together at irreconcilable cross-purposes, their liaison was too fragile to last, but for now, he'd be like his Elodie and suck every iota of joy from an already glorious day that promised, once he'd taken care of provisions for the morrow and found her a room with a bed, to become even more wonderful.

He twined his fingers in hers as they went back to their horses. 'How glad I am to be out of those monk's robes! I've been dying to touch you as we travel.'

'Good thing,' she agreed. 'Since you're grinning like a farmer who's just out-bargained a travelling tinker. I doubt anyone could look at us now and not know we are lovers.'

He stopped to give her a kiss. 'Do you mind?'

'No. I'm grateful for each moment we have to-gether...Will. One never knows how many that may be.'

Happiness bubbled up again as she said his name for the first time, lifting his lips into a smile. He loved how she pronounced it, rolling the 'l's so it was drawn out, like a caress.

He loved her simplicity and directness, her matter-of-fact approach to life, not fretting over problems in-cessantly like a shrew with a grievance, but considering them carefully, making the best plan she could and then putting them out of mind. So she was able to draw sol-ace and find joy...in her garden, beside a river.

This time, she'd brought him joy, too. Tonight, in their bed, he would give that back and more, every-thing, all that was in him.

Only then would he face the dilemma of taking her back to England.

As they approached the village on the outskirts of Paris, they encountered more fellow travellers. After making a circuit of the town, Will chose an inn frequented by respectably dressed men and women—busy enough to indicate its food and service were of good quality, but not elegant enough to attract the wealthy and well connected.

After turning their horses in to a livery, he obtained dinner and a room at the inn he'd selected. It required all his self-discipline, after climbing the stairs and opening the door to a snug chamber with table, chairs and a bed that beckoned, to leave Elodie alone while he went off to purchase a dozen chickens and the cart to haul them in.

Anxious to complete the arrangements, he didn't even bother haggling with the farm woman whose fine fat pullets caught his eye. Settling quickly on a higher price than he'd ordinarily pride himself on getting, he took over the hens, content to leave her thinking she'd struck a good bargain, but not so good that she'd brag to her neighbours about getting the best of a lackwit stranger.

Even this close to Paris, one couldn't be too careful about avoiding notice.

He settled the purchases behind the inn's stables, to the raised eyebrows of the grooms. Farmers, even prosperous ones, didn't usually store their squawking produce at an inn the night before bringing them to market.

But they'd be gone on the morrow before the grooms on duty had a chance to gossip in the taproom, if indeed any watchers had picked up their trail. Will didn't think so; he'd been vigilant—except for a short time at the river—and he'd seen no evidence of their being followed.

Someone would be looking for them in Paris, however. But he'd worry about getting them safely through the city—and out again, Elodie in tow—tomorrow.

Visions of seduction now filling his head, Will hurried back to the inn. For the first time in days, they'd eat a fine dinner and sip wine by their own fire. They'd talk about their adventures, about her life, about Paris.

Maybe she'd even tell him about the mysterious 'Philippe'. Though initially he'd expected during the journey she would try to lull him with lies, when she finally did open up to him, every instinct told him what she'd related was the truth.

Then he'd knead her shoulders, massage her back, take down the honey-brown hair she'd kept hidden and, for the first time, comb his fingers through the long silken strands. Undress her slowly, bit by bit, kissing the newly revealed flesh, as he'd dreamed of for so many solitary nights. Taste the fullness of her breasts, rake the pebbled nipples against his teeth, gauging her arousal by the staccato song of her breath. Finally, he'd taste the honey of her fulfilment on his tongue before he sheathed himself in her and pleasured her again and again.

His body humming with anticipation, he took the stairs two at a time and knocked at the door to their chamber. 'It's Will,' he said softly before unlocking it.

He entered to find the room in semi-darkness, lit by the flickering fire on the hearth and a single candle on the table. From the shadows of the bed, Elodie held out her hands. 'Come to me, *mon amant*.'

She sat propped against the pillows, the bedclothes at her waist. At the sight of her naked breasts, full and beautiful in the candlelight, his member leapt and all thoughts of dinner vanished.

'Nothing would please me more,' he said, pulling at the knot of his cravat, already impatient for the touch and taste of her.

'No, don't! Come here,' she beckoned. 'Let me undress you. I want to honour you, inch by inch.'

Emotion squeezed his chest while his member hardened to a throbbing intensity. Always a success with the ladies, he had been pleasured by blushing maids, loved by neglected wives, seduced by bored matrons who enjoyed the forbidden thrill of bedding an earl's illegitimate nephew. But no woman had ever vowed to 'honour' him.

'Willingly' was all he could choke from his tight throat.

Swiftly he came to the bed, where she urged him to sit. He kissed her head, finding her hair still damp from a bath, that lavender scent enveloping her again. His mouth watered. 'You smell good enough to eat.'

She smiled. 'We shall both eat our fill tonight.' Tilting down his chin, she leaned up to kiss him, slipping her tongue into his mouth.

Not until his brain registered a sensation of coolness at his chest did he realise she'd unfastened his cravat and opened his shirt. Breaking the kiss, she moved her mouth there, licking and kissing until impeded by the shirt's edges. Murmuring, she urged his arms up and pulled the garment over his head.

'Better.' She trailed nibbling kisses along his collarbone while her fingers shaped and massaged the muscles of his back and shoulders. She kissed from his neck down his chest, flicking her tongue teasingly just to the edge of his nipples, until they burned for her touch. He arched his back, manoeuvring his torso until her lips reached them, shuddering as she suckled them and raked her teeth across the tips.

Meanwhile, her fingers moved lower, beneath the back waistband of his trousers, to cup and squeeze his buttocks. He uttered a strangled groan, his member surging.

She glanced up at the sound. 'You must be tired. Lie down, *mon chevalier*,' she murmured, guiding him back against the pillows.

As he reclined, she removed his boots, giving him a delightful view of her naked back and bottom as she tugged.

The temptation was too great; he seized her and pulled her up to straddle his lap while with the other hand, he undid his trouser flap. She gasped, then uttered a little growling sound as she guided his swollen shaft into her slick passage and rocked her hips to take him deep.

He wrapped an arm around her back to pull her closer. As he branded her neck with his lips and teeth, he slipped the fingers of his free hand between them to caress her soft wet nub while he moved in her.

Panting, she arched against him, pushing him deeper. He moved his lips to her breast while his hand cupped her mound and his fingers played at the entrance, sliding into her to the rhythm of their thrusts.

Sweat coated his body, his neck corded and his arms grew rigid with the effort to hold himself near the peak without going over. And then she came apart in his arms, crying his name. Her tremors set off his own, a pleasure so intense he saw stars exploding against blackness as he spent himself in her.

For some time after, they lay limply in each other's arms. All his life, he'd been impatient, restless, driven by some intangible something to keep moving, searching for a destination he could never quite identify. For the first time, he felt utterly content, filled with an enormous sense of well-being. A deep sense that he belonged here, in this moment, with her.

His suspicions, along with the last bit of the anger he'd harboured against her, both gradually dwindling since they'd left Vienna, vanished completely.

He must have dozed, for he opened his eyes to find Elodie, still deliciously naked, sitting on the edge of the bed, pouring a glass of wine. 'For you, *mon amant*,' she said, handing it to him. 'To keep up your strength. You will need it. Now, where was I before I was so pleasantly interrupted? Ah, here.'

She tugged at the waistband of his unfastened trousers. Obligingly, he lifted himself, letting her pull them free and toss them to the floor. 'That's better. Naked, just as I want you.'

Her eyes gleaming, her expression sultry as a harem concubine intent on enticing a sultan, she gave him a wicked smile. 'Now I may see and taste…everything.

She extracted the wine glass from his fingers and took a sip. 'I'll need my strength also. To make this a night you will never forget.'

Some subtle sound roused him from a fathom's depth of sleep. Will rose slowly to consciousness, the room steeped in darkness, his whole body thrumming from senses wonderfully satisfied, like a chord still vibrating after the last note of a virtuoso's performance. *A night you will never forget.*

He certainly never would.

After that first lovemaking, she'd eased him back against the pillows and straddled him again, taking him within. And then sat chatting of Paris and London as if she were conversing at some diplomatic dinner, all the while moving slowly, rocking him inside her, her breasts bobbing deliciously close to his lips.

It was arousing, erotic, unlike anything he'd ever experienced. At first, he tried to match her aplomb and respond to the conversation, but after several times losing track of his sentences, he gave up the effort and closed his eyes, savouring the sensations.

Breathing itself became nearly impossible when, chatting still, she reached beneath him to where his plump sacks lay hidden, squeezing and massaging them while she urged his cock deeper. Pleasure burst in him, even more intense than the first time.

They dozed, roused to eat their cold dinner, slept again. He woke to find her head pillowed on his thigh. Noting his sudden alertness, she leaned over to trace his length with the tip of her tongue. As his member surged erect, she captured him in the hot velvet depths of her mouth, driving him to another powerfully intense release.

Just thinking about her made him smile. Maybe he could talk her into staying one more day at the inn. What would one more day matter? They'd already spent almost four weeks on a journey envisioned to take just over two. At odd times on the road, he'd considered trying to stretch it out even more, eking out every last second of joy from an experience as unparalleled as it had been unexpected.

Now, for the first time, he was beginning to envision a bond that might last not just a handful of nights, but weeks, months…into the hazy future.

As he stretched languorously, savouring the prospect, suddenly Will realised he was alone in the bed.

He sat bolt upright, his heart hammering. Not the faintest glimmer of dawn showed yet under the curtained windows. Probably she'd gone to the necessary, he thought, trying to force down the alarm and foreboding welling up in his gut.

She'd given him all of her freely, everything, as honestly as he had given it back to her. Stripped bare, with no defences, holding nothing back, they'd created a union of souls as well as bodies. She wouldn't just… leave him without a word.

His anxious, clumsy fingers struggled with flint and candle on the bedside table, but the additional flare of light just confirmed she wasn't in the chamber.

He jumped out of bed. Although the saddlebags he'd given her in exchange for the bandbox she'd packed in Vienna sat against the wall, they were empty; the gown, shift, chemise, stockings and shoes she'd donned after giving him back the monk's robe were gone.

Emptiness chilled him bone-deep as he admitted the unpalatable truth.

Damn her, she'd reduced him to a pudding-like state of completion, not out of tenderness, but so she could escape.

Escape him—and run off to her Philippe.

Nausea climbed up his throat and for a moment, he thought he'd be sick.

Betrayed. Abandoned. An agonising pain, worse than he'd felt after being shot by Spanish banditos, lanced his chest.

He dammed a rising flood of desolation behind a shield of anger. With iron will, he forced back deep within him an anguish and despair he'd not felt since he'd been a small boy sitting beside his dying mother.

It was ridiculous, he told himself furiously, carrying on like a spinster abandoned by the wastrel who had deceived her out of her virtue. The circumstances were nowhere near the same as the tragedy suffered by that five-year-old. He hadn't lost his only love, he'd merely been tricked by a lying jade.

But she'd not got the better of him yet.

Stupid of him to forget one rogue should know another. He'd forced this journey on her, giving her no real choice. Their adventure had been based on a bargain, each of them getting something they wanted.

She was trying to cheat him out of doing her part.

The sound that had roused him moments ago must have been Elodie, sneaking away. Without the instincts for survival Seven Dials had honed so well, he might never have heard her. It had already been nearing dawn the last time they'd coupled, so she couldn't have got far.

If Elodie Lefevre thought she'd seen the last of him, she was about to discover just how hard it was to dupe Will Ransleigh.

Chapter Thirteen

Her few remaining worldly goods concealed beneath the chickens in one of the baskets she carried on each arm, Elodie hurried in the dim pre-dawn with the press of other farmers heading into Paris. Too impatient to stroll at the crowd's pace, docile as the birds in the dove-cote on the pushcart in front of her, she darted around the vehicle, causing the startled doves to flutter. Driven by an irresistible urgency, she only wished their wings beating at the air could fly her into Paris faster.

She had to escape Will, before he woke to find her gone. As skilled as he was at tracking, she must lose herself in the safety of the great rabbit warren of Parisian streets well before he set out after her.

There, as she began her quest, she'd also lose this nagging temptation to go back to him, she reassured herself.

It didn't matter how energised and alive he made her feel. Their time together had been an idyll and, like all idylls, must end. Besides, what they shared was only the bliss of the night, no more permanent or substantial than the lies a man whispered in the ear of a maid he wanted to bed.

A dangerous bliss, though, for it made her wish for things that life had already taught her didn't exist. A world of justice not ruled by cruel and depraved men. A sense of belonging with friends, family...a lover who cherished her. Safety, like she'd felt in Lord Somerville's garden. Illusions that should have vanished long ago with her childhood.

It ought to have been easy to leave him. She knew what he planned for her. She'd allowed herself the reward she'd promised, a spectacular night of passion more fulfilling than any she'd ever experienced.

Up until that very last night, she'd been successful in keeping her emotions, like tiny seeds that might sprout into something deeper than friendship if dropped into the fertile soil of his watchful care, clutched tightly in hand.

Her devotion to Philippe was a mature growth, a sturdy oak planted firmly in the centre of her heart. He was her love, her life, her duty. Returning to him should have shaded out any stray, straggly seedlings of affection germinated by Will Ransleigh.

But it hadn't. Even as she hurried to fulfil the mission that had sustained her for the last year and a half, she ached. A little voice whispered that the wrenching sense of loss hollowing her out inside came from leaving a piece of her soul back in Will Ransleigh's keeping.

Very well, so passion had forged a stronger bond

than she'd anticipated. She'd been privileged for one brief night to possess her magnificent Zeus-come-to-earth. But she could no more cling to him than had the maidens in the myths. She'd not been transformed into a cow or a tree; she mustn't let leaving him turn her into a weakling.

She'd just have to blot out the memory of their partnership on the road, forget the sparkle in his eyes and warmth in his smile as he spun tales for her. Obliterate all trace of the feel of him buried in her, catapulting her into ecstasy with skill and tenderness.

She wouldn't have to worry about *him* pining over *her*. When he woke to find her gone, he'd stomp the life out of any tendrils of affection that might have sprouted in *his* heart.

Time to put Will Ransleigh and the last month out of mind, as she always put away troubles about which she could do nothing. Time to look forwards.

The sun just rising in a clear sky promised a lovely summer day. She should be excited, filled with anticipation and purpose. She suppressed, before it could escape from the anxious knot in her gut, the fear that, despite all her scheming, she would not find Philippe.

Losing him was simply unthinkable.

Her agitation stemmed from fatigue, she decided. Certainly it couldn't be pangs of conscience at deceiving Will, she who wouldn't have survived without honing deception to a high art.

Besides, she *had* given him passion—the only honest gift within her keeping. She had no regrets about that.

As she rounded a bend in the road, the walls of Paris towered in the distance, casting an imposing shadow over the west-bound travellers. She forced her spirits to rise upwards like her gaze.

No more time for fear, regret or repining. The most important game of her life was about to begin. After waiting so long and being so close, she was not about to fail now.

Fury and contempt for his own stupidity fuelled Will's flight from the inn, which he quit within minutes of discovering Elodie's deception. Since they'd be entering the city separately, he'd no need to play the farmer. Let the innkeeper roast the fowl for dinner and chop the gig into firewood, he thought, his anger at fever pitch.

Unencumbered by cart and poultry, he was able to move swiftly.

Just a half-hour later, he spotted Elodie as she entered the city gates—his first bit of luck that day, for, once inside, despite her farm-girl disguise, there was no guarantee she'd actually make for Paris's largest market.

Walking quickly, two baskets of squawking chickens on her arm, she did in fact continue towards Les Halles. Camouflaged by the usual early-morning bustle of working men, vendors, cooks, housemaids, farmers, tradesmen, soldiers and rogues returning from their night's revels, he was able to follow her rather closely.

If he hadn't been in such a tearing rage, he might have enjoyed making a game of seeing how close he could approach without being observed. Though anger made him less cautious than he would have normally been, he was still surprised he was able to get so near, once reaching her very elbow as she crossed a crowded alleyway.

Hovering there had been foolish, as if he were almost daring her to discover him.

Maybe he was. With every nerve and sinew, he wanted to take her, shake her, ask her *why*.

Which was more stupidity. He knew why she'd fled, had been expecting it, even. He accepted that she'd out-played him in the first hand of this game, and in the one tiny objective corner remaining within his incensed mind, he realised it was unusual of him to be so angry about being outmanoeuvred. Normally he would allow himself a moment to admire her skill, learn from the loss and move on.

He would not—*could* not—examine the raw and bleeding emotions just below the surface that contributed to his unprecedented sense of urgency and outrage.

He paused on the edge of the market square, watching as she sold off the chickens and one basket, then moved on to purchase enough oranges to fill the other. He could corner her immediately, but it was probably wiser to wait until he could catch her where there were fewer witnesses who might take her part in the struggle that was sure to follow.

After Elodie left the market area, Will dropped back further, though he was still able to follow much closer than he would have expected, based on how alert and

careful she'd been during their escape from Vienna. As
consumed as he was by fury, he still wondered why.

Basket of oranges on her arm, she proceeded south-
west to the Marais. This area of elegant town houses, so
popular during Louis XIV's reign, had been already in
decline by the Revolution, and many of the magnificent
hôtels with their courtyards and gardens looked shabby
and neglected. Elodie paused before one of impressive
classical grandeur which, unlike its unfortunate fellows,
was well tended, its stone walls and windows clean, its
iron fences painted, its greenery freshly clipped. After
staring at the edifice for a few moments, she turned
down the alleyway leading to the garden entrance at
the back.

Was this the abode of the mysterious 'Philippe'?

Watching her walk towards the gate, Will pondered
his next move. Prudence said to take her before she
could disappear within, if that's what she intended.

But if he stopped her now, he might never learn who
occupied that house. She had to know he'd be furious if
he caught her; if she hadn't revealed the secret of this
elegant Marais town house to an accomplice and fellow traveller, there was little chance she'd do so to an
angry pursuer.

Curiosity—and, though it pained him to admit it,
jealousy—battling logic, Will hesitated. If he waited
here, intending to seize her after she came back out, it
was possible she might exit by the front door and he
would miss her. But in her disguise as a farm girl, it

was unlikely she'd be permitted to leave by the grand entrance.

Unless Elodie de Montaigu-Clisson Lefevre had resources he wasn't aware of. During his stay in the city after Waterloo, he'd learned enough about official Paris to know this fine mansion wasn't Prince Talleyrand's home, though it might belong to one of the Prince's spies or associates.

While he dithered, uncharacteristically uncertain, she trotted down the pathway and disappeared through the kitchen entrance and his opportunity to grab her was lost. Exasperated with himself, he retreated down the alleyway bordering the *hôtel* and scrambled up the wall beneath a tree conveniently clothed in thick summer greenery that camouflaged him while allowing him a clear view of the kitchen and garden.

Huddled on the wall against the tree, calmer now, he considered his options. There was no point berating himself for not nabbing her when he'd had the chance. After a night of little sleep, his reflexes and timing were off. It had been a long time since he'd enjoyed a woman so much, longer still since he'd met one who affected him as powerfully as Elodie Lefevre. As the sensual spell she'd created continued to fade, these atypically intense emotions would subside and he'd recover his usual equilibrium.

With that encouraging conclusion, he set himself to evaluating whether to wait where he was, within view of the servants' entry, or move towards the front. Before he could decide, Elodie exited the kitchen.

At the sight of her, his pulses leapt and a stab of pain gashed his chest, giving lie to the premise that his intense emotions were fading. Think, don't react, he told himself as he tried to haul the still-ungovernable feelings under control.

Fortunately, after exiting the back gate, she turned down the tree-bordered alleyway and walked right towards him. This time, he'd grab her at once, before she could elude him again.

Heart rate accelerating, breathing suspended, Will waited until she passed beneath him. He jumped down, landing softly behind her, and seized her arm.

She'd been trained well; rather than yelping or pulling away, she leaned into him, slackening the tension on her wrist while at the same time dropping to her knees, trying to yank her arm downwards out of his grip.

Being better trained, he hung on, saying softly, 'Hand's over, and this time all the tricks are mine.'

At his voice, a tremor ran through her and she stopped struggling. Slowly she rose to her feet and faced him, expressionless.

Will wasn't sure what he'd expected to see on her face: shame? Regret? Grief? But the fact that she could confront him showing no emotion at all while he still writhed and bled inside splintered his frail hold on objectivity with the force of an axe through kindling. Fury erupted anew.

He wanted to crush her in his arms and kiss her senseless, mark her as his, force a response that showed their passion had shaken her to the marrow as it had him.

He wanted to strangle the life from her.

Sucking in a deep breath, he willed himself to calm. He hadn't allowed emotion to affect his actions since he'd been a schoolboy, when Max had taught him channelling anger into coolly calculated response was more effective than raging at his tormentors.

It shook him to discover how deeply she'd rattled him out of practices he'd thought mastered years ago.

But one thing *she* couldn't master. The calm of her countenance might seem to deny he affected her at all, but she couldn't will away the energy that sparked between his hand and her captive arm. An attraction that sizzled and beguiled the longer he held her, making him want to pull her closer as, despite the hurt and anger he refused to acknowledge, his body, remembering only passion between them, urged him to take them once again down the path from desire to fulfilment.

Though he didn't mean to follow that road now, just feeling the force crackling beneath his fingertips was balm to his lacerated emotions. He clutched her tighter, savouring the burn.

'*Bonjour, madame.* I had to hurry to catch up to you. Careless of you to leave me behind.'

'Ineffective, too, I see,' she muttered.

'What of our bargain? Did the heat of the night's activities scorch it from your mind?'

When she winced at that jab, he felt a savage satisfaction. No, she was not as indifferent as she tried to appear.

'I merely wished to begin early to take care of a family matter, just as I told you I would.'

'Here I am, ready to assist.'

'It's better that I do it alone.'

Will shook his head. 'I'll go with you, or you can leave Paris with me now. I move when you move, like lashes on an eyelid, so don't even think of trying to give me the slip again.'

The last time he'd warned her about escaping, he'd talked of crust on bread and she'd licked her lips. A flurry of sensual images from their surrender to passion last night flashed through his mind. In the light of this morning's abandonment, each gouged deep, drawing blood. Cursing silently, Will forced back the memories.

'So, what shall it be?' he asked roughly, giving her arm a jerk. 'Do we head for Calais or...?'

She opened her lips as if to speak, then, shaking her head, closed them. A bleak expression flitted briefly over her face before, with one quick move, she wrenched her arm from his grip and walked off.

In two quick strides he caught back up, grabbing her wrist again to halt her. 'Tell me what we're about to do.'

Freeing her wrist again with another vicious jerk, she said, 'Follow if you must, but try to stop me and, *le bon Dieu me crôit*, I swear I'll take my knife to you, here and now. Observe what I do if you must, but interfere in any way and our bargain is finished. I won't go a step towards England with you, whatever retribution you threaten.'

She delivered the speech in a terse blast of words, like a rattle of hail against a window, never meeting his eyes. Even working with his normally keen instincts diminished, Will was struck by her ferocity and an odd note in her voice he'd never heard before. Something more than anxiety, it was almost…desperation.

Her urgency also shouted of danger, finally giving him the strength he needed to bury emotions back deep within the pit into which he'd banished all loss and anguish since childhood. They weren't in England yet; his first duty to Max was still to protect her so he could get her there.

She resumed walking at a rapid pace, eyes fixed straight ahead, seemingly oblivious to her surroundings. Falling into place beside her, he asked several more questions, but when she continued to ignore him, abandoned the attempt. Instead, he transferred his efforts into assessing all the people and activities in the streets they were traversing, alert for any threat.

While keeping a weather eye out, he was still able to watch Elodie. Her unusual abstraction allowed him to stare at her with greater intensity than she would have otherwise allowed. He tried to keep warmth from welling back up as he studied her striding form and set face, every nuance of the body beneath those garments now familiar to his fingers and tongue.

When his gaze wandered back to her face, he noted it was abnormally pale, her eyes bright, her expression as tense and rigid as her body. She paced rapidly, almost leaning forwards in her haste.

Whatever 'family matter' she was about to address, it was both urgent and vitally important to her.

From the *hôtel*, they passed through the streets of the Marais towards the Seine, south and west until they reached the Queen's gate at the Place Royale. Though some of the houses inside that beautiful enclosure, like those of the Marais, were shuttered and forlorn, even shabbiness couldn't mar its Renaissance beauty.

Rows of lanes, presided over by trees serene in early summer leaf, were well populated by nursemaids with their charges, finely dressed ladies followed by their maids, men with the self-important air of lawyers conversing and a few couples strolling hand in hand. In the distance, on the lawn, several children frolicked.

'Stay here,' she demanded, startling him as she broke her silence. Where her face had been pale before, now hectic colour bloomed in her cheeks. Her eyes blazed, the tension evident in her body ratcheting tighter. Without checking to see if he heeded her directive, she set off.

Neither curiosity nor prudent surveillance permitted him to obey. Will followed at a cautious distance, alertness heightened in him, too, as he sought to identify which of the wandering figures had seized her attention.

As he inspected the several strolling gentlemen, his gaze caught on one who'd paused, leaning over the maid accompanying him. He was too far away to hear their conversation, but the hand the man rested on the girl's shoulder, the juxtaposition of their bodies, nearly rubbing together even in this public space, hinted at intimacy. Had Elodie returned to find the man she loved romancing another woman?

She stopped so abruptly, he had to catch himself before he got too close, though she now seemed so absorbed, he probably could have run right into her without breaking her concentration. Will was scrutinising all the people in the vicinity of her mesmerised gaze, trying to fix upon its object, when a nursemaid nearby called, 'No, no, bring the ball back here, *mon ange*! I'll throw it to you, Philippe.'

A gasp of indrawn breath made him turn back to Elodie. She stood immobile, her gaze riveted on a dark-haired little boy, the basket clutched so tightly in her hand that the knuckles went white. Hope, joy, anxiety blazed in her face.

Philippe. *Philippe.* Comprehension slammed into Will with the force of a runaway carriage, knocking all the preconceived notions out of his head.

A 'family matter', she'd said. It wasn't a lover she'd been so desperate to search for, but a little boy, he realised, even as he recognised her smile, her eyes, in the face of the child. She'd come back to Paris to find her *son*.

Chapter Fourteen

As she neared the children playing in the grass beside the gravelled *allée* in the Place Royale, Elodie picked up her pace. Her heart pounded and her skin prickled as if the mother's love, trapped within her and denied expression for so long, was trying to escape her body and reach him before her feet could get her there.

Discovering from the cook at the Hôtel de la Rocherie that Philippe was, indeed, still in Paris, playing with his nursemaid only a few streets away, had made her desperate to reach him, see him, clasp him once again in her arms. Frantically she raked her gaze from child to child while her thoughts chased one another as quickly as hounds after a fox.

Would his hair still be ebony-black, his eyes still dark and alive with curiosity? He'd be slimmer now, more like a child than the sturdy toddler she'd left, ready for games and to sit a horse. Would he still love balls, play at soldiers, cajole for sweets?

Then she saw him. Her heart stopped, as did her feet, while everything around her faded to a blur.

He was taller, as she expected, his face more angular, having lost the roundness of babyhood. Pink-cheeked from exertions, his skin glowing with health, his eyes bright, his uninhibited laughter as he chased after his ball with that stubborn lock of hair curling down as always over his forehead, made her heart contract with joy.

As her eyes left his face, she noted that his clothing had been fashioned from quality materials and fit him well. The nursemaid tossing him the ball regarded him with an affectionate eye and a husky footman stood nearby, obviously keeping watch.

One anxiety dissipated. She'd for ever blame herself for not recognising the trap before she walked into it, but at least her instincts about the Comtesse de la Rocherie had been accurate. Philippe was well treated and cared for.

But he was *hers*, she thought with a furious rush of determination. Despite all the odds, she'd survived her ordeal, connived her way back to Paris. She would reclaim her son at last and nothing but death would prevent her.

Another swell of emotion shook her and she almost tossed down the basket to run to him, starved for the feel of him in her arms.

She took a shaky breath, fighting off the urge. He hadn't seen her for eighteen months, an eternity in the life of a young child. She mustn't startle him, but approach quietly, let him notice her, inspect her, rediscover her at his own pace.

Then she would work out how to steal him back.

Hands shaking now on the basket, she strolled down the path, on to the grass near her son.

It took two attempts before she could get the words to come out of her tight throat. 'Would you like an orange, little man?'

He looked over at her, his gaze going from the fruit to her face. Elodie held her breath as he studied her, willing recognition to register in those dark eyes, as lively and energetic as she remembered.

After a moment, he looked away, as if concluding she was of no interest. 'Jean, get me an orange,' he commanded the footman before turning back to the maid. 'Throw the ball again, Marie, harder. I'm a big boy now. See how fast I can run after it?'

Hands raised to catch his ball, he trotted off, all his attention now on the maid. Consternation welling within her, Elodie set down the basket and hurried after him.

'Come back, young gentleman,' she coaxed. 'Let me show you my fine oranges. They'll please you as much as your ball.'

'Not now,' he said with a dismissive wave in her direction, eyes still on the maid.

'No, please, wait,' she cried, catching up to him and seizing an arm.

He tugged away from her, but she held on, desperate for him to look at her again, really *look* at her.

He did indeed look back at her, but instead of recognition, as his gaze travelled from her fingers clutching his shoulder to her face, the puzzlement in his eyes turned to alarm. His chin wobbling, he called out, 'M-Marie!'

He didn't recognise her. Even worse, she'd *frightened* him! Aghast, appalled, she stared at him mutely, while denial and anguish compressed her chest so tightly she couldn't breathe.

The tall footman strode over, menace in his face as he pushed her roughly away from the child. 'What d'ya think yer doing, wench?' he growled, while her son ran from her towards the outstretched arms of his nurse. 'I'll call the gendarme on you.'

Then, somehow, Will Ransleigh was beside her, one hand protectively on her shoulder while he made a placating gesture towards the footman. 'No harm meant, *monsieur*. Just trying to get the gamin a treat, that's all. Gotta make a living, you know.'

'Better she sells her oranges at the market,' the man retorted before walking back to the nursemaid, who handed him the child's ball and hefted the frightened child into her arms. With a wary glance at them, the maid hurried off, the footman trotting beside her.

Philippe, his small hands clutching the maid's arms, didn't look back at all as he buried his head against the nursemaid's shoulder.

Just as he used to nestle into her embrace, Elodie recalled with an agonising stab of loss. Had it been that long? Could the eighteen months of separation have erased from his memory every trace of her three years of tender love and constant care?

She stood, staring after them, heartsick denial rising in her, watching until the small party turned the bend of the *allée* and disappeared out the gate. She couldn't, wouldn't believe it.

Suddenly she felt as if the pressure of all the anguish and anxiety, fear and doubt churning within would make her chest explode. Her feet compelled into motion to try to relieve it, she set off pacing down the pathway, light-headed, nauseated and only dimly aware of Will Ransleigh keeping pace beside her.

How could Philippe have forgotten her? His image was etched into her brain. With her first conscious thought every morning, her last every night, she recalled his face, wondered what he was doing, worried about his welfare.

In the depths of her pain after St Arnaud's savagery, his image burning in her heart had given her the will to struggle out of the soothing darkness of unconsciousness. Determination to return to him kept her from despair and lent her patience and courage during the long slow recovery, through tedious hours of needlework, each completed piece adding one more coin to the total needed to fund her journey back to him.

When she pictured their reunion, she always imagined him fixing on her an intent, assessing gaze that would turn from curious to joyful as he recognised her. Imagined the feel of his slight frame pressed tightly in her arms when he threw himself against her, crying, *'Maman! Maman!'*

Instead, he'd called for Marie. He'd clutched *her* arms, buried his head against *her* shoulder.

But he was only a small boy and she had been missing almost half as many years as they'd had together. It had been unrealistic and probably foolish of her to expect he would remember her after so long.

What under heaven should she do now?

Despite the footman being alerted and the maid alarmed, Elodie knew that with a change of clothing and manner, she could weasel her way close to him again, into the house itself if necessary. She'd always envisioned picking him up, telling him to hush as they played a 'hide-and-seek' game while she stole away with him.

She couldn't do that if he were afraid, crying out, struggling against her to escape.

She couldn't do that to him, even if he didn't struggle. The idea of tearing him from all that was comforting and familiar and carrying him off, alone and terrified, filled her with revulsion.

Yet she couldn't simply give him up.

She walked and walked, circuit after circuit, her thoughts running in circles as unchanging as the perfect geometry of the Place. In continuous motion, but always ending up at the same point.

He was young, he'd recover from the trauma, she argued with herself. He'd adjusted to living with the comtesse; he'd adjust again to living with her...even if he never truly remembered her. He was flesh of her flesh; he belonged with her. No one else alive had as much right to claim him as she did.

But could she live with herself if she put him through such an ordeal? Other than the closest kinship of blood, what could she offer him that might compensate for the terror of being stolen away by a stranger?

As she worked patiently in Vienna, she'd always imagined taking him away to a little village somewhere. Using the funds she'd obtain from selling the last of her jewels to buy a small farm in the countryside, where she could plant a garden, eke out a living selling herbs and doing needlework, watch her son grow to manhood. But now?

She was alone with no friends, no allies and very little money. Somewhere St Arnaud might still lurk, a dangerous enemy who might be the force behind those who'd been trailing them. She'd fallen back into the hands of Will Ransleigh, whose tender care was meant to ensure her delivery to England, where he'd press her into a testimony that might send her all the way to the gallows.

Leaving her son, if she stole him away, an orphan in an alien land.

Was it right to catapult him into poverty, peril and uncertainty? Cut him off from the love, security and comfort of a privileged life in Paris?

If he truly was loved, secure and comfortable.

A sliver of hope surfaced, and she clung to it like a shipwrecked sailor to a floating spar. Perhaps, though his physical needs were being met, he was not well treated by the comtesse. Perhaps his adoptive mother neglected him, left his upbringing to servants. Kind nursemaids and protective footmen were well enough, but wasn't it best for him to live with the mother who doted on him, who would make his comfort and well-being the focus of her existence?

If St Arnaud's sister, the Comtesse de la Rocherie, was not providing that, wouldn't she be justified in stealing back the son she'd been tricked into leaving, despite the dangers and uncertainty of her present position?

Elodie would never have the funds to provide the luxuries available in the household of a comtesse. But did the comtesse love and treasure Philippe, as she would?

Elodie had to know. She would have to return to the Hôtel de la Rocherie and find out.

And then make her terrible choice.

Watching, as Elodie was, the footman and nursemaid's rapid exit from the square, Will was startled when she suddenly set off down the gravelled path. Quickly he caught up, about to seize her arm and warn her he'd not let her escape again, when the stark, anguished face and hollow eyes staring into the far distance told him she was not trying to elude him; she was barely aware of where she was or who walked beside her.

Knowing he would likely get nothing from her in her current state, Will settled for keeping pace, while he wondered about the story behind Elodie Lefevre—and her *son*.

He couldn't deny a soaring sense of relief that the mysterious Philippe had turned out to be a child of some five summers, rather than a handsome, strapping young buck. Thinking back, her soft laughter and oblique answer—'something like'—to his question about whether Philippe was her lover should have alerted him to the fact that the 'family matter' might not involve the rival he was imagining. He might have realised it, had a foolish jealousy not decimated his usual ability to weave into discernible patterns the information he gathered.

'Something like' a lover. Ah, yes; he knew just how much a small boy could love his mother.

The son in Paris was obviously what St Arnaud had used to compel her co-operation in Vienna. How had he finagled that? A man who'd beat a woman half to death probably would not have many scruples about kidnapping a child.

Had she thought, once she'd got back to Paris, she would give him the slip and then simply go off and steal the boy out from under the noses of the family with whom he'd been living?

Will smiled. Apparently she'd thought exactly that. With her talent for disguise and subterfuge, she probably had in her ingenious head a hundred different schemes to make off with the boy and settle with him somewhere obscure and safe.

Until Will Ransleigh had turned up to spoil those plans. He understood much better now why she'd run.

He wondered which of those hundred schemes she intended to try next. After he gave her time to recover from the shock of seeing her son again, he'd ask her. There was no reason now for her not to confess the whole story to him.

And then he would see how he could help her.

He startled himself with that conclusion. It was no part of his design to drag a small boy back to England. But he had already conceded, despite his anger over her duping him, that he'd moved far beyond his original intention to barter her in whatever manner necessary to win Max's vindication.

Somehow, he'd find a way to achieve that and still keep Elodie safe. Elodie, and her son.

Because, as much as he had initially resisted it, a deep-seated, compulsive desire had grown in him to protect this friendless, desperate woman without family or resources, who with courage and tenacity had fought with every trick and scheme she could devise to reclaim a life with her son. Too late now to try to root that out.

He was beginning to tire of the pacing when, at last, she halted as abruptly as she'd begun and sank on to a bench, infinite weariness on her face. Quickly he seated himself beside her. He tipped her chin up to face him, relieved when she did not flinch or jerk away from his touch.

'Philippe is your son.'

'Yes.'

'St Arnaud used him to make you involve Max in his Vienna scheme.'

'Yes.'

'Why did he choose someone he had to coerce? Surely he knew other families with Bonapartist sympathies. Why did he not ask one of their ladies to join his plot?'

She sniffed. 'If you were at all acquainted with St Arnaud, you wouldn't need to ask. He thought women useful only for childbearing or pleasure, much too feeble-minded to remain focused upon a course of action for political or intellectual reasons. No, one could only be sure of controlling their behaviour if one threatened something they held dear.'

'How did he get the child into his power?'

'Because I was stupid,' she spat out. 'So dazzled by his promise of a secure life for myself and my son, I fell right into his trap.'

Having been homeless and penniless, he could well understand the appeal security and comfort must have had for a war widow with few friends and almost no family. 'How did it happen?'

'As I told you, my brother, Maurice, suggested to St Arnaud that I serve as his hostess at the Congress of Vienna. I dismissed the possibility, for with all his contacts, why would St Arnaud choose a shabby-genteel widow with little experience of moving in the highest circles?'

'Why indeed,' she continued bitterly. 'What a fool I was! I should have been much more suspicious that he invited a woman with few resources and no other protector but a man already deeply in his debt. Instead,

I was surprised and flattered when he confirmed the offer, insisting that my "natural aristocratic grace" would make up for any inexperience. St Arnaud promised if I performed well, in addition to letting me keep the gowns and jewels he would buy me for the role, he would settle an allowance on us. Later, when my son came of age, he'd use his influence to advance my son's career.'

'Inducements hard for any mother to refuse.'

'Yes. At least, until he informed me that Philippe would not accompany us. Upon learning that, I did refuse his offer; there was no way I would leave my precious son behind in Paris.'

She laughed without humour. 'That insistence, I now suspect, probably sealed St Arnaud's conviction that I was the perfect victim for his scheme. Utterly able to be controlled through my son—an easy loss to explain away to the brother who depended on him for the advancement of his career, if something happened to me. In any event, St Arnaud urged me to reconsider. It would only be for a few months, he said. I would be so busy I would hardly have time to miss the child. His sister, the Comtesse de la Rocherie, had recently lost her young son and would be thrilled to look after Philippe.'

She rose and began pacing again, as if propelled by memories too painful to bear. 'When I remained firm in my refusal, he told me he'd promised the comtesse I would bring Philippe to visit her—could we not at least do that? Surely I couldn't be so cruel as to disappoint a grieving mother! And so…we went.'

'He kidnapped the child on the way?'

She shook her head in the negative. 'We did call on her. The comtesse was good with Philippe; he liked her at once, and when she offered to take him up to the nursery to play, he begged me to let him go.'

A sad smile touched her lips. 'She told him she had a toy pony with blue-glass eyes and a mane and tail of real horsehair. What child could resist that? Philippe had grown restless and St Arnaud urged me to send him up to romp while we finished our tea. And the comtesse…there was no disguising the yearning in her eyes as she offered Philippe her hand. So I let him go.'

'I let him go,' she repeated in a whisper, tears welling up in her eyes. 'The next thing I remember, I was in a travelling coach, groggy, nauseated, my hands bound, too weak even to push myself upright. Not until we reached the outskirts of Vienna did St Arnaud allow me to regain consciousness.'

'Vienna!' Will burst out, incredulous that St Arnaud had managed to kidnap, not a child, but a grown woman, and transport her hundreds of miles. 'That's outrageous! Did no one at any of the inns notice anything?'

'I expect it was easy enough for him to spin some story about my being ill. The actions of a man of wealth and authority are unlikely to be questioned by post boys and innkeepers.'

Realising the truth of that, Will nodded grimly. 'Go on.'

'As soon as I was strong enough to stand, I told him

I was returning at once to Paris. That was the first time he struck me.'

'Bastard,' Will muttered, wishing St Arnaud would appear on the pathway before them—so he could strangle the life from him.

'He told me if I loved my son and wanted to see him again, I would do exactly as he instructed. Not to waste my time trying to escape him, for he had swift messengers at his disposal and employees back in Paris. Children, like his sister's son, were so frail, he said. Playing happily one evening, dead of a fever by morning.'

'He threatened to kill your son if you didn't co-operate?' Will said. 'He truly was evil.'

She nodded. 'He said my life, my child's life, was nothing compared to the importance of restoring France to glory under Napoleon. When I asked what assurance I had of ever seeing Philippe again, regardless of what I did, he said he was a "reasonable man". Reasonable! If I did my part to make sure his plot succeeded, he would provide everything he'd promised: clothes, jewels, a handsome financial settlement. I might even be acclaimed in Paris as a heroine of the Empire for helping him restore Napoleon to the throne. But if I refused to play my role…I was finished, and so was Philippe. So I did what he wanted.'

'What about your brother?' Will asked. 'Did he not try to find you when St Arnaud disappeared after the failure of the plot?'

'I don't know. Napoleon escaped Elba within days of the assassination attempt. Maurice's regiment, like all the French regiments, was called up as soon as the authorities learned Napoleon had landed back in France. He died at Waterloo.'

'I am sorry. Did the comtesse know where St Arnaud went to ground?'

'Perhaps. I don't think she was involved in planning this. We were both just pawns in his game, me in my poverty with a young son to raise, her in her grief and need. When I was reported dead, naturally she would raise Philippe as her own.'

'But you still want him back.'

'Of course I want him back.'

'Very well, I'll help you steal him.'

Her eyes widened, surprise and a desperate hope in their depths. 'You'll help me?'

He shrugged. 'I doubt you'll leave France willingly without him.'

A worried frown creased her brow. 'It won't be easy. He's not a purse you can pick at a Viennese market, but a small boy. He'll feel alone after we grab him. Frightened.'

Remembered anguish twisted in his gut. He knew what it was to be a small child, frightened and alone.

'First, I'll need to get back into the house,' she said. 'Locate the service stairs, find the nursery, manage to see him again.'

'How do you propose to do that? The "orange seller" is unlikely to be welcomed.'

'Probably not,' she admitted.

Thinking rapidly, Will said, 'We'll go as a tinker and

his wife. While I keep the staff occupied in the kitchen, distracting them with my wares and wit, you can slip up to the nursery.'

She gave him a wan smile. 'Have you a cart, pots, pans and fripperies in those wondrous saddlebags of yours?'

'No, but I've the blunt to buy some. Have you another gown, one that will make you look like a respectable tinker's wife?'

'I have one more gown in this basket, yes.'

'Good.' Will held out his hand. 'Partners again? No more disappearing at dawn?'

'Partners.' Meeting his steady gaze, Elodie clasped his hand and shook it.

Threading his fingers in hers, Will exulted at the surge of connection, as potent and powerful as ever. It was all he could do to refrain from hugging her, so absurdly grateful was he for this chance to begin again. Abducting a child from the household of a wealthy comtesse was a mere nothing; to keep her beside him, he would have pledged to abscond with the entire French treasury.

His heart lighter than it had been since the terrible moment he'd awakened to find her gone, Will contented himself with kissing her hand. 'We passed a café just outside the entrance to the Place. You can wait for me there.' He offered her his arm.

She took it and he tucked her hand against his body, savouring the feel of her beside him as they walked together. Comrades again, as they'd been on the road.

A few moments later, they reached the small establishment he'd noted. After he'd escorted her to a table, rather than release his arm, she held on, studying him. 'You're a remarkable man, Will Ransleigh,' she said softly.

It wasn't exactly an apology. But it was close enough. 'So I am,' he agreed with a grin. 'Give me about two hours to obtain the necessary items.'

She nodded. 'I'll be ready.'

A spring in his step, Will headed off to the market, running through his mind a list of items to procure. Having spent much time wandering around in markets in his youth, perfecting his skill as a thief, he knew just the sort of shiny objects that would tempt footmen, housemaids, cooks and grooms, and where to obtain them quickly.

He paced through the crowded streets on a wave of renewed energy and purpose, buoyed by the knowledge that Elodie hadn't, after all, abandoned him for another man. She'd been pulled away by a bond he, more than anyone, could appreciate: that between a mother and her son.

That loyalty would no longer stand between them. In fact, her gratitude for his help in rescuing her child would reinforce their powerful physical attraction.

Bit by bit, like a clever spider creating its web, fate and circumstance were adding strand after strand, linking them together. Mastering this last challenge and then completing the voyage to England would take time…time to examine the many subtle threads of connection. Time to sample passion and see if it tasted of a future.

He hadn't solved yet the problem of how to vindicate Max while protecting Elodie from retribution, but he'd figure out something. All in all, he felt more hopeful than at any time since he'd smuggled her out of Vienna.

Chapter Fifteen

Three hours later, in his latest guise as a travelling tinker, Will Ransleigh was putting on his best show for a staff happy for a bit of diversion during the break between the preparation and serving of dinner. After convincing the housekeeper to allow all the employees—including the nursery maid—to come down to the servants' hall, Will's witty repartee, glittering wares and a magic trick or two kept his audience preoccupied enough for Elodie to slip unnoticed to the service stairs.

Before they began their charade, he'd told her he'd give her half an hour to find the nursery, bundle up her son and get him out of the house. He'd then finalise any purchases and meet her with the cart, its contents conveniently configured to hide a small boy, on a side street a short distance away, ready to make all speed out of the city.

She'd nodded agreement. She just hadn't told him that she might not be bringing her son. Her gut twisting at the very thought, she ran up the service stairs, heart pounding in anxiety and anticipation.

As she hurried up, she recalled with perfect clarity every detail of her visit to this house that infamous day eighteen months ago. *Please, Lord*, she begged silently, *let this day not end as that one did, with me leaving without my son.*

The comtesse had told her the nursery was on the third floor. Exiting into the hallway, she peeked behind several doors before, beyond the next, she found a small boy playing with soldiers.

His eyes fixed on the toys he was meticulously placing in assorted groups, Philippe didn't look up as she stealthily opened the door. Taking advantage of his preoccupation, she studied him, her heart contracting painfully with joy at seeing him, with sorrow for the years together that had been stolen from them.

He was a lithe-limbed, handsome little boy where she had left a toddler just out of babyhood. He had her eyes, her lips, his now pursed in concentration as he positioned the soldiers just so, Jean-Luc's nose and sable hair that always fell over one brow and his long, graceful fingers.

Just then he looked up, his bright blue eyes curious. 'Who are you? Where is Marie?'

'Down in the kitchen. She asked me to come stay with you while she looked at some fripperies my man is selling.'

'"Fripperies"? Is that something to eat? I hope she brings me some!'

She smiled; Philippe obviously still loved his sweets. 'No biscuits or cakes, I'm afraid. Things like hair ribbons or lace to trim a collar, glass beads for a necklace, or a shiny mirror.'

Suddenly his eyes narrowed and he frowned. 'You were selling oranges in the Place today. You're not going to grab me again, are you? I don't like being grabbed.'

The wariness in his eyes lanced her heart. 'I won't do anything you don't like, I promise.' Trying to buttress her fast-fading hopes, she said, 'What nice soldiers you have! And a pony, too.' She gestured towards the infamous glass-eyed toy horse against the wall behind him.

'I'm too big for it now,' Philippe said, seeming reassured by her pledge. '*Maman* says this summer, she'll get me a real pony. I love horses. I shall be a soldier, like my papa.'

If you only knew, Elodie thought. 'Is your *maman* good to you?'

Philippe shrugged. 'She's *Maman*. Whenever she goes away, she brings me a new toy when she comes back. And reads me a story before bed at night.' He giggled. 'She brings me sweets, too, but you mustn't tell! Nurse says they keep me from going to sleep.'

Elodie pictured the comtesse in her elegant Parisian gown, sitting on the narrow nursery bed, reading to *her* son, ruffling his silken hair, kissing him goodnight. Tears stung her eyes. *It should be me*, her wounded heart whispered.

'I won't tell,' she said.

Philippe nodded. 'Good. I don't like storms. When

wind rattles the windows, *Maman* comes and holds me.'
His eyes lit with excitement. 'And in summer, when we
go to the country house, she lets me catch frogs and
worms. And takes me fishing. But she makes Gasconne
put the worms on the hook.'

Each smile, each artless confidence, drove another
nail into the coffin of her hopes. Anguished, frantic, she
said, 'I could take you to the bird market, here in Paris.
They have parrots from Africa, with bright feathers of
green and blue, yellow and red. Wouldn't you like to
see them?' She held a hand out to him.

His smile fading, he scuttled backwards, away from
her outstretched hand. 'Thank you, *madame*, but I'd
rather go with *Maman*.'

She'd frightened him again, she thought, sick inside.
'Can I ask you one more thing? Will you look very
closely and tell me if I remind you of anyone?'

Obviously reluctant, he focused on her briefly. 'You
look like the orange lady from the park. Will you go
now? I want Marie.'

He scuttled back further, seeming to sense the fierce,
barely suppressed instinct screaming at her to seize him
and make a run for it. Keeping a wide-eyed, wary gaze
on her, he clutched two of his soldiers to his chest…as
if hoping they might magically spring to life and defend him from this threatening stranger.

From her. From a desperate need to be together that
was *her* desire, not *his* any longer.

Agonising as it was, she couldn't avoid the truth.
With her own eyes, she could see her son was healthy,

well dressed and well cared for. From his own lips, she'd heard that the comtesse was an attentive, loving mother. One who could afford to give him a pony, who had a country manor probably as elegant as this town house where they could escape the disease and stink of the city in summer.

He was loved. Happy. *Home.*

Her breath a painful rasp in her constricted chest, she stared at him, trying to commit every precious feature to memory.

A patter of approaching footsteps warned her the nursery maid was approaching. Though her mind couldn't comprehend a future beyond this moment, she knew she didn't want to risk being thrown into a Parisian prison.

Even so, only by forcing herself to admit that fear of *her* lurked behind the mistrustful stare of her son, only by repeating silently the plea that had stabbed her through the heart—*will you go now?*—was she able to force her feet into motion.

'Goodbye, Philippe, my darling,' she whispered. With one last glance, she sped from the room.

To Will's surprise, Elodie returned to the kitchen well before the thirty minutes he'd allotted her…and alone. Pale as if she'd seen a ghost, eyes staring sightlessly into the distance, she took a place at the back of the crowd, not meeting his gaze. Wondering what new disaster had befallen her, Will wrapped up his cajolery with a few short words, curbing his impatience as the customers he'd enticed took their time purchasing laces, ribbons and shaving mirrors. At last, he was able to pack up the remaining merchandise and bundle them both back outside.

As soon as they turned on to the small street bordering the Hôtel de la Rocherie, he halted and turned to her. 'What happened? Is the child ill?'

'Oh, no. He's in excellent health.'

'Then why did you not seize him?'

She shook her head. 'I couldn't.'

'Ah, too difficult in full daylight?' he surmised, well understanding her frustration. 'No matter. You know the lay of the house now. We'll come back tonight. It's clouding over, so the sky will be—'

'No,' she interrupted. 'We won't come back.'

Will frowned at her. 'I don't understand.'

Shivering, she wrapped her arms around herself, as if standing in a cold wind, though the summer afternoon was almost sultry. 'He was playing with soldiers. Very well made, their uniforms exact down to every detail. His own clothing, too, is very fine. He summers at a country manor, where there are streams to fish and ponies to ride.' A ragged sigh escaped her lips. 'I can't give him any of that.'

'What does that matter?' Will asked, his gut wrenching as from the depths of his past rose up the anguished memory of losing his own mother. 'You're his mama!'

'I used to be,' she corrected. 'I'm just the "orange lady" from the park now; it is the comtesse that he calls *Maman*. She dotes on him, reads him stories, even takes him fishing. All I could offer is love, and he already has that, along with so many other things I could never provide.'

'Besides…' she turned to face him, her expression pleading, as if she were trying to convince him—and herself '…bad enough that stealing him, tearing him away from everything familiar and comforting, would terrify him. The comtesse married into a powerful family; she would very likely utilise all her contacts to track him down and drag him back, putting him through another round of terror and uncertainty. He's only four and a half years old! I can't do that to him.'

'So you're just…giving up?' Will asked, incredulous.

Elodie seemed to shrink into herself. 'He doesn't need me any more,' she whispered.

Abruptly, she turned and moved away from him down the street. Not trying to escape him, he realised at once. There was nothing in her movements of the purposeful stride that had taken her from the Hôtel de la Rocherie this morning into the Place Royale, or even of the frenzied tramp around the pathways that followed her first rendezvous with her son.

This was the aimless walk, one plodding foot in front of the other, of someone with no goal and no place to go.

When he had obtained the cart and goods necessary for their current reincarnation as tinkers, Will had also provisioned them for a rapid flight to the coast. Avoiding the usual crossing points at Calais or Boulogne, he intended to engage a smuggler's vessel from one of the smaller channel ports to ferry them over to

Kent, where several easy days' travel would get them to Denby Lodge, Max's horse-breeding farm.

They had no need for a cart now—and no reason to linger any longer in Paris. With some additional blunt, he could exchange the vehicle and its wares for horses, and they could head for the coast at once.

An instinctive itch between his shoulder blades kept telling him to put as much distance as possible between them and the danger posed by Paris. Philippe, intelligent child that he was, would doubtless have told his nursemaid about the 'orange lady's' return. It wouldn't take any great leap of imagination for that woman and the footman who'd guarded the child in the park to connect the sudden arrival of a tinker and his wife to the man and woman who'd accosted Philippe in the Place Royale. After viewing the sumptuous, well-tended Hôtel, he didn't need Elodie's warning to realise the comtesse had powerful connections who wouldn't hesitate to set the authorities after anyone who threatened her child, an annoyance Will would rather not deal with.

But Elodie looked so limp and exhausted, her face and body drained of the fire and energy that normally animated them, Will wasn't sure she could stand a gallop to the coast now. Perhaps he should settle for obtaining horses and getting them to an inn north of Paris, and start the journey in earnest tomorrow.

Remaining within easy return distance of the city would probably be prudent in any event. Though at the moment Elodie seemed to have lost all the purpose and determination that had driven her to survive St

Arnaud's brutality, evade pursuers on the road—and elude *him*—in order to find her son, that might change, once she'd had a chance to rest her exhausted body and spirits. No point getting her halfway to England aboard some smuggling vessel and having her decide she must return to Paris and try again.

He knew only too well the agony of thinking you'd lost the one person you loved most in the world. But unlike a mother claimed by death, Elodie's son was very much alive. Though he understood that love made her put her son's best interests over her own desires, everything within him protested the unfairness of forcing her to make such a sacrifice.

He ached to ease her pain by urging that they return to reclaim her son, but at the moment, he had no reasonable answers to the objections she'd raised to simply stealing him away. By dint of skilful gaming and even more skilful investing, he was no longer the penniless orphan who, at Eton, had taunted the boys into gaming with him to earn a few pence to buy meat pies. But the property and modest wealth he'd thus far accumulated was no match for the resources of a comtesse, even if he could persuade Elodie to accept some.

As for influence, his only elevated connection was his uncle. Not only was the earl highly unlikely to embrace any cause supported by his black-sheep illegitimate nephew, he might well forfeit even the loyalty of his Ransleigh Rogue cousins if, after pledging to restore Max's reputation, he appeared instead to champion the woman who'd ruined it.

He wouldn't suggest they do anything, raise her hopes to no purpose, until he could consider the matter more carefully and come up with a better plan.

An inn north of Paris it must be, Will decided.

After a quick exchange of cart and contents for horses, Will had got a listless Elodie mounted. For the rest of the day, they had ridden north at a pace he thought easy enough for her to tolerate. Just before dark, they stopped at a village along the coaching road, where Will located a suitable establishment and engaged a room.

For the whole of their journey there, Elodie had neither looked directly at him nor spoken, seemingly lost in an abyss of despair and fatigue too profound for anything to penetrate.

Gently he led her to the room and helped her to the bed. 'Sleep. I'm going to arrange our horses for tomorrow and get some food. I'll be back with your dinner very soon. Men's clothing, too, perhaps, for this last leg of our journey?'

But even that mild jest produced no response. Sighing, Will stripped her down to her chemise and guided her back against the pillows. She was still staring blankly into space when he closed the door.

Darkness had fallen by the time he returned. As he quietly lit a candle, he noted Elodie dozing in the same position in which he'd left her, head thrown back against the pillows like a broken doll, her face pale and her hands limp beside her.

Will considered setting out food and wine and leaving her in solitude with her grief. The last thing he wanted was to witness her pain and be dragged into remembering the anguish of his own youth. Yet, aching for her, he realised he couldn't leave her so alone and vulnerable, even if it meant fending off memories he had no wish to revisit.

Dragging a chair beside the bed, Will settled himself to watch over her.

Suddenly, she shuddered and cried out. 'Hush, sweeting,' he soothed, gathering her in his arms.

Her every muscle tensing, she jerked away before her eyes opened and her hazy gaze fixed on his face. 'Will,' she murmured. Going limp again in his arms, she slumped back.

He plumped up the pillows and eased her up to a sitting position. 'I've brought food and drink,' he said, going over to fetch the supplies from his saddlebag. 'You must eat. It's after dark and you've had nothing but a little wine since before dawn.'

She didn't reply, but when he put the cup to her lips she sipped. After asking how she felt and what she wanted—and receiving no answers—he lapsed into silently feeding her bits of cheese and bread, which she ate mechanically, without seeming aware of him or the nourishment she was consuming.

When she would take no more, Will finished the wine and bread. As he was returning the remaining meat and cheese to the saddlebags, Elodie wrapped her arms around her torso and began rocking back and forth.

Tears welled up in her eyes and, a few moments later, she was weeping in earnest. Tossing down the saddlebags, Will climbed into the bed, gathered her into his arms and held her as deep, racking sobs shuddered through her body.

He cradled her against his chest as she wept out her grief, wishing there was some way he could ease that terrible burden. Finally the sobs grew shallower, slowed, stopped, then she fell asleep in his arms.

He must have dozed, too, for when he woke some time later, the candle had burned out. Too weary himself to light another, he slid far enough away from Elodie to divest himself of his clothing, then rolled back into the bed's inviting warmth.

Gathering her against him, he found her lips in the darkness and kissed her tenderly. 'Sleep, my darling. We've a long journey tomorrow.'

To his surprise, she reached up, pulled his head down and kissed him back.

This was no gentle caress, but a demanding capture of lips, followed by a sweep of her tongue into his mouth that banished grogginess and instantly turned simmering desire into boiling need.

While her tongue probed and demanded, her hands moved up and down his hardness. Still caressing him with one hand, she urged him on to his back and, breaking the kiss, in one swift motion raised her chemise and straddled him, guiding his swollen member to her soft inviting heat.

'Love me, Will,' her urgent voice pleaded in the darkness.

This was anguish seeking the oblivion of pleasure, he knew. But if pleasuring her would keep the pain at bay, he was happy to assist. Grasping her bottom, he thrust hard, sheathing himself in tight, seductive heat.

He would have stilled then, slowed, made it last, but Elodie was having none of it.

Pulling his thumbs to her nipples, she angled her hips and moved to take him deeper still. With him buried within her, she thrust again and again, riding him faster, harder, deeper, her nails scoring his shoulders, her teeth nipping his skin, until she cried out as her pleasure crested.

An instant later, he reached his own release. Wrapping her in his arms, still joined, Will rolled with her to his side and snuggled her there as together, sated, they fell into the boneless sleep of exhaustion.

Chapter Sixteen

Will woke just after dawn the following morning. At the feel of Elodie beside him, her head nestled on his shoulder, a glow of joy and well-being suffused him. The warmth lingered even after his groggy brain, lagging behind his senses, grew alert enough to remember how despondent and grief-stricken she'd been the previous night.

She'd also come alive in his arms, allowing him to sweep her away for a time from the anguish and sorrow. That had to count for something.

As long as her son was alive and well, there was hope. If whoever had been watching Elodie wanted to harm the boy, they could have done so long since, so there was every reason to expect he would continue to be healthy and content, living with the comtesse. Eventually, Will would figure out a way to reclaim him that would place no hardship on the boy. For now, he must get Elodie, who might still be in danger, safely back to England.

She stirred and he kissed her lips, his joy multiplying when she murmured and wrapped her arms around his neck to kiss him back. Desire surged as she fit herself against him and, for a time, the problems awaiting them outside their bedchamber receded as he made love to her, long and sweet and slow.

Eventually, they could avoid them no longer. 'You wanted to leave early for the coast?' Elodie said, sitting up. 'It's long past dawn now. I'd better dress.'

'You're sure you don't want to return to Paris and try again to take your son?'

Her jaw clenched and she closed her eyes briefly, as if reeling from a blow. 'He doesn't even recognise me, Will,' she said softly when she reopened them. 'Even if he did—what was I thinking? I have a few paltry jewels I could sell, enough, perhaps, to buy a small cottage somewhere in the country. But beyond that, I have no money, no family, no resources. Nothing to fall back on, nothing put away to pay for schooling or to assure his future. If Maurice were still alive…but he's not, and there's no one else. Besides, who's to say what will happen after we get to England? How could I drag him into that? No, we should just leave today, as you wished.'

Much as it pained him to see the bleak look back in her eyes, empty platitudes wouldn't comfort her. Until he formulated some intelligent plan that offered real hope, it was better to say nothing.

Apparently taking silence for agreement, she slipped from the bed and picked up her scattered garments. 'So

I travel as a woman this time? Or have you yet another disguise in that bag?'

Trying not to be distracted by the arousing vista of Elodie, naked but for the bundle of clothing she held, he forced himself to concentrate on the imperative of getting them quickly to the Channel and on to England, before Talleyrand or whoever else had been following them discovered their current location. Realising now what her objective in Paris had been, any French agent worth his pay must know her story and would have kept the comtesse's house under surveillance. So their pursuers must know they'd made it back to Paris.

'I'm afraid the bag of tricks is rather empty and the funds are running low. We'll travel as we are for now and, as you suggest, go at once.'

Giving him a wan smile—so pale an imitation of the brilliant ones that had warmed his heart during their journey that his chest ached—she dressed quickly. He did the same, then assembled their bags and walked down to pay the landlord. After retrieving their newly hired horses from the stables, with Elodie waiting listlessly beside him, Will fastened their bags on to the saddles.

At first, he paid little attention to the private coach that was progressing slowly down the street, the roadway already filling with the usual early-morning assortment of farmers, maids, vendors, clerks and townspeople going about their business. Until, its driver apparently distracted by an altercation between two tradesmen whose carts had collided, the vehicle began heading almost directly at them.

Will had been about to shout a warning to the driver, when the coach inexplicably began to pick up speed. Preoccupied with controlling their now shying, stamping mounts, he was trying to shift both sets of reins into one hand and pull Elodie back out of harm's way with the other as the coach swayed by them, dangerously close.

Suddenly, the door opened, a man leaned out and grabbed Elodie by the arms. Before Will could finish transferring the reins, the assailant dragged Elodie into the vehicle. Will caught one last glimpse of her struggling figure before the door slammed shut and the driver sprang the horses, scattering people, poultry and produce in its wake.

An hour later, the bruiser who'd muscled Elodie into the closed carriage and bound and gagged her, dragged her from the coach and up the back stairs of an inn. After shoving her into a room, he closed the door behind her. Her anxious ears were relieved to hear no key turn in the lock before his footsteps retreated.

Since the henchman who'd grabbed her had said nothing the entire journey, she still had no idea who had abducted her or why.

Furiously she worked at the bonds, desperate to escape before anyone else arrived to manhandle her. After a few moments, she succeeded in freeing her hands. She'd just ripped off the gag when, her eyes finally adjusting to the dimness of the shuttered room, she realised she was not alone.

Her skin prickled and the sour taste of fear filled her mouth as she recognised the shadowed figure seated at the table of what appeared to be a private parlour. 'St Arnaud!' she gasped.

'Indeed,' he said, giving her a nod. 'You appear to be as delighted to see me as I was to discover you'd apparently come back from the dead. I must admit, I was quite distressed when Prince Talleyrand informed me you'd been sighted in Paris. He advised me to take better care of you this time.'

Fury and loathing coursed through her, swamping the fear. 'You *took care* of me before. You took my son!'

He shook his head. 'Very maladroit of you to be manoeuvred into it. A bit of money, some promises of advancement dangled before you, and it was done. So distastefully predictable. Ah, well, your foolishness has made my dear sister very happy.'

Never in her life had Elodie truly wished to harm someone, but at that moment, she would have bartered her soul for a weapon. She wanted to pummel St Arnaud, carve the sardonic smile off his face, make him scream with pain. Not for the beatings he'd inflicted on her in Vienna, but for the blow to the heart from which she'd never recover.

'Bastard,' she spat out, her eyes scanning the room for anything she might use against him.

'Not me, my dear! That epithet belongs to the hovel-born Englishman who's been attempting to assist you.

And don't bother to agitate yourself searching; I'm not foolish enough to leave lying about anything you might use to defend yourself. Now, how shall we dispose of you this time? Something quick and merciful?'

'You mean to do it yourself? You haven't the stomach.'

His gaze hardened. 'You think not?'

'You let others do the difficult work before. What happened to the poor wretch who pulled the trigger on Lord Wellington?'

St Arnaud lifted an elegant brow. 'He was hanged, I suppose. Only what he deserved for being sloppy and inaccurate. Anyway, he was just a means to an end.'

'Like me.'

'Like you. Although unlike Franz, whom the Austrian authorities took care of long ago, you're much more trouble, turning up again after all this time.'

'Then let me relieve you of her,' said a voice from the doorway.

'Will!' Elodie cried, her fear and anger swamped in a surge of surprise, relief and gladness.

St Arnaud's eyes widened with alarm for an instant before he smoothed his features back to a sardonic calm. 'Ah, the bastard appears.'

'Surely you were expecting me. A horse can easily keep pace with a carriage and, with the driver on the box and only one flunky within, there was no one to prevent my following. It's about time you had to deal with someone more up to your weight. And after I do, we'll go.'

'You think I'll just let her leave with you?' St Arnaud laughed. 'How quaint, that you survived soldiering and a childhood in Seven Dials with such naïve notions intact. I would have thought you'd expect me to go for the kill.'

'She's no threat to you.'

'Is she not? What about the testimony you want her to give in London? Dredging up that old scandal could cause a great deal of unpleasantness, just as I'm re-establishing my career.'

'Re-establishing?' Will echoed. 'There's a king on France's throne now. What of your love for Napoleon?'

St Arnaud shrugged. 'He'll never escape from that speck of rock in the Atlantic. I don't deny I regret that France has been saddled with fat old King Louis, but one must adapt to changing circumstances, as Prince Talleyrand always says. I'm a St Arnaud; I belong at the centre of France's political affairs. Now, *monsieur*, I don't know how you convinced Raoul to let you in, but I've no quarrel with you. Leave now and I'll not call the gendarmes and have you thrown in jail.'

'Magnanimous of you,' Will said, showing his teeth.

'Quite. I doubt your uncle would bestir himself on behalf of the bastard branch of family and French prisons are so unpleasant.'

'At least I earned that title by birth. Being a bastard, though, don't you think I would have taken care of such small details as a few retainers? As you said, I was breeched in Seven Dials. It's not wise to leave loose knives lying about that might get thrown at your back.'

Had he really eliminated St Arnaud's henchmen, or was he bluffing? Elodie wondered, shooting him a glance. He gave her a wink.

After weeks on the road from Vienna, witnessing all his skill and ingenuity, she'd bet on Will against odds much higher than these.

St Arnaud wasn't sure, either. His arrogant confidence wavering a bit, he stepped towards the door.

Will stationed himself in front of it, his gaze challenging. 'Let her leave with me now and I might consider letting you live.' He moved his hand so quickly even Elodie didn't follow it and extracted a knife from his pocket.

Making no attempt now to disguise his alarm, St Arnaud reached into his own pocket, uttering an oath when he found it empty.

'Didn't bring a weapon with you? How careless!' Will taunted. 'But then, against a slip of a woman, I suppose you thought your fists would be sufficient.' His eyes narrowing to slits, his expression so murderous the hair raised on the back of Elodie's neck just watching him, Will stepped towards St Arnaud.

Swallowing hard, St Arnaud retreated behind the table. 'Raoul!' he called. 'Etienne! *Venez immediatement!*'

Will laughed and took a step closer. 'Bellow all you want. Your watchdogs are "taking a nap" and the landlord's gone deaf. I outbid you, you see.'

Looking around wildly, St Arnaud fixed his gaze on Elodie. 'Do you really want to go with him? Hanging's an ugly death. I'm sure we can settle our little misunderstanding after all.'

'She knows better than to trust a miscreant like you. Elodie, step behind me, please.' He gave her a quick, pleading glance, as if he weren't sure she would choose him over St Arnaud.

How could he have any doubt? Swiftly she crossed the room. He gave her arm a reassuring squeeze as she passed him, then tucked her behind him. 'His men are tied up, unconscious,' he murmured in an undertone. 'Our horses are at the back. As soon as I deal with this abomination, we'll go.'

Twirling the knife between his fingers, Will looked back at St Arnaud and sighed. 'This is awkward, isn't it? Whatever am I to do with you now? Should I upset my uncle by committing murder? Ah, well, he's upset with me most of the time anyway.' He stepped purposefully closer to St Arnaud.

As he advanced, St Arnaud put his hands out in front of him. 'I'll pay whatever you want! Talleyrand told me the earl never settled on you the sum he promised. I can have a handsome amount transferred to any bank you like.'

'Can you?' Will halted, as if he were considering the offer. Before St Arnaud, looking relieved, could say another word, Will extracted a pistol from his pocket. 'Perhaps I should make it look like you shot yourself instead? Crazed by worry that the old scandal might compromise your new position? I'm sure Elodie could write quite a convincing suicide note.'

'No, please!' St Arnaud wailed. '*Monsieur*, reconsider! What benefit to you if I die? Let me live and I can—'

'Silence, vermin,' Will spat out. 'I've never met a man more deserving of murder, but I'd not soil my blade. However, I might just work the itchiness out of my fists by beating you into the carpet...like you beat her in Vienna.'

'Will, if you're not going to kill him, don't beat him,' Elodie urged, unsure she didn't prefer murder as an option. 'He might hurt my son. He couldn't best you, but he could handle a little boy.'

'Ah, yes, your son.' Will frowned. 'That does present a dilemma. If I let him live, what assurance do we have that he won't harm the boy after we've gone?'

'Of course I wouldn't harm him!' St Arnaud cried with a show of indignation. 'My sister has claimed him as her own, which makes him nearly a St Arnaud. Prince Talleyrand himself dotes upon the boy.'

'I don't know,' Will said, twirling the blade again. 'It would be simpler to gut you and be done with it.'

Elodie didn't know what to think. Much as she detested St Arnaud, she wasn't sure she could live with her conscience if she allowed Will to murder him. Which she was nearly certain Will would do, coolly, cleanly and efficiently, if she told him to.

She didn't trust St Arnaud one bit, but she'd seen for herself that Philippe was treated as the comtesse's beloved son, and she knew St Arnaud was inordinately proud of family and position. Nor would he be foolish enough to cross a man as powerful as Prince Talley-rand, whom he must have already had to appease after the débâcle in Vienna.

'*Madame*, I swear to you, the boy will come to no harm!' St Arnaud cried, recalling her attention.

Will glanced back at her. 'Elodie?'

While Elodie hesitated, agonised, there was a knock at the door, followed by the entrance of a tall, imperi-ous figure.

He halted inside and surveyed the scene, seeming neither surprised nor perturbed to have come upon a woman clinging to the back of a man who was threat-ening a second man with a knife. 'Madame Lefevre,' he said, bowing to her. 'And you must be Monsieur Ransleigh.'

Glancing at the knife, he wrinkled his nose in dis-taste. 'Please, *monsieur*, there is no need for such vul-garities. Allow me to introduce myself. Antoine de Montreuil, Comte de Merlonville, assistant to the Duc de Richelieu, who succeeded Prince Talleyrand last au-tumn as Prime Minister of France.'

Turning his gaze to St Arnaud, he sighed. 'Thierry, must you ever be rash, acting without thinking? When the Prince learned you had rushed off to…detain this lady, he informed Monsieur le Duc at once, telling him he'd made it quite clear to you that you were to speed her on her way.'

'Speed her on—' St Arnaud echoed. 'He told me to "take care of her"!'

'Precisely. However, though the Prince, ah, advises,

it is the Duc who makes policy now. Only your family name and lineage persuaded Talleyrand to retain you after the Vienna fiasco. Monsieur Ransleigh has sought *madame*'s assistance to deal with a matter that is of personal interest solely to his family, and perhaps the British Foreign Office. His Highness the King does not need to be troubled about it, so I suggest that you cease obstructing their progress immediately...or I must warn you, the Duc is likely to be much less forgiving than the Prince.'

Turning from St Arnaud in clear dismissal, de Merlonville addressed Elodie and Will. '*Monsieur* and *madame*, I am so sorry you were inconvenienced. The Duc would be happy to offer you an escort to the coast, to ensure no other...recalcitrants trouble you.'

After studying the Duc's self-professed assistant warily for a moment, Will shook his head. 'Thank you, but I don't think that will be necessary.'

'What of the child?' Elodie cried, needing to be sure about this.

'Child?' de Merlonville repeated.

'Philippe. Philippe...de la Rocherie.'

'What has the Prince Talleyrand's godson have to do with this?' the official asked.

'Philippe is Prince Talleyrand's godson?' Will interjected.

'Well, not officially. But the comtesse's late husband being a close associate of the Prince for many years, he watches over the widow.'

'I see.' Her relief that the comtesse did, in fact, have

a powerful protector who would ensure her son's safety faded rapidly when she realised the full implications of the association.

In her wildest imagining, she might envision some day acquiring a settled home and enough coin to challenge the comtesse's control over her son. But never in any imagining could she hope to find Philippe a sponsor who had the wealth, power and influence of Prince Talleyrand, who'd been at the highest level of France's political life through three successive governments.

Will seemed to sense her dismay, for, after stowing his knife and pistol, he reached over to take her hand. 'Are you ready to leave?'

There seemed nothing further to do or say. 'I suppose so.'

Looking to de Merlonville, Will gestured towards St Arnaud. 'If we might have a moment?'

'Only if you'll promise me not to carve him up once my back is turned. So distressing to the innkeeper and so damaging to the carpet, all that blood.'

'I give you my word.'

De Merlonville nodded. 'Monsieur Ransleigh, you will convey my kind regards to your uncle, the earl? I had occasion to meet him and some other leaders of Parliament when I visited London for the Duc last fall. And, Thierry, I trust you now understand your position? The post to the Caribbean for which the Prince recommended you has not been confirmed…yet. I'm certain you would not wish to compromise your political future by delaying these good people any further.'

'Of—of course not, my dear Comte.'

'Then I suggest you gather up your effects and make ready to return to Paris, while they continue on their way.'

Nodding quickly, St Arnaud pivoted to collect his coat and a snuffbox and some other items strewn about the table. While his back was turned, the comte murmured to them, 'A lovely island, St Lucia. But an area rife with tropical fevers, not to mention the danger of pirates. Many venture there and so few return.'

He gave them a wink, then bowed himself out of the room.

After he departed, Will turned to St Arnaud. Having retrieved his personal items and shrugged on his greatcoat, he was careful to keep the table between himself and Will, while his still-florid face gave evidence of his fury and chagrin.

'Well, vermin, it appears that you'll get to live after all. Though I don't count *your* assurances about the boy worth a ha'penny, I do respect the Prince…and his plans. Still, I want you to know I'll be watching. You'd better pray that Madame Lefevre's son lives a healthy, happy, prosperous life. If I learn he's suffered so much as a sniffle, I'll track you down and snuff out your miserable life.'

Taking Elodie's arm, Will said, 'I believe there's a packet at the coast awaiting us in Calais.'

Chapter Seventeen

Though Will and Elodie had politely declined de Merlonville's offer of an escort, even in her state of diminished awareness, Elodie sensed a subtle presence trailing them during the long days of riding towards the Channel. It wasn't until after dark of the fourth day, when Will hustled her from the room he'd engaged at a Calais inn down narrow back stairs to a pair of waiting horses and rode off with her into the night that she realised he, too, had noted—and mistrusted—whatever force was following them.

Silently he led her horse along narrow back lanes, with only the stars and the distant lights of Calais to guide them, until they reached a small port some miles further south down the coast. Will finally brought them to a halt before a mean-looking inn which boasted only one smoky lantern by its entrance to announce its calling.

Warning her in a low voice to remain outside, he disappeared into the structure. A few moments later, he returned to lead their horses to a lean-to barn at the rear and then escort her up the back stairs to a low-ceilinged room under the eaves whose tiny window overlooked the road and the harbour beyond.

'Sorry to drag you out of your comfortable accommodations for something I fear will be much inferior,' he said as he waved her to the table by the window. 'Not that I don't appreciate the good wishes of the Prime Minister's own man. But I'd rather return to England on transport of my own choosing—and hopefully without the Duc or the Prince's knowledge.'

'On a smuggling vessel? This certainly looks disreputable enough to be a smuggler's inn. You have the most interesting contacts, Monsieur Ransleigh.'

His eyes lit at the gentle barb in her response. 'Are you feeling better?' he asked, pulling a flask of wine from his saddlebags and pouring them a cup.

Better? she asked herself, accepting the mug. She'd gone from agony to numbness, like a recent amputee after the opium took hold. Other than that, she felt… empty, barren as a seashell-dotted beach after a storm had swept it of its treasures, scouring it down to elemental sand.

'I'm feeling…here, I suppose.'

'That's progress. You've been gone quite a while.'

It occurred to her that Will had been unusually taciturn for the whole of their journey north from Paris, trotting steadily beside her with minimal chat, stopping to share bread, cheese and wine at midday without attempting to regale her with any of his stories, settling them in an inn long after dark with only a brief caress before they both fell into the sleep of exhaustion.

Not surprising. In the paralysed state in which she'd existed since emerging from the first shock of leaving Philippe, she'd probably been oblivious to any conversational attempts he might have made. The awful reality of losing her son again had been like staring into the sun, the terrible brilliance blinding her to everyone and everything else around her.

Aside from the vivid encounter with St Arnaud north of Paris, she scarcely remembered anything about the days between walking out of Philippe's bedchamber at the Hôtel de la Rocherie and arriving at the coast tonight. Trying to piece events together now, she could come up with only snippets of memory.

Will, walking beside her across Paris. Settling her into a bed. Feeding her with his own hands. Cradling her against his warmth while grief smashed her like a china doll into shards of misery. And when the anguish had been past bearing, helping her escape into the oblivion of passion.

No friend, companion or lover could have treated her with more gentleness and compassion. A tiny flicker of warmth—affection, gratitude—lit the bleakness within.

'Thank you, sweet Will,' she murmured.

'For rescuing you from St Arnaud? That was my pleasure, though I would have preferred to have beaten him into pudding, if I was not to be allowed to gut him.'

'Would you have gutted him?'

He paused. 'I don't know. Would you have wanted me to?'

'Yes. No. Oh, *je sais pas*! How can I know, when it would make no difference? Killing him wouldn't get Philippe back.'

'It would have guaranteed Philippe could never fall under his power. Although it does seem both Talleyrand and the Prime Minister have united to send him far away, far enough that your son will be safe—and they will be freed from his scheming. Apparently they've also given us their blessing, or so it seems. What do you make of de Merlonville's appearance?'

Like an old iron wheel gone rusty from disuse, she had to scrape away a clogging coat of apathy to focus her mind on the question.

'Talleyrand has been replaced. I didn't know that.'

'Nor did I, but it seems he retains a good deal of influence.'

Thinking more swiftly now, she ran back through her memory the whole exchange between St Arnaud and de Merlonville in the upstairs parlour. 'De Merlonville said Prince Talleyrand had informed the Duc about St Arnaud snatching me, so he must still have agents trailing us…but apparently the Duc now controls who takes action. St Arnaud is tolerated, but just barely. With his thirst for power, I expect St Arnaud will be very careful not to make any further moves against us—or Philippe—without the Duc's approval.'

'In any event, it appears he will soon be leaving France—permanently, de Merlonville seemed to suggest,' Will said. 'The comte also seemed to want to make clear that the French government had no interest in any testimony you might give.'

She nodded. 'Which seems logical—with the king's throne secure, no one would wish to remind Louis of the unhappy past by bringing to his notice a long-failed Napoleonic plot.'

'That matches what George Armitage told us outside Linz—neither the French nor British governments want to dredge up the old scandal now. Which would leave those de Merlonville called "recalcitrants" as the most likely group looking to harass us.'

'Yes, St Arnaud and any of his remaining associates trying to claw their way back into government would be keen to make sure no embarrassing evidence of their former Bonapartist leanings came to light,' Elodie summed up. '*Eh bien*, de Merlonville was instructed to provide us an escort to prevent them from harrying us.'

'Perhaps. Unless de Merlonville's offer was intended to put us off our guard and we are still in danger from Talleyrand's forces, too. Although, since they could have apprehended us any time during our travel north, that seems unlikely, I prefer to remain wary. Hence, this draughty inn.

'A precaution of the wisest sort.'

'I hope you continue to think so after you've slept in bedclothes clammy from its dripping eaves.'

She tilted her head at him. 'You have slept under its dripping eaves before, perhaps?'

Will grinned at her. 'Never underestimate the contacts of a former thief, cut-purse and salesman of illegal goods.'

'You were involved in smuggling, too?'

'Smugglers make landfall all along the coast, then use a network of agents to move the goods inland. The boss for whom I worked used to have us distribute lace, silk and brandy that had never had duty paid on it to eager, if clandestine, clients. A profitable business, as long as the revenue agents didn't catch you.'

'You *have* led an adventurous life.'

'No more so than you. *Émigrée* creeping from Nantes in the dead of night, returnee to the "New France", soldier's bride, grieving widow disguised as a wounded soldier passing through the detritus of two armies, Vienna hostess, seamstress in hiding, old man, valet, monk, farm girl, orange seller...' Will ticked them off on his fingers.

She'd been smiling at his list until the last disguise reminded her of Paris and the final resolution of her quest. 'Then back to Elodie again,' she said quietly. 'Without home, without family, without my son.' Her voice breaking on the last word, she slumped back in the chair, despair and weariness suddenly overtaking her.

She felt Will's hand cover her own. 'At least you need no longer worry about St Arnaud's interference.'

'Perhaps not,' she replied with a sigh, looking over at him. 'Praise God, my son is safe. But he is still lost to me.'

'Where there is life, there is hope, so—'

She put her hand to his lips, stopping his words. 'Please, Will, no more schemes!' she cried. 'I can't bear it.'

He must have realised how close she still walked to the precipice of falling apart completely, for when she removed her finger, he let the topic drop. Silently he took her hand again, stroking it, his sympathetic gaze on her face.

'I wish I could help. I know how much you've lost.'

Though her rational mind appreciated his attempt at empathy, the wounded animal in her turned on him.

'You *know*?' she spat back. 'How could you? *Je te jure*, you have no idea what I feel!'

'Swear if you like, but I do. I held my mother's hand and watched her die. I was five years old.'

The expression on Will's face struck her to silence, her anger withering in its wake. No wonder he'd never wanted to talk about his childhood.

Five years old—almost the same age as Philippe! And she had thought stealing her son from his home a trial too great for any child to bear.

Compassion—tinged with shame—filled her.

'I'm so sorry,' she whispered.

'She was the only being in the world who'd ever cared for me or tried to protect me,' he said softly, staring beyond her, seemingly unaware of her presence. The anguish in his eyes said he was reliving the experience. 'Though I was always hungry and ragged, even at that age, I knew she was doing the best she could for me.'

Elodie hesitated, unsure what to say that might bring him back from the emotional abyss into which he'd tumbled. Then he shook his head, as if throwing off the memories, and turned to her with an apologetic smile. 'I told you the tale wasn't edifying.'

'How did you survive?'

'I already knew the street boys, though Mama had tried to keep me from running with them. They found me at the market, going through rubbish piles with another, smaller boy, looking for the bits thrown away by the vendors as too tough or rotten to sell. When two of them tried to take away what the younger lad had gleaned, I fought them off. Their leader, an older boy, stopped us. He probably could have finished me with one fist, but instead, he ordered them to leave me alone. Said he liked my spirit and they could use another fighter. So they took me in, taught me the ways of the street.'

'How to thieve?'

He nodded. 'Thieving, house-breaking, lock-picking, card-sharking, knife-fighting. Sleight-of-hand and how to do a few magic tricks to beguile the gullible while a mate picked their pockets. The real trick was to become skilled enough to win without using a weighted deck or marked cards.'

'It must have been quite a change, when the earl brought you to Swynford Court.'

Will laughed, a rueful smile on his lips. 'By then, I was in line to become a street leader for the boss, and resisted mightily being dragged into the country by the brother of the toff who had abandoned my mother. Nor was I interested in exchanging my mates for three dandified cousins. Alastair and Dom were as unimpressed by me as I was by them. But Max…for Max, it was different. I was a Ransleigh by blood and that was that: whatever it took, he would turn me into one.'

'What did it take?' she asked, curious. 'I don't imagine you would have made the task easy.'

'I did not. After beating some respect into me, he used a bit of everything—coaxing, challenging, empathising, daring, rewarding. By the end of the summer, much to the chagrin of Alastair and Dom, who had bet him the transformation couldn't be done, he'd instilled in me a sufficient modicum of gentlemanly behaviour that the earl agreed not to return me to Seven Dials.'

Elodie thought about the dangers of a child's existence on the streets and shuddered. '*Grace à Dieu* he didn't send you back!'

'I thank God, too. Max saved my life, plain and simple. But passing muster with the earl was just the first step. In many ways, Eton and Oxford were more difficult, not a single test but a limitless series of them. It was Max who taught me there would never be an end to bullies wanting to pummel me, or better-born snobs trying to shame me, and it was smarter to outwit and outmanoeuvre them rather than fight. A born diplomat, even as a boy, he knew I was too proud to take money from him. Though the earl paid my school fees, I had no allowance; it was Max and my cousins who lured the other boys into playing cards or dice with me, or betting on my magic tricks. I'd always win enough for a meat pasty at Eton, or steak and a pint of ale at Oxford.'

'So that's where you perfected your beguiling pedlar's tricks.'

He cupped her chin in his hands and tilted her face until she met the intensity of his gaze. 'So you understand why I'm so loyal to Max and my cousins? Why the bond between us is as strong as the one between a mother and her son?'

He wanted her to realise why, despite all they had shared, he was still willing to sacrifice her to redeem his cousin. Though she'd thought by now she was incapable of feeling anything, a sharp, anguished pang stabbed in her gut.

'Seeing all you've done since Vienna, I already understood. I respect Monsieur Max, too. He was kind to me, even tried to protect me as best he could from St Arnaud's abuse. Nothing but the imperative to get my son back would have forced me into tricking one of the very few true gentlemen I've ever met. A gentleman who offered to assist me, not to further some scheme of his own, but out of genuine concern.'

As everything else, that story led back to her loss. Recalling it like a knife slash across her heart, she said, 'Ah, *mon Dieu*, it's even worse, knowing I entrapped him and lost my son anyway. At least now I can attempt to make amends by fulfilling our bargain. I will testify to whatever you wish to vindicate your cousin and clear his reputation.'

Will hesitated. 'That might not be such a good idea.'

'Not a good idea?' she echoed, confused. 'Haven't

you just spent the last few weeks dragging me across Europe to do just that?'

'True, but your testimony might have…severe consequences if, instead of viewing this as a personal matter concerning only Max's reputation, the Foreign Office decided to open an official enquiry. The penalty for being judged an accomplice in an attempt to murder the allied commander…' His words trailed off.

Would be a long sojourn in prison, or death, she knew. 'That outcome is always a possibility, although both de Merlonville and Armitage said neither government wants a formal investigation. But if they should, it would be as you told me in Vienna: a life for a life. Not so bad a bargain. Monsieur Max would become a great man, who could do much good. I could do this one thing and then I…I am of no more good to anyone anyway.'

For a long moment he held her gaze. 'You're good for me,' Will whispered.

The tenderness of it made her already-decimated heart ache. 'Sweet Will,' she said, attempting a smile. Their strong mutual attraction didn't change the melancholy facts. The unique, incomparable interlude of their journey from Vienna, wary co-conspirators who'd become mutual admirers, then friends, and then the most passionate of lovers, was almost over.

The silly, battered heart she'd thought was beyond feeling anything contracted in a spasm of grief that she must lose Will, too. She stifled its instinctive demand that she find some way to extend their time together.

But the English coast loomed just beyond a narrow

stretch of restless sea and she'd never been one to deny reality. It was time to see the bargain she'd made to its conclusion.

Gently pushing Will's hands away, she took the last sip from her mug. 'I imagine you've conjured a vessel and some good sailing weather for tomorrow. We should rest now, if we're to be away early in the morning.'

Looking troubled, Will opened his lips as if to speak. Elodie stopped him with a hand to his lips. 'There's no more to say. Rest easy, Will. *C'est presque fini.* Your quest is almost done.'

Putting aside her mug, Elodie swiftly disrobed down to her chemise and climbed into the uneven bed, settling back on the pillows with a sigh. In the hollow emptiness within, lit only by the warmth of tenderness for Will, the decision to testify, come what may, sat well.

She wasn't sure when she'd made it. Some time during the long silent hours of moving north from Paris, probably, as the reality of life without Philippe settled into her shredded heart. She could repay the debt she owed Max Ransleigh, even the balance between. Like a person suddenly blinded, she could see no future beyond sitting before a green baize table in a Foreign Office enquiry room.

'May you have a happy, distinguished life, Philippe, *mon ange*,' she whispered, as a rip tide of exhaustion swept her towards sleep.

Bone-weary, Will climbed in bed beside Elodie. During the last of their discussion, he'd wanted to interrupt her, to disagree, to tell her how unique and beautiful she was. But as he hadn't yet worked out a remedy for her stark assessment of her condition—a woman without home, without family, without her son—she would have seen any such speech as pretty, empty words.

He wanted to tell her she meant too much for him to let her become a sacrifice to Max's redemption. But how could he expect her to believe him, when every step he'd taken since arriving in Vienna had been directed towards doing just that?

Unable to voice or reconcile the conflicting claims of loyalty clashing within him, he fell back to the only language that wouldn't fail. Gently he turned her pliant body towards him.

She murmured when he kissed her, then encircled his head with her arms and pulled him closer. He took the kiss deeper, moving his hands to caress her, filling her when she opened to him, showing her with his mouth and hands and body how much he cherished her.

Afterwards, as she dozed in his arms, exhausted and satisfied, Will lay awake, unable to find sleep. Tormented by a dilemma with no satisfactory answer, his mind spun fruitlessly round and round the final points of their discussion, like a roulette wheel before the croupier settles the ball.

For all his early years and then his time in the army, his survival had depended on making the correct, lightning-quick decision. But from the beginning of his doubts in Vienna through betrayal and reconciliation in Paris, he'd put off deciding what the final move in his game with Elodie would be. With arrival in England imminent, he could put it off no longer. And he was still not sure what to do.

He owed Max his life. But, he might as well admit it, Elodie now held his heart.

A vagabond all his life, he'd never thought of settling down on any of the small properties he'd been acquiring the last few years. Never thought of finding a wife or begetting children.

No more than she had he a home to offer her, and his only family were his cousins. The earl would sever their tenuous connection in a heartbeat, and if he were to betray his vow to Max to side with the woman who had ruined his cousin's life, he wouldn't have them, either.

He wished Max lived in the far reaches of Northumberland, so he would have longer to figure out what to do.

He would still willingly give his life to save Max's. But he was no longer willing to let Elodie give hers. Though he'd been dodging around the fact since the attack on her outside Karlsruhe, after almost losing her again to St Arnaud, he finally could no longer avoid admitting the truth. He'd fallen in love with Elodie Lefevre.

He wasn't sure what he'd expected love to be, but it wasn't the hearts-and-flowers, bring-her-jewels-to-woo-her-into-bed sort of fancy he'd imagined. More a gut-deep bond that made the air fresher, the sun brighter, the taste of wine sweeter because she shared it with him. A deep hunger to possess her, to be one with her, to satisfy her, that seemed to increase rather than diminish the longer they were together. A sense that losing her would suck all the joy, excitement and pleasure from life, leaving him like a mechanical doll, gears and levers taking it through the motions of life, but dead and empty inside.

He simply couldn't lose her.

Admitting this didn't make the way ahead any clearer. Though Elodie desired him, she'd given no indication that she felt for him anything deeper than fondness. But whether she returned his affection or not, he now had no intention of bringing her to the Foreign Office to testify. Despite what Armitage and de Merlonville avowed, it was too risky, when her testimony could too easily detour down a path to prison or the gallows.

Instead of leaving Elodie at one of his properties and going first to London to snoop around the Foreign Office and see if he could discover what evidence would be sufficient to clear Max, perhaps they should proceed straight to Max himself. Max, much better attuned to the intricacies of the Foreign Office, would be in a better position to know if there were a means for Elodie to absolve him without her having to testify in person. By means of a sworn deposition, perhaps, which he could have delivered after he'd gotten her safely out of England.

His heart quickened at that solution, then slowed and he frowned. But if Max thought there was no way to clear his name but for Elodie to appear before a tribunal in London, he might press Will to take her there. And Elodie, in her current state, would agree to go.

Perhaps it would be better to sail around the south coast to Falmouth and catch a ship to the Americas... except he didn't have sufficient funds with him for such a trip; he'd need to visit his bankers in London first.

Maybe he should just go to Max, explain to him privately why he was breaking his solemn vow. Max had never been vindictive; even if Will's betrayal meant Max would lose for ever the life that should have been his, he knew Max wouldn't force him to risk the life of the woman Will now realised he loved.

But at the thought of facing the man to whom he owed more than anyone else on earth and admitting he was reneging on his pledge, his gut churned. The earl would say that Will had no honour to lose. But Max had always believed in him.

So, if he was prepared to betray Max, and it seemed that he was, he might as well make a clean break. Travel through Kent without stopping to see Max, go to London, obtain funds and head at once to Cornwall to take ship. He could write to Max later, when Elodie was safe in America, beyond the reach of French or English law.

His heart torn with anguish at the thought of leaving behind the only family he'd known—and losing the respect of the one man whose good opinion he valued more than any other—Will sprang up and paced the small room. After several circuits, as he gazed down again at Elodie's sleeping form, he knew if he must choose between Max and Elodie—between cousins, friendship, family, honour and Elodie—he would choose her.

They would go straight to London, obtain funds and leave for the Americas.

Then, the thought of betrayal bitter in his mouth, it struck him that leaving England immediately would only compound the dishonour. Max had believed in him, counselled him and championed him since they were boys. He couldn't just disappear without facing him. If he was going to break his pledge and for ever doom his cousin's government aspirations, he owed it to Max to tell him face to face.

He'd not add the white feather of cowardice to his disgrace.

Max might try to change his mind, but Will knew, on the bond they shared, that Max would never try to prevent him from leaving, or put Elodie in danger by sending the authorities after them.

So tomorrow they would sail in the smuggler's cutter to the Kentish coast and make their way to Max's farm. He'd confess his intentions to Max, receive his curses or farewells, then take Elodie to the safety of the Americas.

In her present despairing and listless state, Elodie might not agree to go with him. Well, he'd figure out a way to persuade her. She'd probably end up liking it, with new adventures to share and a whole continent to explore, not a town or river or meadow in it tarnished by anguished memories of the past. Maybe they could

end up at the French-speaking colony at Nouvelle Or-
léans. He could contact his friend Hal Waterman, investigate the possibilities of investing in this new land.

Some of the terrible burden lifted from his chest,
leaving lightness and a peace that testified to the right-
ness of the decision. Though the agony of abandoning
Max still hollowed his gut, Will returned to the bed,
took Elodie in his arms and slept at last.

Chapter Eighteen

On a drizzly grey afternoon three days later, mud-spattered and weary, Will and Elodie pulled up their tired mounts before a set of elaborate wrought-iron gates with the image of a running horse in the centre. 'This must be it—Denby Lodge,' Will said, dismounting to knock on the gatehouse door. 'I have to say, I'll be glad of a bath and a good dinner.'

'I still think we should have engaged a room for me at the inn in the last village,' Elodie said. Now that the moment to confront Max Ransleigh had almost arrived, anxiety was filtering through the fog of lethargy that had cocooned her through their Channel crossing—Will having managed to order up fair seas and a swift passage—and the two days of hard riding since. 'I'm sure Monsieur Max will be happy to offer you hospitality. I'm not so sure he'll be willing to offer it to me.'

'You needn't worry,' Will told her as an elderly man trotted from the brick house to unlock the tall gates. 'Max is a diplomat, remember; he'll receive you with such perfect courtesy, you'll never be able to tell what he's really feeling.'

Turning to the gatekeeper, Will asked, 'Is the Lodge straight on?'

'Aye, sir,' the man replied, bowing. 'Follow the drive past the barns and paddocks. The manor will be to your right once the drive rounds the parkland.'

After handing the gatekeeper a coin and acknowledging his thanks, Will ushered Elodie through the entry gates, then remounted and proceeded with her down the gravelled drive.

'The Denby Stud is quite famous,' Will told her as they trotted past lush, fenced meadows. 'Several army comrades purchased their cavalry horses from Sir Martin and swore by their quality. Swift, strong-boned, long on stamina and well mannered.' He laughed. 'Though I can't imagine what Max finds to keep himself busy here, I am curious to meet his wife, Caroline. My cousin Alastair says she's nothing in his usual style. Max always preferred ladies of stunning beauty and alluring charm. A horse breeder is definitely a departure.'

Surprised by Will's sudden loquaciousness, when they had travelled mostly in silence the last few days, Elodie was about to question him when she realised that, so attuned had he become to her, he must have sensed her uneasiness. His commentary was meant to inform her about the farm and the owner she was about to meet—but also to distract her from worrying about Max.

Once again, his thoughtfulness warmed the bleakness within her. How she wished they might have met years ago, when she was young and heart-whole, when she believed the future bright with possibilities.

She would just have to appreciate each moment of the very few she had left with him.

And if he was kind enough to try to cheer her, she could rouse herself to reply. 'It seems a very handsome property.'

'Yes, the fields and fences are in excellent condition. And look, there on the hill!' He pointed off to the left, where a herd of several dozen horses roamed. 'Mares with their foals. Beauties all!' he pronounced after studying them for a moment. 'It seems Max's wife is maintaining her father's high standards.'

After riding steadily for thirty minutes past pastures and occasional lanes leading to thatched cottages in the distance without encountering barns or paddocks, Elodie said, 'The farm seems very large.'

'Larger than I expected,' Will agreed. 'I'm glad I asked directions of the gatekeeper, else I would fear we'd taken a wrong turn. Ah, finally—I see a barn over that rise.'

After passing an impressive series of barns surrounded by paddocks used for training the colts, Will told her, at last the lane entered a wood and turned to the right. As the trees thinned, they saw a fine stone manor house crowning the top of a small hill, flanked by oaks and shrubbery.

Trepidation dried her mouth, while the fluttering in

her stomach intensified. Would Max Ransleigh receive her—or order her off his property?

Then they were at the entry, a servant trotting out to take their horses, a butler ushering them into the front parlour. Trying to be unobtrusive, Elodie stationed herself behind a wing chair set by the hearth, while Will stood by the mantel, toasting his hands at the welcome warmth of a fire.

With Will poised on the threshold of accomplishing all he'd set out to do, she'd expected he would be excited, impatient to see his cousin again, triumphant to be bringing home the means to redress all Max Ransleigh's wrongs. Oddly enough, he seemed as tense as she was, almost…uncomfortable, Elodie thought.

Before she had time to wonder further about it, the door opened and Max Ransleigh walked in, as handsome and commanding as she remembered. 'Will, you rascal!' he said, striding to the hearth and clasping his cousin in a quick, rough embrace. 'Though I ought to spot you a good round of fisticuffs for returning to England and then leaving again without even the courtesy of coming to meet my bride.'

Just as Elodie thought she'd escaped his notice, Max turned to her. 'And Madame Lefevre,' he said, bowing. 'My cousin Alastair told me Will intended to bring you back to England and I see he has succeeded. Welcome to my home.'

Elodie sank into a deep curtsy, studying Max warily beneath her lashes as she rose. If he was angry, he hid it well; his smile seemed genuine and his greeting sincere. A diplomat, indeed—or far more forgiving then she deserved.

'It is of everything most kind of you to receive me, Monsieur Ransleigh. When you would have every right to spit on me and toss me out of your house.'

He surveyed her with that quick, perceptive gaze she remembered so well. 'To be frank, a year ago, I might have. But everything has changed since then.'

'I deeply regret the disservice I did you. Let me assure you, I'm fully prepared to do whatever it takes to make amends.'

'We'll talk of that later,' Will interposed.

'Yes, later,' Max agreed. 'For now, I'm happy to see you without bruises, *madame*. Will must have been taking good care of you.'

For an instant, she recalled the whole amazing, wonderful journey and how well in truth Will *had* cared for her. Suppressing a sudden urge to weep that their time together was over, she said, 'Ah, yes. Most exceptional care.'

'Good.' Suddenly Max's eyes lit and a smile of joy warmed his face. 'Caro, I didn't know you'd come down! Come, my dear, and meet our guests.'

Elodie turned to see a slender woman enter the parlour, her simple green day dress setting off the auburn tints in the dark hair that crowned her head in a coronet of braids. Eyes the bright green of spring moss glowed when she looked at her husband, who walked over to meet her, wrapping an arm around her shoulders. 'Are you feeling strong enough to be up?'

'I'm fine. When Dulcie told me there were riders approaching, I had to come down. Isolated as we are, Denby Lodge doesn't often receive unexpected guests.' Turning towards the hearth, she said, 'But this gentleman needs no introduction. You must be Will! Alastair told me you and Max favour each other strongly.'

'Guilty as charged,' Will said, giving her a smile and a bow. 'Alastair said you were lovely and talented. An understatement on both accounts; we've just had a most enjoyable ride past your fields and some of the handsomest mares and foals I've seen in a long time.'

'Flatterer! You could find no faster way to my heart than to praise my horses.'

'I warned you he was a rogue, my dear,' Max murmured to his wife.

Will moved to Elodie's side, putting a protective hand on her arm. 'Mrs Ransleigh, may I present Madame Elodie Lefevre.'

'You, too, are very welcome,' Caro said, holding out her hand to Elodie, who, after a moment's hesitation, shook it.

'Caro, why don't you show Madame Lefevre up to a room, while Will and I get reacquainted?'

When Will gave his cousin a look and tightened his grip on her hand, Elodie murmured, her voice pitched for his ears alone, 'Don't worry. I'll not try to run away again.'

'It's not that. I feel…better when you're close.'

Watching their interplay with an appreciative smile, Max said, 'You needn't worry to let her go. Caro will take even better care of her than you do. *Madame*, you look exhausted—why don't you rest before dinner? And if you don't mind my saying so, Will, after a quick chat, you could use a bath.'

'Won't you come with me, *madame*?' Caro said. 'After a hard day's riding, there's nothing so soothing as a long soak in a hot tub. I'll have some tea and biscuits sent up, too, to tide you over until dinner. We'll see you later, gentlemen.'

And so Elodie allowed herself to be shepherded out of the room, down the hall and up the stairs to an airy bedchamber that looked out over the expanse of front lawn to the barns in the far distance.

She found herself instinctively liking Caroline Ransleigh, who offered her hand to shake like a man, dressed simply and whose unassuming, straightforward manner spoke of a self-confidence that had no need to impress.

Upon first seeing Max's wife, she'd been surprised, even though Will had told her his cousin said Caroline Ransleigh was not in Max's 'usual style'. She was certainly different from the beautiful, seductive Juliana Von Stenhoff, who'd been Max's mistress at the Congress of Vienna. That lady would never have deigned to greet guests in so simple a gown—nor would she have passed up an opportunity to try to entice a man as handsome as Will.

With that observation, Elodie liked Caroline Ransleigh even better. Though she doubted her hostess would return the favour, once her husband informed her just who she was harbouring under her roof.

Waving her to a seat on the wing chair near the hearth, Caroline Ransleigh turned to direct the footmen who were bringing in a copper tub, while a kitchen maid started a fire. A moment later, a butler appeared to leave a tea tray on the side table and a freckle-faced maid, carrying Elodie's saddlebags, bowed herself in. 'I'll be happy to wash up your things, ma'am,' she said.

'Excellent idea, Dulcie,' Mrs Ransleigh said. 'Having been travelling so long, you probably don't have any clean garments.' She gave Elodie a quick inspection from head to toe. 'You're a bit slighter than I, but we're of a height. You are very welcome to borrow something of mine while your own things are drying.'

A clean gown, one no doubt newer and in better repair than the well-worn few she still possessed! The idea was almost as welcome as a soak in a tub. 'That is most kind of you, Madame Ransleigh, and you, Dulcie.'

The offer confirmed her suspicion that Max's wife, who appeared to be a straightforward woman with no diplomat's artifices, could not know what role she'd played in Max's life, else she'd be much less accommodating. Feeling guiltily that she ought to acquaint her with the facts before the woman did her any more kindnesses, she was wondering just where to begin as her hostess seated herself and poured them each a steaming cup of tea.

'Here, this will help warm you. Such a raw day for midsummer! After riding in the damp, you must be chilled through.'

Murmuring her thanks, Elodie had just taken a reviving sip when a knock sounded and an older woman came in, carrying a wrapped bundle. 'Dulcie said you was in here, Miss Caro, and that you'd want to tend the young master as soon as he woke.'

'Andrew, my love!' Her face lighting, Mrs. Ransleigh reached out to take the bundle—a closely wrapped, newborn child.

Elodie gasped, her teacup sliding from her nerveless fingers to clatter against the saucer, her gaze transfixed on the baby's face.

In a sweeping vortex of memory, she saw in rapid succession bright dark eyes, a pink bow mouth and waving arms as the newborn Philippe surveyed his world. His drunken-sailor, wobbling steps as he determined, at nine months, to walk upright. The restless toddler fixing his intent, curious gaze on every object that caught his attention, asking 'What is it? What it do? Why?'

And then the boy she'd left, that intense gaze focused on the soldiers he meticulously arranged in battle formation.

As if lying in wait to ambush her after she had thought she was safely over the worst, the pain of his loss attacked her with the blunt impact of a footpad's club. She couldn't draw breath, couldn't move, could do nothing but stare at Mrs Ransleigh's beautiful child, the very image of all she had lost.

'What is it, *madame*?' Over the roaring in her ears, Elodie dimly heard Mrs Ransleigh's voice, saw her turn to look at her with concern. 'Are you ill?'

Elodie struggled to pull herself together. 'No, no, I

am fine, really.' Her fingers shook as she picked up her cup again and took a determined sip.

'You have children, *madame*?'

Elodie nodded. 'I have a son. Had…a son,' she corrected, biting her lip against the urge to weep.

Mrs Ransleigh's face creased in concern and she hugged her infant tighter. 'He died? How horrible!'

'No, he is alive. But…living in Paris. Another lady looked after him for some years, while I was away. She is wealthy, from an important family. He is happy with her and she can give him many advantages, so I…left him with her.'

'But you miss him,' Mrs Ransleigh said softly.

'With every breath.' A few traitorous tears forced their way to the corners of her eyes. Determinedly, Elodie wiped them away. 'Your Andrew is a handsome child. How old is he?'

'Three weeks today. A lusty lad. His proud papa is already planning his first pony.'

With a pang, Elodie thought of the traitorous toy horse with the glass eyes. 'He may need to wait a few more weeks for that.'

The magnetic power of the newborn still held her. 'May I?' she asked, extending a hand. At the mother's nod, Elodie reached over to stroke the infant's soft cheek. Immediately he turned his mouth towards her, rooting. She gave him her fingertip to suckle.

'Always hungry, too, just like his papa,' her hostess said.

After vigorously sucking for a moment, the baby spat out her fingertip, giving her a mildly indignant look.

Mrs Ransleigh laughed. 'I know that look. I'd better go feed him, before he demonstrates just what a fine pair of lungs he has. Ah, here's your hot water,' she said, as the kitchen maid and two house boys brought in steaming urns of water to pour into the tub, followed by the lady's maid with clean clothing and a towel.

'Ring for me when you're ready, ma'am, and I'll help you into the gown,' Dulcie said, depositing the garments within reach of the tub.

'We'll leave you to your bath.' Mrs Ransleigh rose, cradling her son.

Elodie put a hand on her hostess's arm. 'Treasure every moment with him.'

'I intend to.' About to walk away, Mrs Ransleigh hesitated. 'He's my miracle child. Nearly all the women of my family died in childbed and I almost did, too. So I take nothing for granted. Not Andrew. Not Max. Not the farm and the horses that are my life's blood. They are all precious gifts.'

Elodie smiled. 'You are very wise.'

'Actually, I'm very grateful to you.' At Elodie's startled look, she said, 'Yes, I know who you are and what happened in Vienna. But you see, if Max hadn't been in disgrace after the assassination attempt, I would never have met him. I wouldn't have now the sweetest love a woman could ever desire and the joy of bearing his child. And Max truly is content here.'

With a wife who obviously adored him and a healthy

newborn son, Elodie wasn't about to suggest otherwise, but her hostess continued, 'I did try to resist him, you know. I urged him to return to Vienna, to look for you and do everything he could to clear his name and re-sume his government career. But as he began to work with me, training horses, he discovered he had a real gift for it. He says he's happy with his life here and, of course, I want to believe him.'

It eased her guilt to think that perhaps she hadn't ruined Max's future after all. That their interaction in Vienna had merely sent him down a different path, per-haps an even more rewarding one.

She still intended to do what she could to restore his reputation. For now, he was content training horses, but some day he might long to rejoin the circles of power for which he'd been born and bred. If that happened, she wanted to make sure nothing from their association in Vienna prevented him.

'With a lovely wife and a handsome son, how could he not be content? But I thank you for telling me.'

As if trying to remind his mama of his presence, the newborn squirmed in her arms and gave a prelimi-nary wail.

'My master calls,' Mrs Ransleigh said with a grin. 'Enjoy your bath. We're very informal here, so we dine early. Dulcie will get you anything you need, and then we'll let you rest until dinner.'

With that, shushing the baby with a kiss on the nose, she put him to her shoulder and walked from the room.

Swiftly divesting herself of her grimy clothes, Elodie

climbed into the tub and sank with an ecstatic sigh into the hot scented water. Even in the grimmest of times, one should not fail to savour the wonder of a warm bath.

Tired as she was, the water both soothed and made her drowsy. Perhaps, as his wife suggested, Max was no longer angry at being reduced from a rising star of government to a breeder and trainer of horses. What was it he'd said—'everything has changed'?

For the better, she hoped. But she was too weary and the water too deliciously relaxing to contemplate the matter any more. Doubtless Will and Max were discussing it at this very moment. All she need do was be ready, at last, to fulfil the bargain she'd made with Will.

And then see him walk out of her life.

Chapter Nineteen

Will watched Caroline Ransleigh usher Elodie out the parlour door with a panicky feeling in his gut. There'd been no time to reassure her that he didn't suspect she would try to run away. It was just that, after two attacks against her, he didn't feel comfortable about her safety when she was out of his sight.

He turned from the door to see Max studying him and another layer of dread overlay the first. He'd give anything not to have to say to Max what he was about to say. Anything but Elodie's life.

That thought put matters in perspective, so he swallowed hard and looked for a way to begin. The very idea of cutting himself off from his cousins and losing Max's esteem was so painful he'd not been able to bear thinking about or planning what he meant to say, as he normally would have done before broaching a matter of such gravity.

While he stood there, staring at Max and dithering, his cousin shook his head and laughed. 'I should have known if anyone in the world could have turned up Elodie Lefevre—and I gave it more than a go myself—it would be you. A tremendous, and I fear costly, crusade that Alastair said you insisted on funding and carrying out alone. How can I ever convey the depths of my gratitude and appreciation?'

Wonderful—in his very first speech, Max had made him feel even worse. 'I appreciate your kind reception of Elodie; under the same circumstances, I'm not sure I would have been so forbearing.'

'You always were a hothead, faster with your fists than your tongue,' Max observed with a smile.

'You were responsible for teaching me to use my wits instead.'

'I did my poor best.'

'Whatever improvement there is, I owe to your persistence. As for Madame Lefevre, you know the facts of what she did, but you don't know the "why". I think it's important that you do.' *Maybe then you will understand a little better why I'm about to betray you*, he thought.

'Very well, I'm listening. But something tells me the story would be better heard over a glass of port.'

Will didn't object. He'd need all the reinforcement he could get to force himself through the next half-hour. At the end of which, he would likely be saying goodbye to the best friend he'd ever had.

After a gulp of the fortified wine that warmed him to his toes, Will launched into a halting recitation of how he'd found Madame Lefevre and how she'd become involved in her cousin's plot. But as he began to describe

Elodie and her life, the words flowed faster and faster, the stories tumbling out one after another: her childhood trials as an exile, her struggles as a young soldier's wife and then widow, her courageous tenacity in Vienna, when, abandoned by all but her maid after the attack, she found a way to survive, and finally, the return to Paris and the wrenching second loss of her son.

He finished, his glass untouched since his first sip, to see Max watching him again, that inscrutable, assessing gaze on his face.

'A remarkable woman,' Max said.

Will nodded. 'Yes, she is.' *Now for the difficult, agonising part.* 'Max, you know better than I how much I owe you. I promised Alastair I would find Elodie, bring her back to England and make her tell the Foreign Office how she'd involved you in the plot, corroborating your account of the affair. So your reputation might be restored at last, along with the possibility of resuming the government career to which you've aspired as long as I've known you. But…but if she goes to London and the authorities open an official investigation, she could well be imprisoned as an accomplice to an attempt on Lord Wellington's life. Maybe even hung. I can't let her do that.'

Max frowned. 'Are you sure? If her testimony cleared my name, I might indeed be able to revive my government career. There would be no limit to my gratitude! I don't know how you mean to get on, now that you've resigned your army commission. Papa should have made you an allowance when you returned, but…' Max grimaced '...no great surprise that he'd conveniently forget his promise. If I'm in London, Caro will need help here. She'd never give up the stud; breeding horses is in her blood. You could take my place as manager, be the go-between at Newmarket, take a percentage of the sales. She raises excellent horses; it would pay well. You could have a comfortable position for life, accumulate enough to buy property of your own, if you wished. Become a "landed Ransleigh" at last.'

'Thereby finally earning your father's respect?' Will said derisively. 'Though I thank you for the offer, as it happens, I've accumulated sufficient funds on my own. And even if I hadn't, I'd never bargain for Elodie's life.'

Max's frown deepened. 'You obviously care for this woman. Does she return the favour?'

Will swallowed hard. 'I'm not sure. She's fond of me, I know. But...losing her son again has devastated her. I don't think she's capable of feeling anything now.'

'She's "fond" of you,' Max repeated, a bit dismissively. 'You would betray your oath to me for a woman who you're not even sure loves you, or has any appreciation of the consequences of your dishonouring your pledge?'

Trust Max to strip fine rhetoric down to its bare essentials. Unpalatable as it was, that was truth. 'Yes.'

To Will's utter shock, Max gave a crow of laughter. 'So, it's happened at last! Wagering Will's bet was called by a lady with a better hand.'

Sobering quickly, he clapped a hand on Will's shoulder. 'As I said at the outset, I can't begin to express my appreciation and admiration for all you've done, going to Vienna to find *madame* and bringing her back. I'm not sure any man deserves such loyalty. But you needn't risk the life of the woman you've come to love.'

'So, you're…not angry?' Will asked, amazed, too rattled by Max's unexpected response to dare believe it to be true. 'Then why did you try to tempt me with a position here?'

'From the look on your face when you spoke of Madame Lefevre and how protectively you hovered around her, I suspected you loved her. I've never seen you that way with any other woman. But I wanted to discover just how deeply the attachment ran. True, I might not always have felt so forgiving towards her. After Vienna I was angry, dismayed, disbelieving. My world and the future I'd always dreamed of had been destroyed and I didn't think I'd ever be content or fulfilled again. But then I met Caro. Worked with her. Fell in love with her and the farm. I have what I want now, Will. I think, in Elodie Lefevre, you have what you want, too. Am I right?'

'Would I have abandoned my vow for any other reason?'

Max nodded. 'I thought as much. I suppose I recognised the devotion; I feel the same about Caro, as if I'd battle the whole world to keep her safe. Give up the rest of the world, if that were the price of keeping her.'

'Then you do understand. But you know your Caroline loves you. I'm not sure what Elodie feels or wants. I planned to take her away to the Americas, where she'd be safe, but I'm not even sure she'll go with me. When she lost her son after directing all her efforts for nearly two years towards reclaiming him, it was as if she felt her whole life was over.'

'I can appreciate her grief and despair. I thought losing the career I loved the greatest tragedy that could befall me…until Caro had difficulty in childbed and I almost…' his voice broke for a moment '…I almost lost her and my son. I can't imagine how one recovers from such a blow. But as I understand it, Madame Lefevre's son isn't dead, so surely there is some hope of seeing him again?'

'Yes, I'm examining some possibilities, but they'll take time to work out. Grieving as she is, I don't want to propose anything; if the plans went awry, I don't know how she would bear another disappointment.'

'She'll need time to heal. I did, and I lost only the career I thought I wanted, not the persons most dear to me. Teach her there is still beauty and fulfilment in life.' He grinned. 'And that you can provide them.'

'I'm not sure I know where to begin,' Will admitted. I don't even know if she'll agree to stay with me, once she learns we won't be taking her to the Foreign Office. I wouldn't put it past her to disappear in the night, thinking she offers me nothing and I'd be better off starting anew, without her.'

'Is she that elusive?'

Will thought of how she'd loved him to satiation and then slipped away. 'Oh, yes.'

'If you love her that much, surely you're not going to

despair of winning her before you've even begun! I've seen you beguile women from blushing dairymaids to bored *ton* beauties. I can't imagine you're not capable of beguiling a lady you actually love. True, trying to win her is a gamble. But Wagering Will never met a bet he wouldn't take. Comfort her, stand by her and marry her.'

Will sighed. 'I want to, but what do I know about being a husband, creating a family?'

'I thought your cousins taught you a good bit. My father, you remember, wasn't much of a model, either. But then, when you hold your wife's hand while she brings your child into the world, then touch his perfect, tiny hands…' A sense of awe and wonder passed over Max's face. 'I can assure you, the rewards of fighting for a life with the woman you love far outweigh the risks of failing.'

How Will wanted that, too, a life with Elodie, her lovely face finally freed from the shadows of pain and sorrow! He hadn't thought beyond the dread of this interview and the necessity of making all speed to catch a ship to the colonies. Now, buoyed by Max's encouragement, Will started rapidly examining other alternatives.

Winning Elodie's heart, forging a life here…with his cousins nearby. In time, perhaps, giving her another child to cherish, a complement to the one she'd already borne with whom, if the scheme Will was pondering came to fruition, she would forge a new relationship.

'There is another property I've had my eye on, over in Sussex,' he said, running a vision of it through his mind's eye. 'It has a wonderful garden.'

Max raised his eyebrows. 'Another property? Just how many do you own?'

Will grinned. 'Not as many as Alastair or your family, but several. What, you think I just frittered away all my gambling winnings? You remember Hal Waterman, from Eton?'

'That large, inarticulate lad who'd never be lured into playing cards because, he said, the odds were always in the dealer's favour? A sort of mathematical genius, as I recall.'

'Yes. Two misfits, he and I, who later banded together. I happened to meet him in London after Oxford, when I'd had my first really big win at faro. He said if I liked gambling, he could recommend something for which the odds were as risky as gaming, but the potential rewards much greater. Not just in blunt, but in forging the future of the nation. Turns out he's fascinated by finance and technology, and with that limitless fortune of his, has begun exploring the opportunities to invest in new scientific developments. He talked me into putting almost all the blunt I'd won at faro into a canal-construction project he'd put together. With the earnings from that, I bought my first property. I'm also invested in coal mines, mechanical stoves and what Hal claims will be a system that will revolutionise transport, the railroad.'

Max shook his head. 'Does my father know?'

Will laughed. 'Know that his barely civilised, reprobate nephew has become a man of means without his will or intervention? Certainly not! The shock could probably kill him.'

Max chuckled. 'It might at that.'

'However, manufacturing and commerce are close enough to vulgar middle-class shop-keeping that if he does learn of it, I'm sure he'll manage to maintain his disdain.'

'You could have told the Rogues,' Max reproved.

'I would have, had the war and…other projects not intervened.'

'So you're a man of means.' Max shook his head ruefully. 'It's almost as hard for me as for Papa to think you no longer need my help.'

'I'll always need your friendship.'

'That, you'll always have. So, go buy your manor. Would you like us to watch over your Elodie until you return? I must admit, the story you've told piques my curiosity. I liked her when I knew her in Vienna. I'd very much enjoy becoming better acquainted with the remarkable woman who performed so many amazing feats. Not the least of which was capturing my elusive cousin's heart.'

'Would you let her stay here and watch out for her? Although…' Will hesitated, trying to guess how his complex, devious Elodie might react. 'I know it's not fair to keep the knowledge from her, but could we let her go on believing that a visit to the Foreign Office is forthcoming? Not that you need to tell any deliberate mistruths, just be evasive, if she asks directly. I don't think she will. She's committed enough to making recompense for the harm she did you in Vienna that if she thinks I've left Denby Lodge to make preparations for London, she'll not...wander off before I return. It will also give me a chance to think how best to woo her.'

'I may now be a horse breeder, but I'm still a diplomat at heart; I can finesse anything. Especially if it involves the happiness of my dearest friend. So, if you're not going to linger at Denby—and while you're still muddy and smelling of horse—let me give you a quick tour of the stables and stock. My world now.'

'Do you not miss being involved in government?' Will asked, still finding it hard to believe Max could have abandoned so completely the goal that had driven him for as long as Will had known him.

'The idea that I am working for something larger than myself? A bit. But the back-biting and intrigues of those whose mindless ambition far outweighs their concern for the public good? Not at all. I have considered perhaps some day standing for Parliament. Being elected by the men of the district whose respect I've won, whom I respect in turn, giving voice to their concerns in the halls of power, is a more worthy task than what I would now be doing, had Vienna not intervened. Lurking about the Lords, a lackey for my father.'

'Standing for Parliament is an excellent idea.'

'Well, we shall see. For now, I'm just grateful for the blessings of being able to watch my son grow and spend every day—and night—with my wife.'

'So...' Max raised his glass, motioning Will to pick

up his own '…to your safe return. To finding love, and cherishing it. To Ransleigh Rogues.'

Now that he was recovering from the shock of realising he would not lose Max's friendship after all, Will felt a rising euphoria and an eagerness for the future he hadn't known since that moment he'd awakened before Paris, marvelling at the peace he'd found in Elodie's arms.

'To all of that,' he replied. 'And to "Ransleigh Rogues, for ever".'

Chapter Twenty

Two weeks later, on a mild summer afternoon, Elodie sat embroidering her new gown in a beam of sunlight in the front parlour at Denby Lodge. Strange, she thought as she methodically set small, perfect stitches, that she was now marking time awaiting the trip to London as she'd spent the hours before leaving Vienna. But instead of longing and anticipation, she passed her days numb and drifting, the only small joy on her horizon the hope to see Will Ransleigh again before the final resolution.

She did wish Will had taken her with him when he left to consult with the authorities about setting up her interview. After he returned, there would be very little time left to share with him. It would take them a few days at most to travel back to the metropolis before she gave her testimony, that end of the road beyond which she could envision nothing further.

Dull as her spirits still were, she missed him. His acute observations, his teasing eye, his stories…and the surcease from sorrow she found in his arms, when he loved her so sweetly and completely that nothing, not even anguish and loss, could tarnish the bliss. She'd hoped he would come to her some time during the one night he spent at Denby Lodge before leaving for London, but he hadn't.

The day of his departure had dawned all the more dreary for that lack.

Surprised at first that Max Ransleigh had not gone with Will to instigate the proceedings, she'd thought he must want to consult with her about the now-distant events in Vienna, so her account of it, when she at last spoke to the authorities, would reinforce what he'd told them of the affair. But to her bewilderment, he had not sought her out in private to quiz her about her memories, nor had he referred to the matter in any way when in company.

Her host and hostess had insisted she dine with them, and though Max had initiated several discussions of Vienna, their object seemed more to entertain Caro than corroborate what she remembered. He described some of the most notable balls and receptions they'd attended, asking her to share her recollections, or else he traded impressions with her about the colourful array of notables and hangers-on who'd attended the Congress.

Perhaps he didn't wish to distress his wife, who was still recovering from her confinement, by referring to the scandal. Elodie's initial favourable impression of Caroline Ransleigh had quickly deepened to a friendship she would sorely miss when the time came to leave for London. Not since Clara in Vienna had Elodie had a female friend with whom she could converse freely, and growing up an exile with no sisters, she hadn't ever had a confidante from her same level in society.

Though Caro insisted she might borrow any garments she liked, not used to being idle, Elodie had asked Max to sell one of the small pieces of jewellery she'd carried with her, so she might purchase material to make herself some garments. Accompanying Caro to the village, she'd bought several dress lengths, and was now completing the second of two stylish gowns.

In addition to the sewing keeping her occupied, she thought that, if she wished the officials at the enquiry to find it credible that she had been the hostess of a high-ranking French diplomat at the most glittering assemblage of aristocrats and government leaders ever gathered in Europe, she couldn't appear in one of her tattered old gowns, looking like a rag picker.

If prison were the outcome, she might be able to sell the new garments to obtain the coal and candles that would make her existence less miserable. And, if the worst happened, at least she'd have something attractive to be buried in.

At that moment, her hostess entered the parlour with her characteristic, brisk step. 'Elodie, what exquisite work!' she exclaimed, coming over to inspect her embroidery. 'I can easily believe an exclusive Vienna modiste clamoured for you to embellish her gowns.'

'Hardly "clamoured",' Elodie replied. 'But she did pay me promptly and rather well for a seamstress.'

'I'm so hopeless, I can't sew a stitch! I ought to commission you to make some gowns for me. I've never cared two figs what I wore, as long as it was modest and serviceable, but now that I'm regaining my figure…' A blush heated her cheeks. 'I'd like to have something new to intrigue my husband and remind me I'm more than just a mama.'

'Something that shows to advantage that fine mama's bosom,' Elodie teased, smiling when Caro's blush deepened. 'I would be happy to make you something, if I have time enough before I leave.'

A shadow crossed Caro's face. 'I do wish you didn't have to go. But I don't mean to speak of that, for it will only make me melancholy, and heavens, it seems lately the merest nothing has me wanting to burst into tears! Me, who has never in her life been missish,' she finished with disgust.

'It goes with becoming a mama,' Elodie said.

'The nursery maid is just finishing Andrew's bath. Shall I bring him down?'

'Please do! I've been working on a gown for him, too.'

'You're sure? Sometimes I worry that seeing him must make it…more difficult for you.'

'I should miss Philippe every day, even if I never saw another child. But a baby should be a joy. Not for the world would I want yours to diminish, because of my loss! It lifts my spirits to see you with him and know that such happiness still exists in the world. Besides, who could resist such a handsome charmer as your son?'

Caro beamed. 'He is handsome, isn't he? And demanding. Which is good. If I didn't have him to occupy me, I don't know how I would bear the inactivity. I know the doctor said I must not ride for another two weeks, but I'm feeling perfectly fine and cannot wait to get back to my horses!'

'Go get your son and we'll let him entertain us,' Elodie said.

Smiling, she went back to her stitching. She'd not just reassured her new friend to ease her anxiety; she did enjoy seeing the child. Holding and playing with the infant, recalling as it did memories of happier times with Philippe, always lifted her spirits and eased the dull anxiety that sat like a boulder in her gut, an ever-present worry over a future she didn't want to envision.

What if they only interviewed and then released her? Though she tried to keep herself from contemplating anything beyond that meeting in London, occasionally speculation about a different, better resolution crept into her thoughts.

What was she to do with herself if she did not end up in prison or on the gallows? Though she knew her new friend would invite her to stay indefinitely at Denby Lodge, she didn't wish to be a burden. Perhaps she could get lodgings in London and find employment as a seamstress. Rich women would always need new gowns.

There was no question of returning to Paris. The Ransleigh name might command the attention—and protection—of the Prime Minister and the respect of Prince Talleyrand, but Elodie Lefevre, her brother dead and his rising career with him, was no longer of any importance. Besides, sojourning in the same city that contained her son, but unable to be with him, would be a torment beyond enduring.

So, London it must be. Unless…unless Will wanted her. They had been excellent comrades on the road and passionate lovers. Perhaps he would keep her as his mistress for a while, until he tired of her. Such a handsome, charismatic man would make any woman who set eyes on him try to entice him; it wouldn't take Will Ransleigh long to find another lover to share his bed.

As the door opened, she looked up, expecting to see Caro and her babe. Instead, the object of her imaginings walked in.

'Will, you're back!' she cried, jumping up. Within the dull empty expanse of her chest, her moribund heart gave a small leap of gladness.

She couldn't seem to take her eyes from his face as he approached her, smiling faintly, his sheer physical allure striking her as forcefully as it had that first day.

'Sewing again, I see,' he said. 'Just like when I found you in Vienna.'

Was he thinking of their first meeting, too? 'Although this time, you enter, quite boringly, by the door, rather than thrillingly through a window.'

'I see I am failing in my duty as a rogue. I shall have to redeem myself.'

It seemed the most natural thing in the world to walk into the arms he held out to her, to lift her face for his kiss.

He took her mouth gently, but she met him ardently.

With a stifled groan, he clutched her tighter, deepening the kiss. She moulded herself to him, her body fitting his like a puzzle piece sliding into place.

After a moment, he broke the kiss, his turquoise eyes dark. 'Does that mean you've missed me?'

'I have. I feel…' At home? At peace? As content as it was possible for her to be? 'Safe when you're near,' she finished.

His expression grew serious. 'And I mean to keep you that way.'

'Must we leave at once for London? I…I had promised Caro to make her a new gown.'

'She has treated you well?'

'Very well. We so very quickly became friends, I shall miss her when we leave for London.'

'We're not going to London.'

'Not going?' Elodie echoed, puzzled. 'Is the Foreign Office allowing me to give a deposition here, rather than testifying in person?'

'No deposition. No testimony at all. I don't want to risk it.'

She shook her head, more confused than ever. 'But what of Monsieur Max? How is his name to be cleared, if I do not testify? What of his career?'

'Max is quite happy with the career—and the family—he has at Denby Lodge. And if, in future, he has a longing to return to government, he means to go on his own merits, elected to Parliament by the men of this district, not relying on the prestige of his family or the patronage of some high official.'

'This is truth? You are sure?'

'Absolutely sure.'

She would not have to testify. After girding herself for that trial for so long, she could scarcely comprehend she would not be facing the looming spectre of prison or the noose. Dizzy and disoriented with relief, she stumbled to the sofa. 'What is to become of me, then?'

Will seated himself beside her, took her hands and tilted her chin up to face him, his gaze intent. Taking a deep breath, he said, 'I want to take care of you, Elodie. I love you. I want you with me.'

'My sweet Will,' she whispered, freeing a hand to stroke his cheek. 'I want you, too. For as long as you'll have me, I am yours.'

'I want you in my life always, Elodie. I want to marry you.'

'Marry me?' Never in her wildest imaginings had the possibility of marriage occurred to her. 'But that is not at all sensible!' she exclaimed, her practical French mind recoiling from a union of two persons of such dissimilar resources. 'I bring you nothing, no dowry, no family, no influence. You don't have to marry me, Will. I will stay with you as long as you wish.'

'But you can't be sure of that with a mistress. One night, she shows you the moon and the stars, gives you bliss beyond imagining. And the next morning, poof, she is gone, without a word of farewell.'

Feeling a pang of guilt, Elodie looked at him reprovingly. 'That was under very different circumstances, as you well know.'

'What I know is that all my life, I've been missing something, here.' He tapped his chest. 'But in your arms that night outside Paris, I found what I didn't even know I'd been searching for. I felt…complete. I don't want to ever lose that again.'

He stared at her intently, as if waiting for her to reply in kind. She felt a strong bond, something deeper than just the physical, but within her broken and battered heart all was confusion. Better to say nothing than to profess a love she wasn't sure she felt, or wound him by admitting how uncertain she was.

Instead, she shook her head. 'You can have that. It is not necessary, this marriage.'

He drew back a bit, and she knew she'd hurt him, much as she'd wanted to avoid it. 'I know I'm only the illegitimate son of a rogue, while you are the daughter of French aristocracy—'

'Oh, no!' she interrupted him. 'How can you believe I think myself above you? I am the daughter of French aristocrats, yes, but one who has no home, no title, no influential family, no wealth. It is you who are above me, a man linked to a rich and prominent family that still wields great power.'

That seemed to reassure him, for the pain in his eyes receded and he kissed her hands. 'I want to marry you, Elodie de Montaigu-Clisson, whether you can ever love me or not. But don't give me a final answer now. So much has changed since Vienna. You've lost the hope that sustained you for so long and must grieve for that. You need time to reflect, to heal and find consolation, before you can move forwards. I want you to take that time. Will you come with me, let me take care of you? I pledge to keep you safe, so safe that one day you'll stop looking over your shoulder, worried about being followed or threatened. Come with no obligation but friendship. And when you feel ready to begin your life again…if I must, I'll let you go. No force, no bargains.'

Elodie felt tears prick her eyes. She couldn't let him commit the idiocy of tying himself legally to a woman who brought him nothing in worldly advantage, but she would stay with him as long as he'd have her.

'No force, no bargains,' she agreed. 'I go with you willingly and will stay as long as you want me.'

'That would be for ever, then,' Will said and bent to kiss her.

Chapter Twenty-One

On a sunny morning a month later, Elodie strolled through the vast garden at Salmford House. Taking a seat on one of the conveniently located benches with a view of the rose parterre, where the potent, drifting scent of the Autumn Damask 'Quatre Saisons' never failed to soothe her, she smiled.

Her enjoyment of it this morning was just as intense as it had been the afternoon Will first brought her to the property he'd purchased near Firle on the South Downs of Sussex, a lovely land of rolling hills and meadows. After touring her through the snug stone manor and introducing her to the staff, he'd led her out the French doors from the library into the first section of walled garden.

Her reactions of surprise and delight had been repeated many times over as he strolled her through each garden 'room', from the topiary terrace adjoining the library with its precisely clipped boxwood and yew, to the white garden of iris, daisies, sweet alyssum, campanula and snapdragons, the multi-hued perennial border backed by red-leaved berberis, to the artfully arranged herb-and-vegetable knot garden adjoining the kitchen and finally to the central rose parterre, where the 'Old Blush' and damask roses were still blooming after the albas and gallicas had ended their early summer show.

As he'd coaxed her reluctantly to return to the house for an early dinner, saying he, for one, was famished, she'd thrown her arms around him and kissed him soundly. 'What a magnificent garden!' she exclaimed.

'When I was considering where to bring you, I remembered the agent showing me this property. Is it as lovely as the garden of Lord Somerville?'

'Oh, yes, and larger, too! Did you truly choose this house for me?'

'You have had enough of sadness in your life, Elodie. I want you to be happy.' He tapped her nose. 'Clara made me promise.'

'Oh, thank you, my sweet Will! Only one thing under heaven could make me happier.'

But when she took his arm going back to the house and murmured in his ear that she could show him just how grateful she was, pressing herself against him suggestively, he eased her away from him and primly repeated what he'd told her on the drive to Salmford House; that here, they would be friends only, not lovers.

She hadn't believed him, of course, for the idea of refraining from enjoying the powerful passion they shared made no more sense to her than an English aristocrat from a prominent family marrying a penniless exile.

She was not at all happy to discover he'd not been teasing. 'Why, Will? I give myself freely, for your pleasure and mine. Why do you not want such a gift?'

'Oh, I want you—with every breath. But when I make love to you again, I want it to be with you as my wife.'

She sighed in exasperation. 'Is it not the woman who is supposed to withhold her favours until the man succumbs to marriage?'

'Usually, yes. But you see, I'm enamoured of a very stubborn, peculiar female—the French are often stubborn and peculiar, I find—and persuading her to marry me calls for desperate measures. Passion can be very persuasive, so why should I not dangle before her one of my most potent weapons in securing her consent?' He sighed, too. 'Though, in truth, this remedy is so desperate, it may kill me. But were we not true friends and companions on the road, without being lovers?'

'Yes, but only at first, when our disguises prevented it. And we are not on the road now, but in a *hôtel* of the most fine, with, I am sure, beds of quite amazing comfort.'

'You are distressed. I can always tell; your speech becomes more French.'

'Of course I am distressed. This…this show of chastity is ridiculous!'

'Well, as long as there's a chance this "ridiculousness" might help convince you to become my wife, I am content to wait.'

'It may convince me you are an *imbécile*. And I am

not content to wait!' she declared, stamping her foot, frustrated and furious with him, the surge of emotion seizing her the strongest she'd experienced since the loss of Philippe had paralysed all feeling.

'Calm down, *chérie*!' he soothed. 'You need diversion.'

'Yes, and I know just what sort,' she flashed back.

'So do I. A hand of cards after we've dined should do the trick.'

She'd whacked his arm and stomped away, leaving him to follow her to the dining parlour, chuckling. But she couldn't stay angry, as he coaxed her with fine ham, an assortment of fresh vegetables from the garden, aged cheese, rich wine, followed by strawberries and cream, which he fed her with his own hands, rubbing the ripe berries against her lips and then kissing the flavour from them, until she was certain he was going to relent.

Instead of leading her to a bedchamber—by then she would have been quite content with a sofa or even a soft carpet—he handed her into the parlour and produced a deck of cards.

At first, angry with him again, she'd refused to play. But he'd teased and dared, finally winning her grudging agreement by accusing her of avoiding a hand because she was afraid she'd lose.

Within a few minutes, tantalising her with his skill, he'd drawn her into the game. She'd watched him play enough to know he was not trying to let her win, but challenging her to exercise all her skill, which made her redouble her concentration. Interspersed with the hands, he set her to laughing with outrageous observations about the people and events they'd encountered on their travels. When the clock struck midnight and he gathered up the cards, she was surprised to find the hour so late.

It was the most carefree evening she'd spent in years. And she hadn't thought once of her loss.

The yearning returned as he walked her to a bedchamber. She clung to him, trying to entice him to remain with her.

'Marry me,' he'd whispered against her hair as he held her close. 'Marry me, *mon ange*, and be mine for ever.'

When she'd tremulously replied that she couldn't, he'd sighed and gently set her away from him. And then bid her goodnight.

That same frustrating routine had recurred each night of their stay here.

Though he'd laughed at her anger, teased her, given her deep, thrilling kisses as if he meant to relent, he had not. To her extreme irritation and regret, they continued to live as chastely as brother and sister.

She'd thought about slipping into his chamber and into his bed, pleasuring him with her hands and mouth, when, groggy with sleep and tempted by arousal, he would surely yield to her. For the first few nights, she talked herself out of it, worried about embarrassing herself if she were wrong and he refused her still, even in his bed.

By the time they'd been at the manor for a week,

she'd grown too desperate to worry about embarrassment. In the early hours of the morning, unable to sleep, she'd crept through the silent house to his chamber—and found the door locked against her.

The following morning, grumpy from sleeplessness and frustration, she'd sulkily enquired if he thought she were dangerous, that he must lock himself away from her. He'd replied that he was not so much of a fool as to subject himself to a temptation he knew he'd never be able to resist, a reply which mollified her somewhat, though it did nothing to relieve the frustration.

But for that one—and very major—fault, Will had been a perfect companion. He had encouraged her to take him on walks through her beloved garden, telling him the names of all the plants—and later making her laugh by deliberately bungling them. Noticing how she loved to linger in the rose parterre, breathing in the potent scent of the autumn damasks, he had bouquets of the spicy blooms put in every room.

As she gradually began to emerge from the cocoon of grief into which she'd spun herself, it was impossible not to notice his cherishing care of her. Some might have found it suffocating, but Elodie, who had experienced precious little cherishing in her tumultuous life, drank up the attention and concern.

Sitting here now, she recalled all the ways he'd seen to her comfort. Foods she mentioned liking would appear regularly on the table. When she thanked him for a new gown in blue or azure or gold, several more of similar style and hue appeared in her wardrobe.

He even found her, heaven knows where, a little French girl to be her lady's maid. Chatting with the homesick lass in their native French tongue helped ease the sadness within her at the loss of her home and language.

Whatever activity he engaged with her in, whether cards or riding or billiards, he roused her from her recurrent bouts of melancholy by teasing her or cheating her back to attention—or indignation. Sometimes, in the evenings, he read to her, surprising her with the wide-ranging breadth of his knowledge and interests. He talked about his friend, Hal Waterman, and the fascinating new technologies they were investing in that would, he told her, eventually change the way people heated their homes, cooked their food and travelled.

Methodically, slow day by slow day, he was drawing her out of the greyness of grief and death back into the light of his life. Letting her bask in the brilliant warmth of his love.

She hadn't earned such devotion, probably didn't deserve it, but he gave it freely anyway. Wanting, in return, only her happiness.

For the first time in a long time, anticipation stirred in her. What was wrong with her, moping about as if her life were over? Yes, she'd lost her child, a tragedy whose pain would never fully leave her. But along the way, she'd found a matchless lover, who was trying by every means he could devise to woo her and win her love in return.

Almost every day, he repeated his request that she

marry him and share his life. And then, praise heaven, his bed!

Will being normally an intense, restless man, she was astounded that he had managed to content himself staying placidly here, doing nothing more exciting than riding in the countryside and playing cards with her. Surely he was ready to go off exploring new places, investigating new projects. He'd said he longed for her to come with him and share the excitement, companions on the road again.

A sense of wonder and enthusiasm filled her. Salmford House's gardens and Will's tender care had worked their magic. She was, she decided in that moment, now ready to put her losses behind her and start living again—with Will.

Suddenly, she couldn't wait to see him.

Picking up her skirts, she rushed back into the manor, hurrying from room to room until she found him in the library.

He looked up as she entered, his handsome face lighting in a smile, and her healing heart leapt. How could she not flourish in the brightness of that smile? In such tenderness, as she leaned down for his kiss and he caressed her cheek with one gentle finger?

She'd been a fool, not for the first time. It was time to be foolish no longer.

'Are you ready for luncheon, *chérie*?' she said. 'I'm famished.'

Smiling up at Elodie, Will twisted in his hands the letter he'd received in the morning's post. The position he'd discussed with his friend Hal Waterman had been arranged; in the letter was his authorisation to go to Paris and enter discussions with the French Ministry of the Interior about the possibilities of developing railway lines in France.

Hal had pledged considerable financial backing to make the venture happen and tapped his network of influential contacts to persuade the British government to approve Will for the task and to give the endeavour their support. The challenge of persuading the French government to permit the work was exhilarating and Will would need to leave almost immediately.

He wanted Elodie to go with him—as his wife. They'd grown so much closer over the last month. Several times, the tender light in her eyes as she gazed at him had sent his hopes winging to dizzying heights, sure that he'd won her at last and she was about to confess her love.

But thus far, that hadn't happened. And now, if he was to put into motion the scheme he'd been devising ever since they left Paris, he would have to tell her of his plans and propose again, even if he wasn't sure of her love.

He wanted her to marry him because she'd realised she loved him and could not imagine spending the rest of her life without him, not because doing so would allow her to be reunited with her son. Even if she did come to love him later, he would never be able to trust that she loved him for himself, not out of gratitude for his ingenuity in bringing her son back into her life.

But he knew, if he must, he would marry her on those terms. Loving her as he did, he couldn't withhold from her the one thing she wanted most in the world because he hadn't had the good fortune to secure her love in return.

Dropping the letter, he rose to take her arm. She danced around him as she took it, mischief sparkling in her eyes.

His heart turned over to see it, as it always did when she looked happy. He knew a reserve of sadness would always remain with her, but it delighted him to see her look so carefree. It was deeply satisfying to know he'd played a vital part in banishing the shadows from her eyes.

From the naughty glances she was giving him, she was probably plotting to seduce him again. Maybe this time, he'd let her. Heaven knows, resisting her was about to drive him mad.

There wasn't enough cold water in the lake beyond their meadow to cool his ardour for his bewitching Elodie, and he'd been swimming at least twice daily. He'd lasted nearly a month without her managing to break his resolve, far longer than he'd thought he could.

'I'm glad to see you have an appetite, sprite. For so long, you have only toyed with your food.'

'Oh, I have quite an appetite today.' Turning suddenly to push him against the bookshelves, she said, 'Shall I show you how much?'

Anticipation roared through his veins. If tempting her to agree to marriage by withholding passion hadn't worked by now, knowing the proposal he was about to make would contain a temptation she wouldn't be able to resist, why not give up the futile fight and let her have her way with him?

He kissed her hungrily, opening willingly when she slipped her busy tongue inside his mouth. He groaned, pulling her against his hardness.

With a little mewing sound, she reached down to stroke him, and this time he didn't catch her wrists to prevent her. What crack-brained notion had made him deny himself this? he wondered, revelling in her touch.

He returned the favour, caressing her breasts through the fine muslin of her gown and light summer stays, until her breath came in gasps as short as his own.

Picking her up, Will kicked the door closed. It had been too long; desperate for the taste of her, he couldn't possibly wait the few minutes it would take him to carry her up to his bedchamber. The desk would have to do.

In a few quick strides, he reached it and set her on the solid mahogany surface, kissing her ravenously as he slid her skirts up and peeled her stockings down, smoothing the soft skin as he bared it. After working the muslin up to her waist, he parted her legs and knelt before her.

His thumbs teasing the curls at her hot, wet centre, he kissed the tender skin of her inner thighs, tracking up the velvet softness until his tongue met his fingers and he applied the rasp of it to the swollen bud within.

Gasping, she writhed under him, until a very few minutes later reaching her peak. His fingers still caressing her, he took her cries of ecstasy on his lips, then carried her, limp and pliant, to the sofa and cradled her on his lap.

'Oh, my sweet Will, how I've missed you!'

'And I you, *ma douce*.'

'My love, I've been such a fool and you've been so patient with me! I am of a slowness quite remarkable, but finally, finally, I understand. Can you forgive me for being so stupid, clinging to my grief like a child with a broken toy, too stubborn to let it go? But I shall be stupid no longer.'

His heart leapt. Could she mean what he hoped she did? Trying to restrain the hope and excitement bubbling up within him, he said, 'What are you trying to tell me, *chérie*?'

'That no one has ever cared for or loved me like you. Why I have been so fortunate to have received this gift of wonder, I do not know, but my heart rejoices and I love you with everything in me. I want to belong to you for always, be your companion on your adventures and in your bed. I want to be your wife, and though I still believe it is most nonsensical of you to throw yourself away on so undeserving a woman, I shall accept quickly now, before you recover and change your mind. So, will you marry me, prince of my heart? *Parce que je t'aime*, Will. *Avec tout mon coeur*.'

He'd dreamed of hearing her say those words for so long, he could scarcely believe she really had. 'Truly, *mon ange*? You love me with all your heart?'

'Well, with my body, too, as soon as you'll let me.

And from this position…' she wiggled on his lap, rubbing her soft bottom against his hardness '…I am thinking you are ready for me to do so immediately.'

He knew he was probably grinning like the imbecile she'd once called him, but he didn't care. 'Not just yet, in spite of my need. Perhaps tonight, though, if you'll excuse me so I can collect the special licence I brought back from London with me and go to the village to find the rector. If he's available, he can come back and marry us at once. That is, unless you'd like a new gown, or want to plan a ceremony with Max and Caro—'

She stopped his words with a fingertip. 'They can give us a party later. By all means, find the vicar and bring him back at once. I want to be your wife by tonight.'

'I'll kidnap him, if necessary. We've much to discuss tomorrow, but tonight I want to be in your arms.'

Chapter Twenty-Two

The next morning, Will awoke in his bedchamber at Salmford House tired, well loved and with a euphoric sense of well-being that glowed all the brighter when he opened his eyes to see his wife's silky head pillowed on his shoulder.

His wife. He grinned, loving the sound of the words. Fortunately, since he would rather not have had charges brought against him for kidnapping on the eve of his departure for an official mission to France, the vicar had thought his request to wed them immediately romantic rather than foolhardy. Gathering his prayer book, he'd hastened to accompany Will back to Salmford House, where the staff, along with the blushing French maid, witnessed the marriage and the signing of the parish register.

He wanted to wake up like this, with Elodie in his arms, for the rest of his days, Will thought, bending to give her a kiss.

Her eyes fluttering open, she smiled sleepily at him. 'Can it be daylight already?'

'It's halfway through the morning, slug-a-bed.'

'Well, when one has spent hours attending with much concentration to long-delayed and important work, one becomes exhausted.'

He chuckled. 'I think I fell in love with you the moment "Uncle Fritz" limped on his cane into that inn, the night we left Vienna.'

She traced a finger from his shoulders to his chest. 'I lusted after you from the moment you launched yourself from the balcony into my room. But I never appreciated in full measure how wonderful you are until after…after Paris. I thought my life over, that I would never experience joy again. Until with patience, care and tenderness, you taught me I was wrong. You say your cousin Max saved your life; you have given mine back.'

It was a good opening and he took it. 'I'd like to do more. Are you ready to go travelling?'

She shifted up on the pillows to face him, looking so delectably mussed and seductive that only the gravity of what he must discuss with her kept him from pulling her back into his arms and making love to her all over again.

'You have a trip arranged?' she asked while he curbed his amorous appetites. 'To investigate one of those investments you've been telling me about?'

'Yes. This one will be to Paris.'

The excitement faded from her eyes. 'No, Will, please. Anywhere but Paris. I don't think I could bear it.'

'Nor do I, Elodie. It isn't right that your son was snatched from under your nose and you were prevented from reclaiming him. No, hear me out,' he said, forestalling the protest he could see she was about to make. 'Remember, you are no longer Elodie Lefevre, a woman with no home and no family. Elodie Ransleigh is wife to a man of considerable wealth, whose relations, I have it on respected authority, are rich, prominent and wield a good deal of power.'

Though she still looked troubled, he could tell she was cautiously weighing his words. 'What do you intend to do?'

'I've been given an official mission, sanctioned by the British Foreign Office and arranged and financed by my friend Hal Waterman, to approach the French government about the possibilities of constructing a railroad. So not only will you return to Paris as the wife of a wealthy, well-connected man, but one who will be entertained at the highest levels of government.'

'And that will benefit me...how?'

'While in Paris discharging the mission, we will call on the Comtesse de la Rocherie and propose a bargain. It is true, as you said before, that Philippe doesn't remember you and considers the comtesse to be his *maman*. So we won't demand that she give him up— yet. For the moment, we will insist only that you are allowed to become reacquainted with him. I expect this business regarding the railroad will take some time; if it should terminate more quickly than expected, I have other interests that can keep me in France.'

She pushed herself to sit upright against the pillows, joy and hope, anguish and doubt warring in her face. 'Are you sure, *mon amant*? You really think it is possible?'

'I do. Once Philippe knows you better and is comfortable in your company, he can come stay with us. When you think he's old enough to understand, you can tell him that you, not the comtesse, are in fact his mother. And then he will be yours once more.'

'Oh, that would be heaven! But what if the comtesse refuses? To be so close and be denied again...'

'She won't refuse. Elodie, I've been planning this for a long time. I didn't want to say anything until every piece was in place. It will work, I absolutely guarantee it. Have I ever lied to you?'

'No. Oh, Will, if you can truly reunite me with my son, I will be grateful to you for ever!'

He smiled at her tenderly. 'You can show me how much, right now. And then we'll get packing for Paris.'

After a flurry of shopping in London to equip Elodie for her role as Madame Ransleigh, wife to the economic envoy blessed by the Court of St James to engage in discussions with the Interior Ministry of His Majesty, King Louis XVIII, Will and Elodie sailed for France. Though Elodie remained calm—as she had been in every crisis they'd faced together, whether fleeing Vienna in the middle of the night disguised as a valet or while being held, a knife to her throat, by a British foreign agent—

Will knew that beneath the surface, she was torn between anticipation and anxiety.

Knowing every hour of delay before they visited the Hôtel de la Rocherie would be an agony of suspense for her, Will made only the essential calls to present his credentials to the British Ambassador and King Louis's chief advisors before returning to fetch Elodie from the luxurious hotel in which he'd installed her.

He found her pacing the room, from the gilded mantel to the door to the large windows with their view of the Place de la Republique, like a wild bird frantic to escape a jewelled cage.

As soon as she saw him, she rushed to her dressing table, jammed the stylish bonnet on her head and began dragging on her gloves. So nervous was she, she had difficulty pulling the tight kidskin over her trembling fingers.

He walked over to assist her.

'Quite an improvement over our accommodations the last time we were in Paris,' Will said, nodding towards the view of the Tuilerie Gardens in the distance as he coaxed the soft leather on to her hands. 'Though if it would make you less fretful, I could try obtaining some chickens.'

She tried to smile, but her lips were trembling, too. 'Will, I'm so frightened.'

He took her in his arms, wishing he could make this anxious process easier for her. 'You needn't be, my love! Don't you believe I know how important this is to you? I would never have suggested we attempt it if I were not absolutely convinced we shall succeed.' *Even if Will the Rogue has to make a return engagement to guarantee it*, he added silently to himself.

The concierge knocked to inform them their carriage was ready, and he ushered Elodie outside for the short drive to the Marais.

When they arrived at the Hôtel de la Rocherie, Will sent in his card, telling the lackey who greeted them that though he was a person previously unknown to the comtesse, he was in Paris on important government business and must discuss with her a matter of utmost urgency. After showing them into a drawing room elegantly appointed with striped wallpaper and Louis XVI furniture, the man withdrew.

Too nervous to sit, Elodie walked about, trailing her hand over the back of the sofa, down the edges of the satin window hangings. 'Oh, Will,' she whispered, 'This is where *madame* received us when St Arnaud and I called on her with Philippe. The last place I saw my son, before they stole him from me.'

'It's fitting, then,' Will said bracingly, 'that, in this same room, he will be restored to you.'

A few minutes later, an elaborately gowned woman Will assumed to be the comtesse entered the room. As he bowed over her hand, she said, 'Monsieur Ransleigh? I cannot imagine what business you might have with—'

'And Madame Ransleigh, too,' Will interrupted, nodding towards Elodie, who stood frozen by the mantel.

As the comtesse's gaze followed the direction of

his nod, the polite smile faded and her face went pale. 'Elodie Lefevre?' she gasped, stumbling towards the Louis XVI fauteuil and grasping the arm so tightly, Will thought she might have fallen without its support. 'My brother told me you were dead!'

'Sorry to disappoint,' Elodie replied with some asperity, 'but as you can see, I am still quite alive, *moi*. St Arnaud claimed I'd died, did he? How was I supposed to have met my demise?'

'He—he said you'd been injured during the…the attempt on the Duke's life. He did everything he could for you, but you died in his arms later that night. And then he fled.'

'He got the last part right,' Will said drily. 'Shall we sit, *madame*? This must have been quite a shock. You will need time to recover, before we place our proposal before you.'

'Yes, let me order refreshment. I, for one, could use a glass of wine.'

Even while giving orders to the lackey who responded to her summons, the comtesse kept staring at Elodie, as if unable to believe she had truly survived Vienna. After they'd been served, she drank deeply of her wine, then looked back to Elodie again and asked, 'Are you going to try to take my son?'

'Philippe is not your son,' Will reminded her.

'Perhaps not always, but he is now! For nearly two years he has known no other mother. You have only to ask him, he will tell you I am his *maman*.'

'I know,' Elodie said. 'I do appreciate the tender care you have taken of him.'

'You know?' the comtesse repeated with a puzzled frown. Then her eyes widened and she gasped, 'Was it you who accosted him in the park, two months ago? The servants said someone with an oddly intent manner had approached him. That they came back again to this house the very next day. I was so alarmed, I considered informing the gendarmes, but Prince Talleyrand advised against it.' Her questioning tone turned accusatory. 'You frightened him! How could you, if you care for him?'

'I'd hoped that if he studied me long enough, he would remember me. Can you imagine how it felt to see him again and realise he did not even recognise me?' she burst out. 'When I had thought of nothing but his welfare, every day, since he was taken from me?'

'Taken from you? My brother said you'd agreed to go to Vienna without him.'

'That report was as accurate as the one about my death!' Elodie retorted. 'I regret to disillusion you about your brother, but the only reason I left this *hôtel* without my son was because St Arnaud drugged my tea and abducted me. Once he had me in Vienna, he used the threat of harming Philippe to force me to participate in his plot. Did you truly not know?'

The comtesse dropped her eyes, not meeting Elodie's gaze. 'I am…aware of my brother's strong convictions, and the sometimes ruthless means he uses to carry them out. I knew there was something…suspect about your leaving Philippe so abruptly. But the child enchanted me from the first moment. When St Arnaud told me that he was setting out for Vienna immediately and that you had returned home to finish your preparations without seeing Philippe again, so you wouldn't have to distress him by telling him goodbye, I was too thrilled at being able to keep him to want to question the arrangement.'

'Was he…distressed when I did not come back for him?' Elodie asked.

The comtesse nodded. 'Of course. But I had a nursery full of toys to distract him and he loved listening to me read stories. When he would ask for you, I would tell him you were doing an important task, but you would be back soon. He cried at nights, mostly, so I slept in the nursery with him for the first month. And gradually he stopped asking.'

A sheen of tears glazed Elodie's eyes. 'Thank you for being so kind to him.'

The comtesse shrugged. '*Eh bien*, I love him, too. But what do you mean to do now? It was many weeks after you disappeared before he was happy and comfortable. Surely you won't upset him again, by wrenching him from my care?'

'It was to safeguard his happiness and well-being, and for that reason alone, that I did not take him with me when I had the opportunity two months ago. But as much as I appreciate your care of him, he is *my* son and I want him back.'

The comtesse was shaking her head. 'But you cannot

mean to take him *now*, surely! Give him some time! He is too young to understand all of this. You would only confuse and upset him.'

'We don't intend to take him away from you immediately,' Will inserted. 'Right now, he thinks of this as home and of you as his *maman*. What we propose is that my wife be reunited with him, spend time with him, let him become comfortable with her again. Once he is enough at ease with her to agree to it, we will take him to stay with us.'

Tears gathered in the comtesse's eyes. 'And then I will never see him again? Ah, *madame*, if you only knew what it is like to lose your son for ever, you would not be so cruel.'

'Believe me, I know!' Elodie retorted. 'Mine has been lost to me for nearly two years.'

'He wouldn't be far away,' Will said. 'I was sent to Paris on an economic mission to the French government. If negotiations succeed and we proceed to implement the plans, I could remain in Paris for many months. You would be able to see Philippe daily, if you liked.'

'I would like him to remain here,' the comtesse replied wistfully. 'My own son is dead; never in this life will I hold him again. But your son, *madame*, is alive. Though in taking him back you cut out my heart, I…I will not prevent you. Only, I beg you, don't drag him away until he is ready to go willingly.'

'I would take him no other way.' Elodie walked over and put a hand on the comtesse's arm. 'Thank you. I know how difficult it must be for you to agree to let him go. But as my husband said, we will be in Paris for an extended time. It will be weeks yet, probably, before he is willing to leave you, months after that before we would return to England.'

The comtesse shook her head sadly. 'There are not enough months in eternity to reconcile me to losing him.'

'You shall never lose him,' Elodie reassured her. 'Not completely. How could you, when you will always hold a special place in his heart? I promise I will never attempt to erase your image there.'

'Even though I let him forget you?' the comtesse replied. 'But surely you see that was different. I thought you were dead! Why should I remind him of a woman who would never return to him?'

'As long as you both make his welfare your first concern, I don't see why we can't all come to a sensible agreement,' Will said.

'Can I see him now?' Elodie asked.

Knowing her so well, Will could hear the longing in her voice. Knowing, too, that negotiating the terms of Philippe's custody would cause her anxiety—and wanting to make sure, in case the comtesse possessed any of her brother's perfidy, that the woman understood exactly what Will was prepared to do to enforce the agreement—Will said, 'Yes, comtesse, would you please have Philippe sent down now? Elodie, my love, you're too distracted and anxious to think clearly. Why don't you go out—' he gestured towards the French doors leading out to a small, formal garden that stretched between the *hôtel*'s two wings '—and take a stroll while we wait for the boy? The comtesse and I can discuss the particulars.'

Gratitude and relief in her eyes, Elodie said, 'Thank you. I would like that.'

Will kissed her hand. 'Into the garden with you, then.'

After the doors shut behind his wife, Will turned back to the comtesse. 'I'm pleased that you are choosing to be reasonable, *madame*.'

She sighed. 'I don't wish to be. I should like to pack Philippe up and run away with him to a place where you would never find us. But…I do know what it is to lose a son. I'm not sure I could live with myself, if I were to deliberately cause another such pain.'

'I applaud your sentiments. My wife, too, wants only what is best for her son, else I would have snatched the boy for her when we first found him. But I should also warn you, in case your longing to have sole control over the boy should ever triumph over your more noble feelings, that having grown up on the streets of London, I myself possess no tender sensibilities whatsoever. There is nowhere you could run where I would not eventually find you. I'd steal the boy back without a qualm, and he'd be halfway to a Channel port before you even knew he was missing. Once safely with his mother in England, protected by the influence of my family, you truly would never see him again.'

The comtesse gasped. 'You would do that, *monsieur*? But that is monstrous!'

'Perhaps, but there's not need to do anything "monstrous" as long as you are sensible. Considering that Philippe isn't truly your son, the arrangement we propose is quite favourable for you.'

'Favourable or poor, you do not leave me much choice, do you?'

'That was my intention,' Will replied. 'Some day, when he's older, Philippe must be told the truth, preferably before he works it out on his own. Come now, *madame*, let us put away our swords. We need not be opponents. Both you and my wife love Philippe. How could he not benefit from having two mothers to love him? The arrangement will work, I promise you.'

The comtesse sighed. 'It had better. Your wife has you, *monsieur*. Philippe is all I have left.'

'Then you will do everything necessary to make sure you keep him in your life. So we're agreed?'

At the comtesse's reluctant nod, Will said, 'Excellent. The boy should be down soon; I'll go fetch my wife.'

Will went quickly into the garden to find Elodie, who, pale and nervous, was pacing around and around the intricate knot garden.

As always, her distress made his chest ache. 'Have courage, sweeting!' he soothed. 'Philippe will be with you soon and you'll never lose him again.'

'Oh, Will, I know you promised me this would work, but are you sure? The comtesse is not just acquiescing to get us to leave, with no intention of honouring the agreement?'

Wrapping an arm around Elodie, he tilted up her chin and gave her a reassuring kiss. 'Do you really think I would let that happen?'

She gave him a wobbly smile. 'No. If I've learned nothing else since Vienna, I know I can trust you to make happen whatever you promise you will.'

'Then stop worrying, *mon ange*. All you desire will soon be yours.'

Taking her hand, he led her back into the salon.

Hardly daring to believe that she was truly going to have her son back again, Elodie fixed her gaze on the hallway door, hungry for her first glimpse of Philippe. When, a few minutes later, he skipped in, a joy of unimaginable sweetness filled her.

'Are we going visiting, *Maman*?' he asked, trotting over to the comtesse. 'Will there be cakes?'

That lady bent to give him a hug, as if to subtly underscore to Elodie that he still belonged to her. Magnanimous in her happiness, Elodie didn't even resent the gesture.

With the impatience of a little boy, Philippe wiggled free. 'Will we leave now, *Maman*?'

'No, Philippe. This kind lady is a…family connection. She's visiting Paris and wanted to become acquainted with you.'

Philippe looked up at Elodie curiously. Recognition flickering in his eyes, he said, 'I know you. You sold

Jean an orange in the park, and you came to the nursery and looked at my soldiers.'

'That's right,' Elodie said with a pang, wishing he could have remembered her as well after Vienna. 'What a clever boy you are!'

'This gown is prettier. Why were you selling oranges?'

'I dressed up to play a game of pretend. You pretend, too, don't you, when you play with your soldiers?'

He nodded. 'I am a great general and win many battles. I have a tall black horse and a long, curved sword and I am brave and fierce, like my papa.'

Elodie's eyes misted. 'I am sure you will be just like your papa. He would be so proud of you.'

'You said you would take me to see the parrots at the market. You said the birds had red and green and blue feathers. Can we go now? *Maman*, will you come, too?'

The comtesse wrinkled her nose in distaste. 'I do not wish to visit the bird market, Philippe.'

'Please, *Maman*? I do so want to go!'

'He seems to have a memory like a poacher's trap now. How unfortunate he didn't develop the skill earlier,' Will murmured, echoing Elodie's thoughts.

'Please, *Maman*, let me go now!' Philippe repeated, focusing with a child's single-mindedness only on the part of the conversation which interested him.

'I suppose, if you take Jean and Marie and don't stay long, you may go,' the comtesse said.

'Do let us go, then,' Elodie said. Longing welling

up in her for the touch of him, she held out her hand to the boy.

To her delight, Philippe put his small hand in hers. After closing her eyes briefly to savour the contact, she opened them to see Will smiling at her, love and gladness in his eyes. She mouthed a silent 'thank you'.

'What is your name? Can we not hurry? I know I shall like the red parrots best. Can I bring one home?'

Elodie laughed, revelling in the sorely missed sound of her son's voice. 'You may call me "*Maman* Elodie". Yes, we will hurry. As for the red parrot, you must ask your *Maman* about that.'

'Can I have a red parrot, *Maman*?'

'Not today, Philippe. Perhaps the next time.'

As they nodded a goodbye to the comtesse, who watched them walk away, her expression sad but resigned, Philippe said, '*Maman* Elodie, would *you* like a red parrot?'

Elodie looked up at Will, and he groaned. 'Somehow, I fear by the end of this excursion, I'm going to own a bird.'

Several hours later, having inspected all the colourful flock and narrowly avoided the purchase of the red parrot, they had returned a now-sleepy Philippe and his attendants to the Hôtel de la Rocherie. During the outing, Will had let Elodie take charge, following her indulgently as she wandered through the market hand in hand with Philippe, answering his volley of questions, even purchasing some sweets for him from a market vendor.

In the carriage on the way back to their lodgings, Elodie threw herself into his arms, so euphoric and brimming over with emotion, she wasn't sure whether to laugh or weep.

Hugging her tight, he said, 'Was it all that you wished for, sweeting?'

'Oh, my love, it was wonderful! The blessed angels must have been smiling on me the day you climbed up my balcony in Vienna! I still can scarcely believe you convinced the comtesse to agree to our arrangement—and, no, don't tell me how you managed it. I will sleep better not knowing.'

'My dear, your suspicions wound me,' Will replied, grinning. 'Sheer charm and persuasion, that was all.'

'The charm of a rogue!'

'A rogue whom you've bewitched completely.'

'It is I who am bewitched.' She looked at him wonderingly. 'You arranged all of this for me, didn't you? The mission, the railroads. You could have negotiated investments for your friend anywhere. But you chose Paris.'

He shrugged. 'Paris held the key to your happiness.'

Awed at the magnitude of such selfless love, humbled to be its object, she said, 'I can almost forgive St Arnaud for embroiling me in his scheme, for otherwise, I should never have met you. I thought it already a gift that you brought me from despair back to life. And now, you have given me back my soul. How can I ever repay you for such treasures?'

'Hmm, let's see,' Will said, drawing her on to his

lap. 'You could give *me* a son, I suppose. You, Max, Caro, even the comtesse seem to think having one is so wonderful, it would be rather selfish to keep it all to yourself.'

She smiled, it occurring to her that the only thing as marvellous as having Philippe back in her life would be bearing another son—Will's son.

'Sharing that blessing with you, sweet Will, my husband, my life, would be my greatest pleasure.' Framing his face in her hands, she leaned up to give him a kiss full of passion and promise.

* * * * *

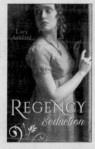

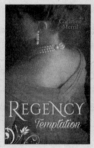